WITHDRAWN

Witch
Cradle

By Kathleen Hills
Past Imperfect
Hunter's Dance

Witch Cradle

A Mystery by

Kathleen Hills

Poisoned Pen Press

First Edition 2006

10 9 8 7 6 5 4 3 2 1

Library of Congress Catalog Card Number: 2005934985

ISBN: 1-59058-254-3

Poisoned Pen Press
6962 E. First Ave., Ste. 103
Scottsdale, AZ 85251
www.poisonedpenpress.com
info@poisonedpenpress.com

Printed in the United States of America

for Zachary Ruben

And now the year of the great decision
Newsweek, January 1, 1951

WASHINGTON—Government, industrial, and scientific leaders came up yesterday with "cloudy but cautiously optimistic forecasts" for 1951.

Chapter One

In the brief brilliant flash John McIntire glimpsed his wife's face, lips waxen, eyes open and staring. He turned to draw her close, but she caught his hand and clutched it to her breast, rigid as a corpse grasping a lily.

"It's only a lightning storm, Leonie," he said. "It'll be over soon."

For a moment the only sound was the movement of her head on the pillow as she shook it in denial. Her chest, under his hand, rose and fell in tandem with her rapidly beating heart.

A crack louder than a shot from any gun ripped through the blackness. Like a dynamite blast in reverse, it was followed by a drawn out electrical-sounding hiss. A power pole struck? McIntire rolled to free his ear from the pillow and imitated his wife's deathlike pose. A flash of light. Again a resounding blast heralded a crackling sizzle. He pried Leonie's chill fingers from his and crept from beneath the blankets, trying not to let too much cold air take his place. He shuffled to the window with only memory and a slight draft to guide him, dragging the bedside rug along under his feet to avoid contact with the frigid linoleum.

Outdoors the night was as solid as it was in the room. McIntire used his sleeve to wipe the steam of his breath from the glass. Lightning flared, exposing a fantastical tableau. In the greenish luminescence, every surface, from the layer of snow on the ground to the twisted limbs of the apple trees and the barbed wire fencing, glittered as in a sheath of glass. The fairytale vision remained for only a second before being erased by the night, like a bizarre half-recalled dream.

Light flickered again, the color of seawater. The cock on the weathervane raised jeweled wings into an ink-black sky. A limb on the maple split from its trunk with an explosive crack, and the source of the hissing became clear as its crystal coating splintered and slid to the ice-encrusted snow.

"It's ice," McIntire said. "It's raining, and ice is building up on the trees. It's breaking the branches."

The almost imperceptible rustle of her head on the pillow was Leonie's only response.

He remained mesmerized at the window. Each flash of lightning, each glimpse, teased for another that would be missed if he blinked. For the briefest possible time, the transformed world was disclosed with perfect clarity and vanished before he could grasp and hold it in his consciousness.

His trance was broken by a blast like an exploding bomb. After what seemed like minutes, a shudder ran through the room, quaking the floor and rattling the windowpanes in their frames. "A tree down somewhere," he said without turning. "It's not close, but it was a big one."

No sound came from the bed. McIntire tore himself from his vigil and slid back under the quilts, mindful of his frigid feet. He gathered his wife's paralyzed body to his chest. Light flickered green. Crashing, crackling, sizzling punctuated the constant background rumble. A war zone. In thirty years of military service McIntire hadn't experienced an enemy attack. Leonie had.

He put his mouth to her ear. "It's almost morning," he said and repeated, "It'll be over soon."

She spoke at last. It was a whisper so low he could barely hear it. "I don't think so," she said. "I don't think this is going to be over for a long, long time."

WASHINGTON—The Defense Department
last week reported 2,424 more
U.S. casualties in Korea. The
new report, running well behind
actual casualty figures, brought
announced U.S. losses in 6½ months
of war to 45,137 men.

Chapter Two

Frosted silver stillness. Saplings twisted into grotesque sculptures; spruce trees turned to slender spires, bowing to one another in a graceful dance, jeweled boughs sweeping the snow; wires transformed into a criss-cross of swags strung with miniature icicles. Soft white and crystal. If there is an afterlife, Mia thought, let it be like this. A mystical secret world she could walk into wrapped in a cape of white fur, gliding weightless among the trees, and disappear forever.

She forced her gaze toward the far edge of the yard where a jagged circle of exposed earth gleamed in a sickening wound. Behind it, an intricate tangle of roots, ripped from their impossibly shallow bed, reared up in a gargantuan lacework fan. How had such a fragile grip on the earth sustained the huge tree for so long? Kept it erect through at least a hundred winters, probably a whole lot more, finally to succumb to the weight of a quarter inch of frozen water?

In the flickering green light, Mia had seen the movement in the branches, had heard the rush of air as it fell and the blast of splintering wood when it met the trunk of its twin. The two towering pines had hit the ground together with the impact of an exploding bomb. The illusion of breaking glass as the coating of ice loosed its hold had merged with reality when the window at which she stood shattered.

She'd spent the remaining hours of night in her mother's old rocker. While all creation cracked and crashed down around her, she rocked, bundled in a patchwork quilt, praying for, and dreading, the approach of day. She knew what the morning would bring, knew that it was going to be yet another irreversible step in a sad and relentless trek away from the past.

She buttoned her husband's plaid mackinaw up to her chin and lifted her blue wool kerchief from the back of the chair.

"Don't, Meggie." Nick shuffled into the kitchen. "I'll go."

"I can do it." She pulled the scarf over her head.

"Do you think I can't?"

She let him take the coat from her shoulders.

His hand shook as he poured a half cup of coffee. He stood next to the pot-bellied wood heater, alternately blowing and sipping.

"It looks like it might have grazed the back of the barn. Lucky they didn't fall this way."

Mia gave a noncommittal "hmph." If luck had been with them, the trees would still be standing. "What do you want for breakfast?"

"I'll wait 'til I get back in." He placed the cup on the table and continued to stare out the window.

At last he moved to the porch and pulled on his rubber overshoes. Minutes passed as he fumbled with the buckles. It would be far easier on both of them if she just did it for him. After fastening only the top two, he straightened up with a look of triumph on his face, and Mia felt a sudden ache in her chest and a twinge of shame at her impatience. "Nick," she said, "be careful you don't get yourself electrocuted."

He pulled his cap over his ears. "I don't think we'll need to fret over any juice coming through those wires for quite a while."

She remained at the window, watching as he walked away from the door. He looked small and...what? Old, that was it, he looked *old*, older than he would ever live to be, leaning into the wind, his hands dangling ape-like at his sides, scuffling uncertainly along the frozen path. When he stepped off the path and put his attention to navigating the litter of fallen branches in the knee-deep snow, he was more the Nick she knew, undaunted and determined to the point of belligerence.

At some distance from the house he paused and turned to look up at the roof. His grimace said that they'd not been so lucky with some of the crashing limbs. He waded to the car and gave a thump on its roof, not budging the ice that coated it. Mia once again felt irritation bubbling in her chest as she watched him disappear into the privy.

At last he emerged, blinking at the light. He tracked a loop around the back side of the sauna, and finally made his way toward the toppled pines that had, for three decades, sheltered the graves of their stillborn infants.

Instantly Mia regretted her cowardice and experienced a pang of jealousy. She had given birth to those babies. She was their mother. If an act of nature had defiled their resting place, maybe exposed it, she should be the one to know, to set things right, to give them back their home. She knotted the scarf under her chin but didn't leave her spot.

Nick hesitated on the edge of the foot-deep crater before gingerly stepping into it. He stumbled on lumps of frozen earth as he examined the ground, making a circuit in one direction, then the other. Standing erect, he gave his attention to the network of gnarled roots above his head. Suddenly he took a step closer and thrust his hand into them. Mia looked quickly away.

When she raised her eyes, he was making his way past the mountain of branches to the point where it met the end wall of the barn.

The pine had punched a substantial hole in the wall, one large enough for Nick to disappear into. Still, the damage couldn't be too bad; the line of the roof was straight. Not that it mattered a whole lot. It had been years since they'd used the barn for anything but storing stuff they should have gotten rid of.

When Nick came back out, it was through the side door. He strode back to the house in a more confident fashion than she was used to seeing lately, clutching an object in his mittened hand.

He entered the porch stomping snow from his overshoes, but came in without removing them. "Looks like your old man was holding out on us." He deposited his find on the kitchen table—a pale green fruit jar encrusted with lumps of frosty mud.

Mia bit back her request to get the grubby thing, and his wet boots, out of her kitchen. She leaned closer and wiped a finger across its developing coat of fog. Her chest gave a leap. "Is that money?"

"I'd say so. Open it, my hands are freezing."

The lid was the kind made of zinc, with a sort of glass lining. It was pitted and misshapen, and covered with a whitish crust, but intact—and stuck fast. Mia poured steaming water from the kettle on the stove into the dishpan, added a dipper of cold, plunged the jar in, swished off the worst of the dirt, wrapped it in a towel, and gave a mighty wrench on the lid. Nothing.

"Ish." She tossed aside the muddy towel and inverted the jar, holding it up to its shoulders in the hot water. "One thousand one, one thousand two…." All the way to twenty-five. This time the lid twisted free with a scrape of corroded metal on glass that set her teeth on edge. She extended the open jar to her husband.

Nick inserted a trembling hand to extract a brown leather wallet speckled with mold. The faded face of Ulysses S. Grant showed through a crack.

He tore open the end of the wallet that was not locked in dripping ice, exposing a lump of folded paper along with a stack of bills of varying denominations and dimensions. He fanned through, counting as he went. "A nice neat seven hundred and twenty dollars," he finally said. "Dead four years, and your old man is still full of surprises."

NEW YORK—The U.N. refused last
night to view a film allegedly
showing American atrocities
against Korean civilians.

Chapter Three

The distant droning of chainsaws intruded on a world bowed low and locked in ice. Only the hips on the shrub roses, beads of scarlet embedded in crystal, gave a spark of color to the surreal landscape of frost and silver.

McIntire's overshoes crunched on the path. It had been an incredible storm, like nothing he'd ever experienced, coming just when the tedium of winter was working its way from oppressive to intolerable. Crashing trees. Thunder and lightning in January. Power out for who knew how the hell long. It would give people something to talk about for the rest of the winter and for years thereafter, most likely. Nothing like some genuine inconvenience, if not adversity, to give a lift to winter-weary spirits.

He set the pail of laying mash in the snow, blew on his bare fingers, and gave a few raps on the henhouse door to crack the ice from the latch. "Get yourselves decent, ladies. It's a man." He ducked inside, scanning the gloom for the Brown Leghorn rooster, a preening show-off, pugnacious and possessing razor-sharp spurs, but too cowardly for a frontal attack.

As his eyes adjusted, he spotted the bird about four feet away, nape feathers lifted, scratching a threat in the frozen litter. McIntire stared him into a corner and waded through the clutch of eager Rhode Island Reds to trade the galvanized waterer he carried for the one that sat waiting with its contents frozen solid. Why did water seem so much heavier when it became ice? And why did his wife persist in giving these creatures ten times the amount of water they could drink before it froze?

The hens crowded in to peck at the snow crystals clinging to his overshoes. "All in good time, dearies."

He kept his eye on the strutting cock as he groped in the nest boxes with his free hand. Empty. Empty. The third contained one egg. The next nest was occupied. He reached under the hen, which gave a squawk and deposited a warm egg into his obviously too cold hand.

"Two? That's it? Angling for an invitation to Sunday dinner, are you?" McIntire stowed the eggs in his pocket and backed toward the door to retrieve the breakfast and dump it into the feeder. "*Bon appetit.*" The hens dived in like ungainly vultures. As he closed the door, the rooster gave a mighty crow of triumph.

Leonie had been considering the possibility of leaving lights on in the chicken house to encourage egg production. She'd have to wait a bit on that. For as far as McIntire could see, the road was lined with mangled wires and fractured poles.

He surveyed the flattened shrubbery and broken tree limbs and found himself feeling a tiny thrill of challenge. Was he on the verge of becoming a Yooper after all? Is this what a few months of snow-induced boredom did to one? When he started seeing clearing up storm damage as recreation, was it time to move on? Get a job? Take a nap?

He glanced toward the barn. The horses would be all right for the time being. Leonie could take care of them later. The single strand of barbed wire on the fence formed a ribbon of spun glass. Beyond it, the snow-covered pasture reflected the hazy rising sun in a flawless sheet to the—his breath caught.

It took a moment to register what it was that was different, what was wrong. At the limit of his vision there was only a naked line, a barren meeting of snow and sky. The treetops that had marked the horizon for as long as he could remember, a feature of the land that hadn't changed since his earliest years, one that gave him a daily connection to the house where he was born, had vanished.

It accounted for the earthquake crash in the night. How could the storm have taken them both? It was incomprehensible.

They had been barely visible, something he'd seldom consciously noticed: two dark clouds squatting at the edge of the earth, a reassuring bridge to the past. Their absence created a void far out of proportion to the physical gap they left. It kindled in him an uneasiness that the destruction in his own yard couldn't match. Maybe Leonie was right. The effects of this storm wouldn't be over so soon.

Mia must be devastated. She'd have seen those trees every day of her life. There were few enough of the giant pines left, something Mia had bemoaned since they were children, and she was proud that her father had saved two of the biggest. Mia's father had done more than that, he remembered. The pines were all that marked the burial place of Mia's sisters, her brother, and her own two infants. McIntire felt a sudden sickness over what might have been torn from the earth if the trees had been uprooted. His mood, as he returned to the house, was considerably less buoyant.

He slipped out of his overshoes and wiped fogged-over glasses on his sleeve. Leonie stood at the kitchen stove, pale in the light of the kerosene lamp. Her wan appearance might have something to do with being awake and vertical at what was, for her, an indecently early hour. McIntire doubted she had gone back to sleep after the storm subsided.

She took the waterer, wrinkling her nose at the collection of litter frozen to its bottom, and placed it in the chipped enamel pan that sat on the floor near the heat register. Her lips formed an unconvincing smile. "Well, we've survived."

"You don't sound particularly happy about that." McIntire put his arms around her, careful to keep his hands off any exposed skin. Her head dropped to his shoulder. She gave a soft sigh followed by a hiccup and clutched him violently about the waist. Whatever emotion had overcome her was arrested by the crunch of eggshells.

"Fancy them scrambled today?" McIntire would be happy to walk around drenched in egg yolk if that was what it took to bring his normally cheerful wife back. Pots rattled as she rummaged in the cupboard for a basin. "Don't expect me to clean it up. Anyone harebrained enough to cuddle with eggs in his pockets deserves whatever he gets."

She turned off the burner under the percolator and filled the cups, while McIntire did his best to transfer the mess to the basin. His efforts produced meager results. He pulled the lining of the pocket out a bit farther and dropped the jacket on the floor. Kelpie roused herself from sleep, turned her liquid spaniel eyes to his in gratitude, and clicked her way across the linoleum to claim the unaccustomed treat.

"Did we lose anything other than that exotic *soufflé* I was planning to whip up for supper?" Leonie asked. "What about the fences?"

"Okay as far as I can see. A lot of branches to clean up. Nothing I'd call an emergency situation." He paused. "Not for us, at least."

McIntire's duties as township constable probably didn't include ice storm patrol. Basically, they boiled down to doing as he was told by the town board, the coroner, the sheriff, and any other official of the country, state, county, or township, down to, and including, the justice of the peace. Harry Truman might claim that the buck stopped at the top. McIntire knew better. The ladder of responsibility is more of a firemen's pole; the more onerous the job, the more rapid its slide to the drudge at the bottom. The constable position's only redeeming aspect was the excuse it gave him to get out and look around. And right now, it might be interesting to see how the rest of the neighborhood had fared.

He sipped and hoped his expression was one of grudging resignation. "I suppose I'd better drive around a bit and see how things are."

Any lingering fear was no match for Leonie's sense of civic responsibility. She nodded. "Do you think the roads are all right?"

"No," he said, "and I doubt I'll be able to get very far."

She removed a pan from the oven and poked a corner of one of the four curled slices of bread. "It sort of resembles toast."

McIntire leaped up and grabbed one to butter it while it was still hot. "It's fine," he assured her. "It looks like the big pine trees at Thorsens' went down. I'd better go see if they landed on anything important, like Nick or Mia for instance, or if there's anything I can do. Nick might not be able to do much clearing up."

"I don't suppose he'll accept help gracefully."

"That's not my problem."

She gave another resigned nod.

He made the sacrifice. "I'll pump some water for the horses before I leave."

"Thank you. Just leave it inside by the feed. I'll give it to them in a little while."

McIntire was grateful for Leonie's understanding that entering those horse stalls was a more daunting prospect to him than battling icy roads or fallen trees could ever be. "Thank you," he said.

She smiled. "Don't put your tongue on the pump handle."

Chapter Four

The Thorsens lived not much over a quarter mile away as the crow flew, but tramping across a field through two feet of crusty snow was not something McIntire felt inclined to do. Eight gallons of water pumped and tongue intact, he slid onto the Studebaker's frigid seat and pulled the door shut. The car's glazing of ice cracked, slipped, and crashed to the ground in a single swoosh.

In the driveway the ice was cushioned by a thick under-layer of snow, but the road beyond gleamed like a well-groomed skating rink.

McIntire left the car running and went back to the barn, passing by the horse stalls for the concrete-floored granary. He shouldered a hundred-pound sack of cracked corn, staggered over the treacherous path to the car, and plopped it next to the bag of sand in the trunk. If the car could still move, it would have a tad more traction.

He eased onto the ice and drove off at a crawl.

It might not have been a good time to leave Leonie alone. On the other hand, she looked like she could use about a three-hour nap. He wouldn't be gone long. He didn't expect to get far before his path would be blocked by a fallen tree or power pole.

The distance by road was upwards of a mile, and it was close to twenty minutes before he inched into the Thorsens' driveway.

A solo emanating from their yard joined the chainsaw chorus of background music. McIntire could see that there would be no saving of the trees. One was reduced to a thirty-foot monolith of splintered wood. It's partner lay full length on the snow, roots in the open air. Close up and horizontal, its size was indeed impressive. Nick Thorsen's red plaid cap bounced among the heaps of broken branches. The buzzing saw hit a higher pitch and one of the limbs fell with a thud. Mia came forward to drag it to a straggly pile. She spotted McIntire and walked over to him. "He's going to kill himself."

Nick seemed to be doing okay to McIntire. Steadier than he'd seen him in weeks.

"Sorry about this, Mia. It's a terrible shame. Both of them."

"Yes." She turned her face to the anemic sun. "There's a whole lot more sky here than there used to be."

"Anything I can do?"

She shook her head, then removed one of her leather mitts and pushed a strand of hair behind her ear. "Well, who knows. Hang on a bit until Nick turns that thing off and we can hear ourselves think. It won't hurt to ask him."

McIntire backed up to take in the soaring mass of roots, a webbing barely a foot thick stretching ten feet above his head. "How in hell," he asked, "could a thin coating of ice weigh enough to yank a tree this size right out of the ground?"

"How in heck did such a flimsy root system hold it up in the first place?"

Mia had apparently changed since the days when she took uproarious delight in shocking young Johnny McIntire with her use of unladylike language.

"It's quite a work of art."

"My mother would have called it a witch's cradle," Mia said.

Nick cut the engine on the chainsaw. The silence sounded strange in McIntire's head.

"Quite a night, eh? Your house still standing?" Nick's face was flushed and beaded with sweat, but there was no sign of tremor in the hand that held the saw.

"Not a scratch," McIntire told him. "Just wound up with a yard full of branches. Power's out of course."

Nick glanced toward the house and quickly back. Not quick enough to prevent McIntire from following suit and noticing the cracked roof slates and the two windows covered with blankets.

"John asked if there was anything he could help us with."

Nick went through the same process of polite refusal and possible assent, then turned to her. "Any coffee, Mia?"

She hesitated for a minute, then nodded and turned toward the house, leaving the men to follow. The thick braid that hung to the hem of her jacket matched the silvery hue of the landscape.

There was no path cleared to the front door. The one that led to the kitchen was only the narrowest of tracks, making it necessary to place one foot directly ahead of the other like a tightrope walker.

Once inside, Mia took her time, fussing over the pine pitch on her mittens, stoking up the fire in the wood heater, making the coffee. Such devoted attention to household tasks was unlike her, but McIntire didn't mind. This wide, warm kitchen was the seat of his earliest memories. Entering it was like a journey back to the womb. Mia had made few changes over the years. The big wood-fired cookstove had been replaced by a gas range. A cabinet with a maple countertop stood where the white enamel cupboard had been. Especially today, illuminated only by the light from the two windows, as it had been in those pre-electric days, the room was much as it had been forty-five years earlier.

An added benefit, Mia's coffee was good. She used a different sort of pot that came in two pieces, one atop the other. McIntire wished he could come up with a diplomatic way of suggesting that Leonie dispense with her percolator in favor of such an appliance.

As Mia's fiddling went on, and he found himself facing the prospect of making small talk with her husband, McIntire's tranquility began to wane. He'd never been at ease with Nick Thorsen; had never liked Nick Thorsen. Even before he learned more about Nick's past indiscretions than he wanted to know, he'd considered the mailman an arrogant little smart aleck. The cocksureness was gone now, buried in tremor and fear. Thorsen's coming down with Parkinson's disease took the edge off some of the overt antipathy McIntire felt, but left him awkward and at a loss for what to say. Should he ask how he'd been feeling? Which was more callous, to refer to his illness or to ignore it?

Mia finally poured the coffee and perched on the edge of a chair. Nick ran his fingers through his hair where it had been glued to his scalp by sweat and a heavy wool cap. "I found something under that tree."

McIntire glanced at Mia before he could stop himself. She pressed her lips together and gave an almost imperceptible shake of her head. Then she turned to her husband. "Oh, I don't think John would be interested in…."

Mia's notion of the aid McIntire might be able to give was apparently not what her husband had in mind. John was suddenly quite interested.

Nick pulled open a drawer and produced a handful of tattered scraps of paper and thin cardboard. "They were in a fruit jar." His voice was low and McIntire had to lean forward to hear. "Along with," he emptied the contents of a brittle leather wallet onto the table, "seven hundred twenty dollars."

"You found it under the tree? Somebody buried it?"

"Looks that way."

Nick had indeed mellowed. His usual rejoinder to such an inane question would have been some remark about how maybe the jar had screwed itself into the ground.

McIntire turned to Mia. "Your father?" She shrugged.

McIntire picked up the largest of the fragments. It was creased and torn and smelled of earth and mold.

"They were stuck together," Nick said. "We couldn't get them apart in one piece."

The ink was faded. The few words retaining some legibility were reversed—ink run through to the back of the paper. McIntire turned it over.

"It's backwards," Mia said.

"I can see that."

"I looked at it in the mirror."

McIntire carried it to the mirror over the sink. He was able to make out a few words. Some kind of tractor, *Jaeger.*... He turned back. "It seems to be a list of tools or machinery."

"You can buy a lot of tools for that kind of money," Mia said.

McIntire held the paper to the light. The faint lines indicating that the paper was some sort of official form showed through. "I don't think it's a shopping list."

Mia fingered an over-sized fifty-dollar bill. An unfamiliar bubble of excitement sounded in her voice. "Maybe we'd better start making one."

"Why would your father have buried seven hundred dollars?" McIntire asked. Eban Vogel hadn't seemed like the miserly type, quite the opposite. "I take it he didn't tell you about it?"

Nick's voice trembled a little. "It can't have been—"

"He must have been worried about it being stolen or something," Mia said. "He'd never have kept that much money in the house, and he didn't trust banks."

"This can't have been Mia's father's," Nick started again. "Eban didn't have that kind of money. If he had, he wouldn't have squirreled it away. Look at the rest of the stuff."

McIntire shuffled through the papers. Two smaller shreds showed faded printing in an ornate script, most of which had been obliterated by the bleeding ink. McIntire could make out a *Bi*, a couple of *L*s and the concluding *ing*. The rest was a pile of stiff confetti.

"I've been thinking about it all morning." Nick said. "I think I know what this is."

"Me too," Mia said. "Indoor plumbing!"

He ignored her. "This one," he held the fragile paper by its edge, "looks like it could be a bill of lading."

Mia put down her cup. "A bill of what?"

"A receipt from a shipping company," Nick said. "And this?" He handed a rectangle of thin reddish cardboard, folded like a small book, its pages stuck tight, to McIntire. Even without the familiar eagle, or a number showing through the small cut-out space, it was readily recognizable.

"A passport."

Nick nodded. "Not enough left of it to say whose." He picked at its corners. "You ever know Teddy Falk?"

McIntire shook his head. "I don't think so."

"He was one of that bunch of communists that went off to find Paradise in Russia—Karelia. Used to live on the old Makinen place. Teddy and Mia's father were pretty chummy."

"I thought it was Jarvi Makinen that went to Russia."

"Jarvi? Hell, no," Nick said. "Jarvi kicked the bucket twenty-five years ago. Pneumonia. Teddy Falk bought his farm, and he married Jarvi's daughter, Rosie. Maybe she came with the place. Or the place came with her. Anyway, it was Rosie and Ted that went off to Karelia…supposed to have, anyway."

"Supposed to?"

"They wouldn't have gone and left this behind. Couldn't have. The people that made that trip needed to pay quite a bit to go. Five or six hundred dollars. The Falks sold everything they had except," he tapped the papers, "some tools and machinery that they shipped over."

"They did leave?"

"They went somewhere."

"But not to the Soviet Union?"

"I don't see how they could have. They might have gone without the passport. I don't know that you had to have one. Though, if they did, there'd be no reason to leave it behind. But if this is their money and the receipt for their stuff…"

"What makes you think it *is* theirs?" Nick's reasoning seemed to be taking some pretty big leaps.

Nick said, "Teddy had a Jaeger saw, and…." He sifted through the tattered fragments and presented one with a scrawl of ink to McIntire. Without excessive imagination, it could indeed be read as *J. T. Falk*.

"But if this guy shipped off his tractor and whatever else it says here, why would he go *anywhere* without the receipt, let alone Russia?"

"Good question."

"Exactly when was this?"

"Exactly, I can't say. Early thirties. Nineteen thirty-three or four. Close to twenty years ago."

McIntire thumbed through the bills. At a quick glance, they all appeared to be pre-nineteen-thirty. Some were the older large-sized kind. The twenties looked surprisingly crisp and new. "But they must have let somebody know where they went. Didn't anyone hear from them?"

"Nobody I know of," Nick said. He rubbed his forefinger rhythmically against his thumb, then lowered his hand beneath the tabletop. "Not that what I know, or don't know, means a hell of a lot."

It did mean a hell of a lot. Nick delivered the mail, and if anybody on his route had been in the habit of getting letters from Russia, he'd have been aware of it and would be bound to remember.

"There were quite a few people that went to Russia," Nick continued, "and a lot of them haven't been heard from since. I don't think anybody knows what happened to them."

McIntire had an inkling of what might have happened to quite a few of them. But then he'd been a bit closer to the action.

Nick went on, "Maybe Sulo Touminen would have some idea. He's got the place now."

McIntire drained his cup. He saw a glimpse of a challenge that could be more satisfactory than piling brush. "I'll see if Sulo's around. I can't think he'd be gone far." He stood up. "I imagine there's some perfectly reasonable explanation, although after twenty years it might be hard to get. Can I take this stuff then?"

Nick shoved the stack across the table. Mia put out her hand to stop him. "No."

"No?"

"You can take the papers and billfold and the jar, too, if you want it. Not the money."

"Mia—"

"That money was in my yard. My father had to have put it there. He wouldn't have done that if it didn't belong to him." She glanced at her husband. "We could have just kept our mouths shut, and nobody would ever have known. I won't spend it right away, just in case, but it's staying here. You don't have any right to take it."

McIntire supposed she was correct. He didn't have any right to do that. Or any reason to either.

Nick Thorsen's readiness to turn the shreds of paper over to him, and his wife's grudging acquiescence, could be a reflection of their reluctance to go to someone of higher authority than township constable. Passing the stuff on to McIntire was a relatively safe method of taking care of any responsibility they might feel. He headed for the door. "I'll let you know if I find anything, but it'll probably take a while." He looked out at the mangled trees and telephone poles. "I might not be able to *get* anywhere for a while."

WASHINGTON—Senator Margaret Chase
Smith, Republican of Maine, lost
her seat on a key Senate investigating subcommittee today. She
is reported to have protested
that Senator Joseph R. McCarthy,
Republican of Wisconsin, "bumped"
her out of the post.

Chapter Five

Mia closed the door on McIntire's retreating back and returned to the kitchen. She avoided meeting her husband's gaze as she gathered the cups.

"What was that all about?" She might have known he wouldn't let her off that easy.

"What?" She tried to sound mystified.

"You know that money didn't belong to your father. He'd never have hidden it from us like that."

"Who else would be burying money in our yard?"

"I'm not saying Eban didn't *bury* it."

"What are you saying? That Papa was stashing away money that wasn't his? That he stole it, maybe?"

"I don't know where he got it, or how, and neither do you. But I'd bet dollars to doughnuts that the money Teddy Falk needed to leave the country is right here in my hand. Teddy went away, and, so far as we know, he hasn't resurfaced."

"Nick! You make it sound like Papa stuck Teddy Falk in the ground out there, too."

Mia felt her stomach clench as she uttered the words, both at her own ever-raw memories and at the pain in Nick's eyes.

"Meggie, sit down. I've been thinking about this. Do you remember when Falk said he was going to Russia? Your father didn't take it so well."

"Of course he didn't. He thought it was unpatriotic. Well, you could hardly be less patriotic! Papa also thought he was an absolute nincompoop to do it. He was right."

"He was furious."

Furious didn't begin to describe Eban Vogel's reaction when he heard the Falks were joining the emigration. "Teddy was a good friend," Mia said, "an old friend. Papa didn't have many friends. He didn't want to see them go."

"They didn't act like good friends as I recollect it. Don't tell me you've forgotten about the fight they had, in this very room."

Mia wasn't likely to ever forget that night. It had been beastly. The two of them shouting, swearing in their respective languages, the sounds of stamping feet and fists slamming on the table until she thought she'd die of fright and embarrassment. She'd begged Nick to go down and put an end to it. He managed to effect a truce and had made it almost to the top of the stairs before bedlam broke out again. The battle had ended with a crash and a blessed, if unnatural, silence. In the morning the kitchen was bathed in the Christmassy scents of cinnamon and ginger, and the cherrywood spice cabinet, a gift from her father to his bride, showed a four-inch gash on one of its lovingly carved corners.

"What is it you're trying to say?" Mia asked.

Nick closed his eyes and pressed his temples with the thumb and fingers of one hand. "I'm just trying to remember."

Mia was trying not to remember. "It doesn't matter now."

"So far as we know, your father never heard from Teddy after he left, and neither did anybody else. I don't recall that Eban ever mentioned being surprised about that."

"Why would he? As you just said, they had a terrible argument before Teddy went away."

"Your old man had seven hundred dollars and the claim for the stuff Falk shipped over. If Teddy didn't go, your father damn well knew it."

"Nick—"

"What if the fight got out of hand? What if Teddy hit his head or something, a heart attack, maybe, and died?"

"I don't want to hear any more of that."

"We can't just ignore it."

"I can ignore it. I know my father, and I know that he wasn't a thief, and he was certainly not a murderer!"

"I'm not saying he was. I knew your father, too, almost as long as you did…and maybe better."

What did that mean? "There was a Mrs. Teddy," Mia reminded him. "You figure she was in on it, too? Maybe Papa and Rosie had a thing going?"

Nick shook his head. "I know, the whole thing is damn strange."

"Papa made money. Even during the Depression he had more money than most people around. It wasn't something he wanted everybody to know about."

"Your father was generous with what he had. He wouldn't have hidden it."

It was true. Mia's father had taken perverse pleasure in helping out the same people who had treated his family with such meanness during the First War.

She took the bills from his hand and patted them into a neat stack. "Nick, we can use this."

"We've done without indoor plumbing so far."

"You won't be able to work much longer." And he wouldn't be able to use the outdoor plumbing much longer.

"So that's what this is all about."

"It's true. We have to face up to it." She leaned toward him with her hands on the table. "You could see a doctor. One that might know something. Go to the Mayo Clinic, maybe."

"Nothing doing." Nick's words conveyed what his spiritless voice could not. "There's nothing anybody can do. That's what we have to face up to. I'm not going to waste what time I have left—or what money we find buried in the yard—on some wild goose chase, so forget it."

"Papa left everything he had to me. That includes canning jars and whatever is in them." She reclaimed the stack of bills and slapped it on the tabletop. "*This is mine.*"

NEW YORK—Adam Hats has decided not
to renew columnist Drew Pearson's
$5,000 a week contract. Company
president Charles V. Molesworth
denied the dropping of Pearson
had anything to do with Senator
Joseph McCarthy.

Chapter Six

The empty feeling in the house hit McIntire as soon as he opened the door. A bleakness that couldn't be explained by the lack of light and heat alone. The light he could do little about, but before he went in search of his wife, McIntire filled both the furnace and the teakettle.

He found Leonie huddled in bed with only her blond curls showing above the quilt. He hadn't really expected her to take that nap. She was a notoriously late sleeper, but once she was up, she generally stayed that way. He touched her shoulder. "Leonie, what's wrong? Are you sick?" He fervently hoped not. They'd raise hell getting Guibard out today.

She shook her head and spoke into the pillow. "I was feeling chilly."

"Why didn't you put some wood on the fire? It was almost out."

He bent to hear the muffled words. "I just didn't feel like it." After a few seconds she added, "It's pitch black down there."

He'd never known Leonie to be afraid of the dark or much of anything else. "Well, I've stoked the fire and put the kettle on. Come on and have a cup." Her cheek felt cold under his touch. "Or should I bring it here?"

The threat of being treated as an invalid seemed to bring Leonie around. She rolled onto her back and pushed aside the covers. She was fully dressed right down to her shoes. "No. I was just about to get up. It must be nearly dinner time." Her smile brought back the woman he knew. "I guess I was pretty tired. I didn't get an awful lot of sleep last night."

"No, I don't suppose either of us did."

She bounced up smartly and seated herself at the dressing table, frowning at her rumpled skirt. "Where have you been?"

"Thorsens'." He told her about the trees. "One was uprooted, and when it fell it hit the other one and broke it off about thirty feet above the ground. I don't know how Nick'll handle clearing it up. He can't even manage to shovel the front steps. There was something a little strange—"

"Where else?"

"Where what?"

"Where else did you go?" She picked up her brush and turned away from him to lean toward the mirror. "You were going to check out the neighborhood."

"That was as far as I got. It'll be a while before this mess is cleaned up. I'll try to get over to Sulo's after we eat."

"I imagine Sulo can take care of himself."

The sharpness was unlike Leonie, and gave McIntire the feeling that there was something he'd missed in their short conversation.

"There are other reasons I want to see Sulo. Come on. I'll tell you about it downstairs." He pulled her to her feet. "If you'd rather I didn't go...."

"Don't be silly," she said. "Sulo is only a hop, skip, and a jump away." She chucked him under the chin. "I'm sure you'll be fine."

McIntire wasn't surprised at Mia's insistence on keeping the money, but it was strange that she was either unconcerned about its implications, or was pretending to be. She wasn't so naive that she didn't know that if Teddy Falk and his family—did he and Rose have children?—had disappeared, and the money to finance their new life had wound up buried in her yard, questions would have to be asked.

It was a puzzle, but one that would have to wait for the snowplow, unless Sulo Touminen could enlighten him. Sulo might know if the Falks ever got to Karelia. He might at least have some idea of what their plans had been. Or should have had at the time; whether he'd remember now was another question. McIntire reckoned his own mother would be a better source of information, and there was no question about her memory. Sophie McIntire had yet to admit to forgetting anything. But his mother was in Florida, and, as Leonie had pointed out, Sulo was just down the road.

Now Leonie stood staring out the window over the kitchen sink, waiting for the kettle heating on the gas burner. She'd been preoccupied over their noon-time meal of pork chops and green beans, but then, so had he. He carried his plate to her.

"I'll be right back."

"Do you think the power will be off overnight?"

"Yes." If the power was restored by Easter, he'd be surprised. He kissed her cheek. "I'll be home long before dark."

He made it almost to Touminens' before finding the road blocked by a horizontal maple. Now what? Should he try to move the thing? It was that or reverse close to a half mile to turn around in Thorsens' driveway. McIntire turned off the engine and got out of the car.

The sky had cleared to a hard sapphire blue. A tinkle of fairy bells filled the air as millions of ice slivers loosened their hold on wires and twigs and fell to the crusted snow.

The song was drowned by the chug of a diesel engine. McIntire squinted into the sun. The brilliant yellow-orange of an Allis-Chalmers crested the hill beyond the fallen tree. Sulo Touminen bounced on its metal seat, hatless. He spent some minutes turning the tractor in the narrow road, leaped down, and attached a chain to the tree. He grunted, resumed his seat, and coaxed the machine into action, pulling the tree a few yards back the way he had come. Only then did he alight once more and stroll to McIntire, leaving the tractor grumbling in the road.

"Quite a storm, eh? Lose anything?" Sulo was not only hatless, but gloveless and with no outerwear other than a heavy flannel shirt. He spit a yellow-brown blot onto the pristine whiteness at his feet.

"Just a night's sleep," McIntire said. "You?"

"A few shingles. You out on official business?"

If it was sarcasm, McIntire chose to ignore it. "I hope not," he said, "but if you've got some time you might be able to help me out."

"Out of what? I'm getting the goldamn tree off the road."

"I mean you might be able to give me some information," McIntire tried again. "If you've got some time."

"I got nothing but time. Follow me."

Sulo remounted his tractor and amply demonstrated his surfeit of time, inching along the road, plowing an icy furrow with his tree, while McIntire crept behind in first gear.

Sulo's imperviousness to freezing temperatures appeared to end at the front door of his narrow two-storied house. Their entry was greeted with a blast of heat that might soon have McIntire stripping to his skivvies. His host loosed the buckles to let the bib of his overalls fall around his waist, but went no further in disrobing. Something for which—at a glimpse of the grayed and tattered necklines of what appeared to be two layers of longjohns under the flannel—McIntire was truly grateful.

Happily, Touminen's home was at odds with his scruffy appearance. Paper in a pleasing print covered the kitchen walls, and the room was bright and tidy, if a bit overstocked with knick-knacks. The ceiling was a shock, enameled a glossy cherry-red. It was all the influence, no doubt, of Sulo's resident sister, Irene. The whirr of a sewing machine treadle sounding from the living room indicated that Irene was at home. Under the circumstances, she could hardly have been anywhere else.

At the sound of Sulo's "Grab a chair" the machine stopped and his sister appeared, her broad shoulders nearly filling the narrow doorway.

With her ball-shaped clefted chin, pointy turned-up nose, and prominent apple cheeks set in a thin porcelain face, Irene Touminen was an unusual-looking woman, bringing to mind a wooden marionette, a female Pinocchio who'd told only one or two harmless fibs. Even her hair looked as though it might have been lacquered on, straight and shiny black, cut to just below her ears with bangs in a ruler-straight line over brilliant sparks of eyes.

She'd had nurse's training, and worked for a time in Lansing before souring on the high life of the big city and leaving it behind to move in with Sulo. Not the smartest move, from McIntire's point of view. He didn't know Irene well, but she seemed friendly and capable, if a little shy. She wasn't all that old, and, as McIntire knew from experience, middle age didn't preclude one's finding a mate. Well, Irene wasn't likely to meet her Prince Charming if she didn't get out of St. Adele more than the weekends she worked as a cook in Chandler's old folks' home.

She smiled gently in McIntire's direction, made a few obligatory comments about the storm and the gumption Leonie exhibited in coping with the Michigan winter, and occupied herself brewing coffee and slicing a loaf of banana bread. When she placed it on the table, McIntire noticed for the first time how tiny her hands were. In contrast to her rangy build, they were as doll-like as her face. She nodded at McIntire's thanks and took herself back to her sewing machine, leaving her brother to handle the pouring.

McIntire's queries were postponed by Touminen's "You mind?" He lifted the sugar bowl and produced a folded letter. McIntire took a ballpoint pen from his pocket and performed the familiar task of transcribing into English still another rambling epistle from one of Sulo's covey of Finnish cousins. Unlike his local cousin, Silent-in-Two-Languages Uno, Sulo was limited to English.

McIntire handed over the letter. Sulo nodded, refolded it, and slid it back under the sugar bowl.

McIntire asked, "You own the old Makinen place?"

A hint of curiosity gleamed in the round blue eyes. "Ya."

"Have you had it long?"

"Oh, ya. I took it over from Teddy. Well, from Rose. It was in her name. You looking to buy some land?"

The light faded when McIntire shook his head and asked, "Have you heard from the Falks at all?"

Touminen studied McIntire's face before filling the cups and replying. "Heard from them? No. Why? No reason I should have."

"Not at all since they left? You didn't need to send payments or anything?"

"Nah, we settled all that before they took off. Well, come to think of it, Teddy'd figured to have a little bit coming from when I sold the potatoes. He wanted it to go to some outfit in New York City. He was supposed to send the address, but I never heard nothing. Potatoes weren't worth the cost to ship them anyway. Maybe he didn't need the money in Paradise, eh?"

Sulo poured coffee from his cup into his saucer and stared into it for a moment. "Anyway, I didn't hear nothing." He popped a cube of sugar into his mouth and raised the saucer to his lips. Sulo Touminen was not an old man, but he was certainly in training for it.

That took care of question number one. Waiting while Sulo slurped his saucer of coffee through the sugar gave McIntire time to come up with question number two.

"When you bought the place, was the house still on it?"

"Not much of a house, more of a two-room shack. I traded it to Earl Culver for a couple loads of hay. He hauled it away and added it on to his house for bedrooms." Sulo chuckled. "If Earl spent a little less time in his own bedroom, he might not have needed to go around buying old shanties. Why Sandra Rindahl married an ugly son of a gun like that—he'd have made a better match for Rose—and to have all those kids…. What do you suppose that guy's got that…?" He shook his head.

The source of Earl Culver's persuasive charm was one mystery that McIntire had no wish to pursue. "I suppose the house was pretty much empty when you got it?"

"Well," Touminen's speech slowed and his eyes showed a definite glimmer of curiosity. "They left some furniture. Whatever wasn't worth either selling or shipping across the ocean. Not much. I let Earl have it along with the house." He refilled his saucer. "Teddy had some pretty good machinery, a dandy cement mixer, and a sawmill, but he shipped every last nut and bolt to Russia. There was Jarvi's car. Twenty-seven Model A. They took off in it, but I don't know if they took it over with them or not."

"What about household stuff, blankets, pots and pans, clothing? Was it all gone when you got the house?"

Touminen spread butter on a slice of bread, careful to cover it to the edges. "Well, sure. They took along anything that was worth bringing. There was a buncha junk laying around. I told Earl to take what he wanted and throw out the rest." He bit off half the slice and held what remained a few inches from his lips, shaking it impatiently while he chewed and swallowed. He stuffed in another bite and spoke around it. "How come you're so interested in Teddy Falk?"

"Oh," McIntire said, "somebody was asking about him, wanted to look him up."

"In Russia?"

"Yeah." McIntire hoped to divert Sulo from asking *who* might be looking to track Teddy down in the Soviet Union and what that had to do with whether he'd remembered to pack his socks and underwear. "It would be interesting to find out what happened to some of those people. The ones that went over. I don't suppose they found that paradise they were looking for."

"They were a bunch of damn fools." Touminen slurped up another saucer of coffee. "I told the whole lot of them they were nuts to do it. Got thrown out of your old man's saloon for my trouble."

"Pa tossed you out?" For speaking out against a communist Utopia? Colin McIntire had been a dyed-in-the-wool capitalist.

"Nah, it was the Saari boys. And I do mean *threw*. They'd of done a whole lot worse, but your old man didn't allow no bloodshed in his establishment, so I got by with a couple sore ribs." Touminen pulled his suspenders back to his shoulders. "If Teddy Falk wrote to anybody, it woulda been that Kraut, Eban Vogel."

"I don't think he did," McIntire said. "But it was a big group that went over, maybe thousands. They'd have left a lot of relatives and friends here. Wouldn't you think there'd have to be people around that have been in contact with some of them? Maybe not since the war, but before then. Somebody must know where they ended up."

"I ain't so sure about that. I heard of a few that came back, but they never said nothing about it. You could try Pelto. At the high school. His old man was a big wheel in the Party. Orville. He traveled around getting people all stirred up to leave, handled the arrangements." Touminen craned his neck to look out the window. "There's smoke coming from the school. Pelto spends the night when the weather looks bad. He mighta got stuck there."

The weather wasn't looking all that good right now. The afternoon's sunshine had given way to low-hanging clouds spitting out snow in sporadic whirling gusts. It was an innocuous flurry so far, but with a determined look about it.

McIntire looked at his watch. Plenty of time for one more stop before dark.

Chapter Seven

St. Adele High School's science, mathematics, and boys' phy ed teacher had put on still another of his hats, and McIntire stood well away while he aimed a gas-fueled blowtorch at an ice-filled keyhole. He stuck in a key, gave it a twist, and grinned as he opened the door to lead McIntire down the hall to the science room.

The school hadn't changed a whole lot since McIntire had served his time there. This classroom had the same gray walls and cracked window blinds, dreary as it had been thirty-five years before. Erik Pelto's foldaway cot and carton of Tenderleaf tea bags did nothing to add a homey, or an academic, touch. It was not exactly an atmosphere conducive to preparing youngsters to take on the world, unless giving them resilience was the aim.

Pelto threw his yellow work gloves on a desk but didn't remove his cap or jacket. He pulled a crumpled handkerchief from his pocket and spent the next half minute blowing his nose, giving McIntire time to look around. He recognized two new additions. A skeleton hung from a metal stand in the corner, and a glass-fronted cabinet contained an impressive collection of what might have been fairly valuable antique scientific instruments. Next to a brass sextant was a cache of home-away-from-home essentials: shaving mug and razor, an array of vitamins and medications to ease the common cold, and a carton of Fig Newtons.

"Come to offer your services?" Pelto asked.

"At chipping ice?"

"We could use a foreign language class."

McIntire parked himself on a wooden stool. "Any particular language you had in mind?"

"Not really. Spanish, French, maybe even German. How about it?" Pelto poured water into a beaker and turned the tap on a Bunsen burner, beaming in triumph again when it responded to his lit match.

"I'll think it over." He might, for about half a second. McIntire had spent too many years incarcerated in these rooms, bruising his knees on the underside of the skimpy desks, to consider voluntary servitude. And his last stint at language teaching was something he refused to be reminded of.

"Seriously, being able to offer a foreign language would…." Pelto gave a shake of his head and opened the cabinet to take out a bottle half-filled with an evil-colored liquid. "But what was it you did come for?"

"I was hoping you could tell me how to get in touch with your father."

"My father? Did you know him?"

"No. I'm just looking for some information. I understand he was once active in politics."

Pelto hesitated with the bag suspended over McIntire's cup as though he might consider reclaiming it. Then he shrugged, dropped it in, and added a stream from the bubbling water.

"That was a long time ago."

"The information I need is from a long time ago."

Pelto didn't respond, only regarded McIntire expectantly. His eyes were a translucent blue that made them seem lit from the inside.

"I'm trying to find out about a couple that supposedly left St. Adele back in the Karelia Fever days. No one's heard from them."

"That's hardly unusual."

It was the usual response, though, and one McIntire didn't quite understand. Several thousand people seem to disappear, and the people left behind just shrug it off. Didn't anyone try to find out what happened? The organization that was responsible for their emigration, for instance.

"It's not unusual *if* they went to Karelia," he replied, "but we're not sure that they did. Sulo Touminen tells me your father was a recruiter of sorts, and that he helped arrange passage. He might remember if the Falks were on the boat as planned."

"Falks?"

"Teddy and his wife. Her name was Rose. You remember them?"

"Nooo." He let the word drag out, slowly stirring his tea, pressing the bag against the side of the cup. "It doesn't ring a bell. Well, that was a while ago. I was just a kid when all that happened."

Erik Pelto didn't look so terribly young, and the exodus had gone on for quite a while. He plopped the soggy teabag into an ashtray and looked up, his contemplative aspect abandoned. "Did you say that the…these people didn't go to Russia?"

"It looks like they might not have. In which case we'd like to find out where they did go."

Pelto opened his mouth, but must have thought better of what he was about to say. Once again he waited for McIntire to continue.

"Can you tell me how to reach your father?"

"No."

The terse reply caught McIntire unprepared. "He *is* still living?"

"He is," Pelto replied, "but he's not all that well. I'm not going to pester him with that stuff after all this time."

McIntire could see that the elder Pelto's communist connections might be a touchy subject, but all he wanted was a small piece of simple information.

"I'm only—"

"My father was, as you put it, a recruiter. He convinced a whole lot of people to give up their homes here, sell everything they owned, leave their families behind, and go off to what he promised them would be a workers' Utopia. It's probable that things didn't go well for those people. He doesn't need to have it brought up now, and…" he turned expressionless eyes to McIntire, "neither do I."

McIntire wasn't ready to get this close and give up. "I'm sympathetic," he said, "but we can't just let this go. We need to find out what happened to Mr. and Mrs. Falk."

"What makes you think anything happened to them? Who is it says that they didn't go to Russia as they planned?"

"Nobody *says* so. It's just that some of their belongings have turned up. Things they would have taken with them. That's why I want to talk to your father. If he arranged for the trip, he should be able to tell me if they backed out." McIntire tried not to squirm under Pelto's expectant stare, a tactic no doubt calculated to elicit confession from the most recalcitrant fifteen-year-old, probably practiced by the hour in front of a mirror. McIntire barely managed to out-wait him.

The teacher wiped his nose on his sleeve and turned his attention to the bottle. He twisted off the lid, releasing an aroma of licorice-flavored acid. "What if they did back out?" he asked. "It's a free country. They had a right to go where they pleased. If they didn't go to Karelia, all the better for them."

"That depends, I'd say, on where they ended up. I'll try to be tactful," McIntire said, and felt himself turning into Sheriff Pete Koski when he added, "It's not like I won't be able to find him without your help."

The gaze went from water to ice, a transformation that left McIntire doubly glad that he was not one of Pelto's students. "Okay, I'll ask my father about this…Teddy Falk," he relented. "He'll remember. He remembers every one of them." He stood up. "It's going to take a little while. I'll have to write. I'll let you know when I find out."

McIntire left Pelto in the darkening classroom spooning down his cough syrup.

He brushed the powder of new snow from the Studebaker's windshield. The sky was heavy with more. The teacher had better get home, or he'd be likely to end up with only fig bars and the Smith Brothers to sustain him over the next few days.

TOKYO—A rejuvenated North Korean
army struck far behind U.N. lines
in a major surprise offensive that
imperiled the entire 8th Army's
fighting retreat.

Chapter Eight

Another few inches of fluffy snow dusted the twenty or so that
had been dropped over Tuesday night's layer of ice. With the
snow had come enough wind to deposit most of it in the network
of paths—trodden more than shoveled—to the workshop, to the
car, and to the biffy. Mia tucked the cuffs of her slacks into her
overshoes. She pulled on her mittens and fumbled to get a grip
on the handle of the white enamel chamber pot. There was no
more expecting Nick to go out in the night to answer nature's
call. Not even to the edge of the porch, which had been about
the limit to his midnight expeditions before his illness.

She proceeded gingerly down the steps and scuffed her feet
to locate the track under the snow. When she was a child, Mia's
family had owned a succession of dogs. Mia had been mystified
at the way the animals always seemed to know where the path
was, even when a heavy snowfall had obliterated every trace of it.
Scent, she supposed now. Whatever the trick, Mia didn't possess
it, and she had no four-footed companion to lead the way. She
inched along, knowing that if she stepped off the hard-packed
snow of the path, now treacherously coated with ice, she'd sink
halfway to her hips and was liable to be doused with the contents
of her pot in the process.

How long would it be before Nick wasn't able to make this trip in the daytime either? How long before he was a complete invalid, maybe bedridden? She used to say that indoor plumbing was something they should have when they got old. Before she knew what had happened, old had sneaked up and slapped them in the face.

Nick wasn't doing so badly right now, though. He was stiff and weak on one side, and sometimes hard to understand when he talked, but didn't seem to be quite so shaky. The tree clean-up was giving a boost to his spirits. Maybe the challenge made a difference physically, too. Still, he'd never be able to finish it by himself.

A long mound of white sprawled like a landlocked Moby Dick showing where the smaller of the limbs were stacked. Other branches, themselves as large as full-sized trees, lay where they'd fallen, most still firmly attached to the massive trunks. Crawling in among them with a saw would be dangerous work, especially for someone unable to move very quickly. Nick would have a tough time doing it, but it sure wasn't going to be her. They'd either have to pay somebody to cut the things up and haul them away, something Nick would never give in to, or they could just stay there. Mia guessed that the pines would be right here, rotting into the earth, long after she was gone and forgotten.

She swished her foot to scrape some of the snow off the concrete block that served as a step, yanked open the outhouse door, and ducked inside.

When she came out, a ribbon of crimson ran the length of the horizon, tying the earth to a sky-full of charcoal cloud, and leaving a streak of brilliant green before her eyes as she bent to scoop the empty chamber pot full of fresh snow. She dumped the yellowed crystals and dipped into the snow once more.

Why hadn't they had the plumbing put in when they could afford it, before they were facing the time when Nick couldn't work? Well, they could afford it now. Seven hundred dollars should cover it. She had every right to spend that money. Nobody could stop her. If Nick hadn't been fool enough to bring John McIntire into it, there'd be no question. They could have given him the few scraps of paper, if Nick thought it was so important. They didn't have to mention the money. Those bills didn't have J. T. Falk's signature on them, for cripe's sake. So what if they were in a jar with an old paper that did? Teddy and Rose Falk were long gone. What difference could any of it make now? John McIntire was a natural born snoop, and he was bored silly. A dangerous combination. He wouldn't rest until he'd dug up something, and she had a queasy feeling that it wouldn't be something good.

One last swish of the pot through the snow and she straightened up.

It was curious, though. Why did her father have that money? And why had he hidden it? Could he really have done something awful? There must have been something he wanted to keep to himself, that was for sure; he'd never have hidden money from her and Nick otherwise. If it really came from Teddy Falk in 1934, that would have been during the Depression. But even then Nick had a secure job, and her father still managed to sell his furniture. The Thorsens were better off than most. Maybe he'd stowed it away as a hedge against the time when that might not be the case.

Her morning ritual ended with the usual contest with herself. The Tossing of the Pot. The object was to throw it as far as she could toward the house while still keeping it near enough to the path to avoid a trek into the deep snow to get it back. Mia drew back her arm.

It was the residue of the ice storm that was her undoing. With a mighty swing, she hurled the pot high into the air and felt the earth slip from under her. Without even a second to catch herself, she fell heavily into the snow, her foot skating off the concrete step and smashing through the privy's rotting siding. The pot, along with her mitten, came to rest a paltry twenty feet away. She lay for a moment, stunned and feeling foolish enough to glance toward the house for reassurance that Nick hadn't gotten up extra early to take a peek out the window. She pushed up onto her hands and twisted around to free herself. A wave of nauseating pain swept up her leg, accompanied by an instantaneous bath of sweat. The foot didn't move. She braced her free one against the side of the building and pushed with all her strength. It wasn't enough.

She sank back into the snow, tears chill on her cheeks.

Nick might not be up for an hour or more, and how much longer might it be before he thought to look for her? She could die of exposure. Frozen in her own sweat, trapped by an outdoor toilet.

Maybe she could pull her foot out of the trapped overshoe. She floundered in the snow, struggling like a turtle on its back, until she could reach to loosen the zipper. Another explosion of pain threw her onto her back, and the dazzling glare of the rising sun turned black.

When the light returned, she was aware only of cold. Then of her husband's voice. His words floated off, carrying no meaning for her.

"I'm caught here, Nick." Mia felt the shivering begin. "Get the crowbar."

LONDON—The prime ministers of
the British Commonwealth nations
will oppose America's attempt to
brand Communist China an aggres-
sor, informed sources said.

Chapter Nine

At the roar of the approaching snowplow, John McIntire halted in his labors and leaned on the shovel that had become his constant companion. For the past three days he'd all but slept with it. He awaited the inevitable. The plow drew near. The driver, a man McIntire didn't know and didn't particularly care to know, glowered from under the brim of his wool cap, eyes straight ahead, apparently oblivious to McIntire and his homicidal thoughts. He chugged by, leaving a three-foot mound of snow and ice decorated with a smattering of gravel blocking the end of McIntire's newly cleared driveway.

Did the county give lessons in sadism? Or was such a level of fiendishness something you had to be born with?

McIntire's frustrated ire abated when he saw, following close in the plow's wake, the Plymouth coupe belonging to Mark Guibard.

The doctor stopped and opened his window a scant three inches. "Top o' the mornin'. You look a little out of your element."

"Well, thanks. That's the nicest thing you've ever said to me." McIntire stepped over the new snowbank into the road. "What brings you out inhaling diesel fumes so early? Retirement getting you down?"

Even Guibard had sacrificed his vanity to a cap with earflaps. He pulled it off now and smoothed back his hair. "I'd like to give it that chance. Some things never change. Why can't people plan their emergencies for a more civilized hour? My professional services are wanted by the Thorsens."

Oh lord, it would have to be something serious. Neither Mia nor her husband would summon a doctor for anything less than imminent death. "Did he take a turn for the worse, or has he lost the battle with that tree?"

"Tree? I don't think so. I haven't heard anything about a tree. Anyway, it's not Nick. Mia went ass over teakettle on ice this morning. Sounds like her leg might be broken."

It could be worse, McIntire guessed, but it was bad enough. "That's all they need. Anything I can do?"

"Piggy-back me up their driveway."

"Maybe next time."

For someone going to the aid of an injured woman, Guibard did not seem in much of a rush. He rolled his window down another notch. "Back in the days when I was driving a horse, a couple feet of snow wouldn't have given me a minute's trouble. I'd have been tapping at the Thorsens' door in twenty minutes, instead of waiting two hours for the plow to come through. And they call this progress."

"Horses ain't extinct," McIntire said. "I got a couple I can spare."

"Throw in a cutter, and I'll give it some thought. There's no more miserable place on a cold day than the top of a horse."

In McIntire's opinion, a seat on a horse was pretty unappealing in any weather. He waved the doctor on his way and bent to clearing away enough of the snowbank to get the car out. No doubt Leonie would be wanting to get over to Mia as soon as she could.

The ice storm had thrown his wife for a loop. When McIntire thought of it, she hadn't been herself for a while, maybe since around Christmas time. Having someone to fuss over would do her good.

He planted his feet and plunged the shovel into the hard-packed snow. He wouldn't mind getting the hell out of these elements. The thrill of battle had long since worn off.

It was nearly an hour later that he hung his cap in the porch. He found his wife seated on a straight-backed kitchen chair with the world atlas on her lap and her feet, in colorful wool socks, on the open oven door. She was still in her robe, but had none of the droopy-eyed look that usually lasted for at least an hour after rising. As he entered, she folded the letter she'd been writing and popped it into an envelope, smoothing down the flap with her knuckles. A flowered handkerchief was balled into the hand. She kept her face turned away while she unfurled it and blew her nose.

"That should appease the snow gods for a few hours." McIntire looked at the clock and wondered if alcohol could legitimately be included in elevenses. "Guibard went by earlier. He was on his way to Thorsen's. He thinks Mia's broken her leg."

The tactic worked. Leonie's eyes widened and the atlas slid to her knees. "A broken leg! What happened? How on earth will they ever manage?"

"Nick should be able to handle things."

"That man couldn't boil an egg. He was helpless as a new-born…ninny even before he got sick. Anything that gets done in the house or the garden is up to Mia."

"Maybe this will force him to finally grow up." They'd never live to see that day. "Otherwise, I guess they'll have to get somebody to come in and help."

"I can't see either one of them wanting to do that."

McIntire couldn't see it either. Mia guarded her privacy, and the first help Nick would accept would be from those carrying his casket.

Leonie bit her thumbnail. "I'd better get over to see what I can do."

"You might want to wait a little while. If her leg is broken, Guibard might be still there."

"It's almost eleven. They'll be wanting their dinner soon."

"He said it happened a few hours ago. They probably haven't had breakfast yet."

With a look of stark horror, Leonie wheeled out of the room and galloped up the stairs. She was back, in a blue sweater and tweed slacks, pulling on her coat and kerchief, before the steam was off McIntire's glasses. She opened the refrigerator, pushing aside the pan of icicles to frown at the four brown eggs in a bowl. "We may have to begin buying eggs." The refrigerator thudded shut. She grabbed a loaf from the breadbox. If Leonie was going to minister to Mia Thorsen's needs in a satisfactory fashion, she was going to have to *stop* buying bread. Mia would never settle for anything less than homemade, and that meant made in her own home. McIntire didn't tell his wife that.

The sudden jangling sounded as foreign as if they'd spent the last four days on the moon. McIntire uttered a groan to commemorate the end of ninety-six hours of blissful isolation. A month ago it would have reflected his true feelings, but in mid-January he craved outside contact more than he was willing to admit. Leonie's broad smile indicated that she had no such reservations. The transformation in his wife was worth the rude jolt into the twentieth century.

"At long last!" She made a leap for the phone. After a short conversation over what newsworthy activities St. Adele High's science classes might have been up to, she beckoned to McIntire, blew him a kiss, and headed for the door.

Pelto hadn't wasted much time in finding what McIntire wanted to know, and didn't waste any now on pleasantries. "As you thought," he said, "the people you mentioned didn't show up."

McIntire put his hand on his wife's arm as she reached for the doorknob.

"Did your fath—"

"They didn't turn up at the headquarters in New York. The person I spoke to wasn't there at the time. He doesn't know if they just changed their minds or if they missed the boat and might have gone later."

The person I spoke to. Odd way to refer to Dear Old Dad. "Did he follow it up? Try to find out what happened?"

"He left the organization about that time."

"Their belongings had already been shipped," McIntire said. "Didn't anybody wonder about that?"

"I couldn't say. It had nothing to do with me. I was just a kid. I imagine those in charge were happy to get the stuff and didn't ask too many questions."

The school teacher was being pretty cryptic, even taking into account the constable's six-party line. And wasn't that nameless person he'd spoken to one of those who'd been in charge?

Pelto's voice lost some of its *here's the facts, now get lost* stiffness. "What makes you think that...the man you're looking for and his wife are still in this country? Do you have any real reason to believe that?"

"No, but what you've just told me backs up the reasons I have to believe they *didn't* go to—" McIntire adopted Pelto's wariness—"go where they had planned."

"What do you suppose could have happened?"

"Your guess is as good as mine on that," McIntire said. "But I intend to find out."

"Good luck." The teacher sounded almost like he meant it, even adding before he hung up, "If I can be of any more help, let me know."

"I'll drop you at the Thorsens'," McIntire told his waiting wife. "I'm going to go see Earl Culver."

She nodded and picked up her gloves.

"You can bring your letter over to Nick," McIntire reminded her. "He should be back on the job this afternoon."

Leonie picked up the sealed, unaddressed envelope. "Oh, I guess not." She tucked it into the pages of the atlas. "I might want to add something."

SAN FRANCISCO—Ida Rothstein,
executive secretary of the
civil rights congress here, was
arrested yesterday on an immigration department warrant charging
she violated the subversive pro-
visions of the McCarran Act.

Chapter Ten

The township road that led to the Culvers' home was never in the best condition and this morning was no exception. Fortunately Earl had been in and out enough times to create two well-packed tracks. Unfortunately, the wheel base of his truck was consider-ably wider than that of McIntire's Studebaker. McIntire poked along with an unnerving margin for error.

He'd been here once before. That was in June, shortly after the death of Earl's and Sandra's oldest daughter. In summer the place had been shabby but picturesque—weathered wood buildings overrun with greenery and half-naked children. Now with the leaves gone, the yard strewn with sawdust and dog droppings, and the foundation of the cobbled-together house banked with bales of hay, its aspect was decidedly less cheerful. One thing new had been added. A double black wire ran from a pole in the yard to the ramshackle enclosed porch. The Culvers had moved into the twentieth century. Electricity. Or at least the potential for it, if the power was ever restored.

The screen on the door into the porch was torn near the bottom, and a dog's black nose protruded through the hole. The animal, of no identifiable breed, gave a single deep-throated woof. Sandra Culver appeared behind it and shoved open the door.

"Come on in. Don't pay any attention to Brutus."

The packed snow covering the two front steps continued through the porch to the slightly more substantial kitchen door. The rhythmical thumping of a washing machine told McIntire that the Culvers had been a step ahead of him in getting their power restored.

They entered a room steamy and redolent of Fels Naptha soap.

"Excuse the mess." Sandra switched off the washing machine and dipped water from a copper boiler simmering on the wood-stove into a percolator.

She had aged since her daughter's death. The harsh light cast by a naked bulb on an extension cord showed little of the honey-colored beauty that had made her the object of fascination and of wonder at her marriage, and bearing of eight children, to the Rumpelstiltskin who sat at the table with the youngest of those children on his knee.

"Hop off to play, Audie."

The little boy didn't move his wide-eyed stare from McIntire's face, but slid to the floor and sidled toward his mother until Earl stopped him. "Audie," he said sternly, "I said 'hop.'"

Audie halted in his crabwise steps and grinned a similarly sideways grin. With great concentration, he put his feet together and made for the living room in a series of tiny leaps. Earl seemed to have regained some of his old sense of humor. McIntire wasn't sure that was all to the good.

The toddler navigated the piles of laundry waiting on the slanting linoleum floor, climbed to the back of a sagging sofa, and began scratching ditches in the frost on the window pane.

"What brings you out?" Earl pushed a chair in McIntire's direction and took a pipe from his pocket. "Something criminal going on?"

McIntire looked for signs of mockery, but saw none. The chair gave an ominous wobble as he sat. "I won't keep you long. I know you need to get back to work."

"No rush." Culver whacked the pipe into his palm and deposited a blackened lump onto the side of his plate.

After a few exchanges about the newly installed electrical power—*Place ain't wired yet, just an outlet on the porch*—McIntire asked, "You bought Jarvi Makinen's old house from Sulo?"

Earl nodded. "Ya. I added it onto this one."

"Must have been quite a job. How'd you get it here?"

"I didn't move it in one piece. It's log. You can see when you get outside. I took it apart, hauled it over, and put it back together, which took a hell of a lot longer than tearing it apart did. Remember, Sandy?"

His wife took his gravy-smeared plate from the table and put down three cups. "I remember."

Earl dipped his pipe into the can of Prince Albert and packed it down. "Any special reason you're asking?"

McIntire could see no need to keep it a secret. On the contrary, the more people who heard about it, the better the chance that somebody would turn up who knew the whole story. Maybe even Earl Culver.

He didn't. "I didn't talk to Teddy about the house at all. Bought it offa Sulo after they took off. They said they were going to Russia. Can't think why they'd of gone somewhere else and not told anybody."

"Neither can I," McIntire agreed. "When you took over the house, what was in it?"

"Not much. Just some crap they didn't want. Rubbish mostly."

"Like what?"

"A couple pieces of furniture that weren't so bad, but the rest was junk. Some stuff in the cupboards, tin cans, jars. Like I said, rubbish."

"What did you do with it?"

"I took the bed and mattress, and a chair or two. Most of the rest I threw down the well."

"Can't have done the well much good."

"It was a pretty damn worthless well, anyway. Sulo said to just throw whatever junk we had into it. He wanted to fill it up so nobody'd fall in, you know. There wasn't much room left. They'd already dumped in a lot of crap."

"It wasn't just a pipe in the ground then, I take it."

"Oh no. Well, there was a pipe in the ground somewhere, I guess, but what I'm talking about was more a cistern. The well didn't ever put out a hell of a lot more than a trickle, so they needed some kind of place to hold water. They had this big hole in the ground, lined with concrete, with a pipe coming in at the side. It just had a wood cover over it that was supposed to keep out rain."

What else might have found its way into the Falks' water supply, McIntire didn't want to think.

"We had bad drought then and there probably wasn't nothing in it but a few inches of slime. They had put down a sandpoint closer to the barn, and they were getting their water from that."

McIntire nodded. "How long after Teddy and Rose left did you buy the house? Was it sitting empty for any length of time?"

"I don't remember for sure, but it wasn't long. They left late in the summer, and we had to get it back together here and roofed over before it filled up with snow. So it didn't sit more than a couple of weeks or so at the most. Sulo was pretty anxious to get rid of it."

McIntire didn't know what else he could ask. He struggled. "Did you notice anything odd. Anything you didn't expect?"

"Well, there was that body in the attic." Earl chuckled and gave a suck on his pipe. "I don't remember anything, but that was a long time ago. One of the windows was smashed. In the bedroom."

"Could somebody have broken in? A tramp, maybe? Looking for a place to spend the night?"

"No need, the door wasn't locked."

"You kept the bed and the mattress?"

"I *took* them. Kept the bed, burned the mattress. Sandra didn't want it."

Sandra Culver stood up quickly and turned to the washing machine. "It wasn't clean."

McIntire nodded. Not wanting to sleep on Teddy Falk's old mattress was understandable.

"That was only on one side. We could have scrubbed it up." Earl grunted at his wife's finicky ways. "It was a pretty good mattress."

Sandra switched on the wringer and stuffed the corner of a dingy towel between its rollers. A flush spread up her neck. Stained mattresses might be a bit tawdry but…. "Mrs. Culver, not to be…." McIntire stumbled. "This could be important. Are you saying…?"

She snatched her hand back from the voracious wringer. "I thought maybe Rosie Falk miscarried. Maybe that was why they left without much of a fuss."

For someone who'd spent a good share of her adult life in the family way, Sandra Culver was certainly modest. "Blood?" McIntire asked.

She nodded.

"A lot of blood?"

"Quite a bit."

McIntire swallowed his coffee and pushed back his chair.

Sandra walked with him onto the porch. Once again she seemed overcome by embarrassment, wrapping her arms about herself and scuffling her feet. Maybe it was only the cold.

"I never thanked you."

"Thanked me for what?"

The dog rubbed against her knees and she reached to scratch behind its ears. "Finding my little girl. If it wasn't for you, she'd still be lying there, and we'd still not know."

The discovery of Cindy Culver's body was a horror that would stay with McIntire forever. How much greater nightmare for her family?

"It must have been awful for you." She straightened up and pulled her faded cardigan closer at her throat.

McIntire struggled for something to say. Leonie would have known exactly the right words. He patted her arm, then the dog's head.

"Say hi to your wife." Sandra slipped back inside.

McIntire gave a thump on the door to dislodge newly fallen snow from the screen. Would it never stop?

DULUTH, MINN.—The request of Knut
Heikkinen to move his deportation
hearing to New York City has been
denied.

Chapter Eleven

The only thing worse than the pain in her leg was the miasma of dank and musty odors issuing from the mattress, the blankets, the curtains, the varnish on the floorboards.

Mia lay back on the narrow bed in the room where her father had slept in the years after her mother's death. It hadn't always held this dead, fusty atmosphere. When she was a little girl, the room had been a special place, warm and scrupulously free of dust, where the furniture Eban Vogel built with such artistry received its final polish. She'd spent the too short winter afternoons playing on the floor, building houses with the scraps from his work; watching the patterns and colors of the wood appear as if by magic from under his cloth: the golden swirls in the oak, the deep red rivers of the mahogany. The room had held its own distinctive aroma then. The smells of his mysterious waxes had permeated the house and still trickled through Mia's dreams. But when Charlotte Vogel died, her husband had moved the wardrobe and the creaky iron bed into this room, and Mia had seldom entered it again.

And she'd hardly entered it since his own death. Four years without the touch of a dustcloth or soap and water is a long time, and the present-day aroma was not blended of shellac and carnauba wax. She'd better get used to it; she wouldn't be climbing stairs for a while. It might not be long before Nick, too, would be confined to the main floor. A silver lining—her accident gave an excuse to get this room ready for him.

She wriggled into as near a sitting position as she could manage. *Manage.* How was she going to manage? There was no point in thinking about it. She simply wasn't going to manage, not for a while. It would be all up to Nick now—water, firewood, cooking, washing, ironing. Ironing? That would never happen. Mia had been contemplating—shuddering at—the prospect of taking over Nick's chores, not passing more onto him. She'd taken the car out a few times before the snow fell, trying to prepare for the time when Nick could no longer drive. That was out of the question now. He'd just have to keep on a while longer. And kill himself, most likely. He'd come close enough a few times already, and that was back when he was supposedly healthy. Guibard said she'd have the cast on for about six weeks. You couldn't starve to death in six weeks. For the first time in her life, Mia wished she'd been more ambitious when it came to putting up vegetables. And she also couldn't help feeling a bit cheated. When this chance to be coddled had at last come her way, she had nobody to do the coddling.

She gave a mighty shove to hitch herself up a little farther. One of the slats holding the bed spring hit the floor with a crack. Nick's footsteps sounded on the living room linoleum.

"You awake, Meggie?" He stood in the doorway. "I thought Guibard gave you enough to knock you out for a week."

"No such luck," Mia said. "The bed's broke."

Nick sank to his knees and peered under. "God!"

"What?"

"It's pretty dusty under there."

"Forget that. I'll try to move so you can put the slat back in before the whole bed goes down."

"Here." Nick grasped her legs and eased her around to a sideways position. "Just sit tight."

He slid under the bed. "Whatever you do, don't make any sudden moves." His words were followed by a twanging of springs and a scraping of wood. "Don't make any moves at all."

After a few seconds he emerged, dust-covered but smiling. He sucked in his breath but got to his feet without struggle. "That should hold for a while. We can bring the big bed downstairs. I'll get Touminen to help." He swung her legs back onto the bed. "Don't bounce around too much."

"I don't plan to do much bouncing for the foreseeable future."

"You want some coffee?"

Had Nick ever in his life made coffee? If he had, Mia didn't remember.

He plucked a curl of dust from his neck. "Did it hurt a lot?"

It still hurt a lot. "Not too much," she told him.

"Leonie McIntire came over to see how you were. She cooked me some breakfast. She insisted on breakfast even though it was past noon."

"Oh, please Nick! Don't let her in here! Tell her I'm still sleeping. Tell her I'm dead!"

"She's gone. I gave her a ride home."

Lord, how had she found out so soon? "She's not going to put this in her paper, is she?"

"Probably. It's the biggest news around here in months." He tucked the blankets around her feet. "She said she'd come back over tomorrow to see what she could do to help. She'll probably be wanting an exclusive interview. Too bad she doesn't print pictures."

For an instant Nick was his old boyish self. The image was reinforced by his parting words, "How much water do you put in?"

John had probably told his wife about their discovery under the pine tree, too. Mia could only hope she didn't decide to put *that* in her so-called newspaper. The story of her broken ankle would be bad enough: a plea for sympathy and aid for poor Mrs. Nick Thorsen who broke her ankle trying to see how far she could throw an empty thundermug. The last thing she needed was Leonie McIntire in this room, helping out by rounding up dust bunnies.

She leaned back against the headboard. The iron scrollwork bit into her spine, and she wriggled down to lie flat on her back.

Her feet popped from the covers and extended past the end of the mattress. She hoped Nick was on the phone to Touminen now. Preferably both Touminens, Sulo *and* Uno. Getting the bed down the stairs could be more than a two-man job. Especially when the strength of one of those men might give out without warning.

What would it be like to sleep in the bed where, presumably, she'd been conceived? Would she be warm and comforted, cradled in the arms of her parents, or would her mind, vulnerable in sleep, be helpless against the intrusion of their restless spirits? Was the soul of Eban Vogel, right now, seething in the frustration of unjust suspicion, suspicion it was powerless to fight from the grave?

Mia didn't even try to curb the morbid flights of fancy. She would have little enough to occupy her time, and indulging in intercourse with the dead was as good an entertainment as any.

The idea that her father might have committed some terrible act of violence or larceny was absurd. Eban Vogel had definite views of how things should be and he didn't hold back in trying to convince anybody within earshot of the logic of those views, but he was not impulsive and certainly not violent. She had almost never seen him lose his temper. That night with Teddy Falk had been all the more terrifying because of the freakish change in him.

It was the money that was the most difficult to accept. It was conceivable that anyone could be driven to an act of passion, pushed beyond his capacity to endure. But theft? Stealing wasn't something done in the heat of the moment. Mia's father was impeccably honest. And he wasn't poor. He would never have stolen a single penny, let alone $700. It had to have belonged to him. But why would he have hidden it?

Besides, Eban had always been fond of Rosie Falk, treated her kindly, complimenting her, and doing things for her that she could easily have done herself. He felt sorry for her, Mia knew. She wouldn't have traded places with Rose for all the money in the world, but she had sometimes wished her father would show that kind of chivalry toward her.

LONDON—A measure of wartime gloom
returned to London last night with
the switching off of advertising
and shop window lights.

Chapter Twelve

McIntire was relieved to see a snake of smoke issuing from the chimney. It wasn't like Leonie to balk at going into the basement to fill the furnace, even in total darkness.

It also wasn't like her to be sitting as he found her, hunched at the kitchen table with her chin barely above the rim of her teacup.

He kissed the top of her head. "Taken up reading the leaves?"

"Maybe they can give me a hint on when it will stop snowing."

"I can tell you that," McIntire said. "You'll be pretty safe around half-past June."

"I don't seem to recollect that it snowed every day last winter."

McIntire recollected it all too well. "It's like childbirth," he said. "You forget."

"Childbirth," she said, "I *do* remember." She stood up to refill the kettle and went about rinsing the teapot.

When his wife was giving birth to her daughters, McIntire was…where? On the other side of the world from her in one of those cramped desks; a gangly, pimply-faced high school sophomore. What would she have been like then? Much the same as now, he suspected, determined and pragmatic. But what had she really felt, evicting those twins from the shelter of her body into a world wracked by war, while her nineteen-year-old husband lay dying a few miles away? What did she feel now, separated from those daughters by an ocean and half a continent?

"What have you discovered about the elusive Teddy and Rose?" She held up the pot with a questioning look, and McIntire nodded.

Teddy and Rose. It sounded like a team of oxen. "I don't think they're elusive," McIntire said. "I think they're dead."

"A lot of people who were in Russia before the war are dead."

"No, Leonie." He accepted the steaming cup. "I think at least one of the Falks, maybe both, died before they could leave, right here, at their farm, in their own house."

Leonie looked as befuddled as McIntire felt.

"Just because nobody got a letter from them? On that basis my sister in New Zealand has been strumming a harp for the past four years."

"If I dig up her handbag in the back yard, and discover bloodstains on the sheets, I'll be alerting the authorities."

"You'd turn me in? You never met Esther, did you?"

Had Teddy or Rose Falk, or both of them, instead of finding a socialist Utopia, found death in their bed? All those years when anyone who thought about it probably assumed they had met with some terrible fate at the hands of Joe Stalin, had it happened right here? How? And what could be done about it now? There was no statute of limitations on murder, but the chances of finding how it came about were slim. If they were both dead, it could have been a case of murder-suicide. No. If that was what happened, at least one body would probably have been found. If they were dead, what did happen to the bodies?

There was, or had been, one other person who must have known that the Falks hadn't gone to Karelia—the person who buried their passage money in Eban Vogel's yard. Most likely to have been Eban Vogel. So why had he let everyone think that the Falks had gone abroad if he knew different? And why had he secreted the money?

McIntire examined the dregs of his own cup, found the leaves unhelpful, and walked to the phone. He picked up the receiver and cranked his way through to the Flambeau County sheriff's office.

Marian Koski's voice on the phone sounded pinched. "The sheriff," she said, "is flat on his back *because* of his back. Shoveling snow." Her sigh was audible even over the static on the lines. "Cecil Newman is in charge. Would you like to speak to him?"

Speak to Cecil Newman? It was too early in the day. Too early in the year. "Oh, I don't think we need to bother Deputy Newman right now," McIntire said. "It's not urgent."

"All right then. Let me know if I can be of help."

"Same here. Give my best to Pete."

Babyface Newman in charge? Well, with any luck, the weather might keep anyone with otherwise criminal inclinations at home.

McIntire made one more call. This one to Harald Anderson. "Harald," he asked, "you still got that Ten-B?"

WASHINGTON—The Defense Department raised its manpower sights to 3,462,205 men under arms by June and indicated an even higher goal may be announced soon.

Chapter Thirteen

It had taken a bit of convincing to get Sulo Touminen to agree to McIntire's digging up the old well. He limited his revelations to the finding of the Falks' bill of lading. He didn't say where, but if Sulo had the mental powers of a walleye, he could easily figure that out. Given road conditions, there could have been only a limited number of places McIntire visited prior to coming to see Sulo himself on the morning of the storm. Limited to one—the Thorsens'.

Sulo's grudging acquiescence meant that McIntire didn't have to try to talk St. Adele Township's bristly justice of the peace, Myrtle Van Opelt, into issuing him a warrant. McIntire hoped his lack of discretion wasn't too large a price to pay.

Sulo was vague about the cistern's exact location, and he had no interest in joining the constable in digging around to look for it under two and a half feet of snow. *About ten yards west of where the house used to be*, was the best he could do. "I dumped in some sand and put the cover—a buncha planks—back over the spot," he'd added, "just in case things loosened up. Didn't want the horses falling through. It's pretty much rotted away now, but there might be some sign of it."

His sister had been a little more precise, sitting silently at her oil-cloth covered table, drawing a neat map on the back of the envelope the electric bill had come in, using the barn and remaining lilac bushes as landmarks.

McIntire stuck his shovel into the snowbank and rotated the chart to find some correlation with the scene before him.

Touminen used most of the acreage for hay, which he stored in the swaybacked barn, the only structure left to show that anyone had ever lived here. He hadn't begun using the fodder yet this winter, so the road into the place wasn't cleared. And it was a long road, a quarter-mile, McIntire reckoned. The Falk homestead would have been an isolated spot even in the thirties, when the area's population was considerably higher than it was now.

McIntire shouldered his shovel and waded into a drift up to his thighs. An investment in a pair of snowshoes was an increasingly attractive idea.

Map in hand, he spent over an hour scuffing through the crusty snow, prodding with a shovel, before he hit what sounded like wood. After getting rid of what felt like a ton of snow, McIntire had only to remove a few rotted splinters of board. Still, it was mid-afternoon before he'd cleared the space down to the slightly sunken frozen ground.

Leaning on his shovel, feeling the snow in his overshoes turning to slush and the sweat chill on his neck, he hesitated. What was he doing here? Was there really a chance that he was going to find some Robert Frostian truth at the bottom of a well, or was this excursion just another manifestation of cabin fever? An exercise to stave off the crushing monotony of the Michigan winter? Would his time be better spent ice fishing?

On the face of things, this seemed senseless, a shot in the dark, but maybe Occam's razor would prevail, the simple explanation would be the correct one. Mr. and Mrs. Falk had disappeared. It was as good a place to start looking as any.

He looked at the threatening sky, dragged a few of the bountiful supply of broken spruce branches to mark the spot, and drove off to the home of Harald, *aka* "Gopher," Anderson and his Bucyrus-Erie 10-B shovel.

◇◇◇

McIntire pulled his car into the shadow of a genuine man's vehicle.

After the war, Anderson had got hold of a couple of retired army trucks, including the flatbed on which he transported the masterpiece of his fleet, the real tribute to testosterone: the Bucyrus Erie 10-B shovel. He'd bought it from one of the mining companies, and he claimed to be able to dig up, move, or knock over anything smaller than a courthouse. The man was the envy of every male over the age of three. McIntire was no exception. He coveted the tractor-mounted plow with which Gopher, aided by the small daughter on his lap, was clearing away snow, scraping it down to his nicely graveled driveway. If snow removal could be considered an art, the precise rectangles and orderly banks in Anderson's yard made him the Picasso of the Plow.

Anderson left the child bouncing on the tractor seat, gleefully fiddling with the various levers, and came to lean on the hood of McIntire's milksop Studebaker.

"Can you do it? When the ground is frozen?"

Gopher chewed a grease-embedded thumbnail. "I can try. Might not be froze that far down. We got snow pretty early on. Anyway it's sandy around there, and it was a dry fall. Might not be too hard."

"I could build a fire," McIntire offered, "try to thaw the ground a little."

"Heat goes up, not down. Wouldn't do much good. The Ten-B can do 'er."

Anderson seemed illogically optimistic. Eager even. His next words gave a clue as to why.

"How come you want to dig out Rosie Makinen's old well?"

McIntire remembered the rock-hard feel of that earth under his shovel. Maintaining Anderson's zeal could be crucial. "Because I think Rosie might be in it," he said, "maybe along with her husband. You think we can get at it tomorrow?"

Gopher nodded.

WASHINGTON—President Truman signed a bill giving FBI agents authority to make arrests without a warrant, for any federal offense committed in their presence.

Chapter Fourteen

McIntire chose his wardrobe for the day by a simple rule: two of everything, three to cover the really important parts. It was going to be a long, cold day, with little for him to do but stand around and shiver. He stuffed his trouser cuffs into his overshoes and wrapped his neck in his Christmas muffler. It was knit with Leonie's own hands in a becoming red and black snowflake pattern. Something Gopher Anderson and his fellows would not be caught dead in.

When he reached the Falk place, the flatbed truck was blocking the road, and Anderson was huddled in the cab of his shovel, face in a thermos cup, scoop poised over the cleared spot.

"I thought I'd better wait for you to give the go-ahead."

"Go ahead."

The engine growled, a confusing system of cables and pulleys clanked into action, and the claw at the end of a ten-foot steel beam descended with a screech and a deafening crash.

A half-hour later, Anderson was still hammering and scratching at the frozen earth, making inch-deep clefts in the frosty sand. McIntire was still stomping his feet and blowing on his frozen fingers, remembering why it was he had *not* taken up ice fishing.

After forty-five minutes, the teeth bit through the crust to expose a darker, loamier soil. The next time the bucket rammed into the ground, it brought up a bushel or so of black, lumpy earth. McIntire felt a surge of excitement. Gopher didn't seem to share it. After three more scoops he leaned out of the cab and beckoned to McIntire.

"This ain't it," he shouted.

"What?" McIntire moved near enough to hear over the grumbling engine.

"It ain't no well. It's a shithouse hole."

"Are you sure?"

He pointed to the mound of black earth. "That stuff ain't water. Besides, there ain't no casing."

He switched off the engine.

The blissful spell of silence was broken by the sound of a car approaching from the south. As McIntire stood staring into the unfruitful cavity, the noise stopped and a door slammed shut, then another. A few minutes later, Sulo Touminen trudged into view, accompanied by his cousin, Uno. Sulo and Uno, dubbed the Touminen Twins. They shared the same birthdate, albeit a dozen years apart.

They did indeed make an identical pair, treading one foot ahead of the other in the shovel's tracks, dressed in plaid mackinaws, noses the same hue as the bills on their deer-hunter red caps.

Sulo looked at the pile of dark soil. "That ain't it."

"We figured that out," McIntire said. "Thank your sister for me."

Sulo nodded and walked about twenty paces toward the barn, then tracked to the left, swishing his feet through the powder.

Uno voiced the opinion that if Teddy Falk didn't feel like writing home that was his own damn business. Snow began to fall, soft feathers floating on currents of air.

Anderson stretched his legs out the door of his cab, but kept to the seat of his shovel, snowflakes decorating his knees. Once he had that seat warmed, he obviously intended to keep it that way.

Uno Touminen had begun amassing a pile of fallen limbs when his cousin gave a grunt, "Uh-huh." Uno dropped the log he carried and trudged through the snow to join him in conference. Twin wool-covered backsides bobbed amid withered bramble fern and the naked stems of wild rose as they pawed in the snow with unmittened hands. The two stood erect. "Here we go," Sulo announced.

Gopher went into action once more. The shovel shuddered and crunched thirty yards to the east.

Uno stomped off, scratching at the thorns in his fingers, retracing his tracks to his car. Sulo ambled back to McIntire, hands in pockets. "I hope you ain't expecting the township to pay for this."

McIntire hadn't thought that far ahead. Was he going to end up with a hole full of trash and a whopping bill from Gopher?

"You ain't gonna find anything there, anyway," Sulo added.

"I hope you're right," McIntire said.

Uno trundled back into view carrying a can of gasoline, with which he gave the stacked branches a liberal dousing. McIntire backed well off, while the silent Finn struck a match on the seat of his pants and transformed the brushpile into an inferno.

The roaring of the fire died, and once again Anderson's bucket rumbled and clanged and scraped frozen earth. Uno stared into the flames from under the brim of his red cap, thumb in mouth. McIntire hoped the pose was occasioned by the brambles and not his usual habit. He turned his back to the warmth and waited.

The falling snow turned the scene monochromatic, like a scratchy movie reel, and lent a ghostlike quality to the figure that now strolled into the clearing. Adam Wall, deputy sheriff when he happened to feel like it, or when Pete Koski figured he was up to it, materialized out of the gloom. He pulled off his gloves and extended his hands over the fire. "I'm not even going to ask."

"You're wise beyond your years."

The bucket brought up sandy soil mixed with stone and cracked concrete. The well casing. On its next descent, it sank deeper and the booty included a glint of broken glass. McIntire moved forward, Wall at his heels. Another scoop produced rusted tin cans, a few small bottles that had once contained extract for making root beer, a gray pottery snuff jar. McIntire peered into the hole. Tangles of rusted wire pierced shreds of rotted fabric. He signaled to Anderson to continue.

The claw dipped into the well once more and deposited a heap of soil and debris into the snow. The excavation was now about six feet deep. Chunks of concrete tumbled onto the crumbled remnants of an abandoned home—a broken stool, fruit jars, a rubber tire. A stick-like object, knobbed at the end, mottled sooty black, protruded through what looked like the sodden remains of a sheep.

McIntire spoke to Adam Wall. "What do you think?"

"I think you might want to go down there and have a look."

McIntire turned to look at the stolid pair regarding him from their spot by the fire, then into the questioning eyes of Harald Anderson. He put up his hand. "That'll do it," he said.

NEW YORK—Officials of the world's
tallest building—the Empire
State—said they are ready to cope
with any bombing.

Chapter Fifteen

The fervor with which the Michigan State Police took on the job of cleaning out a ten-foot-deep hole in frozen earth at six degrees Fahrenheit was spooky. McIntire didn't participate. One day of standing around freezing his backside, and frontside, watching others do the work, was all he needed for the time being. Anyway, he didn't expect that his help would be necessary or appreciated.

He also hoped to be well out of the way when someone thought to ask what had led the township constable to take it upon himself to dig out Jarvi Makinen's cistern. Telling the state police that he just got to wondering what had become of good old Ted and the missus wasn't going to do it. He'd have to fork over the fragments of the bill of lading and the passport, but McIntire wasn't sure about the money. Mia might have a point. It had turned up in her yard and, so far, there was no one to say it hadn't belonged to her father. In the thirties banks weren't the best place to put that bit of extra cash. If Eban feared the Depression catching up with him and his family, he might have wanted to put something aside, somewhere out of the reach of immediate temptation. You'd think he'd have let somebody know about it in the event of his unanticipated death or disability. Eban had died from an untreated cancer. His death hadn't been unanticipated. Not by him. He'd had plenty of time to tell Mia about the stash or to retrieve it himself. It was hard to imagine that he'd simply forgotten about it.

No two ways about it, if the verdict was homicide—and how could it be anything but?—Eban Vogel was going to be the prime suspect. In the absence of evidence to the contrary, the state police could very well just close the book and look no further. Or, they might brush the dirt off their hands and turn the whole thing over to the county sheriff.

McIntire hadn't spoken to either of the Thorsens since the morning after the storm. He was going to have to see them soon. Wasn't one expected to visit the ailing? Commanded to, even, in his father's Catholic religion? Mia and Nick would know by now that he'd found those bodies, and they'd also know that their own discovery couldn't be kept secret. They must be expecting, and dreading, the sheriff's knock on the door. McIntire would have to talk with them before turning over any evidence.

Rose and Teddy Falk were still only names in McIntire's mind. No one he'd talked to had much to say about them, what sort of people they were, if they had a family. Even if they didn't have children, there must have been some relatives. There would be people to notify.

McIntire turned back to his work, the translation of that epic morality tale, *The Saga of Gösta Berling*. It was a thorny process, converting nineteenth-century Swedish to modern American English without making it sound…silly. Still, he supposed he had an advantage in that many of his neighbors *spoke* nineteenth-century Swedish.

"What will they do with the bones?"

Leonie's words came as a surprise, and not just because he hadn't realized that she'd come into the room. Until now she'd shown scant interest in the fact that a young couple from the community had apparently been murdered in bed and their bodies dumped into their well. She'd only responded to his news with a few appropriate words of sympathy and had barely looked at the newspaper accounts.

"The state police took them over to let Guibard have a look," McIntire said. "After that, I don't know. They'll have to find a way to make a definite identification."

"They're at Dr. Guibard's *house?*"

"That's what he wanted." When he left Makinen's farm after what he knew was a futile plea for confidentiality on the part of Anderson and the Touminens, McIntire had stopped at Mark Guibard's home to request an official coroner's visit to the scene. He'd been turned down.

"Anybody wants my professional opinion that the owners of some pile of bones are legally dead," the doctor had stated, "they'll damn well have to bring 'em to me."

McIntire said, "I was thinking of taking a drive over to see if he's made any progress."

Apparently he'd been wrong about his wife's interest in the Falks. She seated herself on the davenport, put her feet up, and spread a striped wool blanket over her legs. "Do you think Mia's father killed them?" she asked.

"No." McIntire didn't hesitate. "I can't believe that Eban Vogel had anything to do with it."

"He had the money."

"It does seem that way."

"I expect you just don't want to believe it."

"Damn right I don't!" McIntire could hardly imagine anything he wanted to believe less. He added feebly, "Eban wasn't that kind of person."

Eban Vogel could be dogmatic and was never reluctant to point out, at whatever length he saw fit, the flaws in one's beliefs, behaviors, or opinions. But he wasn't quick tempered or malicious. He seemed to genuinely believe that he knew exactly how things should be, and that it would be shirking his responsibility not to do his utmost to bring the entire world around to his right-thinking ways.

"Eban would never want to kill somebody he was at odds with," McIntire said. "He'd want to keep them around to convert if it took until doomsday."

"The Falks weren't staying around."

Leonie had a point. "It sounds like *you* do want to believe that Eban Vogel killed them."

"Of course I don't!" She looked suitably shocked at the suggestion, an impression not reinforced by her next words. "I'd prefer not to believe that it happened at all, but it was a long time ago. Mr. Vogel is dead. He can't do any more harm, and no more harm can come to him. Maybe it's best if it's just left at that."

"And if Mr. Vogel didn't do it?"

"I don't know. It happened a long time ago. I know we can't just ignore it, but...it's liable to stir up all sorts of...." She tucked the blanket around her toes. "It's so cold."

It was over a year and a half since Leonie had accompanied her then-new husband to his childhood home. She'd made a few disparaging remarks about the mosquitos, and she wasn't crazy about his mother's choice of kitchen curtains, but in most ways she'd taken to Northern Michigan like it was she who was the native. She had settled in much more quickly than had McIntire himself. And, unlike himself, she'd never before complained about the cold.

"Would you rather I stayed home?" McIntire asked. "I can call Guibard instead." And get him to say absolutely nothing on the telephone.

"Certainly not." She held up her paperback western. "Mr. Grey and I will be just fine." She pulled a second blanket from the back of the sofa. "You might put a stick or two of wood on the fire before you go."

The smell of damp earth permeated Mark Guibard's dining room. The doctor looked dressed for a dinner party, pinstriped waistcoat over his white shirt, and he moved with uncharacteristic sedateness, footsteps silent on the carpet. He folded back the sheet with precise movements.

McIntire had expected to see a collection of moldering bones and fragments. The yellow light of the brass chandelier illuminated a macabre feast. Two skeletons lay side by side on the narrow table, finger bones touching. They were pitted and discolored, but largely intact, if he discounted the fact that the one on the right lacked a skull. Only a row of vertebrae, longer than McIntire would have thought a human neck would be, extended from its circle of ribs. A fragment of jaw with a yellowed molar, and a single shard of cupped bone, bits of sand clinging to its surface, lay on the cloth next to it.

"I didn't expect them to be in such good shape."

"Not much to happen to them down there."

"What about the head?"

"So far that's all we've got."

"They still looking?"

Guibard circled the table as if he, too, were viewing the remains for the first time. "They hauled everything they dug from the well, and a few yards of dirt from around it, down to the lab in Lansing. They'll be sifting through it for some time to come."

McIntire touched the gold band that still encircled the third finger of the left hand of the smaller skeleton, the one with a head. "It would have happened in 1934. You were here then. Who knows more about people than their doctor? Who do you think could have killed Teddy Falk and his wife days before they planned to leave the country?"

"No opinion on that. But I do know enough to tell you that this ain't Teddy Falk."

McIntire's ears seemed to buzz. "What?"

"Teddy was a little guy. Shorter than Rose. I don't know who this man might be, but it ain't J. Theodore Falk."

"You sure it's a man?"

"Pretty sure."

"Rose was in bed with someone else?"

"That's entirely possible. If that was Rose's blood on the mattress."

"Maybe this isn't Rose, either." Maybe it was the Falks who were the killers. Dispatched some unfortunate couple and left the country quick, without their life savings.

"Oh," Guibard spoke with sadness, "it's our little Rosie Makinen, all right. I'd recognize those fractures anywhere." He ran a finger across a lumpy collarbone. "This is where she landed when she took the family milk cow for a ride, when she was about five. The two cockeyed ribs are from a collision with a tree on the maiden voyage of her Super Ice Skis. The left wrist and the chipped tooth...hmmm. I believe that was the high wire incident."

"Your little Rosie Makinen sounds like quite the daredevil."

"Ah yes. I'd be able to retire for good and all now, if Jarvi'd had any money. Rosie was a pistol. And tough as they come. All the times I sewed her up, I never heard her make so much as a whimper."

"Maybe not above risking a fling with...whoever the hell this chap is." McIntire couldn't help but feel relief. "I imagine that wraps it up. Falk came home, found his wife in bed with another man, killed them, dumped them in the well, and took off. End of story."

"Could be." The doctor didn't sound convinced.

It could very well be. Teddy Falk would have been understandably eager to leave and not be disposed to stay in close touch with those he left behind. He wouldn't be wanting awkward questions like "How's the little woman?" It didn't explain how his money ended up under Eban Vogel's pine tree, but knowing that Teddy was quite possibly still alive cast that in a different light, too. How, McIntire could figure out later.

"Any indication of what killed them?"

"I have a pretty good hunch what killed our mystery man." He flipped over the fragment of jawbone and pointed to a tiny greyish lump wedged at the base of the single tooth. "A shotgun blast..." he fanned his fingers and placed his hand over the skull fragment, "right here."

"It that all that was left of it? Of his head?"

"Close range with a shotgun ain't gonna leave a hell of a lot. Like hitting a melon with—"

"I'll take your word for it," McIntire said. "What about Rose? It doesn't look like she was shot, too. At least not in the head."

"Damned observant fella you are. No it doesn't. Left scapula a little beat up, but that could be from anything. Before or after she died. Hard to say what." He wiped his fingers on the edge of the sheet. "Especially with Rosie. I wish now I'd gotten off my backside and been there when they pulled these two out."

McIntire waited. The grave-smell was oppressive.

"When they brought them in, the guy here was basically what you'd have expected, a jumble of bones in a box. They say that's pretty much how they found him—without the box. But this one," he took a long breath, "Rosie…Rosie was more in one piece, embedded in bits of wool and different material. Like she'd been bundled into something made from scraps, a patchwork quilt or maybe a rug, and laid out carefully, gently, not just thrown in the hole like a sack of grain."

Which meant that Rose Falk might have been killed by someone who cared about her. Someone like her husband. Or it might simply have meant the murderer was getting rid of blood-soaked bedding evidence. Or that a body is easier to dispose of if it's neatly wrapped.

Wads of soggy fabric lay on the sideboard next to what looked like the fruits of an archeological dig: some shreds of leather; a clump of hair, long and dark; a few chipped buttons; a tin cup.

"Are these part of the spoils or some of your evil medical instruments?" McIntire pointed to a couple of pieces of twisted metal.

"This is what's left of Rosie's spectacles." Guibard picked up the rusted wire. "And I believe that one's a crochet hook."

"If you say so. Is this all there was?"

"It's only what came along with the bones. The state police have the rest. How'd you know to look for them?"

The question had been bound to come. McIntire wished he had prepared a plausible evasion. "I came across a passport and the receipt for the machinery and household goods they shipped. The bill of lading. They would have needed it to claim the stuff.

After I asked around a bit, it seemed like nobody really knew for sure they'd gone. Then I found out that they hadn't shown up for the trip, and Earl Culver mentioned blood on the mattress and throwing the trash in the well, so…." His breath ran out, but the hurried explanation seemed to satisfy Guibard and draw his attention from the way it began. He didn't ask *where* McIntire had come across that passport. Nevertheless, McIntire thought it best to change the subject. "What will happen to the remains now?"

"They'll go to the state police laboratory in Lansing. The guy, they'll hang on to until they get some identification. When they're done with Rosie, I suppose they'll let her be buried."

Something besides the death of the intrepid Rosie Makinen might have been contributing to Guibard's bleak demeanor. "Palmerson figures he'll be drafted," he said. "I'm going to have to take over part of his practice for a while."

"But he just got here."

"And now he's going to Korea."

"He must be past forty years old."

"Forty-six, and with a wife and four kids. Uncle Sam ain't planning to run short this time. Palmerson got his medical training compliments of the U.S. government in the last war. They don't figure they got their money's worth out of him."

What would it be like to be conscripted into the military at about the age McIntire had left it? McIntire could imagine all too well.

He buttoned his coat and made for the door. Guibard looked up from pulling a sheet over the two skeletons. "You're gonna have to come up with a better story than that for Pete Koski."

LONDON—Grave diggers worked in
the light of flares as the death
toll soared in Britain's great
influenza outbreak.

Chapter Sixteen

McIntire let the earpiece dangle and walked upstairs to knock
on the bathroom door.

"It's a Mr. Patrick Humphrey's secretary, returning your call.
What do you want me to tell her?"

The only response was a gurgle of water.

"Leonie? You still with us?"

"I was just trying to think. It must be a mistake. I've never
heard of any Patrick Humphrey."

McIntire relayed the information to Mr. Humphrey's secretary and went back to the problem at hand. The visit to the
Thorsens couldn't be put off any longer. Besides hashing over
what to do about the money, it wasn't very neighborly to make
no show of sympathy for Mia's broken leg. McIntire couldn't
expect Leonie to be his surrogate forever. Leonie, for that matter,
hadn't been spending as much time tending to Mia as McIntire
had envisioned. Not surprising now that he thought of it. Mia
wasn't one to accept help with any more grace than did her
husband. Well, McIntire wouldn't embarrass her by offering to
spruce up her cupboards. He'd cluck over her leg, try to get his
hands on the seven hundred, and be gone.

But first he intended to drop a short line to Special Agent
Melvin Fratelli. If J. Theodore Falk had been a card-carrying

communist, and if he was still alive and living in the USA, the FBI might be just the folks to know his whereabouts. They might for damn sure have an idea where he'd gone when he left St. Adele. Agent Fratelli, after his successful stint undercover in Flambeau County, instead of riding off into the sunset or back to the bureau's field office in Detroit, had been hanging around Marquette, the better to periodically badger McIntire about what kind of subversive activities might be going on in St. Adele Township. McIntire wasn't keen to be in Fratelli's debt, but desperate times called for desperate measures. He went to the dining room for paper and pen.

"Who you writing to?"

For someone so secretive about her own correspondence, Leonie was being pretty nosy.

"I thought I'd see if G-man Fratelli can find out anything about Teddy Falk." He added, "I'll go over to Thorsens' this morning to let them know that it wasn't Teddy in the well, if they haven't heard. That should come as a relief. But the state police, and maybe even our very own Cecil Newman, will be questioning them regardless. They'll have to fess up to finding that money."

"Good luck." Leonie adjusted the towel on her head. "Mia hasn't been eager for company. You might do better to wait until Nick is at home."

The excuse for further procrastination was tempting. "No," McIntire said. "Nick will hear all the gossip when he's on his route today. I don't want it to look like I'm not bothering to let them know what's going on, or worse yet, holding out." Leonie looked small in her thick dressing gown. "Want to come with?"

"I don't think so. As I said, it seems as if Mia would rather muddle along on her own." She opened the cupboard. "I'll send along some of the fairy cakes."

When he again picked up his pen, McIntire's apprehensions about consulting Melvin Fratelli returned, especially if it might end up involving his neighbors. Fratelli was tenacious in his pursuit of wrongdoers, and no doubt the Michigan winter was having the same effect on him as it was on McIntire. Looking for someone who might, or might not, have skipped out to the Soviet Union twenty years ago would give the agent great amusement. It probably couldn't lead to much trouble for the current residents of St. Adele. With Falk transformed from expatriate to fugitive from justice, the FBI would get into it anyway. Still, McIntire worded the letter judiciously, only asking for advice on locating an old acquaintance, J. Theodore, no mention of why and certainly none of double murder.

McIntire paused with his hand raised to knock. Maybe Mia would be in bed. Maybe he *should* have waited until Nick was there or insisted that Leonie come along. Leonie wouldn't hesitate to walk in without expecting Mia to hobble to the door and open it for her.

He entered the small porch, treading softly across the grey painted boards, feeling like a bandit, and rapped timidly on the kitchen door. If Mia had been forced to come from another room, she'd begun her hobbling at the sound of his car. She called out to him to come on in.

She sat on a wooden chair, her left leg, in a plaster cast nearly to the knee, resting on another. A pair of crutches, extended to their full length, leaned in the corner. On the table in front of her a ball of grey yarn, skewered with knitting needles, sat next to an open magazine. Her hair was damp and hung loose, something McIntire hadn't seen in thirty-five years. It rippled over her shoulders and past her elbows. A silver waterfall. For a moment neither of them spoke.

"I saw your car." Mia sounded apologetic. "I thought it would be Leonie."

"No," McIntire said. "I'll be the one playing Clara Barton today."

Mia pushed the damp tresses behind her ears. "It takes a long time to dry."

McIntire wondered how she had managed to wash it. Could she stand up? Maybe Nick had done it for her. He deposited the plate of cupcakes on the table. "How're you doing?"

"Not so bad." She didn't look good, her complexion barely a lighter shade of blue than her eyes, but then Mia had never had what might be called a robust appearance.

"I never did hear exactly how it happened."

"And you never will."

"Guibard said ass over teakettle on some ice."

"It wasn't a teakettle." She smiled a little but didn't say more.

"Anything I can do?"

"You can sit down, instead of looming over me like a buzzard." She gave the yarn a shove. "I decided to put my time to use by doing some knitting. I didn't get far. I can't remember how you put the stitches on the needle."

"Leonie can probably show you."

"It'll come back to me." She hitched herself up in the chair. "I don't suppose you came over to hold my hand. Are you here to tell me my father's body will be dug up so he can be hung?"

"Your father is probably off the hook. It looks as though Teddy Falk might still be alive."

At the news that Rose Falk's partner in death was other than her husband Mia's eyes sprang to life. She leaned toward him. "You mean Rose was fooling around, and Teddy caught them?"

McIntire nodded. "Looks that way. Any idea who it might have been? Were rumors making the rounds? Maybe somebody showed up missing at the same time she did? Was there anybody else expected to emigrate?" It was hard to believe Rose could have gotten away with anything in this neighborhood.

Mia frowned and shook her head. "I can't think of anybody off-hand, but that was a long time ago. There wouldn't have been a shortage of men around, what with the mines and the logging. Rose got around to all the meetings, so she'd have had a chance to meet a few. If one of them paid some attention to her, who knows? I find it hard to believe she'd really have gone so far as to….But I'd be the last person to ask about what Rosie was up to. I never get off the farm, and I didn't even then. Which is fine with me. I'd as soon stay above the fray—or below it."

He might as well get to the crux of his visit. "Being a homebody won't help you out this time."

"Help me out of what?"

"The stuff you found under the tree. The sheriff will have to hear about it."

"You didn't tell him?"

"Pete's thrown his back out. Cecil Newman is at the helm. But Koski and the state police are going to have to know about the documents *and* the money."

"What for? You say Teddy's still alive. What has any of this got to do with my father now?"

"It's possible Falk's alive, but he's still missing."

"Of course he's missing. He killed his wife! He'd hardly have hung around."

"He'd have needed that money."

"If he's got along without it this long, he doesn't need it now."

"It's evidence in a murder case," McIntire pointed out. But it wasn't his problem, and he knew that when Mia got into one of her stubborn moods, trying to argue with her was a waste of time. "I'll let you fight it out with Pete Koski. But he's going to ask me why I first suspected that the Falks hadn't gone to Karelia, and I'll have to tell him."

"I suppose you will. It's just that…John." She sounded conciliatory, almost pleading. "You know Papa wouldn't have stolen so much as a penny. If he had money, it had to be his own."

And hence, would now be hers. Maybe she had more of a need for it than McIntire had considered. He nodded and looked out the window at the slowly growing mountain of pine branches. "How's Nick doing?"

Mia pulled a handful of hair through her fingers. "Not so good. He gets weak and stiff. Sometimes he can't so much as tie his shoes. It comes and goes for no reason. He's not going to be able to work much longer."

"That'll be tough on him." Possibly not nearly so tough as on his wife.

"He's been delivering mail on that same route since he was sixteen. He'll have to keep up with driving the car for a while longer, though, if we have to get to town. I'm in no shape to take over."

"You know we'll do anything we can to help."

"We'll get along."

"Leonie is never happier than when she's fussing over somebody. She'd be glad to drive you anywhere you need to go."

"I know that."

"I think she might be a little hurt that she hasn't been able to help you more."

"I know that, too."

McIntire stood for another awkward leave-taking. His social graces seemed to be failing. He hoped it didn't have some connection to those urges to take up ice fishing.

DULUTH, MINN.—Knut Heikkinen, held in Duluth under the new Internal Security Act, will make another bid for freedom Friday.

Chapter Seventeen

A light wind sent an eddy of snow off the pumphouse roof, obscuring what appeared to be an arctic explorer waddling to the door. Only when the man pulled off his cap and looked up into the sun did McIntire recognize Melvin Fratelli. The former bogus detective's abundance of clothing impeded his progress up the path, giving McIntire sufficient time to speculate with horror on what he might have said in his letter to bring this rapid personal response. It also gave him time to consider if not being at home might be the best course of action.

Unfortunately, before McIntire could lock the door and draw the curtains, Nanook was in his porch, peeling off layers of wool and flannel.

"Heater ain't worth a shit," was all he said until a few swallows of coffee with cream and a dollop of brandy reduced the frequency of his teeth chattering. Then he gave a monumental shiver. "Aren't you going to ask what brings me out on a day like this?'

In McIntire's estimation, this was one of the best days they'd been blessed with in weeks. The mercury might be low in the tube, and the breeze a little brisk, but the sky was blue as anyone could want, and he hadn't moved so much as a teaspoon of snow. "No," he said. "My manners are too good. I'll just wait for you to tell me."

The agent wasn't reluctant. "Why you looking for that Red?"

The Melvin Fratelli that McIntire had met a few months before had been the stereotypical bumbling detective, an act McIntire couldn't believe he'd fallen for. He knew better now and spoke cautiously. "Teddy Falk used to live around here. He left back in the thirties. A few days ago two skeletons were found in his well. You'd have heard about it."

His nod was brisk. "You were the one found them. I heard that, too."

It sounded like an accusation. McIntire went on, "One of those skeletons was that of Mrs. Theodore Falk. That makes Mr. Theodore suspect number one. It has nothing to do with his political persuasion."

"Nothing that you know of."

The flatness of Fratelli's voice gave McIntire to know that life was soon going to get a hell of a lot more complicated. It was too late to back out now. "I don't suppose you can tell me where he might be?"

Fratelli drained his cup and half-filled it from the bottle. "He's right here in the state. Been here since he came back from Russia in 1948."

Had it really been so easy? He'd located that missing Red with nothing more than a two-cent stamp. Maybe he was getting the hang of this detective stuff. McIntire poured a celebratory drop into his own cup. "So he did go after all."

"He was in the U.S.S.R. for thirteen years."

"That long? I wonder how he managed to get out."

The self-assured agent's cynical snort left a sparkling drip below his nose. "Don't we all?"

It was something McIntire did not want to be drawn into. "If you suspect Teddy Falk is an enemy agent, that's your problem. I only want to inform him of the death of his wife, in the highly unlikely event that he doesn't already know."

Fratelli tipped up the cup, swallowed, and gave another convulsive shudder. "How'd you know Falk was back in this country?"

"I didn't think he'd left."

"Then why the letter to me?"

This was getting into treacherous territory. "All I knew," McIntire responded, "was that Teddy Falk was once involved in the Communist Party, that he was scheduled to go to the Soviet Union, but that he hadn't shown up for the trip. Apparently I was wrong on that last point."

Fratelli pasted on his *I don't get it* face. All the more effective with that drip trembling on his upper lip. McIntire, knowing what a sucker he was, relented and gave a sketchy version of Nick Thorsen's discovery under the pine tree—sans money—and his subsequent conversation with the schoolteacher's father. "I only want to locate J. Theodore Falk. I expect you'll be hearing from the sheriff or the state police before long. I can have the satisfaction of letting them know where he is myself, soon as you tell me."

"He's working as a taxi driver down south." Fratelli fished a small notebook from his shirt pocket, tore out a page, and handed it to McIntire. "Mr. Falk's most recent address."

Detroit. Detroit was "down south"? Well, all things are relative. "Many thanks. Do I need to memorize it and eat it?"

Another, even less agreeable, idea as to what the constable might do with the paper lurked behind the gleam in Fratelli's eyes. Apparently his training won out; he sat back with an indulgent smile.

"Melvin," McIntire said, and saw the agent flush. "Melvin, you didn't come all the way from Marquette, in a car with no heater, to give me Teddy Falk's address or to chat about why I wanted to get in touch with him. What's on your mind?"

Melvin rubbed the bridge of his nose in a meditative pose, frowned, and dug a handkerchief from his pocket. "These are dangerous times." He dabbed fastidiously at his nostrils.

"For who—whom?"

"For you and me and every other citizen of this country."

While McIntire couldn't claim to feeling any sense of personal peril, he didn't argue with the overall sentiment. "True. There've been better than six thousand kids killed in Korea just in the past six months."

"Beats fighting the Reds right here."

"Are you expecting an invasion?"

"We are smack-dab in the middle of the worst kind of invasion, one from the inside."

The agent sounded seriously concerned, and McIntire was seriously afraid that the invasion was going to involve him. Whether as defender or perpetrator, he wasn't sure. "What is it you're leading up to?"

"We have to keep our eyes and ears open. This is a strategically touchy area. You got iron mines and uranium."

There'd been no big uranium strikes so far as McIntire had heard, in spite of Fratelli's relentless prospecting efforts of the previous fall.

"And you got railroads and docks to load it onto ships."

"Melvin, spit it out."

The spiral-bound notebook was never far from Fratelli's hand. He flipped its cover with a flourish and passed it to McIntire. "Do you know any of these people?"

There were about a dozen names. McIntire knew them all, some better than others. He handed the notebook back. "I find it hard to believe this bunch is plotting a coup, even from the inside. Although," he added, "Grandma Jarvinen always did seem a little shifty."

"Who's that?"

"Helmi Jarvinen. Number three on your list of subversives."

"Helmi is female?"

"Female, and old enough to have gotten some practical experience in the original revolution, I'd reckon, and she's the spring chicken of this bunch." He slapped the book on the table. "What is this supposed to be?"

Fratelli reclaimed his notebook and penciled in a question mark after Mrs. Jarvinen's name. "These are people the United States Government has good reason to want information about. Information that you are in a perfect position to get."

"Such as?"

"What sort of organizations they belong to, donate money to, where they go, what they read...."

McIntire looked again at the list and at Fratelli's unsmiling countenance. It was his turn to not get it. "I can answer those questions right now," he said. "They have no money to donate, they don't go much of anywhere, and they read anything they can get their hands on to keep from going stir crazy."

The rectangle of light on the linoleum blinked out. Kelpie gave a disappointed whimper. Clouds once more obscured the sun. It had been nice while it lasted.

Fratelli leaned forward. "We need an agent here. Somebody who speaks the language."

"The language in question being Finn?"

"I understand that the nationality of most of these people is Finnish." His tone became conspiratorial. "There is an organization that these people all belong to."

"I'm sure you'll tell me what it is."

He flashed a new page in his notebook. "Star of Hope. Meets every other Wednesday."

"The Star is a subversive group?"

"Any organization that receives funding from the Communist Party is required to register with the federal government."

"What funding?"

"Where do you think they get money to run this club?"

"I expect they each kick in two bits for coffee and cardamom cake."

"The Temperance Society."

"Is that a fact? Well, I can't say I share their philosophies, but—"

"The Temperance Society is a communist front organization. That's the only philosophy I give a shit about."

"You're asking me to start going to Temperance meetings so I can inform on my neighbors?" It was perversely tempting—John McIntire, St. Adele's own Herb Philbrick.

"Inform on, hell! It ain't informing if they ain't done nothing. I only want to know things that no innocent person would bother to hide."

"So what's keeping you from asking them yourself?"

Sadness invaded the detective's face as he peered into his cup, perhaps the result of McIntire's recalcitrance, more probably disappointment at the level of remaining liquid. "There could be those who would question your patriotism."

"My patriotism! I spent thirty years working for Uncle Sam. Still do, now and again. How patriotic do you want?"

"Thirty years, was it?" His pensive gaze moved from the cup to the ceiling. "Except for a slight gap."

McIntire felt his heart speed up, and he struggled to keep his expression bland. "What now?"

"A little matter of February 1948 until—when was it?—May? June? Oddly enough, about the same time your old buddy turned up here."

"I never met Teddy Falk in my life."

"That's not what your letter said."

"I figured if I said anything else, you'd be sticking your oar in where it doesn't belong. Looks like I was right about that."

"Why didn't you just leave finding Falk to the sheriff? Why stick *your* oar in?"

McIntire had no reply that wouldn't serve to remind the G-man that he was the one who found those bodies, which could lead to those awkward questions about why he had gone looking.

"Where were you?" Fratelli persisted, "in the spring of 1948?"

"I was in Moscow, in the service of the United States Army."

"You might have been behind the Iron Curtain once. You weren't there in forty-eight, not in February."

McIntire couldn't believe what he was hearing. "You've obviously taken the trouble to check up on me. So you know that my service record is white as that snow out there."

"And I'm pretty damned sure you'd like it to stay that way."

"Are you trying to blackmail me into spying on a bunch of old Finns, just because they get together to drink coffee instead of booze once or twice a month?"

"Did I hear the word blackmail?" Leonie came in, suppressing a yawn. "Good day, Mr. Fratelli. How lovely to see you. What brings you our way?"

"Just in the neighborhood." Fratelli pushed back his chair. "And I'm afraid I need to be going. It's a long drive to Marquette."

"Surely you can stay for tea."

Fratelli wasn't to be persuaded. "It's starting to snow again. I'd better be on my way. Thanks anyway." He turned to McIntire. "Think about it. I'll be getting back to you."

McIntire allowed Leonie to take care of the parting chit-chat, listening with half an ear while Fratelli packed himself back into his woolens. It was a lengthy process. Their mutual acquaintance, McIntire's pseudo-youthful Aunt Siobhan, was still in San Francisco. Fratelli spoke to her now and then. Yes, working out of a hotel room was not pleasant, but a special agent got used to it. He'd get a new heater for his car tomorrow.

When he heard Fratelli's Buick pull away, McIntire found himself shaking like Nick Thorsen on his worst days. What could that moron possibly know about where he'd spent that wretched winter of 1948? He hadn't told anyone, not even Leonie. Especially not Leonie. It wasn't part of his service record.

"Oh, dear, you're freezing." Leonie lit a burner under the teakettle and sat down. She took one of his hands between her own and rubbed it briskly.

"What brought on this call?" she asked. "It *is* a long drive to Marquette."

"He's trying to recruit me."

"Really? How exciting! But won't that put you in a sticky position?"

"I didn't say yes."

"Did you say no?"

"I didn't figure the proposition was worthy of reply."

The kettle whistled, and she dropped his hand. "What was the blackmail about?"

"Just a joke."

WASHINGTON—The Defense Department said yesterday replacements for casualties and battle weary soldiers will start reaching Korea in quantity in early March.

Chapter Eighteen

After sleeping on it, or lying awake because of it, it seemed apparent that Melvin Fratelli knew nothing other than that McIntire'd been out of touch for a few months in 1948. Almost four months. That wasn't unusual, given McIntire's line of work. If Fratelli dug hard enough, he might find a fraction of the truth. Know just enough to be dangerous, as the saying went.

McIntire shoved Agent Fratelli into the deepest dungeons of his mind and barred the door. He sipped his morning coffee and forced himself to concentrate on the puzzle that was the fate of Rose Falk and her nameless partner—her husband, too, for that matter. He'd have to go all the way into Chandler, he supposed, to let Koski know that he could find Teddy in Detroit.

What had happened to Falk during those years in the Soviet Union? How had he gotten out? There was not much question about why he hadn't made a trip back to St. Adele to say howdy to the home folks.

Rose Falk had been dead more than sixteen years. It wouldn't be easy to figure out what might have happened on a small slice of a single day or night that long ago. It'd be even harder to prove it. McIntire could start with trying to find out exactly which day it was. If he assumed that Rose and her companion died near the time she was meant to leave St. Adele, it might not be too hard to discover the exact date. Possibly Orville Pelto had records or knew where to get them, or Sulo Touminen might recall. If Sulo didn't remember, he might be able to work it out from the date on his deed to the farm.

"I might drop by to see Sulo for a bit. Will you be okay?"

Leonie put down her dish towel, returning from wherever her own thoughts had meandered. "Of course." She appeared mystified. "Why wouldn't I be?"

McIntire wished he knew the answer to that question. "I won't be long," he said. He looked at the swirls of white pelting the window and hoped that he spoke the truth.

Leonie moved toward the window. "What was that?"

McIntire listened. "A chickadee. That's its spring song."

At his wife's brightened expression, he added. "Don't get excited. Chickadees are notorious liars."

One of Arnie Johnson's favorite adages, *It only warms up to snow*, was definitely not holding true today, McIntire discovered. He ducked his head into his collar and faced the wind. It might be snowing, but warmed up, it was not. It was, also in Arnie parlance, colder than a witch's tit.

The Studebaker's seat was like an iceberg. He pulled shut the door and pressed the starter to the floor. The engine whined, groaned, whirred, and finally chugged. McIntire crossed his fingers and returned to the house for his muffler, ice scraper, and broom. Why hadn't he built a garage? It might not make the car easier to start, but at least he could dispense with the tedious scraping of frost. Why did it make a difference? Why would a car in an unheated garage not build up frost on its windows just as it did outdoors? Maybe he'd put the question to Erik Pelto one of these days.

Irene Touminen answered his knock. Sulo wasn't home. Nick Thorsen had called to get him to help with moving some furniture. He probably wouldn't be back for awhile; afterwards he was going to haul some sawdust for Simon Lindstrom's ice house. Once he dumped that, he planned to stop at the old Makinen place to pick up a load of hay and see what was going on with the excavation, fast becoming a major local attraction.

"There was a whole family from over in Ishpeming on Tuesday." Irene shook her head. "Three kids. Took them out of school for the trip." She shut the door against the wind. "What on earth are people expecting to see?"

What they saw would basically be a gravel pit. "Winters get long." McIntire pulled out a handkerchief to wipe the steam from his glasses. "We have to take our entertainment where we can get it. You could set up a stand. Sell cocoa and peppermint schnapps."

"Might not be a bad idea right now. We could have a cup if we had cocoa—if we had schnapps." She pulled out a chair. "As it is we'll have to settle for coffee, unless you'd like some tea."

For some inexplicable reason, McIntire found that he would like tea. He might have preferred it with a drop of brandy, since the subject of spirits had arisen, but the offer was not forthcoming.

A bowl heaped with apples of such a glossy green that they made McIntire's teeth ache sat on the table. Irene moved it to the counter and replaced it with china cups and Lipton tea bags.

"Did you want Sulo for any special reason?" she asked. "Of course I know you're here about this awful...I still can't believe it. All the time when we thought something terrible had happened to those two, it had! How many times have I walked around that old place thinking about Rosie, remembering her picking the apples or weeding the garden, and wondering what she might be doing.... Maybe she was right under my feet. How could I not *feel* it? Sense she were there somehow?"

Even washed in the blush of the cardinal-red ceiling, Irene looked hollow-eyed and weary.

"Did you know Rose well?" McIntire asked.

"Sure. We went to school together from first grade. You must have known her, too."

"Not that I recall. She'd have been quite a bit younger than me."

"I'm surprised you don't remember her. I suppose you don't remember knowing me then, either."

Was Irene Touminen flirting with him? McIntire looked into the frank brown eyes and could detect no sign of the coquette.

"I certainly do," McIntire lied. "You always had a lovely voice." It was a lucky guess. The cupid's bow lips curved in a shy smile; pushing up high, round cheeks. She glanced down, and the sleek ebony hair swung toward her chin. McIntire wondered if she put something on it to give the look of lacquer. She didn't seem like the type to indulge in such vanities.

"We lost touch for a while, but after I moved in here with Sulo, Rosie and me visited back and forth. At least once a week, I'd say. There really weren't any other ladies around even close to our age—only Mia. I guess she's not all that much older."

Mia wasn't much for visiting back and forth, age notwithstanding. McIntire asked, "How's she doing? Did Nick say?"

"Doing what?"

"Didn't he tell you?" McIntire could hardly believe that he was the first to give Irene Touminen the news of Mia's mishap. He supposed it might have been overshadowed by the other recent events.

"Oh, goodness! That idiot, he didn't mention a thing. Just wanted to know if Sulo could help with lifting something. That's Mia for you. She'd probably have belted him if she heard him tell anybody. I'd better go over and see what I can do. She'll starve to death if she has to depend on Nick." Another fleeting smile. "She doesn't have all that far to go."

McIntire steered things back to the non-living skeleton. "Were you terribly worried when you didn't hear from Rose?"

Irene folded her diminutive hands and raised her eyebrows. "Well, that's the funny thing." She studied McIntire's face as if a clue to that funniness lay there.

"Hardly strange," McIntire said. "She was dead."

"The funny thing is," she said again, "I did hear from Rosie. She sent a postcard from New York City."

"That's not possible. Guibard was positive the remains were hers."

"I spent half the morning digging around in a freezing attic." Irene reached into the pocket of her striped apron and produced a postcard, quite an interesting one, as postcards go. A reproduction, McIntire supposed, of a watercolor. The painting showed blue water and small fishing boats with the city skyline in the background, not the usual conception of New York City.

The few lines, in a childish, backward-slanting hand, were in Finnish. McIntire translated: *Here in New York. It really does look like this! Off tomorrow. Wish me luck. Hope we meet again this side of Heaven.* It was signed *R.*

"Do you know that's Rose's handwriting? Would you recognize it?"

"I couldn't say now, but I'd think I'd have noticed at the time if it wasn't hers. Unless it was a good imitation."

It probably wouldn't have had to be all that good. Irene wouldn't have been looking for a forgery.

"Her husband might have been able to fake it," McIntire said.

"Do you really think it was Teddy killed them? I can't imagine him doing such a thing. But I guess it must have been him. And he must have sent the card. It's just that.... Well, I suppose if he caught Rose with another man.... There's no telling what people might do if they're pushed hard enough."

"Have you got any guesses who that other man might have been?"

"None at all. Rose was a bit of a...flirt, I guess you might say. Frankly, it was a little embarrassing sometimes. But it's hard to believe she would have had a real affair. I can't think who it could have been." She screwed up her mouth in concentration, then shook her head. "No idea. Wasn't there anything about the body? Couldn't Guibard or the police tell anything from the remains?"

"Only that he was taller than Rose, and so, taller than Teddy," McIntire told her.

"Lassie is taller than Teddy."

Irene had more of a sense of humor than McIntire had suspected. It didn't show up much with Sulo around.

"It must have been somebody from around here," he said. "Can you think of anyone else who might have left about the same time? Maybe someone who was going to the Soviet Union, too?"

"The Karelia Fever had pretty much died out by the time the Falks signed up to go. Earlier on, there were whole shiploads that sailed. Hundreds at a time. The summer before quite a few families from here went. There was a party at the Finn Hall and a big send-off for them at the train station. They had flags and music, the works. There was a good-bye party for Ted and Rosie, too, but it was nowhere near so much folderol, just a pot luck at Houtaris'. It was only for the two of them. I never heard of anybody else that planned to go that summer. Not from around here."

McIntire picked up the postcard. The message wasn't dated, and the postmark was smudgy. Maybe it could be read with a magnifying glass. Sherlock Holmes would have been better prepared.

"Do you remember when you received this? How long after they left did it come?

"I wasn't even sure that I really got it—hadn't just dreamed it up—until I dug it out this morning. I only remembered about it last night."

"It's a nice picture," McIntire said. "Not the usual Statue of Liberty or Empire State Building."

"Rosie was a different sort of girl."

"Is this the kind of thing you could see her choosing?"

"Yes, it is. But I suppose Ted would have gone out of his way to find something.... Can you imagine what must have been going through his mind? I don't know which one I feel sorriest for, Rosie or him. Well, I suppose he's paid for what he did. Maybe he's suffered a lot more than she did."

McIntire agreed that it was a sorry business for everyone involved. He'd leave it to the sheriff to spread the news that Theodore Falk was still with them—or with them once again.

"I don't suppose you recall exactly when the Falks were scheduled to leave the country?"

"It was late in the summer, I think. I wouldn't know what day for sure."

"What about the deed to the farm?"

"What about it?"

"The date the farm changed hands should be shortly before the date they were planning to go to Karelia, and so, supposedly, shortly before Rose died. And," he added, "it might also give us a sample of her handwriting."

Rose hesitated, then stood up. "Fortunately, since this morning, I have it all at my fingertips."

She was gone less than two minutes. "August 13, 1934. That's when Sulo signed. Rose's signature is dated August sixteenth."

The long, narrow sheet Irene handed him wasn't a deed. It was a contract for deed, whereby Rose Theresa Falk, nee Rose Theresa Makinen, agreed to sell the property described to Sulo I. Touminen, a single person. In contradiction to what Sulo had said about having the transaction taken care of before Falk left, the agreement provided for a down payment of $350 followed by six installments of $200 to be paid annually. McIntire placed the postcard next to Rose Falk's blurred signature. The two might have been written by the same hand, but McIntire was no expert, and the sample was small. J. Theodore's name did not appear on the contract.

"Is this the only document pertaining to the sale?"

"I don't know that much about my brother's business dealings." Irene took the paper from him and refolded it. "Poor Rosie." Her eyes glistened. "She was the restless sort. Always looking for something new, but soon as she got it, she couldn't wait to move on to the next thing. I thought she was crazy to throw everything over to go off to Russia, but I hoped she'd found the life she wanted at last."

There didn't seem to be anything more Irene could tell him. She folded the card into a piece of wax paper and handed it back to him. He left her tackling the pile of apples so that she might not go to Mia Thorsen empty handed.

WASHINGTON—Senator Joseph R. McCarthy (R-Wis.), the State Department's bitter and tireless antagonist, has now reached membership on the Appropriations subcommittee-the subcommittee that is decisively influential in granting or withholding that department's funds.

Chapter Nineteen

McIntire peered cautiously into Pete Koski's office. No Cecil Newman. No sign of life at all. The desktop, ordinarily littered with the paraphernalia of law enforcement and fishing excursions, contained only a bell and a handwritten sign telling anyone who needed help to ring it.

He retreated to the stairs that led to the sheriff's living quarters. As he raised his hand to knock, the door swung open and Marion Koski gave a yelp. "I almost jumped out of my skin!" She backed to let McIntire enter. "Come on in. I'm about to give our boarders their noon feeding." She lifted a tray from the table. "The sheriff is in—" With a slight raising of her eyebrows, she cocked her head toward the living room and stepped sideways through the doorway. McIntire pushed the door shut and went in search of her husband.

Sheriff Pete Koski was stretched out in a platform rocker, his feet extending about eighteen inches beyond the matching ottoman. The German shepherd, Geronimo, sat at his side. The dog's eyes followed McIntire's approach, but his chin didn't stir from its spot on his master's knee.

The sheriff's scowl thwarted any intention McIntire might have had of issuing a greeting that included such terms as "goldbricking." He contented himself with a simple hello and a glance out the double windows overlooking Chandler's main street and winter-bound harbor. The snow had abated, and, to the north, a frothy line showed where open water lapped at the edge of the ice.

"Hear you're up to your old tricks," Koski said.

McIntire nodded. "Two of them this time."

"Congratulations, a new record."

"I suppose the state police have clued you in."

"More or less. One of your local Reds caught his wife with another man, plugged them both, dumped them in a hole, and took off for parts unknown."

"That's about the size of it. I don't know if they were both shot, but the Other Man had a shotgun pellet in what was left of his jaw." McIntire stopped waiting for an invitation and shoved aside Marian's knitting to sit on the scratchy green sofa.

"Police can't quite figure why in close to twenty years nobody's missed any of the three," Koski said, "or wondered what became of them."

McIntire handed over the postcard.

The sheriff held it a couple of feet from his aging eyes. He flipped it over, extended his arm a bit farther, and squinted. His expression of curiosity blossomed into baffled. "What the hell does it say?"

McIntire told him.

"So it ain't exactly signed *Mrs. J. Theodore Falk.*"

"No," McIntire agreed, "but I don't suppose Irene Touminen was acquainted with a lot of *R*s that sailed from New York City in the thirties." Although if what she said was true, that hundreds of people emigrated, she might have been at that. "She admitted she'd forgotten all about the card. Maybe it was from somebody else and she got confused."

"Ya." Koski sighed in pain or disappointment. "That's probably it."

"Or maybe whoever did sign it wanted to lessen the chance of Irene recognizing that it wasn't Rose's signature, so they just put the R," McIntire said. But Irene's postcard was not the reason he'd come. He tried to keep the smugness from his voice. "I've located the absent Red. That might perk the state guys up."

"No shit!" He flipped the card onto a stack of newspapers and *National Geographic* magazines on the floor beside his chair. "We've got a warrant. I'll send Adam Wall to bring him in." He gave a few thoughtful tugs on Geronimo's ears. "Maybe I'd better let Cecil go instead. Whereabouts is he?"

When he heard that Teddy Falk was living in Detroit, Koski said, "Oh hell, the police can do it." He squirmed himself into a more erect position. "Didn't take you long to find him, considering he's been on the lam for better than fifteen years."

On the lam? Koski must have been convalescing with Philip Marlowe.

"It's easy if you know the right people." McIntire wasn't in the mood to discuss Melvin Fratelli. "Any luck figuring out who the other victim might be?"

"Maybe I should be asking you that. No, nothing about that pile of bones that would show who owned 'em, as far as Guibard could tell, but he ain't exactly an expert. We sent them on to Lansing along with a lot of shit from the hole. Some of it might mean something to you." He rummaged through his chairside stack and handed McIntire a sheaf of typewritten carbons. McIntire scanned the pages, an extensive listing of items the state police had removed from the excavation. It was indeed a lot of shit. "They must have come to some kind of conclusions from all this."

Koski went back to fondling Geronimo's ears. "They figure the female was wrapped in a scrap quilt. She was wearing something made outa silk, some kind of nightgown or under-skirt. Underwear, anyway, probably nothing else. Parts of it were eaten away, maybe the parts that had blood on them. She was laid out straight, like she'd been put in careful. The male victim was in a heap, like he'd just been dumped in on top of her. A whole lot of clothes and blankets and crap was tossed in over them. The stuff she had packed up to leave the country, I guess. The murderer would have wanted to make it look like they did leave. And he'd want to cover up the bodies."

"Her clothing only, not his?" More evidence against the husband.

"Ya, looks like it, near as they can tell. It's mostly rotted rags, but some things last a long time, and it was cold down there." He recited, "Whalebone from a corset, hairpins, lots of buttons. A few things that couldn't have been hers. The remains of a pair of men's shoes. Regular shoes, not work boots. Clips from suspenders." He read on. "A leather belt with a fancy buckle."

"Suspenders and a belt? Must have been a real pessimist. Considering how he ended up, he had a right to be."

"And woulda been a real sissy. The buckle was shaped like a tulip with rhinestones. So it was most likely hers. Nothing to say whether the other stuff belonged to the victim or the husband. Looks more like the husband's stuff. The suspender clips weren't near the skeleton, and the shoes weren't on its feet. They were smaller than a guy that tall probably would have been wearing. We should be able to tell if they would have fit the mister. Matter of fact, there wasn't anything at all that looked like the victim was wearing it. Not even any buttons that might have been on men's clothes. Seems to have been pretty much naked."

The German shepherd's head swung to and fro with Koski's contemplative rocking. "Some of the stuff showed rusty stains that could have been iron ore. Guy mighta been a miner."

"That narrows it down to a few hundred candidates."

"Ya," Koski said, "and plenty of them that could have turned up missing without anybody getting too het up over it. Rust coulda been from a tin can, too." He went on, "There were newspapers. They might be able to get a date from them at the lab."

"After all this time?"

"You'd be surprised how long a paper can last underground if it's folded and doesn't get too wet."

Didn't get too wet? That was indeed a pretty worthless well. "What good does knowing the date on a newspaper do? There's no saying that it was thrown in at the same time as the bodies, and no knowing how old it was when it was thrown in."

"Maybe not, but there was more than one, still folded like they hadn't been read yet, and my guess is anybody packing to leave the country would have used up her *old* newspapers wrapping dishes."

"Good thinking. On the other hand, she might have been collecting them for a while and ended up with more than she needed."

"Ya."

The rocking ceased. Geronimo's ears lifted but his eyes stayed closed. Koski cleared his throat before speaking. "I had a call from an INS agent."

"A what?"

"Immigration. They got a deportation order for another Red from your neck of the woods. Wanted us to pick him up. Maybe you could do it? I'm pretty laid up here, and—"

The proverbial icy fingers began a slow creep up McIntire's spine, inching toward his heart. "Deportation? Who?"

Koski reached to fling around his reading material once again. "They sent a warrant. Here you go."

McIntire took the extended sheet of paper. It contained several printed lines of legal linguistic gymnastics with the name *Erik Antonin Pelto* inked into the blank spaces. McIntire's throat squeezed shut so he could barely get out the words, "What in hell is this all about?"

"They didn't give me the details. Just that they want him out of the country. Or at least in the county jail. Know him?"

"He teaches science at the high school."

The sheriff lurched to a sitting position, dislodging the German shepherd and, if his gasp was an indication, three or four vertebrae. His features locked in a grimace as he lowered himself gingerly back in his seat. "You got a commie for a schoolteacher?"

"He's not a commie so far as I know."

"INS seems to think he is."

"He might have been a party member once. It was probably years ago."

"He an alien?"

"He's been in this country at least since he was a kid. I don't know if he was born here." McIntire had heard stories like this, former and present communists arrested, spending months locked up while deportation cases dragged out. "He's got a wife, two little kids. She's from Australia, a war bride."

"Hmmph. What do you figure he's been up to? Wonder how they got onto him."

No mystery there. G-man Fratelli on the job, aided by his trusty sidekick Constable John McIntire. How could he have been such an idiot? No wonder Pelto had been reluctant to discuss the past. Why didn't the guy say something to warn him? What could he have said? *I used to be a communist, keep it under your hat.* Well, why in hell not? He knew what the dangers were.

McIntire should have known, too. He should have had the sense to realize that the teacher wouldn't keep his job five minutes if the FBI knew he'd been involved with the Communist Party. But arrested? Deportation?

"Well, what about it?" Koski asked. "You wanna bring this guy in?"

"Hell, no!"

"I don't mean today. There's no rush. They ain't coming to question him until next week."

"Forget it, Pete. I'm not arresting St. Adele's only reasonably decent teacher because of his father's misguided beliefs in a better world. If you want it done, get Adam Wall. Or tell this bunch," he shook the paper, "to do it themselves."

The sheriff reclaimed the warrant and studied it for a minute. "I'd like to keep Wall on people's good side for a while. I guess I could send Cecil out. He oughta be able to handle a school-teacher."

Chapter Twenty

As McIntire drove up, Leonie emerged from the office of the *Chandler Monitor*. Juggling a folded newspaper and handbag while clamping her hat to her head with one hand, she battled the wind for control of the car door. If she'd given him time, McIntire would have done the gentlemanly thing and open it for her.

She arranged herself in the seat, pulled off her gloves, and unfurled the paper. "Look, you made page one! *Township Constable Locates Sixteen-Year-Old Murder Victims.*"

"Oh, I think Rosie was probably a little older than that. Don't know if she was a cradle robber, though."

"I managed to resist pointing that out to Mr. Beckman."

McIntire abandoned any discussion of the editor's command of syntax and told his wife of Erik Pelto's impending arrest. "He'll want to kill me and so will everybody else. Hell, I want to kill me."

"It would have come out anyway. I expect those two skeletons are going to multiply like nobody's business," Leonie told him. "You can't blame yourself."

"Oh, yes I can! I sat right there in the kitchen and told a federal agent that Erik Pelto's family was red-hot communist. How dumb could anybody be?"

Leonie didn't dwell on her husband's stupidity or deny it. "Mr. Pelto is far from being the only person around here to have communist, or some sort of socialist, background," she pointed out.

"That's what Fratelli says."

"He's not arresting the rest of them."

"Not yet. So far he hasn't had anybody else fingered by Yours Truly."

The crackling of the paper as Leonie folded it in her lap put a temporary check on conversation. Was this only the beginning—Fratelli's shot across the bow?

"I'm muddled," Leonie said. Mere muddledness put her way ahead of her husband's bewilderment. "It can't be illegal to have belonged to the Communist Party," she went on, "or, surely, to have parents who did."

"It's not illegal to be communist right now." At least, McIntire didn't think so. "But there are laws against communists being on the public payroll. Even having been one in the distant past won't do you any good in getting a job as a schoolteacher, and if you don't happen to be a U.S. citizen, it can get you deported."

"And Erik Pelto's not a citizen?"

"He must not be." McIntire turned off Chandler's main street and reversed a few yards to make a running attack on the hill with its half-inch dusting of new snow. "I'm going to have to go see Erik before J. Edgar Newman shows up with his warrant." He shifted into first gear and stepped on the gas. Neither of them spoke, or breathed, as the Studebaker zigged and zagged to the top.

Leonie exhaled first. "That would probably be best," she agreed. She tucked her coat more snugly around her knees. "*Should* we have a communist teaching school?"

"He's teaching science, not socialism."

"Even so...."

"That is, if he *is* a communist, which I doubt. He wasn't on Fratelli's 'subversive' list until I tipped him off. Anyway, firing him is one thing, but throwing him in jail is something else altogether."

"It does seem a trifle extreme." Was that British understatement, or did Leonie have some sympathy with Pelto's ouster? Her next words expressed more compassion. "What will happen to Delilah and the babies?"

"Delilah *and* the babies? Delilah is a baby." It was possible that Mrs. Erik Pelto wasn't as young as she looked, but it was hard to see her holding down the fort while Papa was in the jailhouse. "I can't imagine what she'll do," McIntire said.

"Delilah Pelto is not the Helpless Hannah that she seems."

McIntire hoped not. "I also can't think it'll be easy to get somebody in to take over for him at the school. Maybe Myrtle Van Opelt will have to come out of retirement. It might give her something useful to do, and she can give off badgering me."

"Did Mrs. Van Opelt teach science?"

"No, I think it was supposed to be history, or civics, maybe geography. We were all too petrified to ask."

Did Fratelli truly believe Erik Pelto was a threat to democracy, or was an arrest warrant for him another method of getting to McIntire? If it was, the agent was every bit as ignorant as he sometimes pretended to be. If word got out that McIntire had been instrumental in getting Erik Pelto shipped off to Finland, he would never get near the scheming Granny Jarvinen and her comrades, much less worm his way into one of their government-overthrow plotting sessions. And could Fratelli possibly believe that McIntire would consent to getting chummy with his socialist neighbors, once he saw what it could lead to?

Thinking about the situation with the science teacher was pointless now. He'd file it away for a better time, along with Fratelli's poorly disguised attempt at blackmail.

"What difference does it make, really?" Leonie sighed. "The Russians have the bomb. What more do they need to wipe us all off the face of the earth?"

"They won't dare use it." McIntire tried to sound more confident than he felt. "They know it would be the end of them, too."

"Do they care?"

McIntire was pretty sure that Stalin wasn't any more eager for annihilation than was Harry Truman, although he might not be overcome with grief at the loss of a few million citizens of the Western World. "I've been there, Leonie. Ordinary Russians aren't all that different from us."

"Different? No, I don't think they are. Every time I pick up a paper all I see is war, war, war. People here don't have any idea what war is."

That was true. McIntire hoped it stayed that way. "What about the papers you picked up today? Did you find out anything?"

"Nothing that seems significant to me. I went through every issue of the *Monitor* for the entire month of August, 1934. Cover to cover. From the date on the deed, the sixteenth, through the next ten days, the news was all about an accident in a mine. Water broke in and fifty-one men drowned."

Massey-Davis. McIntire remembered that. He'd heard about it in detail from his mother. It had even gotten a mention or two in the papers in London. The shaft went under a swamp. It had given way, and in less than fifteen minutes the mine filled up with water, sand, and mud. Two of the dead had been regulars at his father's saloon.

"There was nothing about anybody else leaving or going missing," she went on, "and only a little mention in the St. Adele column about the Falks going away. That was the previous week."

"Well, thanks, Leonie. It was worth a try."

She rubbed at the steamed-up window. "Maybe we could have a bite in town before we go back."

McIntire assessed the size, number, and trajectory of the snowflakes hitting the windshield. "That might not be a good idea. We don't want to end up stuck here or halfway home." He reached to pat her knee. "Sorry."

Her skirt rustled as she moved closer to him. "It's just so dreary."

Silver spirals danced in the beams of the headlights. The street ahead was an unbroken carpet of white. It didn't strike McIntire as dreary. January in London, now that was dreary for you. But

McIntire knew what his wife meant. Life here was…limited, something that, from all outward appearances, his neighbors seemed to accept and even find rewarding. But McIntire was no more able to succumb to the simplicity of survival than was his wife. Maybe less so. And this was only the beginning; winter had barely gotten a good start. "Leonie, you could think about going back for a visit. You'll be wanting to do that sometime before too long, anyway."

She gave the paper in her lap another fold before answering. "I'm not sure this is the best time. I'd rather wait until summer."

"Wait until summer! How could there be a better time to get out of here than right now?"

"If I leave in the middle of July, when it's eighty degrees and sunny, I'll have a whole lot more incentive to come back."

"I'm not incentive enough?"

"Of course you are, Dearest. But when I return here it will be sad to leave home again, and doubly so if this is what I have to face coming back to."

It wasn't the glib reply McIntire had expected, and he wished he hadn't asked.

SYRACUSE, N.Y.—A mother went to
a movie today to catch a glimpse
of her marine son in a film and
was called out during the showing to be told he had been killed
in Korea.

Chapter Twenty-One

It was long past time Mia should be asleep. Although she couldn't think of a good reason why. It wasn't like she had to be up and about early. It wasn't like she was going to be up and about much at all for a good long while. Besides, getting out of bed to turn off the light was just too much effort.

Nick had lain next to her for a time, squirming and turning from one side to the other until she thought she'd scream. He'd finally mumbled that the place was just too damn claustrophobic and gone upstairs.

It *was* claustrophobic. Claustrophobic and dingy, even though a little of the mustiness was dissipating, or else she was getting accustomed to it. Probably the latter.

She turned back to *The Good Earth*. Despite her feeling of sisterhood with the big-footed Olan, after a few pages both her mind and her eyes were once again wandering. The window was a great black hole; she should have pulled the curtains. A stain on the wallpaper resembled an ocean liner with a thread of smoke trailing from its stack. Maybe like the one that should have taken Rose and Teddy Falk to their workers' Utopia. Would Rose have fared any better if she had been on that boat? Or would it have only dragged out her suffering?

She leaned back against the headboard. Aside from the rumpled sheets, it was a comfortable bed. In the past, she'd thought now and again about co-opting it, but she'd hesitated when her father was still alive, and afterwards it seemed like too much of a bother. It weighed a ton. Black walnut, each of its four solid posts topped with a fat pineapple.

When she was a child those carved fruits had fascinated her, never so much as when she discovered that with a little muscle they could be unscrewed, furnishing lovely playthings on lonely snowy days. Somehow one had gotten lost. Her father had demonstrated no anger, only insisting that she replace it with another of her own making. After eighteen attempts' worth of nicked fingers and tears, she'd produced an acceptable substitute, and her fascination with the possibilities locked within a piece of wood was established.

The original had later turned up behind the kitchen woodbox, but her parents had never put it back in the place of the one she'd made, nor had her father given that gouged, lopsided object so much as a touch of sandpaper before anchoring it to the bedpost.

She closed the book, braced her hands against the mattress, and, after a couple of aborted attempts, managed to sit upright. She threw the covers aside, slid down to the end of the bed, and sat facing the mahogany wardrobe.

It was a splendid piece of work, its bulk softened by the simple, elegant lines that made Eban Vogel's furniture unique. Like the bed, it was something Mia would have commandeered for her own room if getting it up the stairs hadn't been a factor. It was in her own room now, if not exactly as she might have wished.

Leaning forward, she could just get her fingernails under the edge of the wardrobe's door. A pull swung it open, and she sat back. A few pieces of her father's meager store of clothing still hung inside, worn shirts, a couple of pairs of work pants. He'd been buried in his single good white shirt. The remainder of the space was taken up, bottom to top, with boxes. All that was left of two lives, one of them much too short.

When Eban died, Mia had eagerly sorted through those belongings of her mother's that he'd kept to himself. There had been disappointingly little. A few letters, articles clipped from magazines, a faded and flowery birthday card from her husband-to-be.

In contrast, Mia had packed away her father's piles of papers with hardly a glance, intending to get around to them someday when she had plenty of time. Someday had arrived. It was possible that he'd left something that would tell the real story of what they'd found under the tree. Information he'd assumed they'd find after he died.

She used her crutch to pull a chair near, swung herself onto it, and began flinging boxes onto the bed.

When Nick came in three hours later with a steaming cup in each hand, she was still engrossed in their contents.

"What the devil is all this?"

Mia grasped the extended cup quickly and put her tongue to the dribble down the side. He'd remembered the cream.

"I've got a bit of time on my hands," she told him. "I should have done this years ago. Look! It's an IOU from Alfred Monson. Papa lent him fifty dollars. I'll bet he never paid it back, and now it's too late. He's dead, too."

"Just like Alf, weaseling out of paying up with an underhanded trick like that." Nick sat on the edge of the bed. "Anything else?"

"No, that's about it for excitement apart from a lot of ranting socialist essays and stuff that has to do with the old Association. They'd be worth reading, if a person had time. Which I do now."

"He was an odd duck, your father."

"He wasn't a thief," Mia said, "and he wasn't a murderer."

"No, but he'd have gone out of his way to protect a friend, even if that friend was a thief or a murderer."

A pounding on the kitchen door kept Mia from thinking about it. Nick scrambled to his feet, slopping coffee onto the chenille bedspread. "Who the hell could that be at this time of the morning?"

He shuffled off without waiting for Mia's conjectures on that. The sounds of the door closing, foot stomping, and soft feminine laughter was followed by, "How is she?" in a brisk voice. A minute later Irene Touminen, pointy nose glowing crimson, burst into the room, bringing the frigid outdoors with her.

"Mia, this is so awful. I came to see what I could do to help." Her coat hit the chair. "Notice I didn't say 'can I help?' 'cause I know you'd say no. I'll just do what needs doing. You're in no shape to put up a fight. Are you warm enough?" After a spell of blanket tugging and pillow plumping, brushing Mia's cheek with tiny fingers of ice, she stood back.

"Looks like you're catching up on your reading." She picked up a brittle newspaper clipping. "Nineteen-oh-three. You *do* have some catching up to do," she said, and peered at the hazy print. "I thought it was just us Finns that read this sort of thing."

"My father was an odd duck, as Nick just pointed out to me." Mia flung the spread over the scattered papers. She didn't need to have her father's life exposed to any busybody that walked in. Mia wondered if Irene Touminen's curiosity meant that she was aware of the role her upended pines had played in locating the bodies in Jarvi Makinen's well. Her brother Sulo's well now. Irene had been pretty chatty with Rose Falk.

"Terrible about Rosie," Mia said. "I know you were close."

"We were. Close as Rosie was to anybody, I guess. Of course I always wondered what had happened to her. I thought maybe she'd died. No one ever heard from her or Teddy, and there was talk some of those people starved to death before the war. But who ever would have thought she could have been killed right here? And by Teddy himself."

Had any of the people who emigrated been heard from? Mia thought a few had come back after a year or so, but didn't know about the ones who stayed. "I suppose it's not easy to send mail from Russia. They can't all be dead, can they?"

"Who knows? Can you picture Teddy doing such a thing? He was always so…easygoing, I guess you might say."

"There's no telling what people might do in a fit of anger," Mia said. What would she do if she caught Nick with another woman? Something that might have happened any time, if she was to believe the gossip. Would she be mad enough to kill him? Would she have a shotgun handy to do it with?

Irene settled on the edge of the bed. "It was the perfect crime," she said. "Nobody noticed they were missing, because they expected them to be."

"We all expected Rosie to be gone, but what about the other guy? Why didn't someone report him missing?"

"Good question, and why didn't somebody on the other end notice when the Falks didn't show up?"

"Maybe Teddy did show up. If he said Rosie'd changed her mind people would probably take his word for it."

"No," Irene said. "Old Man Pelto ran that show. If he thought that Rosie Makinen had stayed here by herself, footloose and fancy free, he'd have been knocking at the door. He was always on the lookout for a new mama for little Erik, and he took quite a shine to Rosie, for some reason. And now to find out she had another one on the string…." Irene shook her head.

"I don't suppose all men are only interested in looks."

"No? Let me know if you find one that isn't. I'm not all that crazy about spending the rest of my days keeping house for my brother."

"Teddy obviously didn't give a hoot about looks," Mia said, "and he's out there somewhere, a free man for the time being. Maybe you can track him down before Pete Koski does." Was that a tactless thing to say? Only if Irene really did consider herself homely, and Mia couldn't see why she would. At least she had the grace to laugh, and Mia went on, "Maybe they liked her spirit. Rose was always the adventurous type."

"Ya, odd, as quiet as she was, you'd never suspect she was a regular Annie Oakley." Irene stood up, smoothed the front of her dress, and took Mia's empty cup from her hand. "I'll bring you fresh as soon as you've had a little nap. You look like you haven't slept in a week." She placed the cup on the dresser, re-plumped the pillow, and went back to tidying the bedclothes.

"Now get under the covers and shut your eyes." She was speaking to Mia, but her attention stayed focused on Eban Vogel's papers as she collected them into a rough stack

Mia lay back and allowed Irene to tuck the quilt around her shoulders. The comforting rustle of paper and the smoothing of blankets went on for a time before she heard the light switch click, and the door softly close. A week? She felt like she hadn't slept in a month.

PRINCETON, N.J.—Civilian defense workers here were shown the first step in how to fight atomic radiation yesterday.

Chapter Twenty-Two

Erik Pelto seemed to be one of those hardy individualists tackling winter with gusto, despite his chronically leaking nose. He exhibited an erudite expression as he swept snow from a bird-feeding table and dumped in a scoop of seeds. McIntire coughed.

The teacher looked up without surprise. "Morning," he said. "I hear you found what you were looking for."

"I did. Thanks for your help."

"Don't mention it." A jay shrieked in impatience. "I'll be with you in a minute." McIntire wasn't sure if Pelto was speaking to him or the bird. Both probably. He waited as the teacher picked up a pail and scuffed through the snow, threading his way between the trees to replenish three more feeding stations, his head encircled by a clutch of voracious chickadees. He was not going out of his way to be so hospitable to his human visitor, and no doubt he was about to become far less so. Before that happened, McIntire had a few questions. As Pelto made his way back to his side, he asked, "Who do you suppose the other victim might have been?"

His reluctant host almost smiled. "It might have been my old man, if he'd had half a chance. He was quite taken with Rosie, oddly enough. But I don't know of anybody else. How the hell would I? I was just a kid. I can't imagine she had admirers breaking down the door."

"So you *do* remember the Falks?"

"Once I got to thinking about it."

It didn't seem to have taken a lot of mind searching. McIntire asked, "Did your family live around here at the time?"

"Not really. We didn't live in any one spot for very long. My father worked for Karelian Aid. Before that he was involved in the Työmies Society and the labor unions. He traveled a lot, and he took me with him."

"What about your mother?"

It was impossible to pass the question off as neighborly chit-chat. The handle of the empty bucket creaked as Pelto twirled it against his knee.

"I don't remember ever having one," he said. "She died back in Finland."

"Is that where you were born?"

The rhythmic creaking ceased. "Why?"

McIntire felt his palms go damp in his gloves. "I saw Pete Koski yesterday."

The pale eyes waited.

"The sheriff," McIntire explained.

"I know who you're talking about."

"He said he'd gotten a call from Immigration."

Pelto tossed the last of the grain onto the snow. "You'd better come inside."

McIntire's position on the narrow path required him to walk ahead of his host. He made it to the door without feeling either a dagger or a snowball hit his back.

Erik Pelto's house was small for a family of four, a probable advantage during the heating season. McIntire pushed his way past the jackets crammed on the wall in the entryway and stepped over a pile of overshoes into the kitchen. It had the ambience of a tropical rainforest, an impression enhanced as McIntire's glasses steamed over. Childish voices issued from beyond the wall, and a small human-shaped blur appeared in the doorway. McIntire wiped the lenses and re-situated his spectacles. The blur resolved into the oldest of the children, Mrs. Erik Pelto. "Hello," she said. "Cold?"

"Cold enough." McIntire had only seen Pelto's Australian wife a couple of times, and had never spoken more than a greeting. Strange. One might have expected a level of camaraderie between Delilah Pelto and Leonie, even though Leonie definitely did not consider herself a "war bride." Leonie had tried and seemed a bit put out that the young woman hadn't shown an interest in moving into the shelter of her wing, but apart from both being subjects of King George exiled to a foreign land, they had little in common. Delilah had come to the country as a pregnant adolescent four years in advance of Leonie. She was extraordinarily shy, and, according to Leonie, totally absorbed in her husband and children. What would happen to her with Erik arrested? What if he did have to leave the country—the country for which he was risking his life when they met? McIntire hoped again that Leonie was correct in her assessment that Delilah was more independent than one might think. Leonie might be in a position to know.

"Mr. McIntire is just here on a little business." Pelto interrupted his wife's advances toward the coffee pot. She smiled, expressed her greetings to Mrs. McIntire, picked up the mopheaded infant that clung to her knee, pulled a Lincoln Log from its mouth, and left the room.

Pelto lifted the lid from a pot on the stove, releasing an aroma of venison and onions to mingle with that of the wool socks hung on the wire above it. He gave its contents a quick stir before turning back to McIntire. "Are you here to arrest me?"

"No, but I expect somebody will be before much longer."

"You turned me in." He sounded more resigned than angry.

"Of course not!"

"You come around asking about my father, and, less than a week later, I'm going to be arrested. You expect me to believe that's just a coincidence?"

"It's not a coincidence. I expect you to believe I'm just a moron."

Pelto didn't argue that. "A moron who can't mind his own business."

Stupidity, McIntire would admit to, but putting his bungling down to simple snoopiness was going too far. "Two people were murdered. One of them you apparently knew fairly well, although you couldn't see your way clear to admit it. It's my business to find out who killed them." That was debatable, but McIntire had made it his business, for better or for worse. "You could have told me you aren't an American citizen, that you've been a communist, and if word got out you'd lose your job."

"You left out getting deported. And I am a U.S. citizen. That won't stop them."

Wouldn't it? If Pelto hadn't owned up to his red roots when he'd applied for citizenship, it probably wouldn't. What the government can naturalize, they can denaturalize. "Why did you give me that line of bull about not knowing Teddy Falk?"

"Whether I was acquainted with Teddy Falk or his wife is none of your damn business." The chatter from the living room lapsed, and he lowered his voice. "For a fourteen-year-old kid to see his old man getting all sweated up over a married woman—a married woman young enough to be his daughter, with a face that would stop a clock—is damn embarrassing. I would just as soon forget all that stuff. That ain't gonna happen now. Maybe you can help me brush up on my Finn."

"Surely you'll be fighting deportation?"

"You just told me about it five minutes ago. How the hell would I know anything about fighting it."

"They can't do it without a trial…or something like a trial." McIntire didn't know what the procedure might be. "A hearing, maybe."

"Of course I won't just turn tail and go. I've got no connection at all to Finland. The government hasn't managed to deport much of anybody so far. But they've kept plenty of people sitting in jail for a long time." He sneezed into his sleeve. "My teaching days are over, that's for damned sure."

"Were you a communist?"

"I grew up in the party." The recollection brought a smile. "For a kid it *was* a party. Rallies, marches, parades, campfires, singing. We were going to change the world. I paid dues myself until after my first year in college. About that time the world changed without my help. Nobody asked about my political beliefs during those four years I spent in the army." He glanced toward the open door to the other room and spoke more loudly. "So you don't know yet who belongs to the other body?"

McIntire shook his head. "What *do* you remember about Rose Falk and her husband, besides her attraction for your father? What made them decide to go to Karelia so late in the game?"

"Orville Pelto made them decide to go, simple as that. My dad was very persuasive. He convinced dozens of Finns to give up their perfectly satisfactory lives here and go off to create that workers' paradise in Hell."

"You said that he left the organization about the time the Falks emigrated."

"Partly from lack of work to do, partly from lack of conviction. Mostly he didn't like the way the Party was going. He thought too much control was coming from Moscow."

"It must have been a big undertaking, arranging an exodus of hundreds of people."

"Thousands."

"How were the trips organized?"

"People had to apply to the Karelian Technical Aid Society before they were accepted. Besides their political zeal, they had to have skills the society wanted—lumber, construction work, fishing. More importantly, they wanted people who had tools and equipment. Plus some good old-fashioned money was always handy. The first line on the application was *How much money can you contribute to the machine fund?* They needed to pay for their own passage. Five hundred dollars each. The applications went to the society's office in New York. Recommendations were sent on to Petrozavodsk, and final approval came from Moscow."

"Five hundred dollars was a lot of money in the thirties."

"It's a lot of money now. People sold their farms and livestock and anything else they didn't plan to take with them."

"What about the stuff the Falks shipped over?" For all his protestations of youthful ignorance, Pelto seemed to know quite a bit. "How would that have been handled?"

"Pa helped take care of that, too. It would have been sent by train to New York City. Then shipped to Petrozavodsk, probably by way of Sweden."

"On the same ship they sailed on?"

"How would I know? I doubt it. What's that got to do with anything?"

"I was just wondering who would be able to claim the goods. Would it have to be Teddy himself, the Aid Society, or would anybody holding the bill of lading be able to pick the stuff up?"

"Beats me. I guess Pa might know."

"So the Falks should have taken the train to New York?"

"I suppose so. The society would have fixed up a place for them to stay until the boat sailed."

"And your father knew that Rose didn't turn up?" If Orville had been so enamored of Mrs. Falk, you'd think he would have checked to find out why she wasn't on the boat, especially if he was aware that her husband sailed without her.

"He knew it when I talked to him a few days ago. I don't know if he knew it at the time. He might have."

"But he didn't bother to check on them?"

"You'll have to ask him. Doesn't look like it."

"Even though they'd sold most everything and already shipped off what they had left?" He could hardly have figured they'd just changed their minds and decided to spend the rest of their lives in a tent on the beach.

"He might not have found out about it until later on."

"Were you in New York at the time?"

"I can't say. I don't remember exactly when it would have been."

"Where does your father live now?"

"Superior. He uses his persuasive powers to further the cause of capitalism now, sells insurance."

"We're going sliding!" Two compact, curly-haired gnomes barreled through the room to hurl themselves on the piles of outerwear. Their mother followed with an indulgent smile.

McIntire said a quick goodbye. The Peltos had things to talk about.

NEW YORK—Ellen Knauff, the German-
born war bride who has spent most
of her time on Ellis Island since
she arrived in 1948, expressed
confidence that late developments were about to clear her as
a "hazard to internal security."

Chapter Twenty-Three

"Pardon me?" McIntire was on the verge of hanging up when he recognized Mia Thorsen's muffled voice. "You're going to have to speak up, Mia, or get off the phone and write a letter."

"It's Teddy Falk. He's here."

"Where?"

"*Here*. In the front room, passing the time with Nick. He says he read in the paper about finding Rose. He came to our house thinking he could see Papa. Now he wants to see you."

Talk about great sleuthing, now the suspects were coming to him. "Send him on over."

"I told him maybe you could come here." Her voice dropped lower still. Did she think McIntire's hearing was that much better than that of the eavesdroppers on the line? "He's not too keen on going out right now. He thinks he might have been followed."

"By who?" Fratelli again?

"He didn't say. Well, he didn't know. Can you come?"

"Give me five minutes."

McIntire returned the earpiece to its cradle and resisted grabbing a drumstick from the plate of fried chicken carried by his wife. "I won't be long. If I'm not home in a half-hour, eat without me."

◇◇◇

McIntire rounded a bend in the road, pumped his brakes, and swerved, fish-tailing past the hulking form of a grey car, lights off, motor running. He pulled into the Thorsens' driveway. When he could no longer feel his pulse hammering at his eyeballs, he walked back to the idling vehicle and rapped on the steamed-over windshield. The driver's side window opened a spare six inches.

"Cecil, what in hell are you up to?"

The deputy's smooth cheeks were pink under his plaid earflaps. "I tailed the suspect from town. He's up there."

"So how come you're down here?"

"I'd a damned sight rather wait and take him when he comes out. He could be armed. I wouldn't want anybody hurt if there's gunplay."

"Armed? The guy's a cab driver!" A Detroit cab driver. Maybe gunplay was all in a day's work.

"He's a murderer, and a communist, and a fugitive. That could mean dangerous."

Newman hadn't plugged "Ruskie spy" into his list. McIntire leaned closer. "Cecil, think about it. If Teddy Falk was a dangerous Red fugitive killer, why would he have come back here?"

The deputy didn't answer that, just turned up his collar. "He's got to come out sooner or later."

"I expect it will be later," McIntire told him. "Maybe after he's tied Mr. and Mrs. Thorsen back to back and cut their throats. In the meantime get this car off the road before somebody that doesn't possess my catlike reflexes comes along. If you don't die of carbon monoxide first."

McIntire left his own car where it was and walked up to the house. Before knocking at the door, he shone his flashlight into the Ford parked in the drive. If Falk had a sawn-off shotgun, it was either at his side or he kept it in the trunk.

Nick opened the door and led McIntire past a sink full of unwashed dishes to the living room. Mia gave a little wave from her spot on the sofa, leg on a stool, hair once again confined in its customary braid.

McIntire had never heard Theodore Falk's age, but the small man who stood to shake his hand wasn't young, and life among the Soviets hadn't been kind to him. His sparse hair and even sparser eyebrows were white, his forehead mottled with brown. He didn't blink at McIntire's greeting in Russian, but he responded in English, pumping his hand like a long-lost buddy.

"Sorry to get you out at suppertime. I want to meet you and say thanks." The words were deliberate and heavily accented, but his English was better than McIntire might have expected; he'd probably spoken mostly Finnish even before leaving St. Adele for Karelia. But then he'd spent the last two years driving a cab in Detroit. He went on, "Since I got back to America, I done everything to look for my wife. It's been a blow, hearing she's dead all these years, but at least now I know."

The amiable smile didn't indicate that Teddy was suffering a whole lot from the blow, and until now the search for his wife hadn't taken him as far as her former home in St. Adele. McIntire was blunt. "What did you think had happened to her?"

"I thought she left me, run off with another man."

Falk sat down and hunched forward with his hands between his knees. "I was just telling Nick and Mia. I was away for a few days, making arrangements for the trip. When I come home, Rose is gone. There's a note on the table saying she left with another man."

"Who?"

"That, she didn't tell me."

"You didn't try to go after her, get her back, at least find out where she'd gone?"

"What was the point?"

Falk answered McIntire's inquiries in a confident, matter-of-fact sort of way, but with a delay, as if running either the question or his response through his mind first. Maybe it was a breakdown in language. Or perhaps the large glass at his elbow, half filled with the purplish liquid that was Nick Thorsen's chokecherry wine, might have something to do with it.

"You must have been…shocked."

"Nothing Rosie did ever surprised me."

"And you didn't tell anybody?"

This response was immediate. "Ya, I did. I told Eban Vogel."

No one commented. Falk picked up the glass. "It was pretty late at night when I got home. I didn't know what to think. I hardly remember what went through my mind. Early next morning I went to see Eban, then I just took off. I didn't know what to do with myself. We already sold the place. Rosie was supposed to sign the contract while I was gone, and I figured she must have done it. Everything else we owned we either sold or shipped off to Petrozavodsk. At first I didn't think I'd go to Karelia without my wife. There didn't seem to be any point in that either. It was really Rose wanted to go. But then I thought, what the hell. Everything was all set. I might as well take the trip and see the world. I could always turn around and come right back." He drained the glass. "It didn't quite pan out that way. But anyway, I drove to Saginaw to see my mother and my brother, like we planned, and got on the train to New York City."

"Orville Pelto says you didn't turn up."

"Orville? What the hell does he know? Far as I know he wasn't even there. He'd set up a place for us to stay, but I didn't go there. I got into New York in the morning and sailed the next day."

Mia shifted her leg to the floor. "You say you told my father that Rose was gone?"

"There was nobody else I could trust. I needed to leave some things for Rosie, in case she came back."

"What sort of things?"

"Some legal documents. A copy of the shipping receipt. I don't remember it all. Her passport. Money. It was Friday, and I didn't want to wait around for Monday to put the money in the bank."

Mia's face was hidden as she bent to shift her leg.

"That was pretty generous of you," McIntire said, "considering your wife had left you for another man."

"It was her money." He shrugged. "I'd cashed some checks from selling the farm and livestock. The place was still in her name only. She didn't get around to changing it when we got married. She had a bank account that Sulo was supposed to pay into. I asked Eban to put the money in it. Like I said, I didn't know what to think. I couldn't figure out why Rosie left me when she wanted to go to Karelia so bad. I thought maybe it was just last-minute nerves, and when she came to her senses she might be back."

Mia straightened up. "Then why did you take off? Why not wait awhile, or try to find her?"

"Well, you know…." Falk squirmed in his seat and gazed into his empty glass. "I married Rose because I felt sorry for her."

"And because she had a hundred sixty acres."

"Eighty, but ya, that didn't hurt. Anyway, once we were married, I found out she didn't really need feeling sorry for." He looked up quickly. "Is Adeline still alive?"

It wasn't a name McIntire knew.

"No," Mia told him. "She died quite a long time ago." She turned to McIntire. "Jarvi's sister. Rose's aunt."

"If Rose had an aunt," McIntire asked, "why didn't you leave the mon—documents with her?"

"I didn't want to tell Adeline that Rose had run off. Rosie asked me not to. In her note she said 'Don't let Aunt Addie find out. Let her think we're together.'"

"So when you got to New York you sent…." McIntire waited.

He hesitated, then nodded. "I mailed some postcards, ya. I signed Rosie's name."

True, or a lucky guess? "Who did you write them to?"

"To Addie, for sure. I don't remember who else. It was mostly for Addie."

It sounded feeble, but McIntire didn't pursue it. "Did you have a shotgun?"

Falk nodded. "Sure. Three of them. I had a couple, and Rose had an old twelve gauge of Jarvi's. She kept it behind the door when she was home alone."

"Loaded?"

"Mostly. Wouldn't have done her a hell of a lot of good if it wasn't."

"Do you remember if it was there when you came home and found your wife gone?"

Falk didn't seem to wonder about the inquisition he was undergoing, or about McIntire's role as Inquisitor in Chief. Maybe he was used to questions. Maybe he was enjoying the attention. "I think it was," he said. "She'd been alone for a couple of days. Anyway I know it was around, because I took it with me. Sold it along with the car. I shipped the other two."

"Was it loaded when you took it?"

"That, I don't remember." He placed his glass on the coffee table and folded his hands in his lap. "Am I going to be arrested?"

"You betcha," McIntire said. "And you were right. You were followed here."

The man stiffened, and for the first time his eyes showed some healthy suspected-killer anxiety. "By who?"

"Cecil Newman, county sheriff *pro temp.*"

Falk relaxed into his chair.

"He's waiting at the end of the driveway, warrant in his frostbitten little hand."

"Cecil is sitting out there? You're kidding! Tell the nitwit to come in and warm up." Mia sounded more amused than concerned.

"Don't bother. I'll go." Falk stood up. "Maybe he'll let me drive my own car in."

After effusive thanks to both Mia and McIntire, Teddy Falk, escorted by Nick Thorsen and his flashlight, made life worth living for Deputy Sheriff Cecil Newman.

McIntire waited until he heard the door close before he asked, "Mia, have you told anybody about that money?"

"No, who would I tell?"

How stubborn could anybody be? "Teddy Falk, for one. It backs up his story. He's got a right to know that you found it, and so does Pete Koski. I'm going to have to tell him, if you don't. He'll have a conniption about not hearing it sooner. And he'll want you to turn it over."

Her face froze to a plaster mask. "Tell him I already spent it."

WASHINGTON—President Truman created a federal commission on internal security and individual rights yesterday to review the government's loyalty program.

Chapter Twenty-Four

Falk's story was marginally plausible. Of course, he'd had sixteen years to work on it. It probably didn't matter a hell of a lot; any evidence would be long gone. He said he'd left the day after he found his wife missing. McIntire would have loved to ask him how he'd enjoyed spending the night on their connubial bed with its blood-soaked mattress, but that would have to wait for the sheriff. He hoped he hadn't fouled anything up by mentioning the shotgun.

It didn't seem possible that Falk had fabricated the story of entrusting Eban Vogel with money for Rose. Otherwise, how could he have mentioned it now? He couldn't possibly know that Nick had found it, so he wasn't simply leaping at the opportunity to cover his tracks or put in a fraudulent claim.

Why would Eban have hidden it away unless he'd been aware that Rose Falk was past needing it? Why not deposit it in her account as Falk had asked? Maybe it was just that he, like most people in 1934, was suspicious of banks. If he'd known that Rose was dead, wouldn't he have said something to her husband? He might be naturally reluctant to bring it up if he thought it was her husband who'd killed her; even more so if he'd done it himself.

If they could figure out exactly when Rose died it would help. If the contract for sale of the farm was dated around the same time as the bill of lading, that would presumably mean that Rose was alive when her husband left for Sault St. Marie to arrange the shipping of their possessions across the world. If she died before he could have made it back, Teddy'd be in the clear. Fat chance of proving that. It might be easier to show that she was still alive *after* he returned. Someone might remember seeing her or the two of them together. Someone could have come to say goodbye. Too bad the aunt was dead, but aunts often come with uncles. It would be worth checking.

It was later than McIntire had intended when he snaked along between the snowbanks into his own yard. The house was lit up like a Christmas tree. Leonie must be making it up to the REA for those five no-electric-bill days. He filled a plate with cold chicken and lukewarm mashed potatoes before joining her on the living room sofa.

She was curled up under a quilt, but there was no trace of sleep in her eyes. A bowl of solid-looking tapioca pudding sat on the coffee table. The radio was off. She had no book. Doing nothing was something Leonie seldom indulged in. She might find Deputy Newman's nabbing of a fugitive murderer entertaining.

"I had a phone call." She yawned. "Well, you had a call. From your mother."

"What's wrong?" McIntire had once or twice availed himself of the long distance operator to speak to his mother. She'd never before done such an extravagant thing herself.

"Maybe that's for you to say." Neither of them spoke while the clock on the wall chimed the half hour. "She said someone phoned her to ask about you. She thought it was queer."

McIntire put down his fork. "To ask what about me?"

"He said he hadn't heard from you for a long time and was trying to track you down."

"What's queer about that? I haven't been around in a long time. Who was it?" McIntire bit into the long-awaited drumstick.

"I'm not sure she got his name. She said this chap seemed more interested in finding out where you were a few years ago than where you are now."

The chicken went down like it still wore its feathers. "Did she tell you exactly what this person said?"

"He said he was an old friend and wanted to know if you were back in the United States. He said he'd tried to find you three or four years ago and had no luck."

"That doesn't sound like something that would send Ma galloping to the phone."

"Not that part. But then he went on and on about how he hadn't been able to get hold of you and worked things around to asking if *she* knew where you were in 1948, or if there was a time when you didn't write. She told him there'd been plenty of times you didn't write, and she's only heard from you in the past six months because of Christmas. Is that true?"

"No, it's not. I sent her a birthday card."

"I sent the card."

"You put my name on it, didn't you?"

"Yes." She pulled her knees up to her chin. "It must have been beastly for her, having you go away when you were just a boy and hardly ever seeing you again. How ever did she bear it?"

The sudden glistening of Leonie's eyes would have sent McIntire into panic if he hadn't already reached that state. What in hell was Fratelli trying to pull? It was a clumsy attempt at getting information that even Sophie McIntire had seen through. Why? A re-staging of his bumbling detective act?

When he'd turned up last fall, Fratelli had appeared inept and naive. Yet he'd come to St. Adele on a mission and had accomplished exactly what he'd set out to do. He'd wavered around but hit what he aimed for, and McIntire didn't much like the feeling that he was the agent's current target.

Leonie swung her feet to the floor. "Why would someone be asking Sophie where you were in 1948? If he was really some old friend, he shouldn't have any trouble finding you. Seems like tracking *her* down would have been a great deal stickier. Anybody looking for your mother would have looked here first, but they would hardly have gone to Florida to look for you. What do you suppose it was all about?"

"I can't imagine."

"Was he right? Were you out of touch somewhere?"

"I was in Moscow." The lie slipped out as easily as it had when he'd said it to Fratelli.

"You mean…?"

"It's not something I can talk about." That might be laying it on pretty thick, but it was true, perhaps not for the reasons Leonie might think.

"Not even to me?"

"Maybe. I'll have to think about it."

"Could this be something dangerous?" Her eyes grew round.

McIntire was hopeless at diagnosing sarcasm, even from his wife, and didn't try. "Oh, of course not. That stuff is all behind us now. It wasn't particularly dangerous at the time." It wasn't dangerous at all at the time, not in the way Leonie meant, and McIntire hoped it wouldn't prove to be dangerous now.

She took his hand and traced the lines of his palm. "There's still so much I don't know about you."

McIntire raised her fingers to his lips. "I sometimes suspect there's even more I don't know about you."

She nodded absently. "Perhaps."

LONDON—Britain will soon begin training its civil defense volunteers to detect radioactivity left by atomic weapons. The gadget used for training will be a pencil-sized Geiger counter.

Chapter Twenty-Five

McIntire would have sworn that he hadn't slept at all if he hadn't awakened to the muffled silence that could only mean one thing. He groaned and turned his face to the pillow.

"What's the matter?"

"Forecast was wrong, *again*. I'll be shoveling *again*."

"How do you know?"

"Can't you tell? Listen."

Leonie lay still for a minute, then shook her head. "I don't hear a thing."

"Exactly. It's like we're wrapped in cotton."

"I thought you liked snow. It keeps people from bothering you."

"I got things to do." Get hold of Melvin Fratelli, for one thing, and wring his scheming neck.

Leonie's thoughts apparently ran along similar lines. "Are you going to ring your mother back?" she asked. "She really did sound worried."

"I will." He lowered his head to her shoulder. "Maybe we should just stay right here."

"I plan to, for a time. You're welcome to join me."

It was tempting. But he had to get out of bed to stoke the fire, and he knew that once he was up, he would find things that needed doing. Plenty of them. "The town board meeting is tonight," he remembered. "It oughta be a humdinger. It'll probably take 'til then to dig out."

It did, or close to it. At seven-fifteen the McIntires swung into the freshly plowed parking area of St. Adele's town hall. It was an exercise in hope springing eternal. There wasn't a spot big enough to stick a tricycle. He drove straight through onto the road and snugged the Studebaker up to the twelve-foot snowbank.

"This has got to be some kind of attendance record."

Leonie didn't reply, just smiled and clutched her green stenographer's notebook and two pencils. She slid across the seat to exit behind him.

The meeting wasn't due to begin for another fifteen or twenty minutes, but the aroma of coffee was already being overwhelmed by that of tobacco.

Whoever had been entrusted with the job of firing up the furnace hadn't gotten himself shoveled out soon enough. The fifty plus bodies huddled on folding chairs, the steam of their breathing mingling with cigarette smoke to create a layer of blue haze floating in the high-ceilinged room. McIntire grabbed one of the few remaining chairs from the stack against the wall and set it up in an advantageous spot for Leonie to record the official proceedings as well as to catch up on the latest unofficial news—in the front row, next to Sally Ferguson. After filling an enamel cup with coffee he took his usual place, standing at the back of the room near the door.

So what was it that had brought out the crowd? A stale murder or the probable loss of one quarter of the high school faculty? McIntire's appearance wasn't greeted with any more than the usual curiosity at seeing the constable there, so either Erik Pelto was still at large, or his own part in alerting the FBI to the teacher's past life hadn't gotten out.

Ernie Jarvinen gaveled the room to silence. "We are gathered here tonight...." His customary opening words were met with the customary groans and followed by a tedious series of housekeeping tasks, from the last meeting's minutes to Myrtle Van Opelt's forking over of the $12.35 her Justice Court had exacted in fines in the past month.

"Any old business?" brought a few snickers and not a few glances in McIntire's direction, but any mention of homicide was held at bay by a discussion of the planting of tulips at the cemetery gate, which had been approved in September, the bulbs duly purchased but never put in the ground. The assembly, in their collective wisdom, decided it could now wait until spring. A consultation on the best means of keeping the bulbs until the frost was out of the ground ensued.

The door opened, letting in a blast of arctic air and Adam Wall, dressed in his brown county deputy uniform. He was sporting knee-high fringed deer-hide moccasins of the sort that might have come mail order from Bill's Wild West Emporium. What was going on with the sheriff's department and footgear? Was Adam Wall making a rebuttal to Sheriff Koski's fancy western boots? Would Cecil Newman soon be showing up in shiny new Buster Browns?

Wall pulled off his hat and moved next to McIntire. "Have I missed anything?"

"Only Hanging Judge Myrtle."

"Damn!"

Wall lived a half mile off the road; he didn't make the trek out often. He must have some good reason for being here, seemingly in his sporadic official capacity. McIntire asked, "Deputy Cecil get his man?"

"Yup. J. T. Falk is tucked up in cell number two, toasty warm, scarfing down Mrs. Koski's cooking."

"And going to be there for some time, I expect."

"Oh ya. Godwin will ask for no bail, and he'll get it."

"What's he worried about? Teddy doesn't seem like the type to run. He didn't have to come back here."

"No," Wall agreed, "and he wouldn't have any chance of disappearing, anyway. He shits, the Feds know what color."

"So why not set bail?"

"When it comes to homicide Godwin's batting oh for two. He ain't taking any chances on this one getting away. And Falk ain't complaining. He's warm, he's fed, he's got nothing to do and a stack of books two feet high." Adam Wall sounded envious.

McIntire lowered his voice a notch. "Any news from Lansing?"

"Two individuals. One adult female, about five foot five, healed fractures of fourth rib and left clavicle. No apparent cause of death. One adult male, at least five-ten, skull blown to smithereens."

"That's it? Guibard had that much figured out."

"They got a date off the shipping receipt. August seventeenth, 1934."

"Didn't anybody ask about it when he was hired?" The strident voice from the front row told McIntire who might be tucked up in cell number one.

"Mr. Pelto hasn't been spreading communism to his pupils." Harvey Muller, potato grower and school board chairman, sounded more defensive than convinced.

Roy Sorenson got to his feet "How do you know? You taking tenth grade math? The kids look up to him, he's a communist...."

"He is *not* a communist."

"He was when he was their age." Roy shook off Mrs. Roy's tug at his sleeve.

"They didn't know that until certain people started shooting their mouths off, did they?" Muller imitated Sorenson's sneering tone to a tee. The certain blabbermouth wearing the constable badge hoped he wasn't going to be called upon to break up a fight.

"Kinda makes you wonder how many more we got." It was Ben Lindstrom, normally a sensible sort, McIntire would have guessed, and, as one whose young son spent more time working in the family fishing business than he did in school, perhaps not one with a legitimate complaint.

"You got anybody to take over?"

"No, and if you think decent teachers are all that easy to come up with around here, now's your chance!" Muller folded his arms and pressed his lips together.

"So keep him on. You know damn well if everybody here that ever belonged to some communist outfit got fired we'd plenty of us be in trouble."

"He ain't being fired because he used to be a communist. We got to let him go if he don't show up for work. He can't hardly teach from a cell in the county jail, now can he?" Muller gave a final huff. "Maybe the state will come up with some extra money to bring in a sub."

"Think maybe they'd go Pelto's bail?" It was Arnie Johnson, miraculously the first time he'd offered the benefit of his wisdom to the group. His comments were ignored.

The meeting concluded with Harvey Muller promising action and vigilance, Mike Maki suggesting that the high school should have been closed and the kids bused into Chandler years ago, and without McIntire needing to exercise his official duty or avail himself of Adam Wall for reinforcement. From the looks of the group around the coffee maker, he might not be in the clear yet.

"Can I have a word?"

An elderly man, bundled in a World War I vintage army coat, nudged McIntire's elbow. He stuck out his hand. "Larry Houtari. Can we sit for a minute? My legs ain't what they used to be."

The basement furnace was finally beginning to spit out some warm air, and McIntire dragged two chairs closer to the grating in the floor. The old man settled down with a barrage of wheezing. His lungs apparently were also not what they used to be.

"My wife, she's passed away, was Rose Falk's aunt. Jarvi Makinen was her brother."

McIntire nodded. "I've been meaning to look you up."

"Adeline—my wife—she was a terrible nag."

McIntire wasn't sure if expressing sympathy was in order. Maybe male camaraderie would be the thing. He satisfied himself with a sympathetic nod.

"She nagged about every little thing. Got so I didn't pay no attention most of the time." Houtari shook his head. "Adeline had a good heart, but that nagging! She was real fond of Rosie, looked after her after her ma died. Rosie needed plenty of looking after, and Adeline worried about her. She was really flustered about them going off to Russia."

"That's understandable."

"I'm glad Addie ain't around to know what really happened."

That was also understandable. McIntire gave another nod.

"Well, I got to remembering. A couple days before Rose and Teddy left it was Adeline's birthday. The ladies, they had a birthday club. The all got together and visited when one of them had a birthday, in the afternoon, you know. Had a little party. Anyway, it was Adeline's birthday, and Rosie didn't show up. Adeline didn't think she'd do that, especially since she was leaving, and they might never see each other again. She got after me to go over to see if everything was okay."

"What did you find out?"

"I didn't go. Oh, I told Addie some cock and bull story about Rose being really busy or sick or something, I forget. I feel bad about it now. But we just saw her and Ted at the going-away party, and Addie was so miserable, crying and carrying on. I didn't want to have to go through all that again. Now I look back, it wasn't like Rosie not to be at Adeline's birthday, but at the time…." He shrugged. "She was just such a nagger!"

"When was your wife's birthday? Do you remember?"

"Oh, sure. Adeline wouldn't let me forget that! Seventeenth of August."

ROME—One person was killed and 8
injured in fighting between Italian
police and communist rioters protesting the presence in Italy of
Gen. Dwight D. Eisenhower.

Chapter Twenty-Six

If Rose Falk was alive to sign a land sale contract on August sixteenth, but was too dead to attend her aunt's birthday party the next day—a day her husband was off shipping cement mixers to New York City—that husband could hardly be responsible for her death.

But if not Teddy, who? Especially if the motive was Rose's affair with…whoever the hell he was. Would that affair have provoked a jealous rage in someone other than her husband? Orville Pelto? Even Eban Vogel? A wronged wife? Or could the murderer been acting out of compassion for the wronged husband? Eban Vogel again.

That Rose Falk might have indulged in some dalliance didn't seem to come as a great shock to those who knew her. Any disbelief stemmed from the notion that she'd had a willing partner. Teddy married her because he was sorry for her. Mia was of the opinion that she might have been vulnerable to anyone who paid attention to her. Irene Touminen said she was an embarrassing flirt, but couldn't believe she'd attracted an actual fella, and her brother thought she'd have made a good match for Earl Culver. Erik Pelto referred to Rose's clock-stopping face. On the other hand, she left his father sweaty, Mark Guibard had gone all misty-eyed with recollection, and somebody had wound up in that cistern with her—without his clothes. And without his head.

McIntire looked out the window. The weather had warmed and brought a light fog that veiled the sun and left the fences and electric wires furred with frost.

Leonie stood by the mailbox, studying an unopened envelope. When she started up the driveway, McIntire turned back to *Gösta Berling*, managing, he hoped, to look completely engrossed by the time she scuffed her feet on the mat in the porch.

"Look at this!" She tossed the only mail she carried, the latest edition of the *Monitor*, on the table. *Communist Finn Jailed in Chandler!* was accompanied by a misty photograph showing a group of youngsters gathered on a lakeshore. At their center, a young man who—according to the caption—was thirteen-year-old Erik Pelto, waved the hammer and sickle flag of the U.S.S.R.

"Where do you suppose Beckman got that?" McIntire wondered.

The article detailed Erik Pelto's childhood traveling the country with his labor activist father, his summers spent at communist youth camps, and finished up with a mention of his adult membership in the U.S. Communist Party.

"How ever did that man manage to find a job teaching school?"

"He had a certificate from the state of Michigan, and he was willing to work for peanuts and act as janitor and general factotum. I expect that put him way ahead of any other candidates. If there were any. He seems to be a perfectly fine teacher," McIntire said.

"Do you think Mr. Lindstrom is right? There might be more of them around? Perhaps we should be paying more attention to what goes on."

"You could get in touch with Fratelli. He's still looking for that spy. He might take you on."

"It's not something to make fun of."

It wasn't. Erik Pelto had two young children and a wife who were going to have a very bad time of it, something Leonie, surprisingly, seemed not to remember. McIntire closed his book. "The Finns who settled here were involved in the labor unions and socialist movements. Some were communists. It pretty much fizzled in the thirties. They aren't plotting to overthrow the government, and, so far as I know, they never were."

"You weren't here in the thirties," Leonie reminded him. "And you weren't here in the twenties or forties either. How could you know? They wouldn't have been writing you to let you know what they planned." She pulled the paper closer to scrutinize the photograph. "Mr. Radosovich wraps the fish in that Russian newspaper."

"It's not Russian. It's Serbian or Yugoslavian. He subscribes to it because it's the only language he can read." The paper did have a left-leaning element. McIntire hoped Chandler's grocer wouldn't end up bunking in with Erik Pelto. Fortunately Fratelli wouldn't be likely to be cooking any fish in his Marquette hotel room.

What was showing signs of turning into the first real quarrel for McIntire and his wife was nipped in the bud by a rap at the door. Uno Touminen stood on the steps. He gave a polite nod. "It's that asshole Thorsen," he said. "He's really done it this time. You got a crowbar?" While McIntire grabbed his coat, he added, "You got a camera?"

◇◇◇

What the asshole had done was put his much-abused Dodge into reverse when he intended third gear, sending it into a swandive through the rail on the Slate Creek bridge to ricochet off a fallen beech tree and belly-flop neatly onto a Frigidaire-sized boulder. There it sat rocking slightly, its three remaining wheels rotating gently in the breeze.

Nick waved from the driver's seat. McIntire snapped his photo and grappled with a major moral dilemma. Sell to Clayton Beckman and possibly win the Pulitzer prize, or turn it over to his wife. Well, she'd provided the camera.

They turned to the task of extracting Thorsen from his cockpit. It proved not to be a simple one. Getting leverage sufficient to pry open the crushed door while maintaining footing on a frozen, rock-strewn streambed was a challenge that McIntire was glad to let Uno tackle. Well, he'd provided the crowbar.

By the time Nick made the five-foot drop to the ice, they'd attracted a small but appreciative audience. Small in both number and stature. A pair of girls, rag-dolls in too large trousers and too small coats, stared from the roadside. Shouldn't they be in school? Apparently so. When McIntire turned in their direction they sprinted off as fast as their scarecrow-clothing would allow.

Nick had been luckier than Mia. The escapade appeared to have resulted in nothing more than a stiff neck. His pride was long past being vulnerable to injury. He stood with his hands dangling limp at his sides and looked with sadness at the impaled vehicle.

"How the hell am I gonna get her off?"

"A couple gallons of Phillips 66 and a match." Uno huffed in disgust and stalked back to his pickup, leaving McIntire to return Thorsen to his wife. It was a delivery he didn't intend to rush. Nick probably had insights into Eban Vogel's character and habits that had escaped his worshipful daughter, and McIntire welcomed the chance to pump him a little without Mia's interference.

"You'd better come back with me and warm up."

"I ain't cold."

"Well," McIntire struggled, "I didn't tell Leonie where I was going. I need to stop and let her know before I take you home."

Nick gave a condescending *Just how in hell hen-pecked are you?* smile but didn't argue. He was not likely to be in a hurry to face his own wife.

Leonie McIntire gave Nick all the sympathy he could have wished for and a slice of ginger cake with his tea. McIntire would have preferred to ply him with a more potent warmer-upper, but didn't know if Nick's illness precluded alcohol. It would undoubtedly take more than Parkinson's Disease to put Nick Thorsen on the wagon, but best not to offer. He realized that he'd never before spoken to Nick without Mia present. Mia might not be getting in the way now, but Thorsen wasn't going to be all that forthcoming with Leonie hovering over him.

"Dear," he said, "I think it may be time for your radio program."

Leonie stared for a moment. "Oh, thanks awfully, Darling. I really believe it is. Won't you both excuse me?"

McIntire decided to abandon subtlety with Nick also. "What do you think your father-in-law was up to, burying that money, not saying a thing?"

"I couldn't say, but I think he had a damn good idea Rosie Falk wasn't going to come looking for it."

"You think he knew Rose was dead?"

The spoon in Thorsen's hand trembled and he put it on the table. "Mia has always thought the sun rose from one of her father's pockets and set in the other. Papa Thorsen was an okay guy, but he wasn't any more perfect than the rest of us. Less perfect than you, that's for sure."

What the hell did that mean? "In what way? Are you saying he *could* have been involved in these deaths?"

"Shit no. I'm just saying he wasn't the saint Mia makes him out to be."

McIntire waited while Nick gripped his cup with both hands, raised it to his lips, and returned it deliberately to the saucer.

"When we got married, I wasn't crazy about the plan to move in with my father-in-law. He scared the hell out of me. But Mia was just a kid, and her mother had died, and it's not like there wasn't plenty of room in the house. It's too damn big now, but then we didn't know there'd never be more than just us two." He picked up the spoon and looked at it like he'd never seen such an implement. McIntire retrieved a fork from the drawer and handed it to him. He grunted, stabbed at the cake, and went on with his story. "Anyway, it worked out all right. I spent most of my time in the car, and Eban spent his in his workshop, and we got along fine. I miss him." He sighed. "Especially when I look at the paint peeling off the barn."

"But he wasn't perfect," McIntire prompted.

"Who is? He kept a lot to himself. We didn't even know he was sick until a couple weeks before he died." He swallowed the last of the cake. "I can't fault him for that."

Nick would die by inches in plain sight of all.

"He wouldn't let Mia clean his room or anything. Liked his privacy."

Was Thorsen ever going to get to the crux of this imperfection?

"Eban was still a pretty young man when Mia's mother died. He didn't seem to have any interest in getting married again, but that doesn't mean he wasn't interested in women. He used to take off to buy wood regular as clockwork, twice a month. Half the time he came back empty handed, but in an improved state of mind, if you know what I mean. There was a woman in Sidnaw he went to for years. But he might not have traveled so far if he didn't have to."

If Eban Vogel had been in the habit of visiting ladies of questionable virtue, that was mildly intriguing, but didn't have much to do with Rosie Falk. Unless the enigmatic Mrs. Falk had yet another side to her personality. "You're not saying that Rose Falk was making a little pocket money in the afternoons?"

"Hell, no. Rosie didn't charge." Nick gave a deprecating humph. "She couldn't have brought in a hell of a lot. But she was the friendly sort, you might say, and not everybody can afford to be choosy."

Not a problem that plagued Nick, apparently.

"Teddy was gone overnight now and then. He had parents down in the Lower Peninsula and a brother somewhere that he went to see. And like I said, Rosie was the friendly sort. I ain't saying that Eban was one of those friends," he went on, "but he did go over to help out with the chores now and then when Ted was away."

"That hardly seems criminal," McIntire said. "He and Ted were good friends. I'd never have pegged Eban as the kind of man to fool around with a friend's wife."

"Me either. But who knows? He was a secretive old bugger, and he was one of those people that can convince themselves that whatever they do is fine and dandy. You know what I mean?"

McIntire did know.

Nick massaged his shoulder as he continued, "I can only see it two ways, either Eban deliberately stole money from Rose Falk, or he knew she was dead and didn't need it. I can't believe he'd have stolen it. Shit, if he did, why didn't he spend it? If he knew she was dead, it can only be that he killed her himself, or he knew who did it and was protecting him. Or maybe he just *thought* he knew who did it and was protecting him."

"How do you figure?"

"Say what Teddy tells us is true, that he came over and told Eban that his wife had run off with another man, and gave him some money. But say Eban found out some way that Rose was dead, and that she had some guy on the side. He might have figured Teddy did it, and if I know Eban, he'd have kept his mouth shut."

Nick's extra time for thinking was turning him into a regular genius.

"Have you mentioned this to Mia?"

"Sure. That Eban might have been protecting Teddy, that is, not about her old man and his whores. But...."

"What?"

"I don't remember Teddy Falk coming over to give Eban any money. But then I get up and out early. He could have come after I'd already gone on the route. I do remember Teddy coming to see Eban not long before he was going to leave. Eban was dead set against the whole idea and the two of them had one hell of a row over it."

"You think it had something to do with Rose leaving?"

"It had to do with them both leaving. Eban thought they were idiots to do it. He was right. Far as I knew, that was the last time Eban and Teddy Falk saw each other. Ted's story about trotting over with a fistful of money a few days later is pretty damn hard to swallow."

"But his plans had supposedly changed by that time. He wasn't going to go after all. At least not to Karelia."

"Well...ya. I guess that's right."

"Back to Rose. From what you're saying, the man in the well, who was definitely not Eban Vogel, could be almost anybody."

"Had to be somebody who could die without people noticing."

"But Rose was the kind that fooled around?"

"I don't know if she did, but she gave a damn good impression that she *would* if she had half a chance." Nick massaged the fingers of his left hand. "You can see why she might...I guess she just wanted to prove she was as good as anybody else."

"Why wouldn't she be?"

Nick looked up. "Didn't you know her?"

"No, I don't think so."

"Rosie had a hare-lip. She was one ungodly homely woman."

WASHINGTON—A military secrets case
that formed the basis for a feud
between Senator Joseph R. McCarthy
(R-Wis.), and Drew Pearson, columnist and radio commentator, has
been sent to the Justice Department
for investigation.

Chapter Twenty-Seven

"It was an accident. It could happen to anybody."

Mia couldn't believe what she was hearing. "No, Nick, it could only happen to you! Face it, you can't drive. You have to quit your job and that's final. We'll find some other way to get along."

"I can get another car. It might have to have an automatic transmission."

"We'll *have* to get another car. There's no question about that. But I'm not letting you near it!"

"Hiring a chauffeur, are you? That's pretty rich, coming from someone who spent less than a minute behind the wheel and managed to demolish two lilac bushes and a telephone pole."

"The car's not still sitting there, though, is it? How much good has your great skill and experience done?" She stuck her crutches under her arms and wrenched herself to her feet. Nick turned back to the door.

"Where are you going?"

"Down cellar for a bottle." He twisted the door knob and gave a yelp.

"What happened?"

"I don't know…I can't…." He stared at the back of his hand, tentatively turned it palm up, and gasped.

Mia sagged on her crutches. "Oh, lord. Don't tell me it's broken."

"My wrist is maybe sprained a little."

His face was damp and the color of cold dishwater, a face Mia had recently been on the other side of. "It's broken," she said. "Sit down and I'll call Guibard."

"Forget it. It's just a sprain. You can wrap it up for me, and I'll see how it feels tomorrow. But open the door first. I'll get that bottle."

"You're crazy. It's not going to get any better overnight."

"It'll be okay. Just open the damn door."

Mia hobbled to the door and flung it open. "Suit yourself," she said. "Bring up a quart of tomatoes while you're at it."

After about ten minutes and a single crash of breaking glass, Nick returned with a bottle in his hand, a jar under his arm, and a splash of red on his trouser cuffs.

"I'll clean it up later."

Mia put the jar of tomatoes on the counter and turned her attention to the bottle, using a knife to flip up the bail on its stopper. Nick took the glasses from the cupboard and poured them each a glass of the dandelion wine. He sat down and swirled the liquid, holding it up to the light.

"What are we going to do?" he asked.

"We'll manage."

"We have to think about moving into town."

"No!"

"This place is too damn big anyway."

"No. Absolutely not. I can get more work."

"Not enough to live on. Anyway, I'm not having my wife support me."

"Go ahead and starve then." Mia said it without emotion. This argument was growing stale. They'd had it too many times. They'd do whatever they had to do, and if it meant that what was left of Nick's pride suffered, so be it. She propped herself on her crutches and hopped off to the living room sofa where she could put her leg up—if she could make room for it on the coffee table among the last of her father's unsorted belongings.

After her initial foray into the fragments of his life, Mia had lost the heart for it, not getting much past stuffing the stacks of paper back into their boxes and recruiting Nick to carry them to the living room. Teddy Falk's visit had changed that.

Teddy had to have been telling the truth about giving her father that money. He couldn't have known they'd found it, so he couldn't have made the story up. If there was some clue in this pile of junk, something to explain her father's strange behavior, she intended to find it. It was impossible to believe that he'd known Rose Falk was dead and kept it to himself.

Still, she could barely bring herself to touch the stuff. It was increasingly painful to see the man these remnants portrayed. The postcards, the clipped advertisements. He'd left so much more, and these tawdry scraps did not reflect the man she knew her father to be. His wish to make the world a better place and his joy in creating something of beauty that would last long after he was gone and forgotten. Eban Vogel lived in clock cases and chests, not in sleazy men's magazines and drugstore receipts for laxatives and worse.

Only two boxes remained. She dragged the largest to her and slid her fingernail across the black electrical tape that sealed it.

A book was on top. It wore a purple dust jacket, a mysterious green symbol, and orange lettering, *The Male Hormone*. It promised "A new gleam of hope for prolonging man's prime of life." A glance through its pages revealed that, although the author, a Mr. de Kruif, began by lamenting the waning of his endurance with ax and crosscut saw, maintaining a good supply of firewood was not his primary aim.

Under it were only more of the magazines. *The National Police Gazette*. Exotic Gypsy Nina wore two veils, neither of which veiled much of anything. Above the title, the headline screamed, "Brooklyn Girls Killed by Woman Quack." She peeked underneath. The next issue's cover girl wore an even smaller costume, but a bigger smile. The box was full. How had he managed to bring them all into the house with nobody noticing? If they had come in the mail Nick would have.... She closed the flaps and shoved the box aside. Too hard. It hit the floor with a thunk.

The last of the cartons was larger and sturdier, but, blessedly, lighter than the others. She lifted its lid and was greeted by more paper. A quick fan through showed them to be receipts for property tax. Forty years' worth. She placed the stack on the table. A smaller box remained inside. Walnut, darkly stained, with ornate silver-colored metal hinges and clasp.

Mia remembered the day the package had come. It was not long after her marriage to Nick, and she'd expected it to be a wedding gift. Her father had cut the string and taken this case from its wrappings. He'd not opened it, only read the short note and informed Mia in a dispassionate voice that her grandmother Vogel was dead. He'd taken the box to his room, and Mia hadn't seen it again until now. Before she opened it she ran her fingers over the smooth walnut and the initials worked into the silver medallion, *LAV*. Lydia Ann? Laura Angela? Mia had never heard the woman's name. She lifted the clasp. Had her father not been curious enough to do the same? Had he never once looked to see what his mother had left?

He should have. Nestled in a snippet of rust-colored velvet was a watch. One he would have liked very much. Heavy, simple engraving on silver. With the tarnish polished away, it would be a handsome piece of work. Maybe it had once belonged to his own father. Inside the cover was more engraving, an inscription. Mia squinted at the ornate script, then set it aside and lifted out the gauzy material beneath.

It swaddled a tiny doll, only six or seven inches tall. Mia smoothed the robe of soft striped wool and the tiny fringed sash that tied it about her waist. The hands and feet were carved of wood. Her eyes were blue and her hair was painted a shiny black. It was old, old enough to have belonged to her grandmother, or even her great-grandmother. Mia propped her erect between two cushions and set the wrapping aside.

All that remained was a square of folded tissue. Inside, tied with a ribbon of faded pink, lay a tiny lock of the softest sooty black hair. Mia let it rest in her palm. Her father's baby hair? Or maybe her own?

Mia's mother had told her of the abundant black hair she was born with. Charlotte Vogel had, like her daughter, lost three babies. Unlike Mia she'd had the courage to become pregnant once more. This time she left her home and husband and traveled to put herself in the hands of her grandmother, a Potowatomi woman she'd never met. When she returned in the spring, carrying the red-faced infant with inky black hair, Eban had been suspicious. In a few weeks all color had faded from both the hair and complexion, but by that time, Charlotte Vogel said, "your father had fallen in love with you and wouldn't have given you back anyway." When Mia's great-grandmother died a few years later, Charlotte insisted that Mia take her name, and little Ramona Vogel had become Meogokwe.

Mia touched the wisp to her cheek. *"Mama."*

A second crash of breaking glass. Nick stood in the doorway, eyes wide, feet in a puddle of pungent wine.

Mia felt her heart quicken. "Nick." She extended her hand with the curl in the palm. "Whose hair is this?"

"Hair? I don't know."

"Tell me."

"How would I know? I never—"

"Tell me!" It was a shriek, but didn't need to be. The look on his face told her the unbearable truth. "How could you? How could you have kept this from me? Part of her, and all this time, all these years and years, you kept it from me?"

"I didn't want to see it. I didn't want to talk about it. I didn't want to ever think about it."

"It was part of *her!*"

He didn't move from his spot in the doorway. "You screamed when we took her from you. Screamed and screamed so I thought you'd never stop. I can hear it still." His deadpan voice was uncaring, cruel. "You were lucky. You got sick and you forgot. How do you think it was for me? You weren't the only one who lost a daughter. I'd have done anything to trade places with you. I'd have done anything to be able to forget."

TAMPA, FLA.—Details of Governor
Fuller Warren's plan to make
Florida a haven for thousands
of retired workers were unveiled
yesterday.

Chapter Twenty-Eight

"Mac, you gotta help me out." Pete Koski had resorted to whining.

"I ain't coming to do your shoveling for you. Get Marian."

"According to our star boarder—"

"Which one would that be?"

"Falk. Murder trumps everything."

"Even sedition? Scheming against Mom and apple pie?"

"Around here it does."

"How are the two of them getting along? It must have been quite a reunion."

"Oh, they're thick as thieves. Which is what I damn well wish they were. The Feds are nagging at me to keep them apart. Only way to do that would be if one of 'em bunks in with me and Marian. They're welcome to take their commie off my hands. His hearing is coming up next week. It's in Duluth, so we'll get shed of him then. In the meantime they're jabbering away in that heathen language, plotting the great escape. I'm tempted to get Marian to bake a file in a pasty."

"What is it you want from me?"

"Well, Falk says that before she left, or died, his wife opened a bank account. She needed it because of selling the farm. It was in her name only."

"The farm or the bank account?"

"Both, I guess. She opened an account so that the payments for the farm could be deposited into it. The plan was that the money would be transferred to a bank in Russia. Talk about dreamers!"

"Did Sulo ever pay it off?" Irene hadn't shown McIntire a deed.

"Damned if I know. Maybe you can find out. If he did, he never bothered to change the title with the county. The place is still in Rose Falk's name. Rose Makinen, that is. Touminen paid the taxes for a while, then not another cent until a couple days ago. Now he's paid them up."

"So he doesn't want to risk losing it. But, I repeat, what do you want from me?"

"Not much." The sheriff's tone of voice gave McIntire to know that it probably was much. "Rose gave power of attorney to one of your neighbors, to take care of transferring the deed when the time came. Maybe you could just go talk to her. If she still has a copy of the document, try to get it so we can make sure it matches the one on file at the courthouse. Find out if the contract was ever paid off, and what the particulars of the deal were. Maybe Falk thought that with Rose dead he could get the place back. It's what he's got on his mind now, anyway. He figures as her husband he'll inherit her estate. "

"Sounds like Teddy's pretty confident that he won't be locked up for the rest of his life."

"He made it through thirteen or fourteen years in Russia. He might be an optimist."

The job that Koski was tapping him for didn't sound terribly onerous. There had to be a catch. "Okay," McIntire asked, "who is it you want me to talk to?"

"Well...."

McIntire waited. Koski coughed.

"You're gonna have to tell me, Pete."

"Rose Falk, in her great wisdom, entrusted her fortunes to Myrtle Van Opelt."

It might have been worse, but McIntire couldn't think how. "Only as a favor to you, Pete. One I'll expect you to not forget."

"I'm sure if I do, you'll remind me."

"Damn right."

"I thought Myrtle liked you."

"Justice Van Opelt is rigorously impartial. She doesn't like anybody."

If McIntire had to face Mrs. Van O, he preferred to tackle it as he had back when he was sixteen years old. Go in cold. Thinking about it in advance only brought on a disabling attack of nerves. "Is Falk still sticking to his story?" he asked. "Still no inkling as to who his wife might have been passing the time of day with?"

"He is, and we haven't come up with a soul who disappeared about that time."

There were fifty-one souls who disappeared in another hole in the ground about that time. McIntire hung up the earpiece and turned to his wife.

"Leonie, when those miners were drowned, were all the bodies recovered?"

"Heavens, no! They only found seven, at least by the end of August. There were forty-four left in the pit. Do you think maybe one of them wasn't really there?"

"Koski said there were rusty stains on some of the stuff in the well."

"Maybe more of the remains were recovered later. I could ask Mr. Beckman."

That's all he needed, Beckman sniffing around. "That's okay," McIntire said. "Maybe tonight I'll make that call to Ma."

Myrtle Van Opelt. *Miss* Van Opelt. *Justice* Van Opelt. Any way you looked at it, the woman struck fear into the very pith of McIntire's bones. He'd like to think it was only an irrational reaction to the memory of years spent anticipating the sting of her metal-edged ruler on his hand, or worse, the sting of humiliation she had such a natural talent for inflicting. But Mrs. Van O didn't need to rely on past ferocity to intimidate. Advancing years had honed her skills to a formidable level.

Pete Koski was usually a match for her. Koski had only contempt for the JPs of this world. And Koski was impartial in his own way. Being female and as old as Methuselah cut no ice with the sheriff.

McIntire simply did his best to avoid contact with her. Which sometimes meant looking the other way as much as possible when confronted with a legal infraction that might fall under Myrtle's jurisdiction. He reasoned that fear of the justice was a major deterrent to petty crime. He wouldn't want to risk criminals becoming inured to her court by dragging them before her for every little thing.

He'd never entered her house before. His concept of the justice's home life was much the same as it had been when she was the dreaded Miss Van O. Then it had seemed that when the last pupil scuttled gratefully out the door at the end of the day, Miss Van Opelt went into a suspended state, scowl fixed, ruler raised, until the first of them crept back in the morning. The concept that she, or any teacher, had a life outside the classroom was ludicrous.

Miss Van Opelt must have had one. For a start, she was not, even then, a Miss, a situation she'd kept under wraps back in the days when marriage would have gotten her booted her out of her job quicker than if she'd been a commie.

Mr. Van Opelt—Hans—kept milk cows and had the distinction of being able to squeeze more profanity into a single sentence than any other man around, and that included the odd visiting Great Lakes sailor.

Hans stood next to his ancient spike-wheeled Farmall wielding a wicked-looking oil can. His greeting contained only two goddamns and a single son of a bitch. Maybe age was mellowing the man in a way it hadn't affected his wife.

He waved McIntire off to the house and ambled to the other side of the old bastard of a tractor's engine.

McIntire knocked. He quavered as he listened to the thunk of Mrs. Van O's cane approach the door. She ushered him through a blanket-hung doorway into the living room with little taps of the stick, like a sheepdog nipping at his heels.

She was bundled in a heavy cardigan, and a glimpse of what must have been a pair of her husband's winter woolies showed below the hem of her 1930s style dress. McIntire hoped they were keeping her warmer than he felt. The room was heated, slightly, by an oil burner. A second doorway was also blanketed. As befitted her former profession, but coming as a surprise to McIntire nonetheless, the walls were filled with books.

She dropped onto a chair and gave the sofa a smart whack. McIntire sat, careful lest his elbow rumple the lace doily.

"What's up?"

"I don't like to bother you—"

"You already have. So what is it? Have you finally caught Stanley Larson in the act? Need a search warrant?"

Mrs. Van Opelt was certain that Larson, known as Chip to all but the rigidly formal JP, was conducting a thriving business dealing in stolen minks.

"No. Chipper seems to be lying low."

The eyes locked on McIntire's and looked straight through to his brain. "Somebody's lying low, but I don't know that it's Stanley. He's waltzing in and snitching those animals right out of their cages."

"I had a call from the sheriff."

"Hah! Maybe now we'll get action from a man who knows a crime when he sees it." The cane gave a thunk on the floor.

"He didn't call about Chip Larson. It was about Rose Falk."

The glint of pursuit faded, and Myrtle rested her chin on the cane. "Poor Rosie. She was bound to come to a bad end one way or another. I remember—"

"Koski says that before Rose left, she signed a paper authorizing you to act as her agent in the sale of her farm."

Mrs. Van Opelt sat erect and placed the cane against the side of her chair. She folded her hands in her lap. "Yes, she did."

The words were politely formal. Almost wary. She touched a liver-spotted hand to her suspiciously black finger waves.

"How was the transaction to take place?" McIntire waited to be told to shove it—in a most judgelike manner, naturally. Myrtle's only expression of displeasure was a slight pursing of her thin lips.

"Rose sold the farm to Sulo Touminen," she said. "He was supposed to make annual payments for six years. I was to deposit them in a bank account in Rose's name. Once she and her husband got settled they would tell me where to send the money. They never did, but there wasn't any money to send. Sulo didn't pay off the contract."

"So the deed was never transferred?"

"No."

"Then as things stand the place would belong to her husband as her sole heir?"

"Would it? Even if he killed her?"

McIntire didn't know the answer to that. "You must have known Rose pretty well if she trusted you with this. What do you think might have happened?"

The old Myrtle flashed in the eyes, but was quashed by whatever had brought on this civil streak. "She was a pupil at the school. When she bothered to come, which wasn't all that often. Always in some sort of trouble. She seemed to think her affliction gave her some special rights, and we should overlook whatever she did." She took a breath and shook her head. "Oh well. Looking at that face in the mirror every morning couldn't have been easy, and she did get teased a lot. Children can be pretty nasty. I suppose she came to me because she didn't really have anybody else she could trust."

"She had an aunt."

"Adeline? Adeline Makinen didn't make it past sixth grade. And she was sickly. Rose didn't think that she'd live six more years. She didn't. Looks like she must have outlived Rosie, though."

"Do you have a guess as to who this other man might have been?"

"I stay away from gossip." A common enough claim. This was one time McIntire believed it.

"Is there anybody else who left or disappeared that summer? Do you remember?"

"There's nothing wrong with my memory!"

Another assertion McIntire did not doubt. "The man in that cistern with Mrs. Falk was most likely from nearby. Was there anybody else who moved away around that time and hasn't come back?"

"No," she said. "Not that summer. I can't think of a soul."

"Which bank was the account in?"

"I don't remember." There was nothing wrong with Myrtle's ability to contradict herself. "It was closed out years ago."

"Do you still have the paper? The Power of Attorney? If we knew what date Rose signed it, we'd at least know that she was alive at that time."

"I probably have it. But I don't need the paper to tell you when it was signed. It was the day of that flood in the mine. I don't recall the exact date, but you can easily find out. We didn't hear about it until the next morning, but I remember thinking that while we were in Walfred Kettil's kitchen signing those papers, making those big changes in Rose Makinen's life, nature was doing the same for a couple of hundred other people."

Nature hadn't exactly been responsible for tunneling a hole under a lake or of sending fifty-one men into it to die, unless the cave-in was an act of retaliation.

The door in the kitchen opened and closed followed by a shuffling, clanking of pans, and the single word *bastard.*

Myrtle got to her feet, thumped across the room, and disappeared behind the blanket. "Ooh, Honey Bun, izz oo chilly?"

McIntire didn't catch the words of the mumbled reply and was glad of it.

"Us has tumpany."

Until now, Myrtle Van Opelt's sugary cooing to her husband had been only a rumor McIntire'd refused to credit. Even hearing it for himself couldn't conquer his disbelief.

"Luvey Buvvy better tum in and get all cozy wozy."

Lovey Buvvy pushed into the room and cozy wozied next to McIntire on the sofa. The stubble on his chin was still coated with frost. "Got that son of a bitchin' bastard purrin' like a goddamn kitten."

McIntire congratulated him and wished the pair good day.

It was not yet four, but Sulo Touminen's barn windows glowed soft yellow. McIntire pushed open the door and stepped inside. A voice from behind the line of Guernsey rumps called out, "Be right with you."

"No rush." The barn was pleasant—warmer than the Van Opelts' living room and suffused with a sleepy aroma of hay and cow's breath. Leonie would not be thanking him for coming home steeped in the odors produced at the opposite end of the cow.

A whoosh sounded at McIntire's back and a cascade of hay dropped through a trap door, sending up a cloud of dust and seed. Sulo came forward and stuck his fork into the stack. He went down the line, pitching hay into the mangers.

A pair of denim-covered legs appeared through the opening, and Irene Touminen descended the ladder. She brushed straw from her knees. "How's by you?"

"Not bad," was all she waited to hear before ducking through a door and returning with a stool and a metal pail. She seated herself under a cow and leaned her head against its flank. A mottled orange cat materialized from a murky corner and lowered itself to its haunches with a demanding meow. Irene bent the teat and sent a stream of milk into its open mouth.

Sulo finished his job and spit into the gutter. "Teddy confess yet?"

"Not so far as I know. Matter of fact, I figured I should let you know, Teddy doesn't seem over worried about a murder conviction. He's looking to get the farm back."

Irene crooned softly to the cow, and milk plinked into the bottom of the pail.

"Hell's bells! How's he got that figured?"

"He says the payments weren't made. Myrtle Van Opelt says the same."

"I made payments. Things got tough for awhile, but I made payments. I got receipts."

"The bank account was closed. Apparently there was no money in it."

"Then maybe you'd just better ask Miss Justice Myrtle what happened to it." His words were emphasized with a shaking of the fork, its tines a foot from McIntire's face.

So that was why the Wicked Witch of the North had died the minute McIntire uttered the words *Power of Attorney*. Myrtle Van Opelt a thief? If she had used the money for her own purposes, it might not have been strictly illegal, depending on the wording of the document, but it was stealing in McIntire's book. Did it mean that Myrtle knew Rose was dead? No, sadistic as the former teacher was, and however outraged she might have been at Rose's youthful misconduct, McIntire couldn't quite see her shooting the two illicit lovers and dumping them down a cistern.

McIntire stepped back from the threatening pitchfork. "Rose was still alive on the morning of August sixteenth. That's when she signed the Power of Attorney and the Contract for Deed. She missed an appointment the next afternoon, so she might have died that night."

"What appointment?" Irene stood with her stool in one hand and a bucket brimming with white foam in the other. The scent of warm milk took McIntire back to those mornings when Sophie had dipped a cup full of just-out-of-the-cow milk for his breakfast. It had gagged him then, and the smell now did the same.

He backed up slightly. "Her aunt's birthday. Adeline Houtari. Were you there?"

"My stars! How would I remember that?"

"The sixteenth was the day all those men were drowned, the Massey-Davis mine accident. You might remember if you saw either of the Falks after that. They weren't scheduled to leave until a couple of days later."

"I think we were gone for a little while then. Do you remember, Sulo? Is that when we were in Escanaba?"

"Maybe. Ya. I think we might have been at the fair." Touminen jabbed his fork into the hay. "I'm going out with Uno tomorrow if you want to tag along."

"Going out" meant going out onto the lake to freeze while staring down a hole in the ice waiting for fish that never came. "Thanks anyway," McIntire told him. "Maybe sometime before the winter's over." And then again, maybe not.

Sophie McIntire sounded far away, as well she might. She did not sound particularly worried.

"It was just strange. I thought I should let you know. He had a sort of funny accent."

"Foreign?"

"Nooo, I don't think so. More like in the movies."

"Cary Grant?"

"Edward G. Robinson. And he was right, of course."

"About what?"

"I didn't hear from you. I couldn't contact you when your father died. You've never told me why exactly. Where were you?"

"I think just mentioning the place where I was can get you thrown in jail these days."

"I won't snitch. Oo-yay an-cay el-tay e-may in-way ode-cay."

"Ma."

"Oh, okay, you can write me about it."

McIntire was glad to switch the topic. As he knew she would, his mother remembered every detail of the mine accident and the two men from St. Adele who were lost.

"Were their bodies recovered?"

"Why are you asking? Or is that another top secret?"

"The man in the well with Rose Falk wasn't her husband."

"Really? Goodness, who ever would have thought? And you don't know who it was?"

"No. And can't come up with anybody else who went missing. It looks like the murders happened about the same time as the mine accident."

"Jack Stewart."

"That was quick."

"Jack used to come into the saloon a lot. Your father felt terrible when he heard. You know how sentimental he was."

Colin McIntire was many things, but sentimental?

Sophie said, "But he didn't mourn very long."

No surprise to McIntire. "Pa was always one to bounce right back."

"John…," she sighed but let it go. "You know Nelda?"

"Ya." McIntire had seen Nelda Stewart, Nutty Nelda, as she was more commonly called, a time or two. He'd never spoken to her. The sight of her was enough to give him the willies.

"Well, a few days after the cave-in, one of the mining company's men went to Nelda. He said that they weren't quite sure Jack had actually been in the mine when the accident happened. The water broke through just before the shift change, and there was talk that Jack might have already gotten out some way. Nelda insisted that he hadn't showed up at home, and he had to be in the mine. They went around and around about it. The company insisted he wasn't there. But Jack had been at work in the mine that day, they knew that for sure, and he wasn't around after it flooded, so they finally had to admit he must have been lost along with the others. They ended up paying widow's benefits to Nelda."

"But they never found his body?"

Sophie hesitated, then apparently decided to throw caution to the winds. "They stopped looking for any of the bodies after a few weeks. Every time they dug, more water came in. But…well, I guess I'm not saying anything everybody doesn't already know. There were definitely people who did not believe Jack was really there. Your father was in a position to hear plenty of talk, and he was sure Jack had just seen his chance and taken off."

"And let his family think he was dead?"

"I guess so. The kids were just little tykes then. It was hard for them growing up, living on next to nothing with only their mother and her being…. Well," her party-line discretion returned, "you can imagine. But they did fine. They were smart. Both of them went off to college."

Jack Stewart. It sounded like a possibility. A strong possibility. McIntire should have felt a thrill of pursuit. Instead he felt only resigned to stirring up more grief.

"Aren't you going to ask about the weather?" Sophie laughed.

"No, Ma, I'm not, and don't you dare tell me." McIntire promised to write and said goodbye.

He walked to the window. The sinking sun cut a path of color across the stark white of the field beyond the barn. A path that led to nothing now that the pines were gone. The sky had gone a deep blue, and a point of light shone bright above the horizon. Too large and too early for a star; it had to be a planet. McIntire didn't know which one.

Nelda Stewart. Another housewife to pump, and this one nutty to boot. McIntire was thoroughly tired of it. Sitting in kitchens with beige or turquoise walls; drinking coffee of varying degrees of unpalatability; asking nosy questions that got him nowhere. He ought to have waited until spring to look for those bodies. They'd been there sixteen years; another five or six months wouldn't have mattered, and he would at least have been able to get out the door without a shovel. His brain might have come out of hibernation.

What had he accomplished so far? A part of his life McIntire hoped was dead and buried was slowly being disinterred. A perfectly fine teacher was locked up. Two babies and a mother hardly more than a child herself would be left destitute in a strange country. Even if Pelto wasn't deported, he'd never teach again, and he might spend months in that jail. In the neighboring cell sat a man who'd most likely already had years of punishment worse than any the state of Michigan could mete out. Mia Thorsen had lost the father she idolized, and now that idol was about to be knocked off his pedestal. Sulo Touminen was set to lose eighty acres. Mrs. Van Opelt would be labeled a thief. Well, every cloud did have its silver lining.

Now Nelda Stewart's dead husband would be dragged from his grave. But not today. It could wait.

"How's your mother?" Leonie rinsed the dregs of chocolate from her cup.

"She sounded fine to me. Warm."

"Did you ask?"

He hadn't. Not in so many words. Not in any words. Was Leonie right? Had he broken his mother's heart when he left home? No doubt he had. He wasn't about to do it again. He wouldn't break his mother's heart or his wife's either. He'd have to make that clear to Melvin Fratelli one way or the other.

WASHINGTON—The government froze wages and prices last night in a stop-gap order designed to hold inflation in check.

Chapter Twenty-Nine

Pete Koski was back behind his desk. The set of his lips said it would be a while before he was behind the wheel of his Power Wagon. "Whatcha got for me?"

"I talked to Myrtle. She confirms what you said. Rose gave her Power of Attorney to handle the sale of her farm. She was supposed to contact her about arrangements to transfer the money to Karelia when the time came. Myrtle never heard from her. She also says Sulo didn't pay up so it was a moot point."

Koski nodded. "The account was in the old Superior Bank. It went under late in 1934. Everything was switched over to Chandler National. Rose Falk's account was closed in 1939, lack of activity. So I guess Teddy's got a chance at getting his hands on the place, if he's not sitting in prison."

"Here's something to take your mind off your back." McIntire handed Koski a slip of paper, *Received from Sulo A. Touminen, 200 dollars, August 30, 1935*, signed, *Mrs. Myrtle Van Opelt.*

"And two more." He placed them on the desk. "Nineteen thirty-six and thirty-seven."

Koski's smile was one of genuine pleasure. "Justice Van Opelt. Petty larceny. My, my, my."

"I don't suppose it was exactly criminal. Rose signed her rights over. Myrtle could legally do what she wanted."

"Maybe not with Rose dead." Koski opened a brown card-board folder. He leafed through the papers it contained and produced the short statement naming Mrs. Myrtle Van Opelt as Rose Falk's agent in all matters pertaining to the property located at the complicated legal description that followed.

Rose Falk's signature was dated August 16, 1934.

"Have you got the bill of lading?" McIntire asked.

Koski signaled McIntire to fetch a heavy, official-looking book from the window ledge. He opened its back cover and removed a folded sheet of waxed paper. Pressed inside, the scraps of document showed the date. August followed by two digits, the second clearly a seven. The twenty-seventh was out. It confirmed what Adam Wall had told him, August seventeenth.

Koski said, "Rose was still alive on the sixteenth. Falk says he went to a freight agent in Sault St. Marie to arrange for shipping. He says he had to sign the papers and pay, but they'd already packed the stuff up and hauled it into Chandler. If Falk drove to Chandler himself and took the train from there, like he says—and he could be lying about that—he'd have been gone at least overnight, maybe two nights. He either had to leave on the sixteenth and stay that night, or leave early on the seventeenth and stay over until the eighteenth. Everybody agrees that he was gone on the sixteenth, so that clinches it. The date on the bill of lading is the seventeenth, the earliest he could have got home would be late that night. So if he killed his wife it was most likely after he got back." He closed his eyes and inhaled a long breath. His words came through a locked jaw. "Could be he got home earlier than the little woman expected."

"It looks like she was already dead by the afternoon of the seventeenth." McIntire told the sheriff about the nagging aunt with the birthday.

"Rose was leaving the country," Koski said. "She mighta been too busy for hen parties."

McIntire turned back to the Power of Attorney. Below Rose's signature were that of Mrs. Van O; Walfred Kettil, Justice of the Peace; and—McIntire pushed up his glasses and looked again—a single witness, Orville H. Pelto. So the senior Pelto had been with Rose that day, which was possibly her last day alive.

Koski returned the shipping receipt to its protective wrapping. "You never did tell me where you got this."

McIntire told him.

"Under a tree? Vogel buried a receipt under a tree? What the hell, was he some kind of…was this a habit of his?"

"Sometimes."

"You do have a bunch of lunatics out there." Koski shook his head but didn't ask for details. "Falk says he had quite a tiff with Eban Vogel before he left."

"I don't imagine Eban was pleased about his leaving. Nick told me they got into an argument over it."

"What they got into was a knock-down, drag-out brawl."

"They came to blows?" Nick hadn't said anything about that.

"They came to shouting, shoving, and throwing furniture around. But," the sheriff added, "Falk also says he got over it enough to go to Vogel and leave him seven hundred dollars."

"He did."

"You seem pretty certain about it."

"The Thorsens found that, too."

Whatever pain it cost the sheriff to lean back and casually swivel his chair wasn't apparent. "How long were they, and you, planning to keep this to yourselves?"

"They didn't know where the money came from until Falk told them."

"It was with the bill of lading?"

"Ya."

"So, until Falk said that he gave the money to Vogel, where *did* you figure he got it?"

McIntire tried not to sound defensive. "I didn't for one minute suppose that Eban Vogel killed anybody for seven hundred dollars. But I think now that he might have known Rose was dead. He could have figured that Teddy did it and pretended to swallow his story about Rose leaving with another man. Nick

Thorsen thinks Eban could have been protecting Teddy, and Nick probably knew him better than anybody."

"Wouldn't a simpler explanation be that Vogel wasn't protecting anything but his own ass?"

McIntire had to admit that was a credible possibility.

"Or," Koski continued, "that Vogel might have been absolutely right when he figured Teddy Falk killed his wife."

That would also not be an unreasonable assumption, but one McIntire couldn't quite accept. "Teddy Falk is behaving like a man with a clear conscience and a bright future," he said. "And if Rose died on the sixteenth of August, I don't see how he could have done it."

Koski's face grew stiff for a second. He sat up straighter and reached for a tin of aspirin. "What sort of guy was Eban Vogel?"

"The sort who did exactly what he thought was right, no matter the cost," McIntire said. "And that included when what he thought was right was at odds with the rest of humanity."

"Wanted his own way?"

"It wasn't so much that as wanting other people to do things his way."

"Hard to get along with."

"Not exactly. He was…it's difficult to explain. He was always good to me."

Eban Vogel had been one of the few men that took the gawky young McIntire seriously. In fact, the only one. Mr. Vogel had shown him respect that he didn't get anywhere else. Knowing now how Eban would have felt about some aspects of the friendship between his daughter and Johnny McIntire…it didn't bear thinking about.

Vogel was a simple man and capturing that in a few words should have been easy. It wasn't. "He had absolute convictions about the way things should be, and he wouldn't settle for anything else. If he couldn't exercise his will, he could at least make it unequivocally clear that he did *not* approve."

"He couldn't exercise his will with Teddy Falk."

"No," McIntire agreed, "but killing Rose and some stranger wouldn't have changed that. It might have prevented Rose from going to live in Russia, but it wouldn't have kept her living in St. Adele, if you know what I mean." It also would have been admitting defeat, something Vogel never would have done.

Koski apparently had no wish to get into a philosophical discussion, but some of his thinking went along the same lines as McIntire's. "You ever hear of Jack Stewart?"

McIntire nodded. "He looks promising."

"Always one step ahead of me, ain't ya? The wife do it for you again?"

"Nah, it was Ma this time. She says Pa was pretty sure Stewart took off for parts unknown."

"Does she know if he had false teeth?"

"Should I have asked?"

"The crime lab has pretty much finished sifting through the shit in the well. They found part of a set of false teeth. Uppers. It wasn't close to either of the bodies, but…maybe you could ask around. See if Stewart had them, or if they belonged to Jarvi Makinen and just got tossed in the hole with the other trash. Falk didn't remember seeing any around the house, but then I don't suppose Rose would have been using her old man's teeth as table decoration."

"Pete," McIntire finally broached the subject, "you've got Adam Wall on the payroll. Why am I still doing the 'asking around'?"

"Don't be an idiot."

"Sorry, it's second nature. You'll have to be patient with me."

"Wall's an all right guy, and he's handy to have around. But if he starts getting on people's nerves he ain't gonna be no goddamn use to anybody."

In other words, Koski was saving Adam Wall for helping little old ladies to cross the road and handling anything that might come up that involved an Indian. Which meant Wall's law enforcement activities in St. Adele would be limited to keeping his father and younger brother on the straight and narrow, since they were the township's only Indian residents besides himself.

"You're forgetting that Adam's granddaddy had my job for about a hundred years. He didn't get on people's nerves too much."

"That old buzzard didn't do shit."

He sure as hell hadn't done Koski's asking around for him. McIntire gave it up.

There had been a lot going on that week in August. The *Monitor* told only a part of it. "Pete," McIntire asked, "do you suppose you could get your hands on some of the Finnish language papers from around that time, say August tenth through the rest of the month? *Amerikan Suometar, Työmies, Paivalehti.* Any other ones I don't know about."

"Sure thing, I'll get Marian right on it."

It was probably a waste of time, but it couldn't hurt. McIntire stood. "Maybe I'll go along to say hello to the troops."

Koski returned to his nonchalant chair swiveling. "Ummm... your buddy Fratelli called."

"Lucky you."

"He asked me not to let you see Teddy Falk."

McIntire stared. Koski fingered the tin of aspirin, perhaps contemplating the driving distance between his office and asking around in St. Adele township. "Just see that you stick to English," he said.

McIntire's reply was not in English, but the look on the sheriff's face indicated that he grasped its spirit nonetheless.

McIntire opened the door to the corridor that fronted the two jail cells. The hallway was more spacious than the cells and contained only a small oak table and a chair. The chair was tilted against the wall and held Cecil Newman, jaw slack, snoring lightly. A narrow trickle glistened at the corner of his open mouth.

McIntire let the door swing shut. The legs of the chair hit the floor.

"Have you got permission to be here?"

"Afternoon, Cecil. Nothing frostbitten, I trust. I'm here to see Mr. Falk."

For someone facing possible life behind bars, Teddy Falk looked chipper. He lounged in the upper bunk with a book on his knees and reading glasses on his nose. The lower berth was occupied by a blanket-covered lump producing more robust snores than those of Deputy Newman.

Erik Pelto, being a dangerous subversive as opposed to a run-of-the-mill killer, had the adjoining cell to himself. He, too, had chosen the upper bunk and lay flat on his back with an open copy of *Life* magazine over his face.

Cecil Newman devoted some period of time to jangling his ring of keys, giving McIntire the opportunity to appropriate his vacated chair to carry it into the cell. Maybe if the deputy had to keep his vigil standing up he'd find something else that needed doing.

Newman paused with his key in the lock when McIntire returned Falk's *"Privet."*

After the hello, there didn't seem to be a whole lot to say, and McIntire began to wonder why he'd come.

That didn't seem to be the case with Teddy Falk. He dangled his legs over the side of the bunk. "Eban Vogel didn't put the money I left with him in the bank."

"No."

"I wonder how come."

"It was 1934. Eban didn't trust banks in the best of times."

"He said he'd deposit it in Rosie's account."

"You knew Eban as well as I did. Why do *you* think he didn't do it?"

Newman returned with another chair and parked it near the bars. Falk slid off the bunk to the floor, quite a drop for someone of his stature, and settled down next to his cellmate's feet. "Eban wouldn't have bothered if he knew Rose was dead. Oh, I ain't saying he killed her. He wouldn't have done that. If he knew Rosie had been killed and didn't say anything, it must have been because he thought I did it."

"That's what I figure," McIntire said. He hitched his chair closer. "Do you think Rose knew Jack Stewart?"

"Koski asked that, too. Ya, we knew Jack. You think he could be the one?"

McIntire told him about the mine accident.

"I didn't know. I didn't know who died, that is. Naturally, I heard about the flood. It happened right about the time I left."

"Stewart's body was never recovered. There were rumors that he wasn't there."

"So maybe it was him with Rosie."

"What do you think?"

"Like I said, nothing surprises me anymore."

The door to the hallway opened wide enough to let Marian Koski sidle through carrying her tray. She placed it on the table and called, "Come on through, Mr. Pelto."

The paper in the next cell rustled, and a pair of feet hit the floor. Falk slowly stood. The door opened again. Orville Pelto flinched when it swung shut behind him.

The two old acquaintances faced each other. Orville must have been the elder by at least fifteen years, but their ages could have been reversed.

"Well," Falk finally broke the silence, "look what the cat dragged in."

"Theodore. I just don't know what to say."

"Maybe you'd like to hear about life in Utopia. You never came to see for yourself, did you?" Falk seemed to hold his breath, then his shoulders sank, and he shook his head. "What the hell, it was a long time ago."

His introduction to McIntire wiped the discomfited look off Pelto's face and replaced it with a glower. "So you're the one that started all this."

"I think it started with you, Pa." Erik Pelto stood close to the bars of his cell.

"Coffee?" Mrs. Koski served the afternoon coffee and cake, charming and chatty as any hostess, while Newman let Pelto into his son's cell. It was quite a gathering, with any attempt at privacy futile. And McIntire made little effort to pretend he was not listening.

Pelto had secured the services of an attorney, a man employed by the Society for the Protection of the Foreign Born. He'd be in Duluth for the hearing. If it didn't go well, he at least hoped to get the federal judge to set bail. "I got a little money," he told his son. "We should be able to scrape together enough to get you out."

Erik responded only with, "Have you seen Delilah and the kids?"

"They'll be fine. I'll stay with them until you're out."

McIntire and Falk looked at each other in some embarrassment. Noises rumbled from the lump on the cot.

McIntire asked, "How could Eban have found out that Rose was dead?"

"He must have gone to the house and found her. Sometimes he came over to help with the chores when I was away. But the stock was already sold, there wasn't really anything to do."

"She was leaving," McIntire said. "He might have wanted to say goodbye, and he might have wanted to do it when you weren't at home, after the fight you had. Did he know you'd be gone? Or would he have come to your house expecting you to be there? To make it up, maybe?"

"Like to apologize you mean? Eban?"

McIntire agreed that didn't sound like Vogel.

"He probably knew I'd be away," Falk said. "I'd have mentioned about going to ship the stuff."

"Somebody also blew the man's head off and put their bodies in the well," McIntire reminded him. "That doesn't sound like Eban either."

Falk nodded. "He was fond of Rosie, but not so fond that he'd kill over her sleeping with another man." He smiled. "After all, I'm still alive."

"Congratulations on that. I imagine it might have been a bit of a challenge now and then." McIntire said it in Russian.

"You speak it like a native."

"Unfortunately." Was he condemned to spend his life dealing with the consequences of that proficiency? No, he had gotten off easy. It was those around him who suffered, and were continuing to suffer, from his mistakes.

Newman rattled his keys and Falk stood up. "It's good to be back," he said in English.

WASHINGTON—Senator Pat McCarran, (D-Nev.), said today that the Senate Internal Security subcommittee, of which he is chairman, would investigate "fully" all matters involved in the records of the Institute of Pacific Relations.

Chapter Thirty

If speaking like she was shouting through a bullhorn and punctuating every utterance with a mirthless chuckle were indications of lunacy, Nelda Stewart was indeed as crazy as a bedbug. Her eyes protruded amphibian-like—no, more reptilian, they held a feral glint you didn't see in a frog. But for a third bulge, an abdomen like she'd swallowed a watermelon seed, she was so gaunt she barely made a shadow. Or, to carry the biological analogies one last step, thin as a water reed.

She stirred boiling water into Instant Postum and handed it to McIntire in a cup wreathed with cat hair. At least McIntire assumed the fuzz came from something feline. It covered every possible surface, but McIntire saw no evidence of a full-fledged, or full-furred, cat. No surprise; if the amount of hair floating around was any indication, the poor thing had probably frozen to death, but not before permeating the air with an odor so strong he could taste it.

There were limits to McIntire's gallantry, and he didn't even make a pretense of drinking the rancid-smelling brew. Nelda seemed to relish her own. A tiny wisp of fur trembled on her upper lip.

McIntire rubbed his nose. "I spoke to my mother the other day," he said. "She asked after you, and I promised I'd visit to see how you're doing."

"Really? That's very nice of her. How does she like California?" Her fixed stare demanded an answer.

"Florida. She likes it a lot. Sunshine twenty-four hours a day, to hear her tell it."

Nelda brushed at her lip. "I like a change of seasons, myself." The self-deprecating chortle, combined with the unblinking gaze of those distended eyes, made McIntire want to bolt for the door.

"I wouldn't mind a change of seasons right now," he said. "Ma asked after your children. Two of them, is it?"

She laughed again and raised her cup. Her hands were long and bony. The nails were chewed to slivers and flecks of blood showed at the knuckles. "A boy and a girl, all grown up and flown the nest."

So something was fully-fledged. "It must be lonely for you."

"It is. But it makes me feel better knowing they're both doing so well. Alexander is…oh, something or other in science, and Katrina is going to school to be a doctor. She's the only girl in her class. Their father would have been very proud."

Was that really true, or a further indication of Nelda's nuttiness? McIntire didn't want to prolong the discussion any more than necessary. He braced his elbow on the arm of the chair and rested his ear in the palm of his hand. "I was sorry to hear about your husband. I never knew him, of course, but I believe he was a good friend of my dad's."

"Lost in the Massey-Davis mine disaster." His ear-blocking ploy did nothing to muffle Nelda's braying.

"And his body never found. That must have been hard to bear."

"Losing my husband was hard to bear."

"Ma says the company put up a fuss about paying compensation."

For the first time, both the voice and the eyelids lowered. "Is this about Rose Makinen?"

Mrs. Stewart might be crazy but she wasn't stupid. McIntire surrendered. "It looks like she died the same day as the cave-in. There was a man with her."

"It wasn't my Jack. Jack was killed in the mine."

"Mrs. Stewart, did your husband have all his teeth?"

"Was Rosie's man missing his?" The old, bellowing Nelda was back.

"I don't know."

"Why not? Did the skeleton have teeth or didn't it?"

"It was hard to say." McIntire was blunt. "He was shot in the head."

"Jack wasn't shot in the head, he drowned in that mine. You must have heard about it." She bit savagely at the base of her thumb.

"The company was pretty sure your husband wasn't in the mine when it flooded," McIntire persisted.

Nelda swept the crusted cuff of her cardigan across her lip and succeeded in depositing a few more hairs. "I didn't know anything about the cave-in until Jack didn't make it home on Sunday. He stayed at the location weeknights. Nobody came to tell me he was dead. I had to go to the mine office and ask what happened." Her voice took on an hysterical edge. "There was an inspector for the company there the day the mine flooded. He claimed Jack came out ahead of the others, that he wasn't in the shaft when the water came in. He wasn't here either, so where could he be if he wasn't dead? Nobody said they saw him after the accident. Massey-Davis finally had to admit that inspector didn't know what he was talking about. Jack was in the mine with the rest of them, and they all drowned."

McIntire didn't know what was making him pursue it. Why didn't he just ask if Jack Stewart had false teeth and get the hell out? He struggled to remind himself that this woman was a widow learning that her husband might have died in another woman's bed. It didn't help. She was sick, he knew that. He should be able to feel some empathy, at least pretend to it, but it was impossible. If he let himself feel anything, it would be terror.

He asked, "Did your husband know Rose Falk?"

"Rose Makinen was always after the men, mostly to embarrass them, I figure. Jack no more than anybody else. Rosie wasn't nothing to fret over. Could they make me give it back?"

"What?"

"The widow's pension. Could they make me give it back?" The eyes opened so wide McIntire half expected them to fall into her lap. "I can't pay it. Do you think they might put me in jail?"

McIntire felt a glimmer of sympathy. "How could they? It would be an honest mistake. You had no way of knowing."

"Please!" The bark turned shrill. "You have to tell that sheriff that Jack died in the mine. I don't want to go to jail!"

"But, Mrs. Stewart, surely you'd want to know if it was your husband in that well."

"Why?"

McIntire couldn't answer that.

"Please." This time it was barely a whisper. McIntire froze as her cracked and bleeding hand touched his knee. "You tell them Jack died in that mine."

McIntire felt himself drenched in sweat. He couldn't spend another minute with this woman, breathing her stale furry air, waiting for her eyeballs to pop out of her head. It wasn't her fault, he knew. Not her fault that she was crazy and lonely and frightened. Not her fault that she evoked in McIntire fears that had nothing to do with her. He got to his feet.

Maybe Leonie could be convinced to pay a call.

He was home, scrubbing his skin raw in the shower, before he could concentrate on what he'd learned. Which was absolutely nothing.

It would be an ironic twist. If Jack Stewart had used a narrow escape from death in a hole in the ground as an opportunity to disappear, stopping off to pay Rose Falk a fond farewell that led to his death in a hole in the ground…. Maybe Nelda could identify the shoes or the suspenders, if she was of a mind to, which would be doubtful. She might be crazy, but she was right; why would she want to know, or let anyone else know?

If Stewart had simply seen his chance and taken it, not bothering with that visit to Rose, he was probably still out there somewhere and might come forward if he heard that exaggerated reports of his death were being circulated. It couldn't matter much now, unless he had a new wife and kiddies.

Of course if the body in the well proved to be that of Jack Stewart, Nutty Nelda would bound past the wronged husband to become suspect number one.

The upper plate could be the key. In his rush to get away from Nelda, McIntire hadn't found out the state of Jack Stewart's teeth. But Stewart was a young man, and if he did wear dentures there would be plenty of people around who'd know it. If the teeth didn't belong to the victim, that left Rose's father. There should also be people around who'd know if Jarvi Makinen had false teeth. Not that they would probably be able to identify a specific upper plate. If Jarvi had worn dentures, would they have to dig him up to see if he was buried with them? McIntire was getting a headache.

ROCHESTER, N.Y.—Scientists reported radioactivity in snow that fell in upstate New York this week, but said the amount was too small to harm anyone.

Chapter Thirty-One

A swirl of snow swept in through the open door. Nick followed, kicked the door closed behind him, and placed the acid-encrusted battery on the kitchen floor.

"I'll let it warm up while I finish shoveling. If she still won't start, I'll call up Sulo to give me a jump."

It was twenty degrees below. The panel truck wouldn't start even if it hadn't been frozen solid since November. It was going to take more than a warm battery and a jump from Sulo to get it going, but Mia didn't utter a discouraging word. They'd have to get it running some way.

"We're almost out of coffee."

Nick examined his mittens, inspecting them for signs of battery acid.

"We *are* out of yeast."

"I'll get into town today one way or the other." He threw the mitts on a chair and held his hands over the heater.

Mia felt a pang of remorse at her meanness. It wasn't Nick's fault that he was sick, any more than she had deliberately broken her ankle. There was a difference; even when she regained two good legs, Mia would still be completely dependent on her husband. And that *was* nobody's fault but her own.

She carried the pan to the table and ladled Malt O Meal into the bowls, keeping the rubber tip of her crutch out of the puddles of melting snow. She lowered herself into her chair and spooned brown sugar onto the cereal.

"No milk?"

"You can have canned." She took a brave mouthful.

"That's okay." Nick opened the butter dish and sliced off a chunk. It melted into the cereal.

Mia sprinkled on a bit more sugar.

Nick swirled the butter in a golden figure eight. "Inge Lindstrom came by."

Mia had seen Inge's car idling at the end of the driveway while Nick leaned on his shovel.

"She said John McIntire's Studebaker was at Nelda's yesterday when she went to the store." He dipped his spoon into the cereal. "It was still there when she came back."

"Was Nelda having some sort of trouble? Not one of the kids?"

"I'd guess that Super Detective was asking about the dear departed Jack."

Of course! Why hadn't they thought of him first thing? The rumors surrounding the death of Jack Stewart had flown thick and fast. Someone whose name no one seemed to remember had hinted that he'd seen Jack after the accident, pushing a "borrowed" railroad handcar. That was all it took to get people talking. He'd taken off for California; he'd been done in by his lunatic wife; he'd been killed by co-workers in revenge for his past strike-breaking.

"He disappeared about the same time as Rose," Mia said. "Some people say he wasn't in the mine. It makes perfect sense, and we should have thought of it right away."

"Maybe."

Despite the talk, most people believed Stewart had drowned in the mine along with the rest of his crew, but, Mia knew, Nick was among those that had doubts. Every Christmas he delivered a card addressed to Nelda and her children. It was always postmarked from a different place, but the handwriting was the same.

"Jack might have made it out of that mine," Nick said. "And if he did, I'm betting he didn't die later the same day."

Mia brought the spoon to her lips and put it down again. She had no wish for extended conversation with her husband, but it was that or eat the icky stuff. "Inge have any other news?"

"Only that Teddy Falk and John McIntire seem to be old acquaintances and Johnny's spent hours visiting him in jail, chatting in what sounds like Russian. She heard that they met 'right in our very home' and was wondering what language they talked in."

"What did you tell her?"

"I said I didn't know. I couldn't understand a damn word they said."

Mia nodded.

"A few days ago that would have gotten at least a little smile out of you."

"Things have changed."

Nick spoke softly without looking up. "I'm sorry, Mia. I didn't do it on purpose. Your father packed everything away, all her clothes, all…. I wanted to put it out of my mind. I didn't want to think about it again."

"You knew what it was the second you saw it."

"I'm sorry. What more can I say?"

"Not a thing."

Nick bundled himself back into his coat. His wool pants hung wet around his ankles. "Do you need anything before I go out?"

She shook her head and turned to the window. The wind had already redeposited most of the snow back into the driveway. He'd be starting over again.

The door closed behind him. Mia remained at the table. She held a knife blade in her hot coffee and used it to slice off a piece of the hard butter. She plopped it into her remaining cereal. It didn't melt. She chopped it up with her spoon and stirred it in.

She tried to recall her father's attitude toward Jack Stewart both before and after his supposed death. Like everybody else, Eban Vogel had little use for scabs. There were also quite a few who saw the labor agitators as the real problem. The mine workers' strikes of 1914 had been close to civil war for those involved. Here in St. Adele they were only newspaper reports, although the battles took place just a few miles away. Most of the workers lived in the mine locations and company towns. They were in their own world. Later on, there were men like Jack Stewart who had jobs in the mine and lived away, in the towns or on farms.

Eban Vogel had talked about the strikes, read the papers, despised the British strike breakers. Mia didn't remember much of anything else about it.

She did recall that Eban had spoken in favor of Nelda's quest for compensation from the mining company. Whatever had really happened to Jack Stewart, he was most definitely gone, disappeared while working for the mine, leaving a deranged wife and two children. They had to be supported, and the amount of money it would take to do it was peanuts to Massey-Davis.

Finding his wife in bed with a former scab could certainly have brought a murderous rage to a man of Teddy Falk's political convictions. But why would a woman of his wife's political convictions be in bed with that scab? Jack Stewart was no Adonis. Well, then neither was Rosie. Who really knew what people might do?

Mia might have been slow in learning it, but she could see that people might not be at all what they seem. Would the kind of woman who'd desert her husband on the eve of the new life they'd planned together be bothered about social principle? Who could say? Maybe Teddy Falk had lured Jack to his house and killed them both. Maybe John McIntire was a Soviet spy. Maybe Erik Pelto was recruiting an army of Kiddy Communists. Maybe her father was a cold—or hot—blooded killer.

"He is not."

Mia had felt her mother's presence often but never before heard her voice, and she had to struggle against turning to look. She knew there would be nothing to see, not a confident nod, not a wisp of fog or a spark of light. But the words were strong and certain, and Mia didn't doubt them.

The telephone rang and she hoisted herself to her feet. The crutches bit into the flesh under her arms.

"Hello, Mia. I just called up to see how you're getting along and find out if there's anything I can do."

Sally Ferguson, who'd no doubt also had a visit from Inge Lindstrom and was interested in getting the real story without Inge's embellishments or misinterpretations.

"Oh, we're doing okay. Thanks for asking."

"Well, I've been a little worried about you, being mixed up in all that business with the Falks, you know. You sure have enough troubles of your own."

"We're fine."

"Is it true that Teddy Falk was actually arrested at your house?"

"No, I'm afraid it was nothing so exciting. Teddy followed Cecil Newman into town and turned himself in." Mia wished she was a fast enough thinker to come up with better stories.

"Well, it's too bad it took almost twenty years for it to come out, but at least he's behind bars now."

"Well, Ted's not been convicted yet," Mia pointed out. "If he knew Rose was dead and he was going to be blamed for it, he probably wouldn't have come back to the country."

"He didn't come *here*, though, did he? Not until he knew he'd be arrested. If he really didn't know what happened to Rose, and if he cared to find out, he'd have come back to St. Adele first thing."

Sally had a point there.

"But my question is," she went on, "who else knew?"

"Knew what?" Mia felt a flush run through her body.

"John McIntire found those bodies. Unless it came to him in a dream, somebody had to have told him. If it wasn't Teddy, then who? How did he find out Rose was dead and where to look for her?"

"I can't imagine."

"I know your father sort of took Rose and Teddy under his wing."

"Sally, it's kind of hard for me to stand—"

"Oh, gracious, I'm so thoughtless. I'll get back to why I called. Wouldn't you like to have some company? A few of the ladies were talking about coming to see you. Maybe having a little get-together to cheer you up."

Mia scanned through her store of polite excuses, then stopped. The ladies were just as interested in what was going on around them in 1934 as they were now. If she wanted to find out what happened then…. She wavered, then heard herself say, "Thank you, Sally. That would be very nice."

The silence that preceded Sally's response showed that she was just as flabbergasted as Mia was herself. "Should we say Thursday afternoon?"

Thursday was as good as any other day to Mia. She said goodbye quickly, before she could change her mind.

Once again she heard her mother's words, this time only in her mind. "No," she replied aloud. "Papa's not a murderer, and I'll see to it that everybody knows it."

WASHINGTON—A special Immigration and Naturalization Service board rejected the ninth appeal of German-born war bride Mrs. Ellen Knauff in her bid to enter the U.S.

Chapter Thirty-Two

McIntire awoke as he had each morning since that visit from Special Agent Melvin, with the hollowness in his mid-section that told him something terrible had happened before he remembered what it was—the sort of feeling that follows a death. He left Leonie sleeping and made his way through the darkness to the cellar.

He poked up the cinders in the furnace and piled on a few sticks of wood. The heavy snow around the house's foundation provided insulation, and the cellar was a much more inviting place than its chill, dank summer self. The shelves filled with Leonie's canning gave a homey sort of feel. McIntire could have done without the tomato preserves, but they gave off a cheery glow.

Leonie had seemed happy when she'd filled those jars, singing along with Hank Williams, packing the sunshine away for winter. She hadn't shown any discontent since they'd arrived, other than the occasional tear over a letter from one of her grandchildren. Until now.

He turned down the damper and ascended to the kitchen. The thought of breakfast repulsed him. Even coffee seemed too…robust, and brewing it too much work. He lit the burner under the teakettle. He'd been drinking a lot of tea lately. Did that mean he was getting old? Or just lazy?

It was black outside the window, but the droplets sparkling on the pane let him know it was snowing again. Well, let it snow. Maybe hibernation was the best course of action.

It was far too tempting. If McIntire wasn't going to surrender to the impulse, he'd have to take some action.

Gösta Berling lay neglected and would have to gather dust a while longer. Somebody else could track down the killer of Rosie Falk and her lover. It was time McIntire concentrated on one thing only: the suspicious, dangerous mind of Melvin Fratelli. It was better than sitting around waiting for the ax to fall. He scribbled a note for Leonie, gave Kelpie a quick rub behind the ears, and went out into the cold.

Icy flakes whipped past his headlights, the car moved through a tunnel toward an ever-receding vortex of dizzying white. The forest of snow soaked up noise; tires crunched softly. McIntire drove as in a dream, without thinking of his destination or what he would do when he reached it.

It was seventy-five miles or better to the hotel room that was the special agent's base of operations in Marquette, but once he got onto the main road, the snow slacked off and McIntire made good time. He should get there about time for Fratelli's morning coffee break.

He might have known better. Special Agent Fratelli did not waste time on sipping coffee, or at least interrupting his work to do it. Not when his nation was under threat. He answered McIntire's knock with an unsurprised nod and a telephone to his ear. "I'll try, but I ain't Superman." He dropped the phone into its cradle. The flamboyant plaid uranium prospector was once more the brown and bland detective. No more intentionally laughable attempts to pass himself off as a native. He shivered as he closed the door. "What brings you out on this kind of…month?"

"I figured it's time we had a little talk."

"Well, sit down. I'm getting a crick in my neck."

There were two chairs; McIntire took the one with its back to the window. At least Fratelli would have to blink when he looked his way. "Calling my mother was going a little far, even for you," he said, with an inward flinch at the pettiness of it.

"What makes you think it was me?" The agent shook a cigarette into his palm and crumpled the empty pack.

"What were you expecting her to tell you? 'Oh yes, my son was off on one of those treason trips'?"

"I didn't need your mama to tell me where you were. And don't give me that shit about Moscow. You'd been out of the Soviet Union for a good year by that time. You were right here in the USA. You kept that to yourself, even from your own Dear Mother. I plan to find out why." He put the cigarette to his lips. "And I will. You might as well tell me and save us both a lot of time and trouble."

He hadn't been doing anything illegal, immoral, or traitorous. He hadn't been doing anything involved in saving the Western World. He'd been doing a job, a demeaning, degrading job, the only one his superiors felt he might be suited for. He'd been far more suited for it than they'd ever imagined.

"Where I was, and who I told about it, is none of your damn business. It had nothing to do with you."

"Then you have nothing to worry about."

"Do I look worried?"

"Ya."

McIntire didn't feel worried at the moment. He felt like throttling the smug little bastard. He wasn't stupid enough to try. "So 'trust me,' is that what you're saying, Melvin? J. Edgar and the boys play fair and square? I asked you for a simple piece of information, to help me find a man whose wife was murdered in her bed, and the next thing I know Erik Pelto is in jail, and you're threatening me with my lack of patriotism and who knows what the hell else."

"You asked me to help you find a man who is most probably a Russian agent who came from your home town, and who left the U.S.S.R. around the same time you did. Came to Detroit by way of Canada same as you did. Went from there to New York, same as you. Ended up back in Michigan, same as you."

"So if I was one of his trusty comrades, would I be so dumb as to bring you into it? Why would I have needed you to find him? Teddy Falk is a pathetic little man who suffered years of Soviet rule and doesn't want anything more than to get his old life back."

"Not, it seems, what you had in mind when you flew into Toronto…ah, when was it?…February 26, 1948, or when you got on that train for Detroit. You were pretty close to your old life then, but didn't even drop in for a quick visit. Why is that?"

It had been the hardest thing McIntire had ever had to do. The bleakest time of his life. The train stopped in the late afternoon at a doll-sized station deep in the Canadian forest. Despite the mounds of snow, the sense of spring was strong. The sun shone warm on his back. Home was a few hundred miles away, and had never been so far.

McIntire ignored the question and asked, "What makes you think Teddy Falk is some sort of agent?"

"How do you think he got out of Russia?"

"If he had a U.S. passport it might not have been so hard."

"Oh, he's got the passport, all right. It's some of the KGB's best work. He also has in his possession a certificate showing him to have been born in Virginia, Minnesota, also faked. And a photograph signed by his loving wife, Olga."

In his possession. So those possessions had been searched. If Fratelli said the documents were fakes, McIntire had no doubt that they were. And a birth certificate wasn't the sort of thing the average person carried around just on the chance that his citizenship was called into question. It probably meant exactly what Fratelli was hinting at. Teddy Falk had been sent back home with the blessing of the KGB, future services to be rendered. If Falk hoped to give his employers the slip, his arrest might not have been unwelcome. The notoriety afforded a jailed murder suspect could lead the Russians to cross him off their list. Afterwards, what better place to disappear to than a farm in the backwoods of St. Adele, Michigan. He might be expecting to do all right, if he didn't factor in Melvin Fratelli, and if he didn't worry a whole lot about what his defection might do for that wife back in the Old Country. Even if he hadn't murdered his first wife, he'd seemingly not had many qualms over walking away from her, and he'd showed no signs of heartbreak at her betrayal. Maybe it was easier the second time.

"If you think J. Theodore Falk and I are two of a kind, why tell me all this?"

"Don't make a hell of a lot of difference. Teddy ain't going nowhere." The agent finally lit his cigarette. "And neither are you."

It had been mostly a waste of time, but McIntire had discovered one thing: Melvin Fratelli didn't know why he'd spent those months in the United States, but he probably knew exactly where. Bizarre as it was, he really might think it was possible that McIntire was, or had been, indulging in espionage. He must not have much respect for McIntire's powers of deception. If he was trying to pull the wool over Fratelli's eyes, would McIntire have balked at the agent's request that he put on his spy suit and infiltrate the St. Adele branch of the Temperance Society? Insane paranoia had probably scrambled Fratelli's mind to the point where simple reasoning was out of the question and counterproductive to his aims.

How had the FBI found out about the flight to Toronto? They couldn't have known all along. Fratelli had only turned surly after McIntire's mention of Theodore Falk. His retirement from the army had gone off without a hitch, so they hadn't been checking up on him then. He'd gone on with the odd translating job for the State Department.

Those three months in New Jersey were hell, but the experience *had* given McIntire his old life back. He'd left Michigan when he was barely grown. Went straight from under his father's thumb to Uncle Sam's; moved from the unforgiving community of St. Adele to the even more rigid European society from which it sprang. The post-war America he returned to as an adult was a world he hadn't dreamed existed, one of fresh air and limitless possibilities. The anxieties of those months couldn't dampen the exhilaration, the opening of his mind, the loosening of the decades of constriction and claustrophobia. He'd gotten his life back, gotten Leonie to share it, and gone back to where he started. He was beginning to be a new person, and he wasn't going to let Melvin Fratelli interfere.

Chapter Thirty-Three

Smoke rose from the chimney of Erik Pelto's house, and a maroon late-model Lincoln stood in the driveway. Insurance agents must do okay, or like to look as if they do. McIntire pulled in behind it.

His knock wasn't answered, and he was about to give up when Orville Pelto waddled from behind the house, red faced and panting, with a pair of snowshoes strapped to his feet. His flush grew a shade deeper when he saw McIntire. "Nothing so boring as sitting around somebody else's house. Thought I'd give these things a try."

"How was it?" McIntire had wondered about getting some himself. The sweat cutting channels in the frost on Pelto's three-day growth of beard wasn't encouraging.

"Awkward as all hell."

McIntire waited while Pelto fumbled his way free of the contraptions and leaned them against the porch steps.

"If you came to apologize, save your breath."

"I didn't. I came to find out why you lied about seeing Rose Falk just before she died, quite possibly on the very day she died."

"Lied to who? Nobody's asked me when I last saw Mrs. Falk."

"When I first asked information of you through your son, you neglected to mention that you had seen her as she was preparing to leave. In fact helped her make those final preparations."

"Why should I think whether I saw her or not is any of your business?"

It was a fair question and one McIntire had no good answer for.

"Not to mention," Pelto added, "that I don't have a ghost of an idea when Rose died."

Pelto pulled open the door to let McIntire enter ahead of him. He removed his gloves and put them on the table next to a stack of papers pencilled with numbers and the hieroglyphics of mathematics. "Sorry it's so damn cold. I haven't got the hang of this stove any more than I do the snowshoes."

He didn't ask for advice, and McIntire wasn't generally pushy, but desperate times…. He opened the damper on the stove, cranked on the grates to let out some ash, blew on the smoldering wood, and fed a few more sticks of maple into the flame. "Anything new with your son?"

"They're taking him to Duluth tomorrow. The hearing is the day after. Enkel, he's the attorney, thinks there's a good chance they'll throw the case out." Despite the words, Orville didn't sound optimistic.

"How can they have a case at all? If Erik is a citizen and a veteran?"

"When it comes to the INS, a case is in the eye of the beholder." Pelto hung his coat on an overcrowded hook. "I took Delilah and the kids into town to see him this morning. They wanted to have a train ride back, so I didn't wait around. That jail gives me the creeps."

McIntire could understand that. Orville had been a lot closer to subversive than his son. He was probably wondering why he wasn't the one in that cell.

"You witnessed Rose Falk's signature on the document giving Mrs. Van Opelt power of attorney," McIntire said. "That was August sixteenth, the same day she signed the contract for selling the farm. The Falks were set to leave a few days later. Rose was dead before then. She probably died on the day she signed those documents."

"Then Ted didn't do it. He was off in Sault St. Marie. That was why I took Rose around to—I don't remember his name—the J.P. He notarized the Power of Attorney and the Contract for Deed."

"How long were you with her?"

"It was twenty years ago, for Christ's sake!" Not quite twenty, but close enough. "Near as I remember, I picked her up in the morning. We had to go fetch that old biddy she signed things over to. The whole business didn't take long. We were done by dinner time."

"Then what?"

"I dropped her off and went home."

"Which was where?"

"I'd rented a little house in Ishpeming for a few months. The people who owned it were away."

"Did Rose mention that she was expecting company?"

"The guy she was with when she died, you mean? She'd hardly be telling me about that sort of thing."

"We don't know for sure that it was that sort of thing. Think hard. Maybe she mentioned a relative? Somebody coming to say goodbye?"

"You keep forgetting this was a long time ago." Pelto shook his head. "I don't think so. I don't think either Rose or Teddy had any relatives nearby other than an aunt. Ted's parents lived somewhere in Illinois. They were going to stop to say goodbye to them on the way to New York."

"Did you ever hear either of them mention Jack Stewart?"

The response came quickly. "No. It's not a name I've heard."

"How did Rose seem that day?"

Pelto's memory came back to life. "She was excited about going. I remember that it surprised me a little, because she'd been pretty jittery for a while before that. I thought they might change their minds. Some nervousness was normal, but with Rose it was more than that. For a couple of weeks, she'd hardly said a word. She looked constantly on the verge of tears, and believe me she wasn't the silent or the crying type. But when the time came she was ready and happy to be getting the last few things taken care of. She wasn't crazy about selling the place to—?"

"Sulo Touminen."

"Right. Rose had no use at all for Sulo, but she didn't have any other offers, and she was friendly with his sister, so she didn't like to make a fuss. She didn't want to meet up with him to sign the contract, that I *do* remember. He did his part and mailed it to her."

"What did she have against Sulo?"

"Some old battle between him and her father. Over that pitiful eighty acres, I think. Sulo's father and Jarvi originally farmed together on a hundred-sixty they got when the old Gitchee-Gumee Association broke up. When the older Touminen died and Sulo inherited, they split the farm. Sulo thought he got the short end of the stick. He did. His half was three-quarters swamp."

"So he got what he wanted in the end."

"What Sulo really wanted was to go to Karelia himself. He applied and got turned down. I handled that application, too, so I was just as glad not to meet up with him myself."

That was a surprise. Hadn't Sulo mentioned being manhandled by the Saari boys for his anti-Karelian views? "Why was he turned down?"

"He didn't have what the Society wanted. Tools and money, mostly, but the conviction, too. After he was turned down, he soured on the whole undertaking, and got pretty carried away ranting and raving and trying to talk people out of going. Sour grapes, I guess, but it turned out he was right."

"I understand you organized the Falks' trip."

"It was through the Karelian Technical Aid Society."

"Which you worked for."

"It should have been a great…. We couldn't know how things would turn out." He folded his hands and placed them on the table. "I worked for the Society. I recruited people, took their applications, and arranged for the passage. They paid in advance. At first it was five hundred dollars apiece. The Society helped out with the Falks. They didn't pay that much."

"And Teddy handled shipping their belongings himself."

"I set it up for them, but Ted took care of the details. It was pretty simple. Once they had things arranged, they just had to get the stuff to the nearest railroad station. The shipping company contracted to get it from there to Petrozavodsk."

"What about picking it up on the other side, how would that work?"

"He would have gotten a negotiable bill of lading. That meant whoever held it could claim the goods."

"And if Teddy had gone and left the bill of lading behind?"

"I think by the time the shipment got to Karelia it wouldn't have mattered."

No, the equipment would probably be put to good use, without much thought to its original owners.

"Falk was definitely away from home when Rose signed over the farm. They were set to leave a few days later." Despite the intervening twenty years Pelto had invoked, his story was seamless. "They were going to drive to Niagara Falls and then on to wherever it was to say goodbye to Ted's mother. They planned to sell the car there—it wasn't worth shipping—and take the train to New York. The society had a rented house in Harlem where people could stay while they waited to sail out. The boat would take them to Göteborg, then they'd go by train on to Petrozavodsk."

"If you arranged for the whole thing, how is it that you had no idea that they didn't leave town as they planned? You might at least have gone to say goodbye."

"I did say goodbye, the day Rose signed those papers."

"To Rose."

"Yes."

"Not to her husband."

"We'd already made our farewells. All the arrangements were set. There was nothing more for me to do." He scratched at a patch of dried milk on the oilcloth. "It was about that time I gave up my position with the Society."

"Why?"

"I was getting disillusioned. The Soviets were taking over the party. More and more it was being controlled directly from Moscow. I'd thought about going myself, to Karelia, but we were hearing stories, a few people were already coming back, and the idea of taking Erik…. If I didn't have the guts to go, I couldn't be sending other people. I went to New York and resigned. Then I came back to Ishpeming for the winter. It was only after my son called, after he talked to you, that I checked and found no record that Rose and her husband had been on that boat. I can't tell you how relieved I was." He stood to open the heater and throw on more wood. "Have the police been able to figure out how Rosie died?"

"Not really," McIntire said. "She might have bled quite a bit. She was wrapped in a quilt or a rug. Whoever put her in that hole was careful about it."

"I guess it had to be Ted. He must have come back earlier than he planned. Or earlier than Rosie planned."

"You were fond of her, I've heard."

"A lot of people liked Rose. There was something about her. Nowadays they can do surgery, maybe they could have then, too, but Rosie didn't get anything but sewn up, and whoever did that was no expert seamstress. She was pretty disfigured, and her speech was affected. She talked through her nose, especially if she got excited. But still…there was just something about her. You didn't notice how different she looked."

If he'd communicated that feeling to Rose, if she, too, had forgotten her ugliness when in Orville Pelto's company, how would she have reacted?

He went on, "I spent sixteen years wondering what had become of her and Ted, if they'd survived the purges and the war, if her hair had turned grey…." He gave a small grunt. "I used to have a dream where I could see her. She was scattering

feed to hens on a little farm next to a river bank. I always hoped
that it might be true."

As McIntire walked to the door, Pelto asked, "What do you
figure Immigration has against my son?"

"Do they need anything special? He was a dues-paying
member of the Communist Party."

"They haven't come after me."

"Maybe your time will come."

"Somebody's been into that jail to question Erik every day,
trying to get him to name people. One of those people is right
in this room." He smiled. "But they haven't asked him a thing
about me, so far as I know."

McIntire made one more stop before returning home. With
Nick car-less and, from what he'd heard, a wrist that he wasn't
admitting was broken, McIntire couldn't bring himself to just
drive by.

Nick waved from his usual spot, chipping away at his fallen
trees, now using his left hand only. McIntire returned the
greeting and continued on to the door. His Good Samaritan
tendencies fell short of cutting wood. As he tramped past the
front of the house, Mia knocked on the living room window
and beckoned him in.

He left his overshoes in the porch and passed through the
kitchen. To call it disorderly would have been charitable. To call
it sweet-smelling would have been an outright lie.

McIntire didn't get close enough to Mia to draw conclusions
about her aroma, but her level of tidiness fell in line with her
surroundings. She slumped on the sofa with her leg, its trouser
leg split to accommodate the plaster cast, on a kitchen chair.
Three grubby toes poked through the end of the cast.

"I just stopped by to see if there's anything I can do for you."

"Were you thinking of the washing?" Her voice was scratchy
and distant sounding. She said it without smiling.

"And if I said yes?"

"I'd faint."

"But you wouldn't let me do it."

She responded with a feeble smile. McIntire sat at the end of the sofa. "Mia, you know you can't keep on like this."

"We'll be all right."

McIntire reached to pat her arm, then pulled back.

"I'll have this thing off in a couple of weeks," she said.

Mia's broken leg was far from being the greatest of their troubles. "Nick's still determined to subdue that tree, I see."

"He'll have plenty of time. He's not going back to work."

"For sure?"

"He says it's only until he gets rested up, but he won't be going back. He's already kept driving that route way longer than he should have."

"Has he managed to rescue his car?"

That brought another ghost of a smile. "Not yet. I have to be the only person in the county who hasn't seen it."

McIntire considered suggesting that he drive her to have a look but thought better of it. "Never fear," he offered. "I took pictures. I'll show you when they get developed."

"Speaking of developments," she threw a knitted blanket over her exposed toes, "any news on Rosie?"

"I suppose you heard about the fella."

"Jack Stewart. I heard."

"What do you think?"

"It makes sense to me. Nick never did think Jack was dead. But he still doesn't think so. He says Nelda gets some pretty fishy looking mail, and he figures it's from Jack. Money for the kids, maybe."

That could account for some of Nelda's skittishness. So could losing mine-widow status and the potential of becoming a murder suspect.

"Knowing that it was Jack, if it was, doesn't help with knowing who killed them," McIntire observed.

"It could provide another motive," Mia said. "Jack Stewart was one of the strike breakers back when we were kids, remember? He'd have hardly been more than a kid himself at that time.

People didn't talk about it after he married Nelda and moved here, but that doesn't mean they forgot."

No, McIntire was sure of that. Forgetfulness was not a local virtue. "Orville Pelto says Rosie and Sulo Touminen weren't too fond of each other."

"Rosie wasn't fond of Sulo. She couldn't stand him. Mainly because Sulo was a bit over-fond of Rosie."

Another suitor? "I'm beginning to wish I'd known this woman."

"Maybe Sulo thought Rosie might appreciate his attention. Anyway, he was always trying to corner her somewhere. She wasn't shy about telling him to get lost, but he seemed to think she was just playing hard to get. I figured he'd laid off once she was married, but maybe not. I was surprised when I heard she sold the farm to him."

"You sure she really didn't like him? Maybe it was one of those protesting too much things."

"Sulo? He spits tobacco into a Campbell's soup can!"

"Even back then?"

"Well, maybe he wasn't so bad in those days. But…nah, if Rose was carrying on with anybody, it wasn't Sulo. You know," she pushed back the blanket and scratched at her leg above the edge of the cast, "I don't think it was Jack Stewart either. I don't believe Rose was having an affair at all." Mia picked up a knitting needle and ran it under the plaster. "She might have flirted a bit, but I just don't think she'd have—"

Through the window McIntire could see Nick making his way, with that curious forward-leaning gait, to the kitchen door. He stood still for a moment before lifting his foot to the first step, then hesitated again. McIntire turned quickly back to the room. "She was in bed. In her flimsies."

"Well, yes, that does seem a bit suspicious."

Nick was visible through the half-open door to the kitchen, shuffling about, feeding wood into the heater. He didn't come through to greet McIntire or his wife, and Mia seemed oblivious to his presence.

"I had to tell Koski about the money."

Mia was resigned. "I suppose he'll be wanting it. Or Teddy will."

"Koski will probably want to hang on to it as evidence."

"And he'll want to know why Papa kept it, and why he didn't tell anybody." She straightened up, and the blanket slipped to the floor. "I want to know, too."

The uneven thumping of Nick's steps echoed as he laboriously ascended the stairs. McIntire stood and spread the cover back over her legs. "Is he okay?"

She pressed her lips together. "I wouldn't know."

TOKYO—The greatest allied tank
thrust of the Korean War jabbed
deep into Chinese and Korean Red
positions within five miles of
Seoul.

Chapter Thirty-Four

The door to the barn stood open, held in place by a shovel. McIntire peered inside. It was unoccupied but for the quarter horses, Spirit and Traveler, munching hay in their separate stalls. McIntire approached as near as he cared to. "You should be ashamed," he said, "sitting on all that horsepower, letting the woman who feeds you shovel the snow."

"I'd say so." Leonie came in the door with a pail of water in each hand. She lowered one of them to the ground with a huff and a splash. "So you're home."

"That I am." McIntire moved forward to take the remaining bucket from her, but she gripped it and walked past him.

"Is it all right if I ask where you've been?" She slapped the burly haunch that blocked her entry into the nearest stall, stepped inside, and waited while Spirit, or Traveler—McIntire was never sure which was which—sank his nose into the water and siphoned it up.

"Didn't you see my note?"

"It didn't say where you were going." She moved to dole out the second portion of water to Traveler, or Spirit.

Hadn't it? "I went to Marquette to see Melvin Fratelli."

Leonie ran her fingers through the thick hair of the horse's neck as he slurped. McIntire moved closer. "Come on inside. It's freezing."

"It's always freezing." She slipped out of the stall and faced him. Her eyelashes were tipped with frost. "You might have woken me up. I'd like to get out a bit, too."

"If you want to argue, it'll have to be indoors."

It seemed Leonie did want to argue. She turned and stomped off to the house. McIntire closed and latched the barn door.

Once inside, she seemed to thaw a bit, both physically and metaphorically. She warmed her hands over the gas burner before sliding the kettle onto it. "I thought you didn't care for Mr. Fratelli."

"I didn't go to pass the time of day."

"What *did* you go for?"

"He can't possibly really think that there's some sort of seditious activity going on in St. Adele. I wanted to find out what he's up to. Why he's making all this fuss over—"

"And did you?"

"Not really."

"So you traveled all that way for nothing?" She didn't wait for an answer. "I don't see why it's so important to you. As you say, the Star of Hope Society is hardly a communist front organization, even if that is what Melvin Fratelli thinks. He's not going to find anything, so what difference does it make?"

"Erik Pelto isn't a Red saboteur either, but Fratelli has managed to ruin his life without half trying."

"Do you think he'll really have to leave the country?"

"I haven't heard of anybody actually being deported. But fighting it can go on forever. Knut Heikkinen has been in jail in Duluth since October. That German war bride is still sitting in Ellis Island after almost two years. Even if Erik gets out of jail, he won't be able to find a job. Not teaching."

"No," she agreed, "and that's the worst of it. It wouldn't be so bad if he didn't have a family to support. It's not their fault."

"Orville's staying with them now. I stopped off when I passed by. The hearing will be in Duluth in a couple of days. They're hoping the charges will be dropped, or Erik will get out on bail."

Leonie poured water into the pot, put down the kettle, and walked to him. She put her arms around his neck and rested her chin on his head. "I'm sorry I was so grumpy. It's getting to be a long winter."

McIntire assured her that it was quite all right. He shouldn't have gone without letting her know.

She kissed the top of his ear. "So that was your day then?"

He leaned back into her throat. "It's not quite over yet."

"I mean, did you stop anywhere else?"

Her neck was warm against him. He only hesitated a second. "No."

WASHINGTON—Information indicating that Moscow had contributed $2,500 to the Institute of Pacific Relations was reported today by Senator Karl E. Bundt (R-N.Y.).

Chapter Thirty-Five

"That one will do." Leonie pointed to the beige crockery mixing bowl on the top shelf. "No! Don't you dare budge. I can stand on a chair." She smiled. "Some of us own kitchen stools."

"Do tell? You have my sympathy."

Leonie wiped the dust from the bowl and proceeded to mix up her New Year's Day Punch. "A bit late, but this is the first occasion I've had. I'll put the ginger ale in at the last minute."

She had come early, as Mia had known she would, and for which she felt guiltily grateful.

"But how could Mr. Stewart have traveled from the mine back here to Rose's without anybody seeing him? How did he get to work? Presumably he didn't drive back and fore."

"No. The mine location had a bunk house. Jack stayed there during the week and came home Sundays. There were a few men that did that, and they'd have taken turns driving I suppose. I don't know how he could have got from the mine to the Falks' house after the accident. If he had a car and he left in it, there wouldn't have been any question about whether he was alive or not. There was talk that he'd taken off with one of those railroad handcars, but he'd still have had a long walk from the tracks to Falks'. There used to be a bus running from St. Adele to some of the towns around, but if he'd been on that, people would have noticed."

"A bus? Here?"

"There were more people then."

"And," Leonie arched her eyebrows, "if anybody had picked him up and given him a ride, they'd have noticed, too."

"But they might have kept it to themselves."

"They would probably still remember." Leonie floated slices of apple in her brew. "How is Nick doing?" she asked.

"As well as can be expected, as they say. I suppose John told you he's not going back to work. The new mailman will be permanent."

Leonie nodded. She was looking a little green around the gills herself, and Mia asked, "How have things been with you?"

"Perhaps a little cabin fever. This winter already seems longer than last year's. There's Sally." Leonie dived into her grocery bag one more time, and brought out another bottle. "Just a wee drop."

"Not gin?" Mia had heard the English were fond of it. She wasn't sure the ladies would be, outside of Elsie Karvonen.

"Vodka. They won't even notice."

"Isn't that unfair?"

"Only if you don't tell."

"Are you going to?"

"I will if they ask."

Sally Ferguson's car was followed by the Lindstroms' Chevrolet. The two vehicles spit forth seven women, each dressed in her best bib and tucker and carrying a pan or a bowl or a box.

"Safety in numbers," Mia said.

"Everyone was a little surprised you agreed to this."

"Me too. When I said okay, it took Sally so long to answer I thought she must have fainted."

"Well, we have you captive now, in your own home. Nowhere to run. You may as well go arrange yourself in regal splendor on your couch." She helped Mia to her feet. "It won't be too bad. Sally doesn't like to drive in the dark."

For the first time in her life, Mia felt some irritation at the lengthening days. She followed Leonie's advice and took herself off to the living room. At least she wouldn't have to see the looks on their faces when they laid eyes on the state of her kitchen. They didn't know the half of it. They should have seen it before Nick's gallant attempt at washing the floor. Fortunately, unlike Mia, none of them was tall enough to see the top of the refrigerator. Those unsuspected layers of dust on her neighbors' high spots were Mia's single source of housekeeping smugness.

Irene Touminen was the first to extricate herself from the buzz in the kitchen that accompanied the unwrapping of bodies and foodstuffs.

"How are you doing? You look well."

"She's lying. You look ghastly." Elsie Karvonen strode in behind her, redolent with the odor of a recent permanent wave. She handed Mia a glass half filled with the lukewarm punch. "This is a hell of a note. When do you get that thing off?"

Mia put the glass on the table. She hadn't consumed an ounce of liquid since her early morning coffee and didn't intend to. They were all probably itching to find out how she managed with a cast on her leg and no indoor toilet. She wasn't about to satisfy their curiosity.

The ladies knew their business, and the period devoted to greetings was mercifully short. In fifteen minutes they were all seated, some in greater comfort than others, each balancing a plate of assorted tidbits on her knee.

"What do you suppose Delilah will do?" Sandra Culver popped a cracker layered with brilliant orange cheese, topped with a pimento-stuffed olive, between her perfectly formed lips. Mia hadn't expected her to come. Since the death of her oldest daughter, Sandra had stuck close to home. Maybe some of that had to do with that daughter not being around to take over the care of her numerous younger siblings.

Inge Lindstrom spoke up. "Go with her husband, what else would she do?"

"Go with him where?"

"Back to Finland," Lucy Delaney said. "Poor little mouse. She hardly sticks her nose out of the house here where she speaks the language."

"*Back* to Finland? Has Erik ever lived there? Stuff and nonsense! He fought in the war, for cripe's sake. The kids are American citizens. They'll fart around for awhile, keep him in jail, but they're not gonna deport him." Elsie Karvonen drained her glass and started to the kitchen. "It seems like sort of a coincidence that it came up now, though." She spoke just as the kitchen door swung shut. "You don't suppose it could have had something to do with the murders?"

"Erik and Delilah? He must have been all of twelve years old, and I doubt Delilah was even born yet."

"How old is that girl anyway?" It was Sandra, and the question sounded bleak.

"Not very," Sally replied. "Makes you wonder how old she was when they…got together."

"I thought of that." Lucy tutted and munched at the edge of a Swedish rosette with understandable hesitance. It was probably left from Inge's Christmas baking. "Maybe there's other reasons he ain't the best choice for teacher."

"That's something we don't have to worry about. He might not be kicked out of the country but he sure won't be teaching again."

"Well, I do feel bad for the family. Whatever he's done, it's not their fault."

Mia wondered if any of them had taken the trouble to visit Delilah to see for themselves how she was faring. Her broken leg at least served the purpose of alleviating her own guilt.

Grace Maki answered the question. "I went to see Delilah yesterday. Orville's there to keep an eye on things. Unfortunately the FBI's taken to keeping an eye on Orville and whoever else might be hanging around. They drove by and gave my car the once over while I was there. Poor little Delilah's scared half to death, and I don't blame her."

"Goodness, she's probably got more to worry about than the FBI what with feeding those kids and keeping them warm. The house is only rented."

"Do you think possibly we might do something to help?" Leonie asked. "Perhaps the church…?"

The short silence was broken by Sandra Culver. "Did you have something in mind?" Her words were cautious. Mia empathized with Sandra's wariness. Leonie McIntire had a good heart, but when it came to Christian charity her schemes were sometimes awkward for the donors and closer to humiliating for the recipient.

"They're going to need help, at least while Erik is in jail and probably after that," Leonie answered. "How will they get along?"

Elsie returned with a full glass. "They'll let him out. He can get another job. He's young and healthy."

It was followed by another self-conscious gap in conversation, eyes focused on plates—or anywhere to avoid looking at Mia.

Grace finally said, "I don't think they'll accept donations."

"We could do something to raise money."

"Wouldn't that be sort of embarrassing for them?"

"They wouldn't have to know," Leonie said. "Anyway, it might be different for Delilah. She's a child, really. I don't think she'd be too proud to accept help." She added, "She's not American."

"You appear to have some plan in mind, Leonie. You'd better tell us." Sally gave Leonie her chance, and they were doomed. Leonie was too good at convincing people. Her accent always made her sound smarter than anybody else.

"I was thinking perhaps we could make up a cookery book."

"Cookery?"

"A recipe book. I saw one from a Methodist church in Saginaw. We just put in our favorite recipes. I can print it up, and we could sell it for a dollar or so a copy." She speared a limp slice of cucumber. "I'm sure people would pay a dollar just to get the secret to these lovely pickles." She smiled at Lucy Delaney, assuring the twin incentives of pride and competition.

"Well…."

"We can talk about it at the meeting on Sunday."

Mia was not a member of St. Adele's Lutheran Ladies Aid, and she couldn't be traipsing off to meetings. Maybe she should hang on to the cast for a while. She used the lull in the discussion, no doubt occasioned by visions of culinary fame, to introduce her own agenda.

"Does anybody know," she asked, "if there'll be a funeral for Rose?"

"I'd certainly think so. Maybe we'd better see to that, too. Her husband's in no shape to organize it."

"Well, what about one for Jack?"

"If that's who it is."

She'd accomplished her task, and Mia sat back to listen, trying to eat slowly. She nibbled Grace Maki's baked beans. She hoped there'd be plenty of leftovers, including the punch. That wasn't likely with Elsie around.

"It's so queer." Irene had been mostly quiet until now. "We thought we'd lost her—and Jack—and now we have to go through it all over again. But life has gone on as usual all these years without them, almost like it didn't matter. Is that how it'll be this time, too? Will it be any different *knowing* that they're dead?" Irene's philosophizing was met with a stares and a few wise shakes of the head. "I just don't know," she went on, "why nobody seemed to realize that Teddy and Rose didn't leave when they should have. Didn't anybody try to say goodbye?"

"If it happened on the same day as the mine accident we probably just weren't paying attention."

Sally Ferguson stirred her coffee. "I'll never forget when I heard about all those men dying. Drowning in mud...in the dark. Grace's husband came over and told us the next morning. I was pouring milk into the separator, and half of it ended up on the floor. I didn't take any notice until I found myself standing in a puddle!"

"I was in Escanaba with Sulo," Irene said. "We stayed with Ma's cousin and his wife. One of the kids had a radio in his room and was up listening to it at all hours. He started yelling. Scared the daylights out of me!"

"It's amazing how fast news spread in those days, even here where we didn't have the radio."

"But we did have Mike Maki."

"That's right," Grace said. "I always say, our three means of communication—telephone, telegraph, and tell Mike."

"Where does your husband find out all that stuff?"

Grace chuckled. "Telephone, telegraph, and turn on the radio. But that night he got it from Eban Vogel."

"From my father?" Mia felt a chill.

"It was late, about eleven o'clock, but still hot as Hades. I was just coming out of the sauna, and Eban stopped when he saw my light. He was on his way back from town, seems to me. Looked like he'd been through the wringer. Ross was just a baby, and I remember thinking I wasn't going to ever let him go down in a mine." Grace shook her head. "And now look where he's ended up."

Ross Maki had spent three years working on and off for Mia, picking up wood and supplies, delivering her finished work. Now he was in Fort Leonard Wood, being groomed for Korea. She sorely missed him, and not just for his driving abilities.

Mia remembered learning about the accident from her father the day after it happened. She'd come downstairs to find him sitting on the porch steps, staring across the yard. It was a still morning, promising a sultry day to come, but not yet warm enough to account for his damp and ashen face. She asked if he was sick, and he told her that more than fifty men had drowned in a mine. She also distinctly recalled that he'd claimed to have heard the news in the usual place—Mike Maki's sauna.

But it was looking like the source of the story, the first to know, was Eban Vogel.

WASHINGTON—The house committee on un-American activities was urged by its Republican members to revive its Communist-in-Hollywood investigations.

Chapter Thirty-Six

"So how'd it go?"

Leonie tossed her mittens and wool kerchief onto a chair but didn't remove her coat. "All right. I don't think Mia suffered over much. I wonder why she agreed to it."

"She might be getting bored. Maybe even an afternoon sipping tea with the ladies looks good when you haven't been able to get out for a month."

"She doesn't normally have much interest in getting out. Perhaps it's different when you can't do anything at home either. But I suspect an ulterior motive."

McIntire suspected one, too.

"She kept steering the information around to Rosie and the mine flood. Not that it was too hard, but I think she was fishing for information."

"Did she get any?"

"None that she could have liked very much. The ladies got to talking about how they heard about the accident. From all appearances, Mia's father was the first in this community to know."

That was strange. Unless Eban Vogel had changed after McIntire knew him, he hadn't been one to go out much more than his daughter, outside of those wood-buying trips. "Maybe he got it from Nick."

"Or from the late Mr. Stewart." Leonie ignored the spot next to him on the sofa and flopped into a chair. "I brought up my cookery book scheme. The group wasn't too keen at first."

"Until you appealed to their cut-throat competitive instinct."

"They agreed to consider it. What do you suppose will happen to that poor girl?"

McIntire couldn't suppose. Importing thousands of soldiers' brides had been a major U.S. government happy-days-are-here-again operation following the war. How would they handle sending their grooms the other way?

"At least she has Orville for the time being."

Leonie nodded. "I think I'll go warm up in the bath. Will you be okay without tea for a time? Sorry I didn't bring you any left-overs. I reckoned Mia needed them more." She stood and let her coat slide off her shoulders. "She mentioned that Nick wouldn't be going back to work. I guess you didn't know."

If McIntire admitted to knowing, that stupid lie would come out. He responded, "That's too bad. He doesn't seem to be in such bad shape, considering."

"Did you know he was giving up his mail route?"

"I figured he'd have to. Especially after the flying car incident."

She dropped her coat on top of the mittens and walked to the stairs.

She looked, McIntire thought with a start, older. Slowed steps, and, now that the frost-induced roses had warmed from her cheeks, washed out and tired. He wasn't sure of Leonie's age. She had to be older than himself by a few years.

If Eban Vogel had been the first in the neighborhood to learn about the mine disaster, he hadn't heard it from Nick. The cave-in had happened in the late afternoon or early evening, after Nick would have completed his daily rounds. If Eban had learned it straight from an escapee and failed to mention his source, that did sound suspicious. Wouldn't Massey-Davis have sent people out immediately to inform the families? Probably, but it would have taken time, and the ones who lived outside of Ishpeming and the company town would have taken a while to find. The families of the two miners from St. Adele could have easily been overlooked in the immediate aftermath.

What kind of a guy would use his fortuitous deliverance from a flood to escape an unpleasant life, leaving his companions to die? Desperate? Confused? Crafty? What kind of guy would blow that escaped miner's head to bits? McIntire could think of only one: the husband who found that miner naked in bed with his wife. If Teddy Falk had killed the two and gone to Eban Vogel that same night with the truth, including the story of Stewart's escape from the mine, Eban might have kept the deaths a secret. But would he have gone out later to pass the news of the cave-in on to Mike Maki?

Leonie's footsteps on the floor above had ceased some time ago, but McIntire didn't hear the tub filling. He put down his pencil, and put the teakettle on to boil.

Leonie sat at the dressing table in her chenille robe, her back to him. He heard a book slap shut and she turned around. "Just doing a bit of tidying up."

"Drink this while it's hot. I'll prepare your bath."

She looked into his eyes, perhaps recalling, as McIntire intended, the time—the first time—she'd spoken those words to him.

"Thank you." She sipped the tea, and added, as he had then, "It's very nice."

McIntire crossed the hall to turn on the water. When he returned he sat on the edge of the bed. "If you're good I'll let you have my secret recipe for your book. Are you going to take all comers or be choosy? That could get dangerous."

"I think we'd better form a committee. As executive editor, I'll excuse myself."

"Coward."

"Well, you know what they say about valor and discretion." She slid the book into the dressing table drawer and stood up. "Are you coming to wash my back?"

"Definitely. Just get yourself comfortable."

She closed the bathroom door behind her.

McIntire stood for a time before he pulled the drawer open. The garish cover leered at him. *Lone Star Ranger*. It was an old book. She couldn't have been reading it, and she didn't ordinarily keep Zane Grey in her dresser. Her age was the least of what he didn't know about Leonie.

He didn't remove the book from the drawer, but lifted the cover and fanned through its pages. Keepsakes were tucked among them. A Christmas card made by her grandson, Chuckie; a tiny pressed daisy; a ribbon bookmark; and, just inside the front cover, a faded news clipping. McIntire didn't touch it, or read it past the headline. He knew what it said. A report of a car accident. *Victim, believed to be a U.S. embassy attaché, was identified as Michael Warren. No enqueries are being made into the death which has been ruled accidental.*

Melvin Fratelli, your days are numbered.

What else had he told her?

"John," she called, "my back is ready for you now."

An insistent rapping at the back door saved McIntire from reliving the events leading to Mike Warren's death as well as keeping him from his wife's back. He closed the drawer and walked to the stairs.

"I come to tell you to call off your dogs."

McIntire couldn't muster the strength for indignance or pretended ignorance of the nature of the dogs.

"Come on in."

Uno Touminen wiped his feet and stepped inside.

"How long before the rest of us end up like Pelto?" Touminen gave McIntire an emphatic poke in the chest. "One of your buddies drives by Erik's place at least three-four times a day. Checking to see who might be there, taking licence numbers. Same thing for the Star Society. Two goons in a black car, sitting at the end of the road, taking numbers."

"What makes you think that has something to do with me?"

"You're the one brought that Feebee snooping around here."

"I didn't bring him!"

"That ain't what Orville says." Another poke. "Didn't he come close to marrying your aunt?"

"No, he didn't." It hadn't been Fratelli that Siobhan had almost married. "And Melvin Fratelli is no buddy of mine." McIntire wondered what Uno would say if he told him that the agent suspected…what the hell, what could it hurt?

"Uno." McIntire glanced over his shoulder and moved closer. "Uno, it's *me* Fratelli's after. He thinks I'm a Russian spy."

"Are you?"

"What do you think?"

Touminen's eyes narrowed. "The judge set Erik's bail. Orville paid it so he'll be getting out for the time being. What I think is that damned well better be the end of it. Anybody else gets picked up, you'll be held responsible, spy or no spy. Tell your Fed cronies that." Uno stomped the last of the snow off his overshoes before he left the house.

Had McIntire been the one to bring the FBI back to town? Melvin Fratelli had his eyes and ears peeled on Flambeau County before he'd ever heard of Teddy Falk. Before he'd heard of him from McIntire anyway. That was why he was holed up in Marquette. That was no excuse. McIntire should have been more careful about throwing around names. He'd opened the genie's bottle or Pandora's box, and there was no closing it. What he wouldn't give to chuck those bones back in that hole and cover them up forever. Maybe.

But someone had killed a young woman in her bed and put a shotgun to her companion's head. That person could still be walking among them. Unless it was Eban Vogel.

Maybe by finding who that killer was, McIntire could atone for his transgressions, assuage some of his guilt. Unless it was Eban Vogel.

CLEVELAND, OHIO—Republican leaders were accused today of attempt-
ing to capture political control
"at the cost of this country's
position in the world and the
civil liberties of its people" by
Americans for Democratic Action
in convention here.

Chapter Thirty-Seven

"Can you get out?"

A plow had rumbled by an hour earlier, but McIntire wasn't about to commit himself to the sheriff until he found out where he would be called upon to get out to. "Don't know for sure, I haven't tried."

"There ain't much point in going on about who killed Jack Stewart 'til we find out for sure whether it *was* Jack Stewart. Which we just might be able to do now."

"How's that?"

"They found more pieces of the teeth. Pieces with lead pellets in 'em."

"That makes it official, then," McIntire said. Unless Rosie had used her daddy's upper plate for target practice, they belonged to the victim. Which might very well be why Nelda had turned evasive when he'd asked about her husband's teeth.

"Did you ever find out if Stewart had his own teeth?" Koski asked.

"No. I asked but didn't get a straight answer. Mrs. Stewart spooked me too much to pursue it. Maybe you'd have more luck getting the information from her kids."

"They must have been only babies when their old man disappeared."

"More like five or six. Old enough to remember if Pa could take his teeth out."

"I'll try to track down one or the other of them. In the meantime, maybe you could just zip over and ask Mrs. Stewart about it. Most everybody I talk to is saying they never for one minute thought Stewart died in that mine. There were ore stains on the shoes. I'm ninety-nine percent sure he's our man."

From what McIntire had heard, people hadn't always been so positive about Stewart's escape. And now the possible rusty tin can residue was ore stains?

Koski might have recognized his own grabbing at straws. "But, I suppose he was pretty young for losing his teeth. It's possible that it wasn't him." Or maybe the sheriff was employing some of his heavy-handed psychology to save his back. He went on, "Could be I'm wrong. You can double-check, and if you strike out we can cross him off the list for good. That way you'll be able to set his widow's mind at rest."

Discovering that the sheriff had concluded that her husband hadn't died in the arms of Rosie Falk might rest Nelda's mind for a time. It was going to be little consolation when she also learned that Koski thought Jack Stewart might be still alive. Massey-Davis Mining had paid out twice the normal amount as compensation to surviving families of that disaster. The mining company would be sure to get wind of it. They would not take fraud lightly. Of course they'd still have to prove it. Here was just another bit of muck he'd been responsible for stirring up. It had done nothing but add another layer of tragedy to a pathetic woman's life.

"I'll go over as soon as Leonie gets back with the car," McIntire told him. She'd been right about those multiplying skeletons.

He'd have to face her with his own skeleton sooner or later. It was amazing the way she was carrying on as if things hadn't changed. She wouldn't have had that news clipping if she didn't know about his role in that fatal car crash. But she was behaving as if she'd never seen it. She seemed morose, but that had been going on for weeks. Sometimes he caught her looking at him curiously, no more than that. Maybe she was playing some sort of game, waiting for him to crack. That didn't seem like Leonie, but how did he know? How well did he really know her? Not much more than when they'd married, and she'd been a virtual stranger then.

Their meeting came about ordinarily enough. When he'd stopped at the unimpressive offices of *H. Harris and Sons, Publishers and Printers,* with his English translation of their twenty-page booklet, *The Railroads of Hungary,* it was Leonie who sat behind the desk. A nameplate said she was Mrs. H. Harris. Before McIntire knew how it had happened, he'd learned that she was the widow of the firm's founder; that she had sold out her portion of the company to her stepsons, changing her status from owner to employee, and that she was free on Saturday evening.

That first social engagement did not get off to nearly such a brisk start. Leonie was a shop window mannikin at his side at the cinema. Over supper she made polite responses to his questions but otherwise sat silently regarding him with an expression he'd seen only once since—when he accompanied her to a horse fair to choose a pony for her grandson. McIntire had tried not to squirm, prattled on like the lunatic he'd so recently been, and made an excuse to see her home as soon as was diplomatically possible. She'd acquiesced with discernible relief.

He was surprised when she invited him into her flat, astounded at his own acceptance of the invitation, and flabbergasted when that invitation extended to morning.

When he awoke, she sat on the side of the bed in a pale blue dressing gown. On the table was a tray holding a teapot, an egg, and two slices of toast. She was once again silently watchful as she poured the tea.

McIntire had sipped. "It's nice."

She'd asked if he might not like such nice things for the rest of his life, and he'd allowed as how he probably would. She'd put aside the both the tray and the robe. Fortunately a short wait could cause no further damage to British toast.

Three weeks later, at her sister's house in St. Mary's in the Marsh, they became man and wife.

The zip of her overshoes sounded from the porch. She came through to the dining room with flushed cheeks, and dropped her purse and a sheaf of papers of various sizes and colors on the table.

"Got the go ahead for the cookbook, I take it."

"Got the raw materials, so we're underway. Unless they prove to be forty variations on tuna hotdish."

Her eager look faded as she leafed through the handwritten scraps. "No, it seems we have forty recipes for the pasty—with absolutely no variation."

"Folks hereabouts don't fiddle with their pasties."

"How did the Cornish pasty get to be Finnish ethnic food anyway?"

"People like Jack Stewart, I imagine. By the way, we should know soon whether or not he was Rosie's man."

"I'm glad to hear that. Irene called in on Nelda a day or two ago. She says the poor dear is getting frightened and seems even more unbalanced. Her standing as a miner's widow is about all she has."

"She might not have that much longer."

Leonie unpinned her hat and listened to McIntire's news. "The children might not be any better source of information than their mother. They're not going to want to believe their father was shot to death."

"Pa didn't think he drowned." Neither did Nick Thorsen, but McIntire couldn't quite remember how or when he'd learned that. *When first we practice to deceive.* "If he lived through that mine accident, Nelda might know it, if she has any real comprehension of the situation at all."

"What do you suppose goes on in that mind?"

"I have enough trouble figuring out what goes on in yours."

She stretched to kiss his chin. "Women are supposed to be mysterious."

"Leonie, has Melvin Fratelli been in touch with you?"

"Mr. Fratelli? Of course not! Now you're the mystery man. What would Melvin Fratelli want with me?"

"I don't know...he was after Ma."

"What makes you think that was him?"

He hadn't denied it. Not exactly. "He might not have been the person who made the call, but I know damn well he was behind it."

"Why? Are you sure you're not just over-reacting? What reason could he have?"

"I don't know," McIntire said again. "I wish I did. I'll get over to see Nelda while the car's still warm."

"Will you be long?"

"Chatting with Nutty Nelda? I should hope not."

"You don't plan to go anywhere else?"

"No."

"Good. It'll be dinner time soon. I'll put some potatoes going."

Put potatoes going? His wife was turning into a Yooper before his very eyes.

◇◇◇

The previous night's snowfall had buried Nelda Stewart's front steps. Near the wall, an eight-inch hole was tunneled through to the underside of the porch. A few black hairs clung to its sides. McIntire stooped to peer in. A whisper of cat urine hung in the air, a harbinger of things to come. He should have tried stuffing some Vicks up his nose. He mounted the bottom step, closed his eyes, willed his mind to go blank.

He rapped on the screen door. It thudded against the ice that kept it from closing completely but made little sound. He gave a yank forceful enough to dislodge the snow heaped against it and leapt back.

He stepped past a heap of frozen washing, stacked like cordwood with clothes pins still clinging to the shoulders of the faded dresses. His knock at the inner door received no response, not even the courtesy of a get the hell out of here. McIntire waited and shivered before knocking again. This time an answer came in the form of a plaintive yowl, nowhere near loud enough to have been uttered by Mrs. Stewart.

McIntire put his mouth to the glass of the small window in the door and blew until he'd melted an eyeball-sized gap in the frost that covered the other side.

The kitchen was devoid of life forms visible to the naked eye but for the cat on the table. It was so heavily furred that only its narrow eyes showed it to be other than a great black dust-mop. Snow clung to its tail and neck ruff, and its whiskers were tipped with frost that wasn't melting. The animal must have its own way in and out. A fruit jar next to it had a neat crack splitting off its base to expose solidly frozen string beans. The cat opened its mouth in another pleading cry.

The door wasn't locked. McIntire stepped over a dead bluejay and went inside. There is no place on earth so cold as an unheated house, but the air was none the worse for being frozen.

"Mrs. Stewart, are you at home?"

It didn't take long to determine that she was not. McIntire walked through the living room to the stairs, as steep and narrow as a ship's ladder but nowhere near so sturdy. It led to a hallway flanked by two tiny bedrooms. Strips of frost on the slanted ceilings showed where the roof beams lay.

The room on his right had no door and had almost certainly been the lair of one or both of the Stewart children. Pictures cut from magazines papered the walls—movie stars and horses.

McIntire rapped on the doorframe and waited a few seconds before he pushed aside the curtain sheltering the entry to Nelda's own room. The double bed was made up, threadbare blankets tucked under the mattress edges, two lumpy pillows stuffed into purple and blue bordered feed sack cases. A pile of moth-eaten wool coats lay at the foot, and two more hung on the bedposts. Whatever Nelda had done with that money from Massey-Davis, fraudulently acquired or not, she hadn't spent it for her own comfort. The only hint that the room's occupant was not a rag-doll was a new-looking cardigan of brilliant crimson lain flat on the bed along with a pale grey dress. The style of the dress showed, even to McIntire's untrained eye, that it was definitely not new, but it looked well made, little worn, and,

like the sweater, brushed mostly free of cat hair. Finery laid out
for a trip to town?

McIntire bent his head under the low ceiling and crossed to
the window. There were no tracks in the snow that had fallen
in the night, so if Mrs. Stewart had gone off it had been the
day before. She could have taken the train into Chandler. That
would have meant a walk back from the depot in St. Adele in a
snowstorm. McIntire wasn't worried that Nelda was frozen in a
snowbank. She'd lived here too long for that.

A narrow vertical box resembling an upended coffin served as
a wardrobe. It held a single plaid dress and a short-sleeved blouse
sagging on a hanger. McIntire approached the chest of drawers.
A book rested on its bubbled veneer, *The Poems of Oscar Wilde*.
Nelda didn't seem like the literary type. He opened the cover.
It was a 1908 edition. Maybe her husband had brought it from
his native England. As he reached to pull open a drawer, the
crowing of a cock brought him to his senses. What in hell was
he doing, lurking around this crazy woman's pitiful bedroom?
Nelda Stewart had a right to leave home, and if a storm kept her
from getting back, it was none of McIntire's business.

He descended the stairs and left the house with relief akin
to joy. Whatever his problems, he had warmth, food, and his
sanity, and, so far, Leonie.

His buoyant mood extended to fetching the shovel from the
Studebaker's trunk and clearing the snow from Nelda's steps. The
cockerel crowed again, and he turned his shovel on what he took
to be the path to the barn. The chickens wouldn't have been fed
or watered, and hens weren't nearly so resourceful as cats.

Clucking led him to a door at the side of the barn. Inside, a
dozen reddish hens scratched in a two-foot layer of manure and
straw. It might have helped to keep their feet from freezing.

A door on the far wall led to the building's interior, but
probably hadn't been opened in ten years' worth of chicken shit.
McIntire backed out and waded through the snow around the
corner of the barn.

The wall afforded some shelter; vestiges of Nelda's path were still visible. Like every other barn door in the county, in winter this one opened only wide enough to admit its largest regular visitor. McIntire was slim, but not so skeletal as Nelda Stewart.

A bulging gunny sack topped with a rusty coffee can was just inside the door. He wedged himself into the doorway and reached to scoop a can-full of cracked corn.

A blast of wind through the open door elicited a creaking of beams and sent a shadow fluttering on the wall. McIntire peered into the dim space. He didn't see the expected barn owl. He saw rubber overshoes lying in the litter, and, some ten inches above them, toe to toe, a pair of feet. They were bare; they were blue; and they swung restlessly to and fro below the tattered hem of a flannel nightgown.

If he looked up into those eyes he'd be sucked into their madness. Wherever she was, he'd go with her. He couldn't help himself. He knew he should stay fixed on those fallen overshoes, back out the door and close it. But his gaze was drawn up the emaciated body, past the sticklike arms and bony fingers dangling limp and frozen, to confront those bulging, accusing eyes. The fear and pleading were gone from them, leaving opaque frosted orbs.

"Where is this all going to end?" he asked aloud.

NEW YORK—Controversy over loyalty tests now has come to the broadcasting industry with the decision of the Columbia Broadcasting System to ask its 2,500 regular employees to sign statements stating whether they ever have belonged to organizations designated as subversive.

Chapter Thirty-Eight

He made it all the way home and had called both the sheriff and Mark Guibard before the shaking started. Then it wouldn't stop.

Tea splashed on the tablecloth and Leonie took the cup from his hand. She put her arms about his neck and pressed his head to her chest.

"It's all right now. Mr. Koski can take care of it. You don't have to go back."

"Yes, I do. I didn't tell them where to find her." He struggled to his feet. "Guibard will only be a few minutes. I have to get over there."

"Then I'm driving you. And not until you've finished this tea."

McIntire acquiesced with relief.

The yard was still empty when they arrived. They didn't approach the barn, or speak of what was there, or of anything else.

McIntire carried coal from the meager store in the cellar and set about starting a fire in the leaving room heater and one in the kitchen cookstove. A car rumbled into the yard. He scratched the frost from the window by the table and watched as Leonie spoke to the doctor, waved toward the barn, then plowed her way through the knee-deep snow to the pump.

The two of them entered the house together less than five minutes later.

Guibard pulled off one glove, then replaced it. "Sad business."

"Who would know how to contact her children?" Leonie dipped water into a teakettle and poured the rest into a chipped enamel basin. She slid the stove lids aside and placed the kettle and the basin over the fire. Her lips were blue.

Guibard shook his head. "Don't know."

Leonie put her hand on McIntire's shoulder. "Can you look around? There must be something with their addresses."

"Koski will search the house." McIntire sat at Nelda's creaky table while his wife plunged hair-coated cups into boiling water, brewed her ever-present tea, and set about scraping flakes from a thin bar of Fels Naptha soap into the basin. She silently began emptying cupboards and scrubbing surfaces.

The kitchen grew warmer. Probably warmer than Nelda had known it. No need to conserve coal now. Frost on the windows melted, puddles formed and were sponged up by the rotted sills. Odors oozed from every corner.

McIntire left the cutting down of Nelda Stewart's frozen remains to the sheriff and Cecil Newman. It didn't take long. Newman scurried off to notify the undertaker.

"Christ!" Koski sucked in his breath as he came in the door, his bulk filling the tiny kitchen. "If this is the way that woman lived, I can't say I blame—" He glanced in McIntire's direction. "It was like picking up an armload of popple sticks."

Just a crazy woman, reduced to an armload of popple sticks.

"She leave a note?"

McIntire shook his head.

"Well, I'll have a look around." He turned sideways to pass through the doorway to the living room.

McIntire heard his shuffling about, followed by an extended period of silence, then the first tentative step on the flimsy stairs. Soon the footsteps sounded overhead. Leonie looked up and moved from directly under the creaking boards. She picked a filth-encrusted rag rug from the floor and carried it through to the living room. McIntire heard the door on the heater open and close, and the rush of a draft up the stovepipe.

"Do be careful, Mr. Koski."

"I'm holding my breath," the sheriff replied. He sidled back into the kitchen, clutching a few sheets of paper. "What the hell do you make of this?" He placed a folded sheet on the table in front of McIntire. "It was on the bed, under her clothes."

The paper was thick and had a ragged edge, the fly leaf torn from a book. The handwriting flowed in bold loops and delicate flourishes: *All that I know about lying in jail is that the wall is strong; And that each day is like a year, A year whose days are long.*

"It's a poem," McIntire said, "slightly paraphrased. She copied it from a book upstairs." They were McIntire's first words in over an hour.

"I guess it puts a cap on things."

"Maybe."

"Maybe? No maybe about it. Mrs. Stewart goes over to say goodbye to Rose and finds her in bed with Mr. Stewart. Bang. That's all she wrote."

"Wouldn't that be a bit of a coincidence? Nelda deciding to pay a call on Rosie just at the time her husband happens to have the same impulse? She couldn't have planned that mine accident."

The sheriff was dismissive. "Coincidences do happen, you know, but I don't see that this is one. The mine *did* flood at the time Rosie was home alone getting set to leave. That would be the normal time for Nelda to make a visit. There's a thirty-two Plymouth rusting away in back of the barn. It probably belonged to her husband, so she'd have had it back then."

"Maybe," McIntire said again. If Nelda had killed herself because of guilt, or fear of being exposed as a murderer, he might be able to feel a little less guilt himself.

"Only funny thing is, she had clothes laid out on the bed. Good clothes. Could she have been planning to go somewhere?"

"Yes."

Koski stared for a moment. "Oh, ya. I guess maybe she was." He strode out the door, giving an audible gasp when he reached fresh air.

Leonie picked up her coat. "We'd better go, too. I can come back later. We don't want those children coming home to...." The choking of her voice brought McIntire back to life and to his feet. Tears welled up in huge drops before finally spilling down her face. Her body convulsed in a single great sob and she buried her face in his jacket. McIntire had never seen his wife cry in earnest before. Only the occasional bright eyes at sad movies or letters from home. Now she appeared to be making up for years of restraint. She finally turned her head to speak, still resting against his chest. "I wonder how much time she put into it."

"What?" Knotting the rope? She would have had plenty of time to think things over.

"Choosing what she wanted to be buried in."

That couldn't have taken long. McIntire was sure of it.

Chapter Thirty-Nine

Nick dropped the phone onto the hook. "It was Nelda
Stewart."

"Why? What's wrong? Where's she calling from?"

"She's not. Guibard and the hearse. It was Nelda they were
going to get."

"Nelda's dead?"

"She hung herself in the barn."

"Because she killed her husband?" Mia felt shame that the
tears that sprang to her eyes were those of pure relief. Whatever
her father might have done, she'd known he couldn't have committed murder.

"So it seems."

"Don't you believe it?"

"That woman was crazy. She could have killed herself over
anything, or nothing."

"But she didn't. Not until people started asking about Jack."

Nick nodded. "I think I'll go lie down a little while before I
get back to work."

It was only after he'd tottered from the room that the full
impact of his words hit her. Nelda, hanging in the barn. All these
years, struggling to survive, raising her children, had she been

tormented by memories of blowing their father's head away? How long had she hung there? Who had found her?

She heard a thud and a long sigh. Nick had made it only as far as the living room davenport. It would be chilly in there. He might want a blanket. He could get it himself; he wasn't completely helpless. Yet. At least he wasn't on crutches. Yet. She struggled. She wasn't sure if it was conscience or martyrdom that won out, but she pulled herself up and stumped past him to the bedroom. By the time she came back, dragging the patchwork quilt, he was sound asleep. She spread the cover as well as she could manage while balanced on the crutches. He needed to get to the barber; hair curled thickly around his ears. The lines of his forehead were smoothed away, leaving a serene and confident aspect. Contrary to the usual cliché, it was the wide-awake Nick who looked vulnerable. And it would only get worse.

They'd had their problems, but most of their life together had gone smoothly enough. He'd not demanded much of her, and she'd forgiven his many trespasses. Maybe she could forgive again. Someday. She looked away.

She jumped at the knock on the door. She hadn't heard a car. She hobbled to the window. There was a car. A car and a half. A sleek black sedan, steam rolling off its hood, sat at the end of the driveway.

A man stood on the back steps, shuffling his feet and slapping his gloved hands together. When he raised his head to knock again, she recognized the private detective who'd been with them on that terrible day in November. Now, according to John, he was an FBI agent in Marquette. What could he possibly want with them?

He knocked again. She glanced at Nick curled under the quilt and at the remains of their dinner fighting for space on the kitchen table with the remains of their breakfast. The FBI was something she only heard about on the radio. Curiosity overcame pride and nerves. She swung off with sweating palms to open the door.

"Remember me, Mrs. Thorsen? Special Agent Melvin Fratelli." He flashed a printed card before her eyes. "Sorry to disturb you at such a time."

What time? Was this something about Nelda Stewart's death? She saw his gaze on the soiled cast. "Oh, this happened weeks ago. What can I do for you?"

"I was hoping I could use your telephone." The hysterical private detective of the previous fall was lost in a voice as smooth as chocolate pudding. "I need to make a rather important call."

Mia nodded and stepped out of the way. He went straight through to the kitchen. "Don't worry about your boots," she said to his back.

The phone call amounted to a few not so important sounding mumbles. The man thanked her and got to what was no doubt his real business.

"As I'm here, do you think we might talk for a bit?"

"About what?" More likely it was *who*. She resisted the urge to wipe the dampness from her hands.

"Just some general information." He slid his heavy coat from his shoulders.

Mia aimed the agent toward a chair. He had the face of someone in a magazine ad and was dressed as if he was on his way to a funeral, black suit and white shirt. At the sight of the tops of his ears, blistered with frostbite, a few of her stomach butterflies closed their wings.

He whipped out a notebook and a pencil. "I understand that Theodore Falk was arrested in your home. Is that true?"

"No."

The agent cleared his throat. "He didn't come to see you?"

"He came to see my father. They'd been good friends. He didn't realize my father is no longer with us."

"What's your father's name, Mrs. Thorsen?"

It was a question Mia hadn't expected. What interest would he have in her father? Was he investigating the murder, too? She couldn't keep it a secret. "Eban Vogel. He passed away several years ago."

Apparently it wasn't the right sort of name to interest Mr. Fratelli. He lowered his pencil.

"Who else was present when Mr. Falk was here?"

"Are you investigating Mrs. Falk's murder? Because if you are, that's been solved."

"We're just looking into a few things. Who else was present?"

"My husband. He's resting now. He's not—"

"Anyone else?"

The agent's demands were becoming more irritating than intimidating. "A sheriff's deputy, Cecil Newman. He was waiting outside. He planned on arresting Teddy."

"John McIntire?"

Mia'd been waiting for it. She wasn't sure why. Should she just tell the agent to go fly a kite? She didn't think she had to answer his questions, but she couldn't help wondering what they would be. John might be interested in hearing what the detective was asking about him.

"He was here."

"Why?"

"Teddy wanted to see him, to thank him for finding Rose."

"That's all?"

"I wouldn't know. What else would it be?"

"What language did they speak?"

Inge had asked Nick that, too. "I don't know," Mia answered, "I couldn't understand a word they said."

Fratelli gravely lifted his pencil.

"I'm kidding!" Mia stayed his hand. The agent's expression clearly said that G-men don't take kindly to jokes. "They talked in plain old English. Or as plain as Mr. Falk can manage, anyway." That wasn't quite true. John had greeted the prodigal Teddy with some outlandish word.

"Did they mention how long it had been since they'd seen each other?" The agent stretched his legs and affected a casual tone, letting Mia know that they were getting to the nub of his questioning.

"Far as I know, they never met before. John left ages before Ted moved here."

His brow wrinkled. "I understand you've been acquainted with John McIntire a long time."

How had he come to that understanding? Had he been asking questions about her, too? "All my life. He was born in this house. So was I."

"And you stayed close friends, you might say?"

What was this about? Mia didn't know how to reply, or whether to reply at all, and Fratelli didn't wait.

"So you might be better acquainted with him than anyone outside his own family."

Was she? She often didn't feel she knew John in the least. "I wouldn't know about that. We both lived here, in this house, when we were small children." The intervening years were none of Agent Melvin's business. "I didn't see him at all from the time he left for the war, that's the First World War, until he came back a little over a year ago."

"Did you keep in contact when he was away?"

"No."

"Still, you know him pretty well."

"Pretty well."

A throaty chuckle accompanied his confidential smile. "Have a lot of stories to tell, does he? About his time in the service?"

"Not to me." John had never mentioned a word about his time in the Army to anyone, so far as she knew.

"And I guess he'd be pretty interested in the changes in the area since he left. All the mining and such."

"Mining? There's nothing new about that."

"I imagine it was quite a surprise to everybody, when he moved back here after so long away."

He imagined correctly, but Mia wasn't about to say so. "He was retired. This was his home."

The agent put his hands together and leaned toward her in a poor imitation of a gossipy housewife. "Anything else about him ever seem funny to you?"

Funny? "Anything else? I didn't say anything was funny about John."

"Strange...you know, odd."

John McIntire? Odd? Mia tried to keep the laughter from her voice. "I'm not sure what you mean."

"Retired army officers of his rank don't get a big pension. He and his wife travel quite a bit. He might seem to be living beyond his means."

If what she'd heard was true, the McIntires weren't living anywhere near beyond that wife's means. "I wouldn't know," she said again."

"What about his family?" He leaned even closer. "Any history of mental problems?"

"Mental problems? What is this all about?"

"You knew his parents."

"You knew his aunt." Melvin Fratelli and John's exotic Auntie Siobhan had been quite an item. But Siobhan wouldn't have troubled herself to answer nosy questions about her relatives, not even from a good-looking G-man.

Mia had apparently uttered the magic words. Fratelli cleared his throat and got to his feet. His conspiratorial tone disappeared. "Thank you for your time, Mrs. Thorsen."

She watched the big car reverse into the road. Why would the FBI be asking questions about John? And why ask her, of all people? Mental problems? The McIntire family seemed about as sane as they come. Were people ever what they seemed to be?

It *was* strange, though, the way John had gone off for thirty years without so much as a postcard and then suddenly turned up to stay. He'd never said much of anything about how he'd spent those three decades. Why would Fratelli think John and Teddy Falk had met before? Had they? No, outside of John's first words—and Teddy hadn't responded in kind—there was nothing about their meeting in her living room to hint that it wasn't the first.

Nick whimpered softly in his sleep. People could be very good at concealing things. She knew that.

NEW YORK—The Peace Information
Center and five of its officers were
indicted yesterday by a federal
grand jury on charges of failure
to register as a foreign agent.

Chapter Forty

"I can't do it. I just can't go."

"You have to. There'll be few enough people as it is." Leonie hooked the hanger over the door and began applying the clothes brush to the sleeves of her blue overcoat. "Think of the children."

"I am thinking of the children. For God's sake, Leonie, it's because of me she's dead. I'm the last person those two are going to want to see on the other side of their mother's coffin."

"It's not because of you. She did it herself." She picked a wad of dog hair from the brush and waved it in the direction of the dozing Kelpie. "You should try hanging onto this stuff. Baby, it's cold out there."

She turned back to McIntire. "Maybe we're all of us at fault. What did we do for her when she was alive? Her children had gone. She was on her own twenty-four hours a day. Even when the rumors started about her husband and Rose Falk, when we knew he might have been murdered, everybody prattled on about whether she was the one who had done it, but hardly anybody could be bothered to call in to see her. We didn't know then that she *had* done it. We still don't know that for sure. We might have shown some sympathy. It must have been beastly. She would have been frightened and very, very lonely. Loneliness can do things to your mind."

She slipped the coat from its hanger. "I'm going, and I want you with me. Do you want to walk or should we drive?"

Snow was falling so heavily McIntire couldn't see to the end of the driveway. "We can walk," he said.

Leonie was wrong about one thing. There was a sizeable group of mourners to see Nelda Stewart off on her final journey; more than might have been expected on a Wednesday afternoon in close to blizzard conditions. It was a far greater number of callers than she'd had in a year when she was alive. Five years. The two young people sat in the front pew, flanked by a pair of elderly women wearing identical collars of the sort made with entire mink pelts. Each sleek animal had its jaws clamped on the tail of the one before it in a gleeful romp around an old lady's neck. One of the women stood and waddled forward to touch Nelda's cloth-draped casket.

McIntire had an irrational wish to fling open the box and look once more into those probing eyes, beg them for some sign that her existence had not always been intolerable. How many of the people of this earth lived out their lives in misery and loneliness? Did Nelda have good memories buried somewhere? Had Jack Stewart been in love with her? Did a sunrise or a rainbow give her joy? Had she been saving that red sweater for a special occasion that never came? Until now?

The service was mercifully short. They'd be spared the trip to the cemetery. Nelda Stewart's earthly remains would be placed in the township vault until the frost was out of the ground and a hole could be conveniently dug, necessitating a repeat of this ritual at about the time people might have begun to forget. For the time being, the casket was left at the front of the church, and the assemblage trooped down to the basement where a few plates of sandwiches and cake awaited them.

McIntire was surprised to see Orville Pelto ambling his way to the table. He couldn't imagine that Orville had known Nelda. If he'd been acquainted with Jack and his reputation as a former strike breaker, it was more likely to have been as adversaries than friends. Maybe insurance salesmen were like politicians and made an appearance wherever people congregated. Or maybe he intended that tin cup in his hand for contributions to his son's bail.

He nodded to McIntire. "This is a sad business, but at least it's over."

Of course, McIntire remembered, Orville had been fond of Rose, and he probably was gratified to take part in putting her killer to rest.

"We can hope so." McIntire doubted they would ever know for sure. Maybe it was best for all concerned if they just followed Pelto's lead, assumed the killer had effected her own punishment, and let it go at that. McIntire ached to be able to believe that Nelda had hung herself over guilt at having committed double murder, not at panic instilled in her by the callous township constable.

"We have to feel for the kids," Pelto said. "Well, young people can bounce back." His voice held more of hope than conviction.

"I heard Erik is getting out."

"On bail, until his appeal is heard."

"Appeal?" McIntire had thought it was only a preliminary hearing, some procedure to decide what to do with the teacher until his case was formally heard.

"He's been ordered to deport himself."

Orville walked off before McIntire could respond. He hoped young people were as resilient as the man professed to believe.

The young people. It could be put off no longer. Nelda's children stood together, accompanied only by one of the fur-clad ladies. The son, the younger of the two, smoothly handsome, shook McIntire's hand and nodded awkwardly at his expression of sympathy. The daughter introduced herself as Katrina and followed immediately with, "Was it you that found my mother?"

She was ruddy faced and strong looking. The word "strapping" came to McIntire's mind. She look more like a Brunhilde than a Katrina. You didn't have to look too deeply into her eyes to detect something of Nelda's wild animal aspect. McIntire suspected that here was one doctor whose orders would be followed to the letter. He nodded and added once more, "I'm sorry."

"People are saying that my mother committed suicide because she didn't want to go to prison." The young man next to her sucked in his breath. The elderly animal lover patted her arm.

She interrupted McIntire's stumbling attempt at denial. "They're right, I think. Ma was afraid of being locked up. She was terrified that she might end up in an asylum, or a jail."

McIntire moved closer that she might lower her voice. It was futile. Katrina was her mother's daughter.

"But not for murder."

"No one has said your mother was a murderer."

"They don't have to say it. I know what they're thinking. Nutty Nelda killed her husband and his girlfriend, and when she was about to be found out, she hung herself in the barn."

Her brother moved off. Several others moved closer. "Ma didn't kill my father. He wasn't in that hole with Rosie Makinen." A clutch of women vied for the job of pouring coffee from the nearby pot.

Katrina accepted a cup and stirred sugar into it. "I'm sorry about Rosie," she said. "She used to let me sit on their horses sometimes, and she showed me how to make a whistle from a willow stick." She finally turned her back to the growing audience at the table and walked off a few steps, leaving McIntire to follow. She spoke into her cup. "If my mother was afraid of being exposed as a criminal, it was fraud, not murder. My father isn't dead."

"Are you sure of that? Have you talked to him?"

"Quite sure, and no, I haven't seen him. We used to get money at Christmas time, and on our birthdays. Once we had cowboy outfits. Ma told us it came from the angels."

Knowing Nelda, she might have really believed angels were behind it.

"My mother was terrified of being taken away and locked up somewhere. I always thought it was because people said she was crazy. But if she was afraid she was about to be exposed for fraud…."

If that fear was what had driven her to the barn with a rope, it had come directly from McIntire. "Miss Stewart, how old were you when your father disappeared?"

"I was six, almost seven."

"Then you'd remember if he had false teeth."

"False teeth? No." She smiled. "I'll bet he does now though. But back then the few he had were his own."

"Have you told the sheriff that?"

"We only got here late last night. Are you saying the victim wore dentures?"

McIntire nodded.

"Then for sure it wasn't my father. Maybe you can tell Mr. Koski."

McIntire's opportunity to do that came sooner than he'd expected.

As he battled his way home through the mounting drifts—Leonie had prudently decided to stay behind to help with the washing up and get a lift home later—the rumble of an engine that could only belong to Pete Koski's Dodge Power Wagon slowed behind him. McIntire pulled the door open and slid onto the ice-cold seat.

Koski sat behind the wheel, ramrod straight.

"We're back where we started."

"Back to being positive it was J. Theodore Falk that murdered his wife and Jack Stewart?"

"Back to still not knowing shit about it. He's old."

"So am I, Pete, way too old to read your mind."

"Looks like Rosie Falk's boyfriend might have been more of a sugar daddy. The police just got the report from Lansing. They're saying the false teeth were made sometime in the eighteen-eighties. The plate was made outa some sort of celluloid crap. Even if the guy had them since he was, say, thirty years old, he'd be seventy or eighty in nineteen thirty-four, unless he was borrowing his grandad's choppers."

Koski pulled into McIntire's driveway. "So ask around," he said. "Maybe you can find out if some old codger didn't make it home that night. Put out a bulletin, elderly male, five foot ten or better, disappeared around the middle of August, 1934. Naked as a jaybird. Got that?"

Eighty years old? Not likely to have been working in an iron mine or tripping the light fantastic with Rose, when she could have had Pelto, or Sulo, or maybe Eban Vogel. On the other hand what other explanation could there be, if Rosie was in bed in a silk nightie and he was indeed dressed, or undressed, like a jaybird?

And once again the question arose, why had no one noticed this naked old codger missing?

Rep. Dewey Short (R-Mo.) hinted
that the nation's armed forces may
rise to 4,500,000 by the summer
of 1952.

Chapter Forty-One

McIntire's satisfaction at being once again in the warmth and privacy of his own home soon began to wane. In the empty house, thoughts kept at bay by the demands of social intercourse pushed their way to the head of the line.

Nelda Stewart had taken her own life after learning that the authorities were interested in her maybe not-so-late husband. Learning it from McIntire. Erik Pelto had been ordered to leave his home forever, after the FBI learned he'd been a communist. Learned it from McIntire.

That was only the worst of what he'd stirred up with the uncovering of those bodies. Could he have done things differently? Aside from his blunder in dragging Melvin Fratelli into it, maybe not. His only other option would have been covering up, looking the other way. Maybe some things are best left buried, but McIntire didn't think a pair of murder victims was one of them.

That was what he'd done with part of his own life, tried to bury it, and it hadn't gotten him anywhere. If he'd told Leonie from the first how things had been, he wouldn't be in this fix. But she'd never have married him if she'd known, so he'd be no further ahead. Those months in New Jersey, and the events leading up to them, had happened before they met. They didn't matter now. Leonie might not see it that way.

She wouldn't be home for a couple of hours. The snow had abated. He had time to do a little more snooping around.

With no particular plan in mind, but a need for some sort of action, he started the car and left it to warm up while he threw some hay to the horses.

A smudgy plume at the far edge of the field created a ghost of the fallen trees. The Thorsens hadn't been at the funeral. McIntire put the fork back in the barn and headed for the car. If an old man who'd been around in 1934 suddenly wasn't, the mailman would know.

◇◇◇

The piles of branches were shrinking, succumbing little by little to Nick's persistence and a can of gasoline. The fire smoldered without his attendance.

Mia called to McIntire to come in. "He went to lie down for a while."

"Is he...?"

"Just played out, I think. He's been chipping away at those things from dawn to dark, and the time of year from dawn to dark is starting to get bigger."

McIntire stepped inside but didn't remove his coat and refused the offer of a chair. He wouldn't stay any longer than necessary. In answer to his question her eyes widened.

"Old?"

"And he had false teeth."

"In his mouth, I take it, not in a glass by the bed."

"I can't say. Right now they're in the police lab in Lansing. Could he have been a relative?"

"Not one I ever heard of."

"Do you really think he might have been a—for lack of a better word—boyfriend?" McIntire asked.

"Some old duffer? Rosie might not have been choosy but she was...lively. I can't see her in bed with some wrinkled old...." She convulsed in a shiver. "Oh, I get eebie-jeebies just thinking about it!"

McIntire mentally counted the years until he would fall into the shiver-evoking category.

"And besides, like I said, I don't think Rosie had a boyfriend, not that sort of one. She just wouldn't have done it. I'm surprised she even got married. But maybe with Teddy…." Mia fingered the end of her braid. "I can't believe Rose would…she really didn't want to have children. She was deathly afraid of getting pregnant."

"Daredevil Rosie?"

"She paled at the thought." Mia twisted the hair tighter. "Rose came to me for advice. I guess she figured…maybe since I didn't…she thought I could tell her how to avoid it. She was dying of embarrassment. So was I."

"Well, I presume Rosie wouldn't have had much to worry about with Grandad."

"I didn't think of that."

"I suppose you're right," McIntire said. "It probably wasn't a romantic assignation. But then why was this old man naked?"

"Naked!"

"According to Koski."

"Ooooh, now I *really* can't think about it!"

McIntire would as soon not dwell on the image, himself.

"John…." Her expression was suddenly grave. "That detective was here the other day, the FBI guy."

"Melvin Fratelli? He want to check what you might have stashed away in that cast?" Did the man never sleep?

"He said he wanted to use the telephone. That he had to call his office."

"Did he do it?"

"He called somebody, but it was just an excuse to get in the door and pump me."

McIntire felt more resigned than angry. "I don't suppose I need to ask about what, or who?"

"He pussy-footed around for a while but your name did come up." She smiled. "He asked about your interest in mining. Don't worry, I didn't snitch."

McIntire relaxed. If Fratelli was asking about McIntire and mining, it was unequivocal evidence that he had no definite suspicions of anything. "I knew I could count on you. What else did he want to know?"

"Not much, just asked how well I knew you and your parents."

"What did you tell him?"

"I mentioned how well he knew your aunt. That put an end to it. How was the funeral?"

McIntire gave the highlights, asked that she put the question of disappearing old men to Nick when he awoke, and took a short detour to Karvonen's store for a newspaper before returning home.

◇◇◇

Leonie stood at the sink peeling potatoes. He told her about the ancient dentures.

"I know," she said. "Cecil Newman was here a few minutes ago."

"For what?"

"He was going door to door, every house. Trying to find anybody might have a hunch who the old man could have been. If we know of anyone who went missing. Why did he waste his time on coming to me?"

"Cecil is conscientious. If Koski said every house, Cecil wouldn't quibble over technicalities."

The sheriff was right. They were right back where they started from. "I guess there's not much else to do," McIntire admitted. "If we're going to find out what happened, we have to figure out who it was in that hole with Rose." Leonie looked weary. He added, "That's where I've been, to ask Nick if anybody stopped getting or sending mail."

"Did you find out anything?"

"No."

"I'm not surprised. And neither will the sheriff. You're going about it all wrong."

"Give me a hint. Maybe I can go about it right."

She rinsed her fingers under the tap and dried them on her apron. "Hunting for an old man who went missing is a waste of time. If that had happened people would remember. You have to give off looking for someone who died here and start looking for someone who lived here. He probably didn't come from a long way off. How many people over eighty lived in St. Adele or nearby at that time? Look at the tax rolls, check who owned property. Find out what happened to them. Everyone who was that old in 1934 would surely be dead by now, and there should be a record of their death. If there isn't one, there's your man. Find somebody who lived here, but doesn't seem to have died. It shouldn't take so long."

CHICAGO—American Bar Association
leaders held today that there was
no reason why lawyers should not
take anti-Communist oaths.

Chapter Forty-Two

It took about four hours, at the end of which McIntire possessed a list showing every taxpayer in Flambeau County as it existed in 1934. Now all he needed to do was discover which of them were from households that included males over eighty years of age and hope the mystery man had been a resident of Flambeau County. That might turn the four hours into four years. But Leonie's original premise was a good one, and if he limited himself to St. Adele Township, population three hundred fifty, he had a fighting chance.

According to his calculations, the St. Adele personal property tax rolls, and the 1930 census report, the number of males over age seventy-five—might as well be on the safe side—numbered seventeen. Eliminating those he was positive, from personal knowledge, had not died in the arms of Rose Falk left McIntire with eleven possibilities.

Birth and death certificates were filed and recorded by the township clerk before being turned over to the county. That meant that McIntire had only to locate those record books rather than seek out the certificates themselves. Those books, up to and including 1945, were stored right here in the county courthouse.

Each of the eleven possibilities was represented by an entry in one of the books. The entries were numbered consecutively beginning with the first death of the year, included the date the death certificate was received, and each entry was signed by the township clerk. One of the elderly had died in 1934. Einar Hegstrom had succumbed to heart failure. Didn't everyone, when it came down to it? That was in late June.

The next octogenarian death was entry number two of 1935, filed July first. Dr. Cedric Hudson had drowned.

McIntire had a single vivid memory of the doctor who'd preceded Guibard. Hudson had come to the house when McIntire had an earache. While he rocked in agony, the doctor, ancient even then in Johnny McIntire's eleven-year-old eyes, had heated one of his mother's darning needles in the flame of a kerosene lamp. It glinted in the light as he held it up. "Hold him still." McIntire had screwed his eyes shut and pressed his face into his mother's arm. A lightning bolt of pain, a pop deep inside his head, and it was over. When he opened his eyes, his savior was turned away, dabbing a handkerchief at a streak of yellowish brown on his white shirt front. Sophie McIntire had turned down the doctor's suggestion that he do the other ear "just in case."

The only other thing McIntire knew about the doctor, or thought he knew, was that he'd drowned when his car went through the ice. Even in Lake Superior that didn't generally happen in July.

McIntire went in search of the ponytailed assistant registrar, Pamela, to ask that she fetch the death certificate. Then he went in search of a chair to settle himself in for the wait. It was less than an hour. Pamela was mastering her trade, or at least the alphabet.

The date of Hudson's birth was listed as December 20, 1848, which would have made him eighty-six when he died, of drowning, on—McIntire looked again—November 3, 1934. So he hadn't gone through the ice after all, even the bay wouldn't have been frozen by that time, but he also hadn't lived until the following July when the certificate was filed.

McIntire felt a tap on his shoulder and gave a leap.

"Must be some great reading if a guy my size can sneak up on you." Pete Koski leaned against the table. "What's up?"

"Do you remember a Cedric Hudson? Lived out my way and drowned in nineteen thirty-four."

"Before my time. Why?"

"He was a doctor. At least he claimed to be. I think I'll take a stroll over to Teddy Falk's sanctuary and find out if Hudson ever treated his wife."

"Falk's getting out. There ain't no point in keeping up feeding him 'til we got some evidence to charge him. He's got too many people interested in him to go anywhere. And I'll just be hanging on to his car for a while. That's why I came looking for you. To see if you can give him a ride out to—guess where."

"Pelto."

"Bingo."

McIntire stood up. "Let Teddy know I'll be back for him in a half hour. I'm going over to the newspaper office for a bit."

McIntire said hello to Clayton Beckman and descended to the basement cubicle where seventy-five years' worth of the *Chandler Monitor* was stacked on pine plank shelving, more or less in chronological order. It was front page news, November 5, 1934. As three witnesses looked on "aghast," Cedric Hudson, retired physician, had taken his fishing boat onto Lake Superior in a raging gale, where it had filled with water and sunk "with awe-inspiring speed beneath the icy waves," in an estimated sixty feet of water. Which meant—same old words, same old tune—his body wouldn't have been recovered. At least not until the following spring or summer.

McIntire put his question to Falk before they were a half mile out of town.

"I don't remember Rosie ever seeing a doctor. She didn't get sick." Falk used his mitten to wipe at the side window. "I'd forgot how much snow you get here."

"I forget every summer," McIntire told him. "It's a surprise every year. Do you remember Cedric Hudson at all?"

"I don't think so, but I didn't live here that long. I only moved here when I married Rose."

"How did you meet your wife? Your first one, that is."

Falk didn't show surprise at McIntire's knowledge of his second marriage. "Finn Hall."

The silence stretched. Falk cleared his throat. "I didn't expect to ever get back to America. Rose left me. There wasn't any reason I shouldn't have got married again."

"No," McIntire said. "I guess not. I shouldn't have mentioned it." He tapped the brakes and lurched across an icy patch. "I understand your second wife is still in her home country."

Falk's response was a movement of his head that could have been a nod. McIntire didn't bother to express sympathy, or to ask how Falk had managed to get out of the Soviet Union. He wouldn't get the truth. He wondered if anybody from the FBI had questioned the man while he was in jail—had tried to find some link between the two of them.

Falk pulled a pack of Luckys from his shirt pocket. "I got two kids. I guess I'll never see them again."

Once again McIntire felt chagrin over his thick-headedness. Of course Teddy might not have come here by choice, other than a choice between the U.S., leaving a hostage family behind, and a Soviet prison or worse. What would happen to him and to his family now, with Melvin Fratelli on his tail?

"I'm sorry."

"They don't know I'm here. They think I'm dead."

"I'm sorry," McIntire said again.

He left Falk at the end of Pelto's driveway and headed for the narrow road that ran past the tavern formerly owned by Colin McIntire and down to the lakeshore. To the northeast, beyond the narrow bay with its village of ice fishing shanties, Lake Superior lay hard and blue, and benign. Not a swallower of old men. He shivered.

He turned in at Mark Guibard's icicle-wreathed house.

He expected to find the doctor with a chair drawn up to the table near the window, reading his newspaper or playing a game of solitaire while he watched the sun setting behind the hills. A glass and a crumb-filled plate testified that Guibard had been in his customary spot, but the paper next to them was still folded, and the cards were in the box.

He pulled out a chair for McIntire and fetched another glass.

"We figured it was suicide." Guibard squinted to pour two precise measures of the Canadian whiskey. "He headed straight out into the lake. The boat flipped and sank out of sight."

"Whose sight?"

"What's that?"

"Who were the three aghast witnesses?"

"Elsie Karvonen and one of her kids, and somebody who'd come into the store. I forget who. Cedric went out onto the bay in one hell of a gale and made a bee-line for the open lake. I suppose he could have passed out or something, had a heart attack or stroke maybe, but I'd put my money on suicide. He sure as hell wasn't out there fishing. And he'd shown some signs—getting his house in order, withdrawn."

"I don't suppose his body turned up?"

"No."

"But you signed a death certificate."

"We had an inquest. All the evidence was that he was dead. He had a grandson that wanted it official."

"Did Hudson have false teeth?"

"Damned if I know. John, if you figure this has something to do with Rose Makinen, forget it. Hudson didn't die until sometime late in the fall."

"When did he stop practicing medicine?"

"Practicing, good word for it. He never really got past the practicing stage, and practice did not make perfect. Maybe I shouldn't speak ill of the dead, but the man was worthless! He didn't have any real training that I know of. He worked for a couple of the mining companies, and took outside patients, too. People went to him because he was all they could get. It wasn't long after I took over in Chandler that he retired and moved out here full time, into the old lighthouse. Not the old lighthouse that's there now, the one on the other side of the point."

McIntire nodded. The *really* old lighthouse. Ironically, it had washed away in a storm.

"It was a nice spot. Nothing there now. He didn't practice medicine after he came here...to any extent...only...." Guibard shuffled his deck of cards. "Maybe you *should* find out about his teeth."

"Who would know? Except you. Did you ever treat him? Get him to open his mouth and say aaah?"

"No, I didn't, and he lived to be a hell of a lot older than the majority of my patients."

"And died still able to get out in his boat."

"People better look out, I'm going to be back at it again."

"Back at what?"

"Curing or killing. It's happened, Palmerson's been called up."

The world was going straight to hell. Old deaths were the best deaths. "Maybe it won't be for so long."

"I ain't counting on it. Take your vitamins."

"Back to the other doctor," McIntire said. "Karvonen's store must be a half-mile from the lighthouse."

Guibard nodded. "More like three-quarters."

"So anybody watching from the store could have seen Hudson's boat on the lake, but wouldn't have been able to tell for sure who was in it."

"I guess not."

"And his body never washed up?"

"You gonna start looking for another stiff, count me out."

"Maybe it was Jack Stewart," McIntire said. "Sorry."

"That boat and whoever was in it," Guibard pointed out, "went into the lake two or three months after Rose Falk died. If Hudson had been gone all that time wouldn't somebody have noticed?"

"Nobody noticed Rosie missing."

"Because people expected her to be gone."

That was only partly true. Rose had family and friends who expected her to be away, right enough, but they knew where she should be and they might have expected to hear from her.

Presumably that was true of Hudson, also. That grandson, for instance. "Who would be most likely to have missed Doctor Hudson?" he asked.

Guibard scratched the back of his neck. "You might have a point. Old Cedric wasn't the sociable sort."

WASHINGTON—The new senate
Communist Investigating Sub-com-
mittee may reopen the investigation into the communists-in-gov-
ernment charges by Senator Joseph
McCarthy (R-Wis.).

Chapter Forty-Three

Mia stared into the open cupboard. It was looking more Mother Hubbardish every day. And she was getting hungrier every day. She was beginning to get an inkling of the way many of her neighbors lived. The way Nelda Stewart had probably lived most every day of her life. No, that was stupid. Her and Nick's hardships weren't even close to Nelda's and a lot of others she could name. Yet.

But there was no yeast. They'd have to make do with baking powder biscuits. Which meant she'd need to wait until Nick tore himself away from hacking at those trees and could go to the cellar for some milk. At the rate he was working, he might have the job done by 1960. He was probably in no rush, he'd nothing better to do and it gave him an excuse to stay out of the house.

His back was turned toward her and he was bent down, struggling to use the buck saw with only one hand. She knew that if he turned, the face she saw would be that of a stranger. If she could bear to look at it at all.

She put her fingers to her chest, where the tiny lock of hair lay next to her heart. A soft, warm part of her baby, her tiny perfect Nicola, and he'd kept it from her. It would be with her forever now.

The irregular rasp of the saw was drowned by the grumble of an approaching car. The arrow-shaped nose of John McIntire's Studebaker appeared from behind the snowbank and turned into the driveway with Leonie at the wheel. She was brave enough, or foolhardy enough, to plow her way through the snow-choked driveway to stop near the house. It gave Mia no time to sweep the crumbs from the table or pick up the dirty towels, but for once she didn't care. If Leonie McIntire was offended by the disorder in Mia's kitchen, let her stay in her own. If she was fussy, she might just try muddling along with a broken leg and a helpless husband, herself. She'd see how her own kitchen ended up.

"I'm on my way to town, Mia, and I stopped to see what I could pick up for you." Leonie smiled and touched Mia's arm, but the words were more of an order than an expression of neighborliness.

"I could use some yeast."

"Milk?"

"We buy it from Irene Touminen. She's been bringing a quart over every couple of days." And it was now in the cellar, Mia remembered. "Do you have time for coffee?"

Leonie hesitated for just a moment. "Yes, thank you. That would be lovely."

She didn't insist on brewing it herself, did not even offer to lend a hand as Mia hobbled to the stove.

She sat at the table and waited while Mia thumped about, getting spoons and filling the cups.

"If you take cream, I'm afraid you'll have to get it from the cellar." Leonie took milk, and Leonie knew that Mia liked cream in her coffee.

"Black will be just fine." Mia was foiled.

It wasn't like Leonie to be insensitive or stubborn. Mia wondered if she'd offended her some way.

They sipped at the bitter liquid.

"It must be awful for you cooped up inside like this, unable to work."

She'd hit the nub of it. Mia found that more than anything, she felt the need to make something. Anything. A maple chest or a loaf of bread, it didn't really matter. She was having a hard time doing either.

Leonie asked, "Wouldn't you like to come with me?"

Amazingly, Mia discovered that she would have liked that very much. But by the time she got herself presentable the sun would be going down. "I don't think crutches and ice are a very good combination."

"No. Perhaps not." Leonie nodded.

"I'll have the cast off in another ten days."

"And looking forward to that I'm sure." She touched the rim of her cup to her lips, then set it down as if she'd suddenly remembered some pressing question. "Mia," she asked, "do you remember a doctor who used to live here, a Mr. Hudson?"

Mia nodded. She remembered him, not with fondness. "He lived in the old lighthouse place. He drowned when his boat sank in a storm." A more recent memory intruded into Mia's consciousness before it flickered out.

"John and Mr. Guibard think maybe he didn't. They think he might have been the man in the well with Rosie."

"Rosie in bed with Dr. Hudson? They've lost their minds! Besides, he died long after she did."

"A couple of months later, and his body was never found."

"Elsie Karvonen saw it happen, and his glasses and some of his clothes did wash up.... No! It couldn't be. Rose Falk was *not* having an affair with Cedric Hudson!"

"Maybe she had gotten sick and called him out."

"We didn't have phones then. If Rose had been sick, somebody would have taken her into town. If she was too sick for that, she'd have had to send for a doctor, and that would have been Guibard or his partner, Doctor Monroe. Not Hudson. Nobody sent for Hudson. Not when they were sick."

"But Guibard was living in Chandler then, almost twenty miles away. Even if Mr. Hudson was old and out of practice, if Rose was desperate...."

"If she was having some sort of emergency, somebody else would have had to go for a doctor, whoever that doctor was."

Leonie relented. "And that person shouldn't have had any reason to keep it to himself."

"Or herself."

"If he or she is still living."

"You have a point."

"Oh dear!" Leonie took a final microscopic sip and leapt up. "I'm afraid I've been gabbing instead of drinking this lovely coffee and need to be off straight away." She slipped into her coat and, after begging the promise of a recipe or two, was out the door.

Mia watched as she backed the car down the winding drive-way. All four tires stayed neatly in the tracks.

Cedric Hudson. Where had she...? She slid her chair to the pot-bellied heater and pitched in the last two chunks of birch from the woodbox. Then she hoisted herself onto her crutches once more and stumped to the living room.

Her grandmother's jewel case still sat on the table. A case her father *had* opened. She carried evidence of that next to her heart. She lifted the lid and took out the watch. Her father would have loved that watch. If it belonged to him he wouldn't have hidden it away, even if it had been left to him by a mother he hadn't spoken to in...how long? She didn't know. Since his marriage most probably. Was it really Charlotte Vogel's Indian-ness that had estranged them? It seemed inconceivable that a mother could end all contact with the child she'd borne simply because of his choice of a wife.

Mia couldn't begin to know why he'd put the watch away any more than why he'd conspired with Nick to hide the lock of her daughter's hair from her. Or Rose Falk's money. She thought her father had been a friend to Ted and Rose Falk. She thought that he was a generous person who tried to see the good, and appeal to the sensible, in everybody. Now she was finding that there was another side to him, but she'd always known that there was one person Eban Vogel truly hated. If he'd gone over to see how Rose was getting along with her husband away and found that she was ill or had some sort of accident, the last person on earth he'd have called upon for help would have been Doctor Cedric Hudson.

Ornate engraving covered the front of the watch case. With some imagination it could represent an H intertwined with a C. Inside, the watch face said that it was a *Russel keyless chronograph*.

The back opened in the same way as the front to reveal the wheels and gears of the watch's inner workings. Mia wound the screw and set it into motion. Two covers were hinged at the back. She closed the inner one over the clicking gears. On the inner surface of the silver cover were engraved words which left no doubt as to the owner of the spectacular timepiece.

Presented to ASST. Surg. C. Hudson J.M.P in acknowledgement of his valuable services as assistant to Civil Surgeon by BR. Surg. Lt. Col. Carnegie, September 1894.

WASHINGTON—Secretary of State
Dean Acheson yesterday compared
Russian and American atomic potential now as like that of a BB gun
and a .38 caliber revolver.

Chapter Forty-Four

Alien Finn Free on Bail. No photo this time. McIntire spread
the week's issue of the *Monitor* on the table. Erik Pelto had been
ordered to deport himself, but was released on three thousand
dollars bond pending appeal.

An article further down the page stated that the body found
in a St. Adele Township well was thought to be that of an elderly
male, and anyone with information should come forward. It
added that the victim would have been missing since the late
summer of 1934 and wore a set of "antique"dentures.

"Do you think he'll come back?"

McIntire could only assume his wife was referring to Pelto,
not the owner of those dentures. "I suppose he will. I don't expect
we'll be murdered in our beds."

The rhythmic squeak of her ironing board ceased and McIntire
looked up.

"I didn't imply that we might." The iron hovered a few inches
above the board. Leonie's expression said she might like to use
it on him, rather than his shirt.

"I didn't mean anything by it."

"Except that I'm a chicken little." She brushed the curls back
from her damp forehead. "If we were murdered in our beds, we
wouldn't be the first. Not even the first to be murdered in our

beds by a communist. You might be more concerned if your children were less than a thousand miles from the Soviet border. You might be more concerned about it if you *had* children."

"I need to go out," he said. What he needed to do was change the subject. "I'll try to find out if Cedric Hudson could have been dead for three months when he took that boat ride."

She pressed the point of the iron into the starched collar of his white dress shirt. The one he'd broken out for Nelda Stewart's funeral. He hoped it could be put away again for a good long time.

"Leonie, are you going to tell me what's wrong?"

"Nothing is wrong. Go off and take care of your investigating."

She couldn't be convinced to say more. McIntire went off to take care of his investigating.

As people pass through life, they leave tracks. If one had passed through and out, what sort of things would have disappeared with them? Bills. Had Hudson paid his bills? Who would he owe? No electricity in 1934, no bottled gas, no telephone. That epitome of certainty, taxes—it seemed even death is not so incontrovertible as it might be—would have been due in January. Did Hudson get any kind of pension? From the mining companies? He must have had some sort of bank account. Had he taken out money? Written a draft or two? Guibard said witnesses testified that he'd been withdrawn before his fatal trip. What did that mean exactly? Had he been moody, antisocial? Or had he been so damn withdrawn that no one had seen him?

The doctor answered the door in slippers and a flannel bathrobe. He led McIntire to a table, shoved aside a stack of mail, and poured coffee into two mugs.

"The records of the inquest should still be at the court house. But as I recall it, there were people who testified that Hudson hadn't been showing up in his usual haunts."

"Which were?"

"I don't remember. He probably would have stopped in at your old man's place now and then. I don't know where else. He wasn't a church goer."

"If he died in November, there might have been quite a bit of snow on the ground."

"Probably. We can check the newspapers."

"The driveway into the lighthouse must be a couple of hundred yards. Who would have done the plowing?"

"The county did it. But you're on the right track. They'd have plowed the driveway, but nothing else. If the car was just sitting all that time, getting buried in snow, no path to the door, somebody should have noticed."

"Somebody put that boat in the lake, and that somebody could have made sure it looked like Hudson was still around until they did it," McIntire said.

"Gone over and shoveled him out?"

"He was old. Maybe he usually got somebody to take care of it for him. Who'd remember after all this time?"

"Whoever it was that did it should remember, if he's still alive."

"No smoke from the chimney?"

"I don't know! We were looking for evidence to confirm that Hudson was dead *after* he went in the lake, not that he'd been alive before that."

It was true, they'd had no reason to think that Hudson's fishing boat had gone out empty.

Guibard added, "He might have heated with kerosene. The lightkeeper's house wasn't meant to be lived in during the winter."

It would have had a chimney. Presumably the residents had to cook. "Why was he living way out here anyway? What would a doctor be doing here?"

"Excuse me?"

"You said he wasn't one of those who lived to fish."

"He didn't even fish to live. The house didn't have so much as a hook in it."

"I suppose the boat turned up?"

"Three weeks later. In Thunder Bay. His coat washed up on shore here a few days after he disappeared. His glasses were still in the pocket."

"Back to my question. What *was* he doing here in the middle of nowhere?"

"Hiding out, in a manner of speaking. He came in 1914 or so, about the time of the strikes. You remember?"

"Barely. I was too young to take much interest, and we were pretty well out of it here. Long as folks kept on drinking, the strikes didn't affect the McIntires."

"There was a murder in Painesdale."

McIntire did remember that. Shots fired into a boarding house killed two English miners, strike breakers, as they slept, both hit with the same bullet. A little girl in the house was injured, and maybe a couple of others.

"They arrested three people. One of them—an Austrian—broke out of jail, and they never did catch him. Hudson was a star witness at the trial that got the other two convicted. After that he retired and moved out to the lighthouse. His wife died a few years before he did. Once she was gone he pretty much kept to himself." Guibard was silent for a time, perhaps thinking of the parallels between Hudson's life and his own. He gave a shrug. "I see by the *Monitor* that our Alien Finn is on the loose. I suppose he'll be back among us."

It was a discussion McIntire wasn't eager to get into again. He pushed back his chair and got to his feet.

"And J. Theodore's out too." Guibard wasn't to be discouraged. "There are some stories going around, speculation on what might have happened, that maybe whatever brought on the murders started way back. Something with Falk and Orville Pelto maybe."

"Orville and the Falks would have been on the same side."

"They would have, and that would have been the wrong side to a hell of a lot of people. There were bad feelings stirred up in those organizing days. The unions might have won out in the end, but people still connect them with communism."

"That's not surprising. There *was* a connection."

"It might be better for Pelto and Teddy Falk to be somewhere else."

"They're out of jail on bond. I don't suppose traveling is something either of them is at liberty to do."

"Maybe not. It might not be pleasant for them around here." Guibard stood and tightened the belt on his robe. "Or for their friends."

"Is there perhaps some particular friend you have in mind?"

"Word is out that you speak the language, and I don't mean Finn. You and Teddy Falk both turned up back here about the same time. People are wondering how you knew that Rose Falk was dead and where to look for her."

"We did *not* turn up at the same time," McIntire insisted. Not as far as anyone in St. Adele knew anyway. "And why would one of Teddy Falk's trusted comrades be the one to unearth his wife's dead body?"

"The evidence is long gone. He'll inherit."

"Inherit what?"

"People don't think that far ahead."

"People don't think at all." McIntire picked up his gloves from where they lay next to the doctor's opened mail. The flamboyance of the signature on the official-looking letter caught his eye. Rigid lines in blue ink over the typewritten, *Patrick J. Humphrey, Attorney at Law.*

ENDICOTT, N.Y.—Dr. David Bradley, a physicist who observed early atomic tests, said yesterday he believed recent explosions in Nevada were tests of hydrogen-type bombs.

Chapter Forty-Five

The sky was the untrammeled crystal blue of the lake. The cold hit McIntire like a knife to the eyeballs—not the dreary grey chill of Europe, sneaking around corners and up trouser legs, seeping into your soul. This bold and merciless frigidity stood up and faced you head on. A worthy opponent to engage in battle. Or to be sensible and stage a retreat from.

What about his newly gained knowledge? Would retreating from it, dismissing his wife's call from a lawyer, a man she claimed never to have heard of, be the sensible thing to do? Had it been a mistake as she said? Or had Leonie simply lied to him?

At least it wasn't snowing. He might as well take the opportunity of the break to make that trek to the Flambeau County courthouse one more time. One last time, he hoped. If Guibard was right, maybe he would be considered too subversive to be trusted with the lofty position of constable and this particular monkey would slide off his back to make room for the troop that was scrambling to climb on. Of course the pragmatic townfolk would be unlikely to go to the trouble of replacing him this close to election time.

First he drove back to his house. He wouldn't make the mistake of leaving without issuing an invitation to Leonie to accompany him on this trip.

Funnily, she didn't seem to be at home. The house was empty and the barn contained only the two grain mills on hooves. The tread marks of unfamiliar tires showed in the snow. Someone must have picked her up. Maybe she'd run off with her attorney. McIntire left another note. More than his wife had done for him.

◇◇◇

Cedric Hudson had not paid his personal property taxes for 1934, but they wouldn't have been due until the first part of January. Nor did his name appear on the voting rolls for November's election.

Just as McIntire was about to offer to help in her search, Pamela produced the transcribed proceedings of the Flambeau County coroner's inquest into the disappearance of Doctor Cedric Hudson.

It contained little more than Guibard had told him. A notarized affidavit signed by Colin McIntire attested that Dr. Hudson had not stopped in at the Lake Superior Tavern in the weeks before his boat was seen sinking into the waters of the lake. Another from a Bruce C. Hudson stated that when he'd written to settle the particulars of his grandfather's usual autumn visit, he'd received no reply.

Elsie Karvonen testified that she had glanced out a window in the second-floor living quarters of her store to see a small boat on the lake. She'd assumed it came from the lighthouse and been surprised because it was almost dark, there was a strong wind and she didn't figure either Cedric Hudson or his dinky little boat could handle the waves. She'd yelled for her young daughter, Gilette, who came upstairs with Ray Hanson. Ray had been in the store buying a can of kerosene and some molasses. They watched the boat head straight out into the open water. All of a sudden, before their very eyes, it disappeared "like a rock."

Her story was backed up by Gilette and Mr. Hanson.

Kaarlo and Betty Saarinen said that they had seen Dr. Hudson from a distance, a couple of weeks before, poking around his yard. He had on the baggy coat and hat he always wore when he went out, but he'd only waved and headed into that funny little house.

Cecilia Torvinen testified that, while out walking along the lakeshore not far from the town hall, she'd found a black coat with a pair of spectacles in the pocket. George Armstrong Wall—Walleye—McIntire's predecessor, said that after asking "everybody and their brother" he'd determined that both the coat and the glasses had been the property of Cedric Hudson. A landing net found a quarter-mile down the shore could have come from anywhere, although nobody claimed to have lost one. The boat had so far not turned up.

McIntire stood up and strolled to the cobweb-curtained window. From now on he was going to start paying more attention to people. Look for that spark of life in their eyes. Maybe a judicious pinch now and then. Alive or dead? He wasn't taking anything for granted.

A black Buick pulled into the parking area below. Melvin Fratelli got out of the driver's seat looking a good deal more svelte than his usual outdoor self. He must have gotten that heater fixed. The man who emerged, blinking at the light, from the other side of the car was wrapped more snugly, but was not so well covered that McIntire didn't recognize him immediately as the reason Fratelli knew so much, and so little, about his recent past.

McIntire stepped back from the window. Had they come looking for him? Probably not. No one but Leonie knew he'd come here, and she only knew if she'd seen his note. She wouldn't "rat to the coppers," as she'd love saying. But they'd be on his trail. Big Bad Buster's being here wasn't a coincidence.

He could slip out and be long gone before they got a sniff of him.

No, he couldn't. The two agents—and McIntire had no doubt that was Buster's line of work—circled his Studebaker like a pair of horse traders. After a short consultation, staring at their feet, hands in pockets, Fratelli handed over the car keys and continued to the courthouse door, while his partner returned to the vehicle. Buster apparently wasn't any more eager for a reunion than was McIntire. But if it had to be, it might as well be on McIntire's terms.

He left the files on the table and bounded down the stairs.

Buster huddled behind the wheel, engine idling, his face hidden by a copy of the *Marquette Mining Journal*. McIntire opened the door and slid onto the seat beside him.

"Buster, old buddy! You're a sight for sore eyes. Haven't seen you in a coon's age. Come up in the world since scrubbing floors and wrestling loonies into straitjackets, I see."

"Have we met?" The words were clipped and came through a wiggle at the corner of his lips.

"Ma mentioned you called. Nice of you to want to look me up."

Agent Buster sighed and folded his paper. "Shut the goddamn door."

McIntire did as he was bid. "What in hell are you up to? No, never mind. I know what you're up to now. What were you up to then?"

"Wilhelm Reich."

McIntire nodded. More or less the same reason he'd been there. In the beginning, at least.

He wouldn't soon forget his first sight of the Marlboro State Hospital, a sprawling structure of brick and timbers, its Tudor grimness in contrast to the light streaming from every window. Home to hundreds of more or less insane individuals and to a few enlightened physicians who followed the principles developed by Doctor Wilhelm Reich.

The U.S. government had had its eye on Reich since he'd been hounded out of Norway in 1939. The suspicions weren't political. The good doctor had made a name for himself as a proponent of free love. Everything from raving psychosis to hangnails could be put down to sexual repression. Who knew what such radical ideas might lead to? What sort of degradation might be imposed on the social structure of the Land of the Free and the Home of the Brave? And who better to pose as one of those repressed males than middle-aged, never wed, social stiff-neck John McIntire? It'd get him out of the mess in London. They'd put him in under a fake identity. A couple weeks should do it, then he could make that long-overdue visit to his parents in Michigan. It stretched from the end of winter and into spring.

The agent pulled a smoldering cigarette from the overflowing ashtray. "How for Christ's sake can you live in a place like this? This is all that's keeping my lungs from turning to icebergs." He took a long drag and seemed to swallow the smoke. "I told Mel you were just an ordinary nut," he said.

"Good."

"He convinced me otherwise."

McIntire didn't know if that was good news or bad. It depended on what that "otherwise" turned out to be. "What's Fratelli's theory?"

"That you were a patient at the Marlboro State Hospital at the behest of the State Department or the KGB…or maybe both."

"What about battle fatigue?"

"You ain't never been near a battle."

"There are all sorts of battles."

"Not to the U.S. Army, there ain't."

That was true enough. "You were a decent guy, Buster. You should have gone over to riding herd on the insane full time and given up working for them."

"Shit! Don't know how the hell people can keep that up, either." He studied McIntire's face. "You weren't so crazy as some," he said. "But you were crazy enough. If you were faking it, you oughta get an Oscar."

"Thanks."

"But if you weren't faking, if you were a psychotic on the up and up, it'd be in your army records. And it ain't. So which was it?"

"I wish I knew," McIntire answered. He opened the door. "Give my best to your partner." The agent nodded and put out his hand. "Joe Hayward."

"You'll always be Big Bad Buster to me." McIntire left the cozy Buick and sat listening to his teeth chatter in his own car as he let the engine warm up.

Buster, or Joe, if that was his real name, fit the mold of G-man precisely, just as he had that of mental ward attendant. Odd that they should be so similar.

How much had McIntire been acting, and how much was genuine? If his craziness act had seemed a *tour de force*…. He didn't recall having had to put much effort into behaving like a neurotic. No late-night rehearsal sessions. Had he really been so convincingly off his rocker? Well, they hadn't kept him around for three months because of his good looks.

The agent hurried into the courthouse, and McIntire headed home.

The former Buster might have been the FBI's source of information about McIntire's sojourn in a state hospital, but that didn't explain why Fratelli had gone looking for the information in the first place. Surely the U.S. government didn't figure Soviet agents were posing as mental cases to infiltrate asylums. Well, maybe it did. The State Department had done exactly that when they sent McIntire in. But had Agent Fratelli just been trolling for Reds, hoping to make a big catch, when he stumbled onto McIntire's non-connection with Teddy Falk, or was he really after something specific? Probably the former. Finnish-Americans had long been the core of the country's Communist Party. Flambeau County was handy, and Fratelli might consider it as good a place as any to drop a line in the water.

An unfamiliar car sat in McIntire's driveway. He considered driving by and stalling for a while. He wasn't in the mood for company or door-to-door salesmen. But he was cold, hungry, tired, and had no place else to go. He pulled in behind the two-tone spruce-green and grey Nash.

The smile he pasted on his face as he opened the door went for naught. The kitchen was empty. The pile of recipes on the table had grown. Leonie hummed as she came up the basement stairs. At least she'd faced up to whatever goblins lay for her there.

He took the fruit jars from her hands. "Who belongs to the snazzy car?"

"It's mine."

McIntire wasn't sure he'd ever been struck speechless before. She looked serious.

"I bought it in Ishpeming. Mr. Davis brought it out today." She sounded serious, too. "I thought it was time I had my own."

"Why?"

"So I don't have to ask to use yours."

"You don't ask."

"Are you saying I should?"

This time McIntire remained silent out of discretion. Leonie leafed through the recipes. "I need to be able to get around." She examined a penciled scrawl. "It's not fair for me to take your car every time I want to go somewhere."

"It looks like a nice car." It did. It made the Studebaker look like a soup can on wheels.

"You can use it any time you like." She smiled.

"Thanks."

"Look at this. It's a recipe for goose blood soup. Do you think it's a joke?"

"Who's it from?"

"Marge Arvidson."

"It's no joke."

Leonie wrinkled her nose. She went back to shuffling the papers. "Mia phoned. She asked if you would stop over as soon as you get back."

"For what?"

"She didn't say."

"Nick?"

It took her attention off the recipes. "I doubt it. Why would she call you about Nick?"

"Maybe it's about getting his car out of the creek. No doubt there've been complaints." McIntire got to his feet. He was ready for this day to be over.

"You can take my car if you like."

McIntire got back into his coat and his own car.

WASHINGTON—The U.S. is now ready
to try for actual construction
of the world's first known atomic-
powered aircraft engine.

Chapter Forty-Six

It was beginning to look a little bit like a mitten…or maybe a sock. Mia sighed and speared her knitting needles into the ball of yarn. She leaned closer to the window. The pile of burning branches made an inviting oasis in the evening gloom and threw a glow onto Nick's face. Green pine spit out sporadic gales of sparks. It would be nice to stand in the glow of that fire. It would be nice to stand anywhere on her own feet, by a fire, at the sink, here at the window. It didn't matter.

Car lights arced across the snow. She watched as John McIntire parked close to the house and got out. Nick lifted a tin cup in his direction. John hesitated before nodding in return and trudging onto the porch.

Mia left the window and opened the door before he knocked.

His took off his glasses. His eyes had dark circles. "That was quick. You must be getting to be a dab hand with the crutches."

A dab hand? She assumed that was good. "I'm making Guibard cut this thing off in a day or two," she told him. "It's only been a month, but I can't handle it any more."

"A month? Is that all?"

"It was a couple of days after the ice storm."

He shook his head. "It seems like years since those trees toppled and the world went to hell."

Her world was about to disintegrate even further. There was no point in putting it off. "Have a chair. I've got something for you." She clumped toward the living room, asking over her shoulder, "Want coffee?"

"No, thanks. I've been out all day. I need to get home." He sounded tired and indifferent, almost irritated. Mia felt a sudden burning of tears. It hadn't been easy to make that call. She should have gone straight to the sheriff. Maybe even Cecil Newman. Cecil would be interested. Cecil would crawl over burning coals to get to her.

The watch gleamed on its scrap of burnt-orange velvet. She could have thrown the damn thing in the lake. If he didn't care, why should she? Well, he was here now. It wouldn't make him any jollier to tell him to forget it. She folded the fabric over the watch and went back to the kitchen. He still stood near the stove wiping his glasses on the end of his scarf.

"Nick says Leonie bought a car," she said.

He nodded. "The whole neighborhood probably knew it before I did." He held a chair while she maneuvered into it.

"We have to be getting another one, too."

"Mia, is this about Nick's Dodge?"

Nick's Dodge?

"No." She tightened her grip on the watch, letting its screw cut into her flesh. "I've been sleeping in Papa's old bedroom," she explained, "because of my leg. There were boxes of his stuff there, old papers and things, so I decided to go...." His eyes were glazing over. She opened her hand. "It belonged to Doctor Hudson. It was with my father's things."

He only stared.

"If you're not interested—"

"Interested? Of course I'm interested. I'm just...." The smile brought him back to her. "Struck dumb. Twice in one day."

She picked up courage from his eyes. "My father had Rose Falk's money, and he had Cedric Hudson's watch."

"There might be some simple explanation."

"That's what I'm afraid of."

He sat and took the watch from her hand. "Mia, what possible reason could your father have had to kill Rose Falk and the naked doctor?"

Mia couldn't think that her father would ever have harmed Rose, but Cedric Hudson might be another matter. "Papa hated Hudson's guts," she said.

"Why? Because he worked for the mining companies?"

"No. That might not have helped, but…." How could she say this? "John, Hudson didn't come to live here until he was more or less retired from medicine. He'd never exactly been considered a terrific doctor, and once he got old…he might have been called out now and then, if somebody was really desperate, but otherwise, no." Mia felt her cheeks burn. "There's one thing he did keep doing."

"Which was?"

"Well, it was…women who were pregnant, if they didn't want to be, knew that's where they could go."

"He did abortions?"

"Ya."

"Abortions? You mean…? Why wasn't he ever prosecuted? Surely it was illegal."

"Of course it was illegal, but fairly common back then. Especially during the Depression. Everybody knew. When it comes to things like that, most people just look the other way."

"You make it sound no more out of the ordinary than going to the dentist."

"Dentist? Are you kidding? It wasn't anywhere near that unusual!" It was amazing how innocent men could be. "Hudson was reliable, far as I know. He kept his mouth shut, made house calls, and was reasonably priced. He was probably pretty much in demand." She pulled one of the needles out of the yarn. "And I expect even Hudson beat using one of these."

His wince was gratifying. "That's why Eban hated him?"

"Papa called him a butcher." Her hand went of its own accord to her chest. "If my father had gone over to see if Rose needed help with anything and found her dead or close to it, and Cedric Hudson there, *and* a loaded shotgun behind the door, he might very well have killed him. *I* might have killed him."

It brought only a nod. He asked, "How do you know for sure it's Hudson's watch?"

She flipped the back open and handed it to him. He read the inscription without comment. Didn't he see how it could have happened? She persisted, "Papa wasn't the kind to fly off the handle, but anybody in that situation would hardly be thinking clearly."

He turned the watch over in his palm, still silent. Mia said, "But he didn't. My father was not a murderer."

"From what you've been saying...how can you be so sure?"

Mia took a deep breath. It was only Johnny McIntire, after all. "My mother told me."

John only gave a grave smile. Maybe he was sort of "odd," as that FBI agent implied. If his acceptance of a chat with her mother was indication of his strangeness, what did that make her? She tried to explain, "The thing is, I can't think he'd have been so sneaky and cold-blooded about it, putting the bodies in the cistern, keeping the money and the watch, going over to clean up in Mike Maki's sauna, sending Hudson's boat out so it would look like he'd killed himself—" She stopped as she realized, "That doesn't add up."

"What?"

"Grace Maki says Papa came by about eleven that night. He took a sauna with Mike, and he told them about the mine disaster. If it had been Jack Stewart with Rose, Papa could have heard about the flooding from him, but he sure wouldn't have gotten the news from Cedric Hudson."

John rubbed at his eyes and replaced the glasses. "If your father didn't get to Maki's until eleven, it might have given him time to go somewhere else after leaving the Falks' place, before he got to Makis'. Maybe he heard about the accident later."

"Gone out for a drink to celebrate after blowing Hudson's head to smithereens, maybe?" What kind of person did he think her father had been? "How could Papa have killed Rose and dumped her body in a hole, and then just headed off to catch up on the latest gossip as if nothing had happened? And how could he have faced Teddy the next day and never let on a thing?"

The springs on the storm door squeaked and Nick's coughing sounded in the porch. Mia hadn't shown him the watch. She resisted the urge to snatch it up and stick it quick behind her back.

"Why is it, no matter which side of a fire you stand on, you get the smoke in your face?" As her husband came into the room, John wrapped the velvet around the watch and slipped it into his pocket.

Nick's eyes were rimmed with red, and he smelled like a roast ham. "Hear your wife got a new car."

It seemed to be a touchy subject; John gave a nod and asked how the storm cleanup was coming along. Nick nodded in return.

"Nick," John said, "if the guy we're looking for was Cedric Hudson, it means he was gone weeks before he officially died. What about his mail? Was it piling up?"

"He never got any to speak of. Or sent any either. He had a long driveway and didn't come out to get his mail every day, so if there was some boxholder stuff left in it, I wouldn't have paid any attention."

Nick turned toward the door leading back to the porch and the cellar stairs. He hesitated and, despite everything, Mia felt the ache of his humiliation. He wouldn't try to tackle those stairs with John McIntire there, no matter how badly he wanted something at the bottom of them.

The cause of his indecision might have been something else. "You know," he said, "if it was Hudson with Rosie, there would have been only one reason for it."

"Mia just mentioned that," John said. "I don't suppose you heard any rumors to the effect that Rose was pregnant?"

"Not me," Nick replied. "Ask Ted. He says he's coming tomorrow to lend a hand with finishing up the sawing."

If Rose was pregnant and had gone to Dr. Hudson, her husband might well be the last person she'd tell. Once again Mia marveled at how naive the human male could be.

"I just might pay you another call." John still seemed exhausted and remote, but his brain was apparently working. "There's one more thing that doesn't add up," he continued. "What about Rose's farewell note?"

Mia had forgotten that. "We only have Teddy's word for it that she left a note," she said, "and if he came home and found his wife had bled to death thanks to Dr. Hudson, he'd have had a lot more reason to go for that shotgun than Papa would have."

"Teddy wasn't around three months later to fake Hudson's suicide," John said.

"And Papa was," Mia sighed. And Papa had his watch.

Nick retraced his steps, said goodnight, and disappeared into the living room. She didn't hear his footsteps on the stairs. McIntire stood up. "Fratelli been back to hobnob with you?"

"Not so far." He joked about it, but Mia couldn't help feeling he might do well to take it more seriously. "You know, John. If that guy talks to other people, he might get different answers from the ones I gave."

"Like what?"

Who knows? People talk. They do wonder what you were up to all that time you were away, and they can't figure why you decided to come back here of all places. I wonder about that, too, a little.

"Call it unfinished business."

What could he mean by that? Mia felt a flush of heat in her face for the second time that evening. "There's talk that maybe you should quit," she told him.

"Quit what?"

"Constable."

Now he did smile. *"There are gains for all our losses, There are balms for all our pain."*

He was her same old John, odd or not. "Say hello to your wife," Mia told him. "She sounded sort of strange when I called."

"It's been a long winter."

Nick hadn't been far off. He returned from the darkened living room, leaned heavily against the countertop to wash his hands under the tap. "What did he want?"

"I'm not sure." It was the best she could do.

He dried his hands carefully and moved a chair close to her. "I want to see it."

Mia's hand rose to her chest.

"She was mine, too. I want to see it." For the first time in weeks he looked straight into her eyes. "Please."

She untied the ribbon from her neck and opened the soft deerskin pouch. She placed the folded tissue on the table and opened it. The tiny wisp lay like angel's breath in its pink ribbon. Nick stretched a single finger towards it. His hand shook and he pulled it back. A second try failed. Mia ached to keep its softness, its silky blackness, for herself. He rested his hand, palm up, on the table. "Please," he said again.

He'd betrayed her, in this and so many other things. And he could remember. It wasn't fair that he should have both this part of their baby and memory of her, too. He'd forced Mia to live all these years, over half her life, with neither. Maybe if he'd given this to her then, if he hadn't taken away every trace of their Nicola, it might have awakened her own memories. But he'd kept it, hidden it away from her, and he'd hidden away his memories, too.

She plucked the lock from the tissue and watched his hand close over it. "Tell me," she whispered.

He didn't hesitate. "She was very, very small. Her hand was no bigger than my thumb. She had the tiniest, blackest eyebrows and her eyes were blue. She curled in your arms like a baby bear. You were so happy. You wouldn't put her down. You wouldn't let us—"

"No." She put her hand over his. "Tell about *her*. Tell me all about her."

NEWARK, N.J.—A former WAVE lieu-
tenant charged with being an unfit
mother because of "association
with communists" won postponement
of a child custody suit.

Chapter Forty-Seven

It would be the simple explanation, and the simple outcome. If Eban Vogel was shown to have committed this homicide, there'd be no arrest, no trial, nobody imprisoned, no complications. It would make things easier for a whole lot of people. Easier for everyone but Mia.

But if Rose Falk was pregnant and had died trying to end that pregnancy, any one of that seemingly bottomless font of male admirers could have lost his head, grabbed the shotgun, and the doctor would have been the next one to lose his head. They had no reason to believe it was Vogel any more than Orville Pelto or maybe Sulo. There was the little matter of the watch, of course. But they had been prepared to overlook Rose's property in Vogel's possession, so why not Hudson's watch?

The crime-of-passion hypothesis didn't explain why the dead abortionist was unclothed, or the note left for the husband, if there had been a note.

The distant whine of dueling chainsaws meant that Falk had made good on his promise to help with dismantling Thorsens' trees once and for all. McIntire put aside the velvet-wrapped timepiece and pulled on his overshoes.

◇◇◇

The two of them were going at it like a pair of mechanized beavers. The reignited brush pile shot flames twenty feet into the air. Acrid smoke battled with the heavy scent of pine.

"I guess it's not impossible. She could have been pregnant. She didn't tell me." Teddy brushed snow from the three-foot horizontal trunk and sat. "I don't really see how, though. We didn't…very much…Rose didn't…she didn't want a family."

To the point that she'd died trying to avoid it? McIntire asked, "Do you know why?"

Falk's skin was shiny with sweat and decorated with flecks of sawdust. "You wouldn't know it from how she acted. She wasn't bashful or anything. But Rose…the way she looked, it bothered her a lot. She was afraid a baby might be the same. Or even worse."

It was understandable, McIntire supposed. Were things like that hereditary?

"Especially when we started talking about going to Karelia. We knew it would be a tough life for a while. She didn't think there'd be a place for deformed children there."

She might have been right about that. "I don't suppose you still have her note?"

"I don't have anything I left this country with."

"Except your passport."

Falk must have been a hell of a poker player. "Ya. I got that," he said. "I don't have the letter, but I can tell you what it said. You don't forget a thing like that."

He proceeded. "'Dear Jimmy T.'" He flushed. At least she hadn't called him Teddy Bear. "'I'm sorry. I am leaving you. Don't feel too bad. There has been another man. Go to do our work without me. Have a glorious life.' She signed her name and under it she put, 'Please don't let anyone know what I've done, let Addie think we are together.' The 'please' was underlined. Three times. That was it."

"English or Finn?"

"English. That was the only thing that was a little funny."

The only thing? His wife leaves him a goodbye-forever note and it's the language that's a little funny? "You'd have expected the note to be in Finn?"

Falk nodded.

"Are you sure it was her handwriting?"

"Oh, ya, I guess so. It was a little shaky, but it was Rosie's writing. She'd missed a lot of school when she was a kid, and her penmanship wasn't so good. Nobody else would of wrote like that, unless it was a nine-year-old kid. English gave her more trouble. Too many letters that look alike, *g*s and *q*s and and *f*s and *b*s. When she wrote for the family it was always Finn."

I'm sorry I'm leaving you. There's been another man. Rose hadn't expressly said she was leaving Teddy in the company of that other man, and she'd died wearing her wedding ring. "She might have written those same words if she knew she was dying."

"She might have."

"You didn't think of that?"

"Hell, no! Why would I? She said there was another man and she was leaving me. She wasn't dead when I got back. She was gone!" A spark of temper from Falk at last.

"Did Rose show any sign of being pregnant?"

"Like what? She didn't get fat." He shrugged. "She kept to herself a lot."

So Rose could have been pregnant. The father of that child might have been someone other than her husband, still another reason she wouldn't have been pleased with her condition.

If not Teddy, who? Eban Vogel? Sulo Touminen? Orville Pelto? Maybe it was Jack Stewart, or how about Nick? He was the only notorious philanderer in the neighborhood so far as McIntire knew. How about Colin McIntire or the Fuller Brush man? It could have been any of them, none of them, or all of them. But they were all McIntire had to work with.

Of the front runners, Orville Pelto was the prime candidate. He was charming and persuasive, offered her travel and an exciting life, and he was the new boy in the neighborhood. Rose was an adventurer. She'd be attracted to novelty. If she'd wanted to fool around with any of the others, they would have been available for years. The pregnancy would have been instigated at about the time Orville was setting the Falks up for emigration, but too far in advance of their departure to be the result of a goodbye fling. Pelto was also the only person McIntire had spoken with who hadn't referred to Rose's ugliness. He'd only said she looked "different." And he was the only one who had never claimed to have conveniently forgotten the events surrounding her leaving. He'd told his story in perfect detail.

McIntire turned back to Falk. "How did your wife feel about Orville Pelto?"

"He might have run second to God or Karl Marx, but I doubt it." Falk stood up with a groan. "Jesus, I forgot what real work was like."

"Orville still around?"

"You maybe can catch him. He's heading back to Superior today."

Chapter Forty-Eight

The blanching of Pelto's wind-reddened cheeks when McIntire mentioned Rose Falk's possible pregnancy told McIntire what he wanted to know. Pelto added one more stick to the bundle of narrowly split birch cradled in his round-eyed grandchild's arms. "Take it to your mum." He turned back to McIntire. "Are you sure about this?"

"No," McIntire admitted, "but it's a strong possibility. The other victim was probably a Doctor Hudson. Hudson was a known…abortionist, I guess you'd have to say. Rose was terrified that any child she bore would inherit her cleft lip."

Pelto's own lip would be shredded if he chewed it any harder. "And you think maybe Rose died from whatever he did to her? She wasn't murdered after all?"

"There are those who would disagree, but, no," McIntire said, "there was no sign of injury on her remains, only a mattress stained with blood. Rose might not have died of natural causes, but she probably wasn't deliberately killed."

"I never could see how anybody would want to kill her."

"The doctor, on the other hand, had his head blown off. That was no accident."

"Maybe he did it himself. Despondent over what had happened."

"And put the shotgun back in the house just before he jumped into the well?"

"Yeah, I guess that's right."

The grandchild, boy or girl, McIntire couldn't tell, bundled as it was with little more than a red nose showing, charged back across the yard and began rummaging through the discarded ends of lumber at their feet.

Pelto removed a knife from his pocket. "Poor little Rosie," he said. "There's hardly been a day in the past sixteen years that I haven't thought about her and Ted. I talked them into leaving, them and a whole lot more like them. If they'd been shot or starved to death, I had to answer for it." He opened the knife and tested the blade on his thumb. "Makes me glad to be an atheist."

He seemed to be evading the point. He may not have sent Rose to starve in Soviet Karelia, but if she'd died aborting his infant, he was hardly absolved of complicity in her death.

The child extended a scrap of wood. "What's in it, Grandpa?"

Grandpa turned the wood over and peered at its cut ends. He held it up to the sun, as if he could see through its grain. "Well, Tony"—ah, a boy—"I can't be positive," he said gravely, "but I'm pretty sure it's a boreal owl."

"Aegolius funereus." The boy smiled, showing gaps a jack-o-lantern would be proud of. "Dad likes owls."

Pelto applied his knife to the wood. "It's been hard to grasp. All that time, wondering, imagining where she was, and she'd bled to death in her own bed and nobody knew it."

"Somebody knew. Somebody who cared enough for her to take revenge on Cedric Hudson."

"You thinking me, for instance?"

"You were with her that day."

"Until about noon." And he supposedly believed she was leaving a day or two later, yet he'd made no attempt to see her again, no saying goodbye.

"Where did you go after you dropped Rose at home?"

"What business is that of yours? Don't tell me you're investigating me?"

Anybody with Orville Pelto's political background knew his rights, among them that he didn't need to answer nosy questions from a passing township constable. Pelto surprised him by chipping away at his stick of wood and murmuring, "What did I do the rest of that day? I don't remember for sure. I took Rose home, and I felt a little down. We'd said goodbye, and I knew I'd probably never see her again. I must have gone into Chandler to file the Contract for Deed with the county. I would have picked up Erik from wherever he was."

"It was the day the Massey-Davis mine flooded."

It brought the former recruiter back to life. "Oh, Jesus, that's right. That's something I won't forget. It was hot as hell that afternoon. I fetched Erik and we stopped at the lake to cool off. Then I did go in to the court house. The cave-in happened around supper time. I went straight to the mine and stayed all night. They brought out seven men. That was all." He went back to talking to himself. "So when I was there, watching them pull those bodies out, Rose was dying, too."

"What about Erik?"

"What about him?"

"Was he with you?"

"No. Of course not. He was at home."

"By himself?"

"He was fifteen years old!"

He was. A grown man in those days. How much had Erik guessed about the extent of his father's friendship with Mrs. Falk?

"When we talked before, you said that Rose seemed happy that day, excited to be going?"

"She'd been nervy up to then. I thought she might back out. That day, when we went to wrap things up, get the papers signed, she seemed more her old self. I thought it had to do with leaving home. I suppose if she'd had another problem, and had come up with a way to solve it, that could account for the change."

It raised the question of why Rose had felt the problem to be entirely hers, one she needed to solve without help. She'd depended on Orville Pelto to take care of everything else. Why not this? A woman's mind was a hard thing to fathom, and Rose seemed inscrutable even to those who knew her best. Once again McIntire found himself wishing he'd been among them.

"You figure it was Teddy after all?" Pelto asked.

"No. It wasn't Teddy." McIntire was reasonably sure of that. "You might have had as much reason as Ted to kill Cedric Hudson. Maybe more."

The door opened and Delilah Pelto came out holding a sheet of paper, a sock monkey, and a well bundled baby. She placed the baby with its leggy companion on a bed of wood-chips and the paper in McIntire's hand. "Could you give this to Leonie? It's a recipe for the church cookbook." The sand-colored locks escaping her kerchief made McIntire long for spring. "It's Erik's favorite." She smiled. "Pasty."

McIntire thanked her and filed the recipe in his pocket.

A graceful owl had, with the aid of Pelto's jackknife, shucked its bonds and lay in its liberator's palm.

At the sound of an approaching car, Mrs. Pelto gave a muffled gasp, snatched up the baby and bolted for the kitchen door. The familiar black Fed-mobile rolled slowly past the driveway.

Orville scraped a tail feather into the owl. "One of us is going to be suspected of keeping bad company," he said. His smile faded as he added, "Poor little Wild Rose. She should have told me."

The female mind might be an enigma McIntire would never crack, but those with them seemed to have an uncanny ability to understand one another. If Rose had told anybody about being pregnant, it might have been another woman. Even if she hadn't said a word, another woman might have suspected, recognized some mysterious signs, as only one with experience could. Sandra Culver thought Rose had miscarried, and Sandra was certainly a pro in such matters. Irene Touminen wasn't. Not from a personal standpoint, so far as McIntire was aware, but she was Rose's closest female friend, and, he remembered, she'd trained to be a nurse.

Sulo opened the door. He was in his relaxing state, feet in grey wool socks, suspenders hanging on his hips. "Come on in. Take a load off." He shuffled back into the room. "Uno brought a cake over." Mount Everest in sugar and coconut occupied the center of the table. Irene cut three man-sized slices and fetched forks from the drawer.

"Pregnant?" She might never had heard the word.

"Do you think it's possible?"

"Sure it's possible. I guess. I don't know any reason that she *couldn't* have been expecting. But I also don't have any reason to think that she was. What difference would it make?" The theory that Rose's partner in death had been Cedric Hudson must not yet have made the rounds.

"Maybe none. But we're no closer to finding who killed Rose than we were when we found her body. Any information might help."

Irene placed the knife on the table, crossed her arms across her chest, and waited.

McIntire said, "If the father was someone other than Teddy, it might have a bearing on the case." *A bearing on the case.* He was turning into Perry Mason. "You were Rose's best friend," he added. "If she told anybody it would have been you."

"She didn't say a word to me."

Sulo left the table to pick up the broom leaning against the cupboard and pull out one of its straws. He returned and sat picking his teeth.

McIntire was willing to put up with the pesky shreds of coconut. Uno Touminen's reputation as a champion baker of cakes was well deserved. He took another bite before asking, "Did you see Rose in the days before she left? Other than at the party?"

"Sure. I went over in the afternoon. It must have been the day before she died. Teddy was off to take care of the last-minute things, putting stuff on the train. I stayed for a while and helped with some packing. Mostly we just talked about the past...and the future. Eban Vogel brought some eggs over. Rose had sold her hens. He only stayed a few minutes. He asked when Teddy'd be home and said he'd stop back the next day." She licked at her fork. "Looking back, he did seem concerned about her, maybe even worried. I thought it was about her going to Russia. He was mad as all get out about that, had a big fight with Teddy, which was why he wanted to know when he'd be home, I figured at the time. But maybe there was more to it."

"You think Eban might have known Rose was pregnant? How?"

"Only one way I can think of." Irene's eyes twinkled. "No. Don't be silly. He couldn't possibly have known. If she *was* pregnant, which I do not believe for one minute."

"Was that the last time you saw her?"

"We went to Escanaba." It was Sulo's first contribution to the conversation. His chair scraped on the linoleum. "The next day, we took the train to the fair in Escanaba." He stood up and shrugged into his braces. "I gotta get back at it." The door slammed behind him.

"Time waits for no man, and neither does a barn full of cow...er...manure." Irene touched her fingertip to a shred of coconut and put it to her tongue. "Don't mind Sulo. He was crazy about Rose once," she said. "So was Eban Vogel. It seemed like a fatherly sort of thing, but who knows?"

LONDON—"Let them wander up and down
for meat, and grudge if they be not
satisfied." (Psalm 59, Verse 15)

Chapter Forty-Nine

McIntire flipped through the latest edition of *Time*. Groundhog
Day had been a bust at the Vancouver zoo when the fisher ate
the groundhog. Otherwise it was the same as last week and the
week before: Death in Korea. Communist hunting at home.
How close was World War III? Should the U.S. get out of
Europe? How high would prices go? The background noise of
existence, a blur of print or a grumble on the radio, something
to tsk over, indulge in a bit of hand wringing, then switch off,
use the paper to start the fire, and get on with peeling potatoes
and mending the fence.

Unless, like Grace and Mike Maki, you had sacrificed your
firstborn to Douglas MacArthur or, like Erik Pelto, you were in
a face-off with Joe McCarthy. However uncomfortable Melvin
Fratelli could make things for McIntire, he couldn't send him
and his family to exile to Finland, and McIntire didn't have a
job to lose.

A sixteen-year-old murder with a handful of suspects, all with
the same possible motive. Anyone who loved Rose Falk might
have walked in, found her dead or dying, her blood on Cedric
Hudson's hands, availed themselves of the loaded shotgun and
blown the doctor's head to kingdom come. Except that it wasn't
quite like that. The doctor died outdoors, near the cistern into

which his body was dumped, naked, or close to it. Had he been undressed after he died? Who would, or could, do such a thing? Had he been forced to undress at gunpoint? Why? To save the jacket and glasses for his eventual suicide? That would involve an element of premeditation.

Would one who truly loved Rose Falk leave her body in a hole, pinned under her killer's, hoping it would never be found? Cheating her out of a grave and her rightful chance to at least be mourned?

How had Eban Vogel got hold of that watch? Vogel was another puzzle. A puzzle who'd been out late the night Rose died and come back spreading the word about a mine flood. Where would he have been likely to have heard that news? Maybe somewhere near the scene?

"Leonie." McIntire shoved aside his unread magazine. "Want to go for a drive?"

She didn't turn from her place at the sink. "Where to?"

"Maybe take a swing down along Forty-one."

"It's snowing."

"It's always snowing. Anyway, I think this is more just what's already here blowing around."

She wasn't hard to convince. "We can take my car." She dried her hands and reached for the bottle of Jergens. "You can drive."

McIntire waited until he was behind the wheel of the Nash before mentioning, "I need to stop a minute to ask Nick about something."

"What's that?" She placed her handbag and *Time* on the seat between them.

"How to find a woman of the streets in Sidnaw."

"There are no streets in Sidnaw."

Which meant that if Eban's lady friend was still around, locating her should be a snap.

"I need you to come up with some devious way of luring Nick away from Mia, or vice versa."

"No deviousness necessary. He'll want to come out to see the car."

He did. Leonie obligingly went to the house to ask Mia if there was anything they could pick up for her. Nick ambled out in his shirtsleeves. "Can I take a look?"

McIntire lifted the hood and ducked under it with him. Nick didn't show surprise at his request.

"Her house is on the corner in back of the filling station. Little place with lots of bushes. Handy for her."

"You think she's still there? Or still alive?"

"She's still there. I don't know that she's in the business anymore though." He prodded some wires. "Claudette."

"Does she have a last name?"

"Damned if I know." Nick straightened up. "Were you planning to pay by check?"

Leonie flatly refused to be a part of the interview. "Much as I'd like to see what a real...*Claudette* looks like, I'll decline. I'm sure she'll be much more forthcoming if you're on your own." She headed for the café a couple of hundred yards down the road. "Join me when you're done. No shenanigans. I'm wearing my watch, and I'm thoroughly familiar with your routines."

Routines? Was that why she'd been so out of sorts?

His knock on the door sounded timid, and he gave another, more emphatic rap.

"Claudette?"

The woman who answered the door would have been a disappointment to Leonie. McIntire was a bit let down himself. No painted lady, no faded and bitter-eyed jezebel with nicotine-stained fingers. Mrs. Mason, as she corrected him, was in appearance similar to his wife, aproned and comfortably rounded, with curls the grey that Leonie's would be without her fleet of bottles.

She waited behind the storm door. McIntire fumbled for a tactful approach, but only for a moment. He supposed anyone "in the business" couldn't afford to be oversensitive. He said, "I think you knew Eban Vogel."

"I believe Mr. Vogel has passed away."

When Mrs. Mason learned that McIntire was a lifelong acquaintance of Eban Vogel's, that he'd been born in his house, that there was an element of St. Adele's bodies-in-the-well in his curiosity, she pushed open the door and invited him inside.

"Yes," she said. "Mr. Vogel used to call from time to time."

"I know it was a long time ago, but I was hoping you might be able to tell me if he visited on a specific day." Maybe she kept accounts, a ledger, a schedule in a log book, saved her old calendars.

That didn't seem to be the case, but from the set of her lips, she'd guessed at his line of thinking.

McIntire tried again. "Do you remember when the Massey-Davis mine flooded?"

"Nobody around here is ever going to forget that. I lost several good…friends that day. And, yes, I remember very well, Mr. Vogel was here that evening."

"Would you have any recollection of what time he left?"

"He usually stayed for a cup of tea," she looked him in the eye, "after. That night there was a lot of noise and carrying on out in the road. He went down to Mitchell's to see what it was all about, and he didn't come back. It wasn't late. Maybe around nine or nine thirty."

Nine. It would have been tight, but it left time to go see Rose before he stopped off for a sauna with Mike Maki.

"A few minutes later my mother came pounding on the back door to tell me the mine had caved in and a hundred men were dead." Her smile showed the glint of a gold molar. "Ma was one for exaggeration."

Ma? McIntire supposed that even Claudettes had to come from somewhere.

"It gave me a start. Ma wouldn't normally have knocked when I had a visitor."

"But Mr. Vogel had gone."

"Oh, he just walked down to the saloon. His car was here for another hour or better."

McIntire could have kissed her, but he'd left his billfold in his other trousers. At last a shred of good news. He'd join Leonie for a celebratory slice of banana cream pie. He felt twenty pounds lighter as he walked to the door.

"Anything else I can help you with?" The gold tooth gleamed.

Maybe she *was* still in the business.

◇◇◇

His ebullience waned at the sight of Leonie's downturned mouth.

He sat opposite her and nodded to the waitress with the coffee pot.

"Look at this." She shoved her magazine across the table. "The government's reduced the meat ration again. It's down to eight pence a week now. That's worse than during the war. The girls haven't said a thing." She sounded more bewildered than angry. "How can you raise a boy on a lamb chop a week?"

As far as McIntire was concerned, a fella could get through an entire lifetime without ever eating a sheep and be the better for it. But it did sound pretty draconian. He looked at the article. It began with reporting the twenty percent reduction in ration, continued into a tirade on the folly of socialism, and concluded with a London butcher's apt quoting of Psalms.

"It sounds grim, but things will get better soon. I'm sure the girls are doing fine."

Now she sounded angry. "And just how can you be so sure? They wouldn't tell me if they weren't. There's hardly any coal, flu going around, and smallpox in Bristol. What can you expect? How can people stay well if they can't even eat or stay warm?" She sighed. "Would you like a pudding?"

"No," McIntire said. "I guess not. I think we'd better be on our way, if you're finished."

He took time to drink the hours-old coffee and let Leonie know what had transpired with Claudette.

"I'll stop on the way back to let Pete know." McIntire backed the Nash onto the road. It handled better in the snow than his Studebaker. "And we'll have to tell Mia."

"I daresay she will be grateful."

Grateful? It was a funny way of putting it. "I'm sure she'll be overjoyed. She hasn't had much good news lately."

"And you must be overjoyed to be able to bring it to her."

Once again Leonie was someone he didn't seem to know. Patrick Humphrey came to his mind. McIntire asked abruptly, "Are you going to stay?"

"I don't know. If there's another war…." After a long silence, she said, "You won't go back with me."

Patrick Humphrey, hidden news clippings, concealed letters. He gripped the wheel of the new car, the one she hadn't mentioned until it stood in the drive. "Leonie…."

"You promised you would."

There was nothing he could say. He had promised. "Give it two years," he'd begged. If, after that, she wanted to leave, they'd go back to England. He couldn't see now how he'd ever be able to keep that promise. "I'm sorry."

"So that's it? I finally get a husband who lives longer than the time it takes to unpack, and…."

"I'm sorry." He didn't know what else to say.

"Not so sorry as me, I'm sure."

"So you do want to go back?"

"What I'm sorry—no angry—about is that promises mean so little to you."

"It doesn't mean little, it's just that…." Just that what? How could he explain? He'd found his home again after half a lifetime. He couldn't leave it behind now. Not forever.

"You lied to me. Why?"

"I didn't know how it would be. I shouldn't have promised that I'd leave here until after I had actually lived here."

"I'm not talking about that."

He'd been afraid that she wasn't. But he had nothing to say to that either. It wasn't important. He'd stopped and talked to

Mia for a few minutes. That was all. He didn't mention it. He'd been gone all day, and she was angry with him already. "You don't always tell me everything."

"I don't lie."

Had she been sleep-walking when she called that lawyer? The one she'd never heard of? He couldn't bring himself to pursue it.

He would have to let Mia know what he'd learned today, and soon. Presumably relief at discovering that her father was miles away when Rose Falk died would override the sting of finding out where he had been. It might not do much to protect Nick when she learned who it was had pointed McIntire to Claudette.

"He could have done it earlier in the day." Pete Koski vigorously polished the watch on his sleeve, maybe hopeful of a genie popping out to make all things clear. "There's no law says Rose had to have died at night."

There wasn't. It just seemed that such a ghastly scene could never have been played out on a sultry summer afternoon.

"Mia remembered that her father had been out the evening that the mine flooded. She didn't mention him going earlier in the day."

"She might not have such a reliable memory where her old man is concerned."

"She didn't have to turn over the watch."

"No. I wonder why she did."

"She's absolutely convinced that her father is an innocent man, and she wants to prove it." Koski would probably not give the late Charlotte Vogel's assurance much more credence than he might Nelda Stewart's angels.

"What do you think?"

"Me?" Koski had sounded like he really wanted to know. What did he think? McIntire leaned back in his chair and stared at the ceiling. "I think that sometime toward the middle of the long, cold, tedious winter of 1934, Orville Pelto came riding in on his four-wheeled charger and swept young Rose Falk off her feet. He was handsome and charming. He didn't notice how ugly she was, and, when she was with him, she forgot, too. He convinced her, and her husband, to give up their life here and take part in a great Utopian adventure. He convinced Rose of a few other things, and she got pregnant. In spite of her courage, or maybe because of it, she couldn't face bringing a child into the world that would suffer the way that she had. And she knew what she could do about it. When it turned out that Teddy would be away for a few days, she called upon Doctor Cedric Hudson."

Koski looked up sharply, but he didn't interrupt.

"He probably did come at night, or late in the evening. The Falks had a long driveway. A car in their yard wouldn't be seen from the road, but, still, Rose would want to be discreet.

"They weren't discreet enough. Someone—someone who cared about Rose—showed up. Rose was in bad shape, bleeding and near to dead."

The sheriff's glanced shifted to the photo of his daughter, then back to McIntire.

"He gave Rose a paper and pen so she could write a note to her husband."

"He-who?"

"Whoever it was that came."

"And Cedric Hudson hung around while this was going on?"

"Why not? He did fancy himself a doctor." McIntire continued, "Rose wrote a note for Teddy, and she died."

"And this person who was so fond of her dumped her body in the well?"

That was the sticky part. "The note asked that Ted let people think they'd gone together. That he not let people know what she'd done. Rose wouldn't have wanted anyone to find out how she died. She might have begged that it be kept a secret."

Koski nodded.

"When she was dead, the visitor bundled her into the blankets and placed her body in the well. Then he marched Cedric Hudson, at gunpoint, to the edge of it and blew his head to smithereens."

"Before or after stripping off his clothes?"

"After," McIntire said. "This person realized that if he was going to keep Rose's secret, he'd have to make it look like the doctor died far away. He might have spent hours sitting by Rose's bed, waiting for her to die. He'd have had a while to plan."

"Enough time to get her to a hospital perhaps? And if he wanted it to look like the old man died far away, why not just put him in the car and see to it?"

A few niggling inconsistencies. "He threw the doctor's body into the well, too." On top of Rose, that was what bothered McIntire the most about his hypothesis. Would someone who loved Rose leave her to spend eternity under her murderer? "He threw whatever was lying around over the bodies. Trash, the clothes, maybe more bedding. Then he cleaned up as best he could, flipped the mattress over, and drove the doctor's car back to the lighthouse."

"Leaving his own car at the Falks'?"

"It's not all that far. He could have walked back, got in his own car, and gone home." Or to watch bodies being pulled from the Massey-Davis mine in Ishpeming.

"Not at all worried about the time that somebody would come by, find that Hudson wasn't around, and go looking for him?"

"And absolutely correct in that. It didn't happen. And what if it had? Cedric Hudson was an old man. He could have wandered into the woods and gotten lost or stumbled into the lake. He might have gone to see a relative and not told anybody."

McIntire hadn't thought about it until he said it. Why not just let people figure the doctor had wandered off? Why bother with the suicide? "Maybe he does get to worrying, maybe people are beginning to mention that they haven't seen good old Cedric in a while. So he punches a hole in the boat, starts it up, maybe throws in a rock or two to make sure it sinks, and sends it off into the waves. *Voila*, everybody knows what's become of the old boy."

Koski spoke from the depths of gloom. "Maybe it was Jack Stewart."

McIntire laughed. "More likely Nelda. It had to be somebody who stuck around long enough to fake the suicide. Or at least lived near enough to make the trip."

"Like Orville Pelto?" Koski asked. "He says he spent the night at the mine."

"A convenient alibi," McIntire said. "And one that's hard to prove one way or the other."

"Have you talked to him?"

McIntire nodded.

"John." Koski fidgeted with his pencil. "Orville Pelto is the closest thing we got to a real suspect."

"I'd say so."

"And he's the only one we got that knows shit about what was going on with Rose and Teddy Falk back then."

What was he getting at?

"I think maybe…." The pencil broke. "We don't want him scared off."

McIntire waited.

"His kid's already been booted out of the country. If Orville thought the same thing might happen to him…."

"We don't want to do anything that could bring him to the attention of Melvin Fratelli, is that what you're saying, Pete?"

"Well, you know—"

"I think I get your meaning."

Koski grinned and nodded. "Good. By the way, I got the papers." A bundle of yellowed broadsheets lay on the window ledge. The Finnish-language news from August, 1934.

"Stick your papers up—"

"Sheriff—" Marian Koski put her head around the door. "Oh, Mr. McIntire, I didn't see you. Pardon the interruption."

McIntire assured her it was perfectly all right, he was just leaving.

"Don't forget your papers."

Chapter Fifty

The coffee had a burned taste to it, or maybe the bitterness came from McIntire himself. He sat in his usual spot by the window. No rising sun to greet him. It was long since up. He hadn't been eager to face this day.

The papers lay where he'd left them when he'd come in last night. He pulled a copy of *Amerikan Suometar* to him and tried to flip the switch in his brain that would enable him to make sense of it. It was no use, he saw only a page swimming with vowels.

He'd never have believed a supper of grilled cheese sandwiches and fried leftover potatoes could last so long. Leonie had gone upstairs immediately after washing the dishes. Writing more letters, no doubt.

Maybe he was being unfair. Of course she was lonely. Of course she missed her daughters and their children. He'd expected that. She'd just lived through one war. She was terrified at the thought of another, separated from her family, with the A-bomb looming. But that wasn't new, and she'd seemed perfectly fine until the past couple of months. It was only after Christmas that she started getting moody—and secretive about the mail. Now she was buying her own car and making phone calls to attorneys, not to mention those unflattering allusions to his "routine."

Although, buying a car was not generally something a woman planning an imminent move out of the country might do.

Her footsteps sounded in the bathroom overhead, and he buried his face in the paper.

It didn't take long to find it, an accounting of the subdued send-off given J. Theodore and his wife. It took even less time to realize it held nothing new, other than the scheduled departure date, Monday, August 20.

Leonie came into the room in her blue dressing gown. "Are you feeling all right?" she asked. "I don't ever remember you sleeping this late."

"Maybe it's contagious," he said. "Or maybe it's my age catching up with me."

"It's not being old that keeps me in bed."

He hadn't meant it that way, but was too tired to try to talk his way out of it. He went back to the papers.

"How old do you think I am?"

"You know I have no idea."

"Guess."

She couldn't possibly have so little regard for his intellect. "Leonie—"

"Oh, forget it!"

Maybe it was time to stop forgetting things, sticking them into the back corners of his mind. "I don't know how old you are. That's only one of the many things I don't know about you."

"Meaning?"

"Like who you've been getting mail from, and writing to, that you keep from me. And why you've been consulting with an attorney."

"What are you talking about?"

"Patrick Humphrey is a lawyer."

"Yes, he is."

"Why didn't you tell me that when he phoned?"

"He didn't."

He hadn't, that was true. The call had come from his secretary. "Why did you call his office? And why did you lie to me about it?"

She leaned back against the sink and folded her arms. Her voice was gentle, patient, infuriated. "I did not lie to you about Mr. Humphrey or anything else. I phoned Mr. Humphrey's office because I wanted to speak to his partner, Mr. Mondale. You asked me who Patrick Humphrey was, and I said I'd never heard of him, which, at the time, I had *not*."

McIntire tried to control his own anger. "All right, I'll rephrase that. Why did you call Mr. Mondale?"

"I need to make a will. I'm getting old, remember." The flint went out of her voice. "We don't know what's going to happen." She turned her back.

"I'm sorry, Leonie." He was only slightly sorry. Maybe she hadn't lied, but she hadn't been strictly open and aboveboard either. She hadn't brought up being in the market for a "solicitor" to make out her will, nor had she mentioned how she planned to dispose of her worldly goods, or her worldly money, of which there seemed to be quite a lot. In McIntire's limited experience, a will is something married couples usually discuss.

"Sorry? Are you? Good! I'm glad to hear it. And if you want to know who I'm writing to, you can ask me. If I think it's any of your business, I might tell you!" She slammed the cupboard door.

McIntire returned to August 17, 1934.

The news of that day and the week to follow was, as everywhere, the death of fifty-one miners. It must have been ghastly, choking, smothering, drowning in a deluge of sand and mud. The incident was held up as a grisly manifestation of the oppression of the worker. An account of the long night of waiting was detailed in an interview with a man who'd been at the scene—Orville Pelto.

So Orville Pelto had probably told the truth. While Rose Falk was dying he'd left his son at home alone and kept vigil at the mine.

So what had happened? It seemed simple. Rose Falk was alone, making ready to leave the country. Someone had gone to see her, to help or say goodbye, or both. They'd found her dead or dying at the hands of Dr. Cedric Hudson, and they'd killed him. It could have been almost anybody. The killer had driven Hudson's car back to the lighthouse, easy enough to do in the night without much risk of being seen. That was all they needed to do. Check the doctor's mailbox now and then. Maybe move the car to make it look like it had been used. Hudson generally went for a visit with his grandson in the fall. He wouldn't be missed for a while. When a letter or two arrived from that grandson, wondering when the old man was planning to arrive, the killer was forced into action. He couldn't be absolutely sure no one had seen the doctor on his way to his call on Rose Falk, or that Rose hadn't told someone that he was coming. It would be best to defuse any sticky questions. He didn't need a complicated scheme. He could let himself be seen in the doctor's coat and hat, "waving and going into his funny little house." He could go out around sundown on a stormy November evening, stick a landing net upright in Hudson's boat, dress it in the man's trademark hat and coat, glasses in pocket, start up the boat, and send it off into the waves. That was the end of it for sixteen years, until a tree went down in an ice storm.

Once again, it could have been almost anybody. Anybody but J. Theodore Falk, who was long gone, but who had done the killer a great favor when he'd sent those postcards from his wife.

Eban Vogel lived in the neighborhood. Eban hated Cedric Hudson and, the most damning evidence, he had that watch.

Orville Pelto and his son spent the winter less than thirty miles away, and Orville was in love with Rose Falk.

But Eban was with Claudette, and Orville had told the truth about where he'd spent that night.

It seemed that everybody had told the truth. Almost everybody. One person had lied every step of the way.

McIntire stood up. "It looks to be a fine afternoon. I think I'll go see what Sulo's up to."

"Are you talking about—?"

"Ice fishing."

"That's a fine idea. Dwelling on murder isn't good. You'd do well to get your mind off it for a time."

What a luxury that would be. To take his mind off those wretched deaths and all the miseries they had brought to the living. To be able to enjoy the hard blue sky and the sun on the snow. To have nothing more pressing to think about than trying to lure a fish to a hole in the ice. To sit in comfortable silence with Sulo Touminen. The time he spent with Sulo would be anything but comfortable.

Sulo, who'd sold Rose's house for a few stacks of hay, and who'd been so eager for Earl Culver to dismantle it. Sulo, who'd encouraged Culver to add more debris to the well; who'd been diligent at filling it in but hedgy about its location. Sulo, who claimed to be in Escanaba when Rose died. Sulo knew Rose would be alone that night. Sulo knew about finding the bill of lading and the passport and could easily guess that it was the Thorsens who had found it. Sulo had gone to Thorsens' to move some furniture the day after Mia's accident. Was it in the room where Cedric Hudson's watch was ultimately found? And finally, Sulo spoke only rudimentary Finnish and needed McIntire to translate letters from his Finnish cousins.

However angry Leonie might be, her domesticity won out. "You'd better take a lunch," she said. "It's getting on for midday already."

Eating would probably be the last thing on his mind, but it was nearly noon, and it might be a long day. Leonie had a lunch bag and thermos ready before McIntire had finished bundling himself into what he hoped would be an adequate amount of clothing. She was suspiciously enthusiastic about his expedition.

"You eager to get rid of me?" He spoke as flippantly as he could manage.

"Yes." The response was straightforward and delivered without a smile. It left McIntire with nothing more to say.

◇◇◇

McIntire was in luck. Sulo was apparently running late, too. He exited the barn, gave the door a shove and a hearty kick, and walked toward the woodshed. At the sound of McIntire's slamming car door, he turned, and the face under the wool cap was transformed into his sister's.

"You're going ice fishing? Wonders never cease!" Irene lifted her hands in mock surprise.

"I thought I'd give it a try."

"Well, you're surely dressed for it."

McIntire tried to ignore the glint of mirth in her eyes. Someone dressed in her brother's bib overalls and mackinaw had little room to snigger. Especially given that they were a perfect fit.

"I hate to disappoint you," she said, "but Sulo left hours ago."

"No matter. I'll just follow his tracks. Or maybe the trail of crumbs." A trickle of sawdust ran across the yard to the road, legacy of Touminen's contribution to Simon Lindstrom's ice house.

She laughed. "His will hardly be the only tracks out there, but you shouldn't have any trouble finding him. First you'd better fill me in on the latest. I hear Erik Pelto has gone off to cut wood in Wisconsin. What's happening with Delilah?"

McIntire hadn't heard anything about that.

"Poor kid." Irene hugged herself against the cold. "What's brought on this sudden urge to take up ice fishing? Or is it to see my brother?"

"I figure it's something everybody should do at least once."

"See Sulo?"

The lady did have a quick sense of humor. At another time McIntire might have appreciated it more. "Irene, after Mia Thorsen broke her leg, Nick called Sulo to help move a piece of furniture. Do you know what it was?"

"Charlotte Vogel's old bed. They wanted it downstairs for Mia. It weighed a ton and he was there forever putting it together. He complained about his back for a week afterwards. Why?"

"No real reason. Who knows when I might need some furniture moved? Leonie might take it into her head to buy a piano." He wasn't fooling her for a minute. "I'd better be on my way before I overheat."

"Good luck."

McIntire made a final stop at Karvonen's store for a can of Sterno and a couple of Milky Way bars. He also sought an informed opinion on where Sulo and his like might be fishing. The hot spot of the day, according to Elsie, was at the mouth of the bay where it met the open lake.

, He took the long way around, telling himself the shorter route might not be plowed. That road would have taken him past Nelda Stewart's home—and her barn.

It was later than he had planned when he arrived at a jumping-off spot, Simon Lindstrom's dock, but he was in no hurry. It wasn't like he was hoping to catch his dinner.

The dock was nearly buried in the great heaps of jagged ice that lay along the shore. Nearby, a narrow space had been cleared away to make a path for dragging blocks of ice cut from the lake to the squat log building where they were stored for packing fish in the coming summer. As he stumbled over a pile of sawdust and onto the frozen lake, McIntire found it hard to believe in summer.

The ice was peppered with figures hunched on up-ended pails, staring between their feet. Here and there a thread of smoke rose where some not-so-hardy soul had dragged out a supply of firewood or a kerosene stove.

One of the fireless was Adam Wall. McIntire crunched across the wind-packed snow to where he sat. Wall seemed even more stunned at McIntire's arrival than Irene Touminen had been, and more poetic. "Is this a vision that I see before me?" He jiggled his line. "You must have the cabin fever really bad. I never thought I'd see the day."

"And you haven't. I'm looking for Sulo."

His eyes searched McIntire's face. "You want me to come along?"

"Tired of fishing already?"

"Got my limit already."

A couple of stiff lake trout lay on the ice.

A little thing like fish and game regulations wouldn't ordinarily get in the way of Wall filling his larder. Maybe his periodic deputy stints had changed his outlook.

"There is something you can do," McIntire told him. "See if you can find out the dates of the State Fair in Escanaba in 1934."

Wall nodded and returned to his jiggling. McIntire walked off.

"Careful you don't tip over," Wall called after him. "You could wind up stuck on your back like a turtle, kicking your legs in the air."

McIntire scanned the headache-inducing expanse of white and spotted the distant but unmistakable Touminen silhouette, head down, hands in pockets. He struck out in its direction.

Though it was only mid-February, the afternoon sun rode high in an achingly blue sky, giving a tantalizing hint of spring. A wind, barely perceptible in the shelter of the trees, flung itself across the lake, stinging his eyes and sucking away any warmth that sun might have offered. McIntire turned his back to it.

Far out on the ice, how far McIntire couldn't tell in the white-on-white landscape, a tiny figure flanked by another much smaller moved across the snow. Was the woman completely brainless? The ice did not go on forever, and the farther she got from shore, the thinner it would be.

He set out with giant strides. The surface of the lake was a marbling of ice swept bare, thin crusts of packed snow, and drifts into which he sank almost to his thighs.

"Mrs. Pelto!"

She turned and watched him for a bit without speaking, then wheeled and walked on. The largest of her children trudged alongside, holding, with its mother, the rope of a small toboggan carrying its younger sibling and the sock monkey.

McIntire trotted up behind her. "Mrs. Pelto, what are you doing out here? It's not safe to go any further." He waved toward the water, close enough to see ripples lapping at the shelf of ice. "This is far enough."

"It's too windy. When we turn around it's cold on their faces."

"Not half so cold as they'll be if.... When will your husband be back?" He might have been demanding to learn the whereabouts of her daddy, he realized. He'd been reminding himself that Delilah Pelto wasn't really a child, but now was beginning to wonder. He added, more gently, "I heard Erik is in Wisconsin cutting wood."

"He has to make some money to pay back Orville for the bail."

"Not Wisconsin." The little boy scuffed through the snow.

"Tony—"

"It's just pretend. Dad didn't go to Wisconsin, did he Mum?"

Why would they have lied about that?

Delilah sighed. "No." She ducked her head against the wind and spoke into her collar. "Erik went to Canada."

He might have guessed. McIntire didn't know what sort of immigration laws they had in Canada. But they didn't have Joe McCarthy.

"He's not coming back. When he gets a place to live, he'll send for us."

It seemed extreme, an overreaction. The government could make life uncomfortable for those it wanted out, but they hadn't managed to actually deport much of anybody. Erik Pelto hadn't committed any crimes that McIntire was aware of. He was a U.S. citizen, and a war veteran. He had a family. Wouldn't running to Canada just make things worse? Still, Erik and his father knew more about the situation than McIntire did.

"Canada isn't such a bad place."

"We don't want to go."

"Well, right now you're getting off this lake. March!"

McIntire lifted the largest child in his arms. He had his mother's cinnamon eyes and his father's runny nose.

Delilah obediently flipped what McIntire assumed to be his sister—she had a pink hood—around to face the back of the sled. She gripped the rope and swung the sled around.

"Were you thinking about going back to Australia?" Would Erik Pelto lose his family as well as his home?

"We want to stay right here."

That might very well be something about which neither of them would have a choice. The first thing McIntire noticed when he turned was a toenail moon high in the eastern sky. The second was a stretch of gun-metal blue water, slicing the ice on which they stood from the tree-lined shore.

Delilah gave a tiny gasp. That was all. They stood silent, staring into the stream that widened perceptibly even as they watched.

The hills were already dark shadows before the sinking sun. The shoreline was long, empty of human life. Except for Adam Wall. By the time he had galloped up to face them across the chasm it had grown to six or seven feet. "Come on." He beckoned.

McIntire lowered Tony to the ice and took Delilah's elbow. "You first."

"No!" It was a horrified whisper.

"You're the heaviest. The crack is getting wider by the minute. These two will be easy." He didn't wait for assent. The months of slinging snow paid off. Delilah sailed across the ice with room to spare. Wall staggered only a little when her weight hit his chest. The children he caught like footballs.

McIntire backed away from the water. He took a few running steps and launched himself across the gap. The next thing he felt was the blinding pain of his knee cracking into the ice and a shock of disbelief when the water closed around his legs. For a moment his layers of wool kept him afloat, bobbing like a cork as he struggled to reach Adam Wall's extended hand. Then he felt numbingly cold water on his skin and the lake reached up and pulled him under.

WASHINGTON—FBI chief J. Edgar
Hoover called on all Americans
to mount guard on the nation's
internal security, but warned
against "witch hunts."

Chapter Fifty-One

Flames leaped into the darkening sky. Gnomelike creatures with peaked heads flitted amid swirls of smoke. Fierce heat seared McIntire's face and naked chest. The rest of him was either numb or missing.

"Am I in Hell?"

"Yes." Delilah Pelto's voice was inches from his ear. "Mr. Wall's gone for a car. Don't fall to sleep."

Did that mean he was awake? This wasn't some bizarre nightmare after all? His cough sent a hot knife through his lungs.

"Get as close to the fire as you can stand."

She wasn't making sense. He'd never be able to stand, not with his smashed knee and ice-armor trousers. He slumped forward and smelled the acrid odor of singing eyelashes. "My glasses?"

"Long gone." She pushed him back. "Not quite that close."

"Abies balsamea." Tony. His announcement preceded a shower of sparks and a rush of flame.

It was short-lived. The firelight died. Not far off, black water gleamed.

"What happened? Did they all get off before the ice went out?"

"No." Delilah rubbed his hands. "I don't think so."

"Betula lutea."

Another burst of flame felt warm on his face. McIntire leaned back. Someone had thoughtfully propped him against a log, taken off his soaked jacket, and wrapped him in a dry one. Adam Wall. Adam Wall had pulled him out of the water. Mr. Wall had gone for a car. Erik Pelto had run to Canada. His wife didn't want to go.

"It'll be okay," McIntire said. "Canada's not that much different from Michigan."

The response was a piercing wail.

"Miranda!" Delilah started up.

The toddler dropped her firewood contribution and held out chubby fingers for her mother's kiss.

"*Rosa acicularis.*" The boy's precocity reared its ugly head once more. "Prickly wild rose," he added helpfully.

Prickly Wild Rose. Little Rosie. Had she been prickly or gentle? Courageous or cowardly? Loving or thoughtless? Ugly or beautiful?

Tony threw a piece of driftwood of indeterminate species onto the pyre and leaned against his mother's knee. Miranda stood clutching her monkey, scratched fingers in mouth, mesmerized by the flames. Her stubby figure brought an eerie recollection. Uno Touminen in miniature. It seemed years since Touminen had stood similarly transfixed by fire, similarly sucking his digits, waiting as Rose Falk's bones were being removed from under the *Rosa acicularis* that had bitten him. Nature, at least, had given Rose a suitable tribute. Or had it? Even wild roses can be planted.

Thoughts of Uno, and flora, and murder, were erased by the sweetest music McIntire had ever heard: The rumble of Adam Wall's Ford pickup.

DULUTH, MINN.—Knut Heikkinen, jailed under anti-communist laws, walked out of St. Louis County jail, free on $2500 bail.

Chapter Fifty-Two

Before he left the blessedly warm truck, McIntire turned to his rescuer. "Find Sulo Touminen."

Ten hours later he emerged from the deepest sleep of his life. His first conscious feeling was of his aching knee. His second was of his wife's warm body against his back.

"Playing Eskimo?" he asked.

"If it's good enough for Nanook…." She lay still for a time. "You might have been dead, too."

McIntire didn't need to ask what other deaths Leonie referred to. "I couldn't have done that to you—left you husbandless for the third time."

"You already have done."

McIntire felt cold all over again. "Don't talk about it now. We'll work things out."

"You took my third husband."

"I'm your third husband, and I plan to stay—"

"Fourth."

He was still dreaming. He might as well go along with it. "And the third?"

"Michael Warren."

Not dreaming, but delirious. Or was he as crazy as Buster—
what was his real name?—said he was. On the other hand, maybe
it was Leonie that had gone off her rocker.

"Michael Warren wasn't married," he said.

"He would have been. He'd have been married on New Year's
day, 1948, if he hadn't been killed the week before Christmas."

It explained a lot, the change in Leonie's attitude toward him,
her sadness, but it brought up more questions, more confusion.
"But how could Melvin Fratelli have known? This can't be just
a coincidence."

The bed lurched as Leonie bounced to a sitting position and
pushed her husband onto his back. "Melvin? What's he got to
do with it?"

"I saw the clipping. I thought…. It didn't come from Fratelli?"
How blind could he have been? Who would be more likely to have
a clipping from a London newspaper? "You always knew."

"I knew that it should have been you in that car. Mike died
because he was taking your place."

"Then why did you…?" He didn't want to say "seduce me
the first chance you got?"

"You owed me."

"So you hunted me down."

"It wasn't hard. I knew Mike had gone that night because
the man who was scheduled to work got sick, and Mike was the
only other person at the embassy that spoke Hungarian. He'd
taken someone else's place, and he died in someone else's place.
That man was still alive. It wasn't hard to find the Hungarian
railroad pamphlet and call the U.S. embassy to see if they could
supply a translator."

How simple, and how gullible he'd been to think that it had
all been the product of fate and his overwhelming charm. How
gullible and how vain. "You couldn't have started out with the
intent of getting me as a substitute husband. For one thing, I
might have been already married."

"I didn't have any particular plan. I only wanted to meet
the man who was responsible for Mike dying. Then I could

decide the best way to get revenge." She tickled her fingers up his ribs. "What better way than torture by inches, for the rest of your life."

"It hasn't been all that bad."

"After I met you, I thought, why not? Mike had taken your spot, you could take his. Of course I never really blamed you. I knew that crash wasn't your fault."

He could let it go at that. But he was too tired for more evasions. "Yes, it was," McIntire told her. "It was my fault."

Leonie's face against his neck went still.

"It wasn't an accident." He pulled the blankets away from his throbbing knee and leaned back into the pillow. He'd tell her now. Quick. Before his brain thawed out and cowardice took over.

"The British Foreign Office had a conference going with leaders of some Hungarian political parties, hatching up plans to keep the Russians from taking over completely. They were scrambling for interpreters. They sent a car for me. I got some ribbing about meeting their new driver, a young woman from America. It was the usual cold December London drizzle. When I came out she was waiting, ready to open the car door. She wasn't American."

"You knew her?"

"Yes, I knew her. She wasn't American, but, to my credit, she gave a pretty good imitation."

"To your credit?"

It was a story McIntire hadn't told before. One he hoped he'd never have to tell. He tried to clear his mind, remember how it happened and remember that it was Leonie by his side. "The U.S.S.R. had, still has I'm sure, a program set up to train operatives in the customs of target countries. A school for spies. The agents were steeped in the culture they were expecting to enter, mostly in Britain and the USA. I was an instructor in the habits of *Homo americanus*. Considering I had almost no first-hand experience, I must have done okay. For a time."

Ludmilla Andropov had been one of the best students. A chameleon, a natural mimic, she was like a recording robot, and with just as little feeling. "It was Ludmilla who began to hint that my Russian wasn't quite what it should be."

"Mr. Falk says it's perfect."

"It is," McIntire said. "Down to the last regional nuance. That was the problem. I was supposed to be from Philadelphia. A turncoat named Kenneth Richards. I had obviously gone to some pretty great lengths to gain such a command of Russian that I could have easily passed as a native speaker almost anywhere in the country. That was troubling."

A knowledgeable ear might have been a whole lot more suspicious of his early twentieth century polyglot American English. But suspicion was aroused, and poor Mr. Richards died suddenly of a ruptured appendix while on a weekend holiday to the Black Sea. He left a pair of better-equipped colleagues behind.

It was concern for the safety of those two agents that caused McIntire to panic.

"She wasn't looking in my direction, but I didn't have any way of knowing if she'd seen me before I recognized her. I fumbled with my umbrella like I couldn't get it open, and went back inside. I could think of one thing and one thing only—if she'd seen me, I couldn't let her leave. If she could get somewhere to contact her bosses.... There was a little conference room where the coffee pot was always on. I poured two cups."

"Thoughtful of you."

"It wasn't a movie. I didn't carry a cyanide capsule," McIntire said. "But I had some pretty potent sleeping pills. I used to take them to knock me out when I had a headache. I crushed three of them and put them in the coffee."

"Which coffee?"

"I didn't think the pills would be strong enough or work fast enough to keep her there, but it was all I had. I asked the young marine at the door to take the coffee out to the driver and let her know it would be another twenty minutes. Then I rubbed my forehead and put on a glassy-eyed look, and went straight to the ambassador's office. I was hardly out of the room before Mike came by. He knew all about my headaches, knew it would be more likely twenty hours than twenty minutes. He said he'd go in my place."

McIntire felt her tears on his shoulder. "I don't know if she saw me. I don't know if she knew I'd seen her, and I don't know if she drank the coffee. Maybe she drank it and it made her groggy. Maybe she knew she'd been recognized and was as panicked as I was. Maybe she chose death over being exposed. Anyway she drove the car into the Thames and took Mike Warren with her."

If he'd drugged her and she died, he'd be guilty of manslaughter at the very least. Double manslaughter. "There was an autopsy. It didn't show drugs." It didn't mean they weren't there.

"I didn't find out he was dead until I saw it in the papers," Leonie said. "There was nothing in the news about that driver being a Russian spy."

"No. There wouldn't have been." He may as well tell the rest of it.

"I was up for retirement soon. I wanted out, and the army wanted me out. Most of all, the State Department wanted me out. They found one last job for me. Investigating a former army psychiatrist who was working with Wilhelm Reich. Reich and his crew had the theory that everything that can ail a human being stems from sexual repression. They wanted somebody to pose as a patient, and I was the perfect candidate, a middle-aged male who understood German, and was about as repressed as anyone could get."

McIntire became a patient of Dr. Richard Grossman. In their first interview the doctor asked about his parents. McIntire told him. He went on telling him for hours, for days, for weeks. He branched out from Grossman. He told doctors, nurses, Buster, floor scrubbers. He talked to crazy people and sane; sometimes he could tell the difference. He talked about his father, his mother, Mia, his various dogs, Myrtle Van Opelt, his father, his father, his father. A father that would have rather seen his son dead than in an asylum.

When McIntire left the hospital on a soft shiny day in mid-May, he was not quite so repressed, and his father had been six weeks in his grave.

They'd all apologized. It had been an unfortunate mix-up. The army had him down as being on leave. The State Department hadn't heard from him in weeks.

He couldn't tell his mother that, when her husband died, their son was not on the other side of the ocean but a four-hour flight away, in a hospital, where he'd been for months without letting her know. He couldn't tell her then, and he couldn't tell her now.

He felt his wife's impatience. Could he tell Leonie? He began, "It wasn't national security at stake. They suspected Dr. Reich of running some sort of sex business. It was demeaning and sleazy, and," he took her hand, "it was in New Jersey."

The pounding on the kitchen door set the windows to rattling. Leonie reached for her robe and headed for the stairs.

McIntire heard only a murmur of a male voice, then the closing of the door and Leonie's tread on the steps.

"It was Adam Wall. He brought your car back, and he wanted to know how you are."

"Did you tell him that now that he's saved my life, he's responsible for it forever?"

"No." She didn't smile. "He said that they haven't found Touminen. They think they got everybody else, but if he's still out there...."

"Which Touminen?"

"He didn't say. Were they both on the lake?"

McIntire wasn't sure about that. He threw off the bed-clothes.

"Where do you think you're going?"

Pain shot up his thigh as his foot hit the floor. "First I'm going to the bathroom, and then I have to make a phone call."

He went to the phone first.

"Did Uno Touminen get picked up?"

Marian Koski's reply came after a flurry of tears and thank God you're alives. "Uno Touminen, yes. He was with the bunch that floated all the way to Munising, but last I heard they haven't found his twin brother. Mr. Touminen says they weren't fishing together."

"That's what I was afraid of."

Leonie took his arm. "Get back to bed. I'm phoning Guibard to come and look at that knee."

"Just give me some aspirin. I'm going to pay a call on Irene Touminen."

HOUGHTON—Three more area servicemen were named on the casualty list issued by the Defense Department last night.

Chapter Fifty-Three

Rubber overshoes flopping and wool kerchief making a hood around her pointy face, Irene Touminen tramped towards the door, resembling a northwoods Baba Yaga. Her face was flushed with cold and exertion; her eyes were the brilliant jet of the coal that filled her buckets.

"John! Goodness me, why aren't you home warming your toes by the fire?"

"Where's Sulo?"

"I was praying that was what you'd come to tell me. I've been frantic! They haven't found him yet, and he's been gone all night. The sheriff says there's nobody left on the lake. They think it was three separate sheets of ice, and they know where they all ended up." She dropped the two buckets onto the steps and flexed her fingers. "Sulo's tough. I'm sure he just got off on shore somewhere. He'll turn up safe in somebody's kitchen. Don't you think that's the most likely thing?"

"No."

The pleading eyes turned bleak. "That's an awful thing to say."

"Where is he?"

"You know where he is as well as I do. He went fishing yesterday morning, and he didn't come back." Her voice turned sharp. "You were supposed to be with him."

"He didn't go fishing. There was only one Touminen out there last night, and that was Uno."

"I hope that's true. I hope Sulo's not in that lake somewhere, but it's cruel of you to say it, if you don't know it for sure."

"Where is he?"

"He told me he was going fishing, he took his fishing gear and he left. That's all I know." Her smile below downcast eyes was barely perciptible. "Am I my brother's keeper?"

McIntire shivered. She turned and picked up the pails. "You'd better come inside."

He followed but remained in the doorway.

She stood with her back to the kitchen table, removed the scarf, and smoothed her hair. The ceiling reflected blood-red on her face.

"Sulo is my brother," she said. "I wouldn't want to say anything that might get him in trouble, but I think maybe he might have been…. Sulo was crazy about Rose. You saw how he acted when you said that she was pregnant when she died." She sighed heavily and bit her lip. "I don't like to think it, but…well, Sulo didn't tell the truth about where we were that night, about being in Escanaba."

"It was you lied about that."

"I went along with what Sulo said. I didn't want him to get into—"

"No. It was Sulo that backed you up. It was you who said it first."

She cocked her head. "It seems to me we were in Escanaba. It was a long time ago. I don't suppose you can remember where you've been every minute in the past twenty years." The response was calm, conversational.

McIntire moved closer. "When you got the postcard from Rose, didn't you wonder why she'd written to you in Finnish? She was your best friend. She knew you didn't read Finn."

"Rose wasn't always the most sensible—"

"You knew that card couldn't have been from Rose, knew it the day you got it. You might not have recognized that it wasn't her handwriting, but you damn well knew she'd never have written to you in Finnish. Still, you didn't question it, didn't mention to anyone that it didn't seem quite right. Why?"

"I thought maybe Ted had done it for her. Rose wasn't a good writer. She didn't like writing."

And, according to her husband, if she was pushed into writing, if she had a choice, she wrote Finn. "And when she was weak, near death, she needed help with her goodbye note to Teddy. She had to turn to someone, someone who could only help her do it in English." McIntire stepped closer still. Irene continued to meet his gaze without flinching.

"It must have given you a bit of a start at first," he said, "to get a message from someone you knew was dead."

"How could I know Rose was dead? None of us knew that."

"You were her best friend."

"I was her only friend."

"It was you who guided her hand to write the note."

Her eyes grew brighter.

"You knew she was dead, and you knew how she'd died…and you planted the wild roses on her grave."

Tears collected in the corners of her eyes. "She begged me to do it."

She leaned back, her hands gripping the table behind her. "Teddy was away, and I'd promised to go over and help with the last-minute packing and cleaning up. I walked over in the middle of the afternoon. It was a strange day, hot and muggy and so very, very quiet. There wasn't a bird singing. No insects buzzing. Nothing. Total silence.

"When I got close to the house I saw a car and thought Teddy must have got back. Then I recognized that it was Cedric Hudson's. At first I couldn't imagine what might have happened, if he'd come to say goodbye, or if Rose was sick. Then the truth dawned on me.

"There wasn't a sound. The door was open. I could see Cedric Hudson in the bedroom. He was half naked. I didn't know why until I saw the blood." A tear trickled down the ski-jump nose. "He didn't want to get her blood on his clothes."

McIntire recalled Hudson's disgusted frown as he wiped fastidiously at his soiled shirt. He also recalled mistaking Irene for her brother. "Did Hudson's coat and hat fit you as well as Sulo's? Well enough to fool anyone who might pass by?"

She stared for a second, then left her spot at the table to pull open a wooden bin. "It was so hot. Poor Rose was drenched in sweat. The smell made me sick. I tried to open the window but it was painted shut. I broke it."

She took out a few potatoes, examining each and placing them in an aluminum colander as she went on. "It didn't seem like there was such an awful lot of blood. She said it didn't hurt any more. I thought she might be all right. I helped her write the note for Ted, because that's what she wanted. Then I sat by her bed. She asked me to sing. It was one of the things she hated most about her hare-lip, that she couldn't sing. Her voice came through her nose. I sang until she fell asleep."

"And Doctor Hudson stayed all this time?"

"Don't call that butcher a doctor!" She opened a drawer and shuffled through it, removing a knife too large for peeling potatoes. "He said it was too late to take her to a hospital, then he said she was dead. At first I didn't believe him.

"I hardly remember the rest. It was hard to think straight. It was hot. Maybe that's what hell is like. It felt hellish. Like the worst dream you could ever have."

She placed the knife on the table and faced him. "Rose didn't want anybody to know what she'd done. It would be so much better if everybody just thought she'd gone to Russia. That butcher went out to the pump to wash himself. He didn't get any water. The well was open. It was big like a grave, and it was bone dry. I wrapped her in the quilts. It was so ungodly hot, but she was starting to feel cold.

"The shotgun was behind the door. I made him go down into the hole. Rose wasn't very big, and I was strong. I carried her and lowered her down to him."

"And then you shot him."

"He started to come out. He stepped on her. He *stepped right on her.*"

"You shot him."

"I shot him and I didn't even care. I didn't like leaving him there, on top of Rose like that, but what else could I do? I threw everything I could find over them—all the blankets and rugs, the clothes Rose had packed, all of it. I hardly knew what I was doing."

"But you hung on to Hudson's clothes. You didn't throw his coat and hat in the well."

"He deserved to die."

"So why not just admit what you'd done?"

"She begged me! She didn't want anybody to know. The baby wasn't Teddy's. She died. Keeping her secret was the least I could do."

"The secret came out anyway. Rose was long past being hurt. Why trot out that postcard to implicate her husband? You didn't do it to protect Rose Falk's memory."

"I was scared, and I didn't know Teddy would be back."

"Not something you had to worry about when you set out to pin it on Eban Vogel."

"Eban?" She frowned. "No. I shouldn't have done that. He didn't deserve it. I don't know what I would have done without him."

Done without him? "Are you trying to tell me Eban was in on this?"

"He came over. Hudson's car was there and Hudson wasn't. Rose wasn't either. There was blood, and he'd heard the shot. I had to tell him. He was mad, furious, but he said it would be all right. We couldn't change what had happened, and letting it get out would only make things worse. He said I should take Hudson's clothes and his bag back to his house, and nobody would ever know he'd been there."

She returned to her original pose, leaning back against the table. "Rosie had such a sad life. To have it end the way it did was bad enough, but to have everybody know…Teddy only married her to get Jarvi's farm. Orville got her pregnant, and then wanted to ship her off to Russia. Nobody cared. Only me and Eban. I shouldn't have put the watch in with his things. I found it that morning when I was looking for the postcard, and I put it in my pocket planning to get rid of it. When I saw all the boxes in Mia's bedroom, I just opened one and popped it in. I regretted it. I shouldn't have done it. But I thought, he's dead, he can't be hurt."

"What about Sulo? Can he be hurt, or is Sulo dead, too?"

"Don't say that!"

McIntire gritted his teeth against a wave of pain. "Where is he?"

"He's still on the ice."

He moved toward her. She snatched the knife from the table and turned its blade to her chest. A squeak, like a frightened mouse, came from her throat, and a tiny circle of blood oozed through her sweater.

"Suit yourself." McIntire went out the door.

There were not many places to look. The woodshed, pump house, chicken coop. Nothing. McIntire walked through the empty barn and climbed the ladder to the haymow. He grabbed the pitchfork and flung hay about, toppled a small stack of round bales. Nothing.

He pushed open the door in the outside wall and stood looking out over the backs of the Guernseys lounging in the sunny shelter of the barn. What had he expected? A woman clever enough to hide a murder for sixteen years wouldn't be likely to be less crafty with her next victim.

The thud of a car door was followed quickly by another, then by the whine of a recalcitrant starter. McIntire leapt to the ladder and felt a wave of nausea as his knee struck the wall behind it. As he charged into the open, the battery won its battle with the cold, and Sulo Touminen's grey Pontiac sped past him.

After what he knew would be a futile glance into the Studebaker—no key—he limped toward the house.

The telephone line lay in the snow by the path. McIntire picked up its snipped end. She'd taken no chances. It lacked a good eight feet of reaching the house.

A quick search of the house was only a formality. Sulo's familiar plaid mackinaw was not on its hook, and it hadn't been on his sister. Wherever he was, Touminen had left dressed for the outdoors.

McIntire began the torturous trek to the nearest phone. Thorsens'.

The Pontiac's tires left no distinguishable tracks in the icy road. Where was that damn snow when you needed it? McIntire hadn't even noticed which direction she'd turned when she left the driveway.

Another perfect crime. Sulo'd gone fishing and been the victim of Mother Nature. Why had she done it? Why not confess to killing Cedric Hudson in a fit of passion? If she went to prison at all, it probably wouldn't be for long. But if her desperate cover-up extended to harming her brother, it changed everything.

Irene couldn't have known that the ice would go out. She'd gotten lucky with that. But there were other ways to freeze to death, other than being on ice…and other places with ice.

A car horn sounded, and the black Buick, all eight cylinders pumping, grumbled to a stop behind him. McIntire used the last of his strength to slide into the back seat. Teddy Falk sat, hands between his knees, at his side.

"Well, well, what have we here, Tweedledum and Tweedledee." Melvin Fratelli gloated in the rearview mirror.

"Lindstrom's dock," McIntire said to his back. "I'll give directions. Just drive."

"This look like a goddamn taxicab to you?"

"Make him do it, Buster. For old time's sake."

Hayward shrugged. "Do it."

The Buick was powerful and sure-footed. If the distance had been another half a mile they'd have caught Irene before she got there.

She stood at the door of the ice house, mesmerized at their approach. For a moment. Then she clasped her hands in front of her. "Thank God you've come! I think my brother might have got himself locked in. I only hope we're in time!"

"And you're planning to get him to a hospital?" McIntire waved toward the Pontiac, backed up to the door with the trunk open.

Irene bolted for the car—and straight into the arms of Agent Buster. His experience in wrestling down fractious patients no doubt served him well.

McIntire walked to the ice house. The jolly red paint couldn't combat the grimness of the structure. Squat, windowless, four solid walls of foot-thick logs. A tomb. He flipped up the iron latch.

Sulo wasn't dead. Quite. His eyes flicked open and shut against the light.

"Nothing tougher than an old Finn." Teddy Falk pushed his way past McIntire and the blocks of ice.

Sulo mumbled through cracked and bleeding lips. "Somebody locked me in. They must of got Irene."

"Or dumber," Falk added.

McIntire reached for Touminen's legs but was shoved aside by Buster, solicitous attendant once again. He cradled Sulo like a baby and placed him tenderly in the front seat of the Buick. The tough, and dumb, old Finn nodded to his handcuffed sister in the back and flopped unconscious.

Fratelli slid in next to his prisoner, the tires spun on the snow, and McIntire and Teddy Falk stood staring at their taillights. The entire operation had taken less than five minutes.

"Shit." McIntire peered into the Pontiac's window, "She's got the key."

Touminen's rusted Ford pickup, bed heaped with sawdust, sat off to the side.

Teddy opened the door. "Key's in this one. Hop in. I'll get you back to your wife."

McIntire was well beyond hopping. He groaned his way into the cab. Falk perched on the edge of the seat and stretched to reach the clutch. They chugged out onto the road.

"The boys taking you for a little joy ride?" McIntire asked.

"Ya," Falk replied. "They found me a job. Place in Minnesota. Honeywell."

Whatever offenses the man had committed in J. Edgar Hoover's and Joe McCarthy's eyes, he was about to atone for them.

"Why'd she lock Sulo in there?" Falk wanted to know.

"Because he figured out what she'd done, and she knew I was getting close to it, too."

"It was Irene that killed Cedric Hudson?"

McIntire nodded. "And buried your wife in the cistern."

Teddy grunted. Nothing surprised him. "Thank you. At least it's over. We can let Rosie rest now."

WASHINGTON—The senate armed services committee voted unanimously
to draft 18-year-olds for 26
months of service.

Chapter Fifty-Four

Rose could rest at last, but she might be about the only one. Did tracking down her killer make things better for anybody? McIntire put the question to Leonie the next day.

She thought for a while. "Her widower has a new job."

Already another moral dilemma. Was he obligated to let Leonie know that Teddy Falk's employment with a major munitions manufacturer might involve some bothersome overtime? That a counter-agent's work is never done?

Leonie went on, "Irene Touminen killed an old man and was responsible for concealing the death of a young woman and her unborn child. She left them all three to rot away under a pile of garbage. She ought not to have gotten away with it for almost twenty years."

"And if she's convicted of any of those crimes, Irene will rot away in some women's prison for who knows how long. What good does that do? She was a frightened and desperate woman. She wouldn't have done it again."

"She almost did! If Irene had her way, her brother would be dead and taking the blame." She knelt on the floor before him. "And shortly after she called in on Nelda Stewart, the poor woman decided to end her life. That might not have been a coincidence."

McIntire wished he could believe that it was Irene's visit and not his own that had driven Mrs. Stewart to her barn.

"Murder will out." Leonie looked up into his eyes. "You couldn't have kept this to yourself, and you can't expect evil to result in anything but more evil. All you can do is try to put a stop to it. Which you did." She pulled the bandage snug around his knee. "Dr. Guibard says I should see that you stay off it for a few days."

"Good."

"You said *if* Irene is convicted. Do you think she might not be?"

"The only evidence that Irene intentionally locked Sulo in the ice house will have to come from Sulo himself. He'll never face up to that, and a jury might well see killing Cedric Hudson as excusable. There's not even any evidence that she did that. If she decides to plead not guilty, deny the whole thing...."

"But trying to pin it on Eban Vogel, and then on her brother? Maybe they'll find her fingerprints on the watch."

McIntire shrugged. "She was tidying up Mia's room. It was a nice watch. She picked it up to have a closer look."

"How could she have done those things? Do you think her mind is not quite right?"

Another crazy? Was he the expert on such matters? McIntire didn't reply. Leonie leaned against his knee and closed her eyes.

McIntire touched her hair. "Are you going to leave?"

"I promised two years. I keep my promises."

The two years would be up almost before the snow was off the roof. "I'll try to keep my promise, too."

"Did you think that it didn't matter? That after we were married I'd whither-thou-goest no matter what you got up to?"

What *he* got up to? How about hunting him down and marrying him under false pretenses? "I suppose maybe I did," McIntire admitted.

"I don't know if I can hold you to our agreement. Neither of us knew enough about what we were promising. Things turned out to be different from what we expected. Things might change again. There could be another war...or things closer to home."

She didn't come right out and say it, but there was no point in ignoring what she meant. Mia Thorsen might, before too long, be a widow. If that happened—*when* that happened—would it change his life with Leonie?

He and Mia were two sides of the same coin, a dismal coin. As a couple, they would have made a slightly bigger shadow, nothing more. Together they'd have lived a life of gloom, feeding on each other's cynicism. Nick had been the perfect mate for Mia, and Leonie was.... "You know I could never have a decent life without you."

"No," she said. "You couldn't. I'm sure of that."

"I didn't finish telling you about the time I spent in New Jersey."

Once again the mention of that sojourn triggered a rap on the door.

Leonie stood and pulled aside the curtains. She mouthed, "G-man."

Now there was someone who'd made quite a lot of hay out of McIntire's discovery of those bodies. Melvin Fratelli had delivered up a Soviet agent and hauled in a murderer. Maybe it would satisfy his blood lust for a while. He knocked again. McIntire called out, "Nobody home!"

Leonie dumped the bag of ice into the sink and opened the door. Her "good day" was slightly more civil but no more welcoming than her husband's greeting.

Fratelli dropped the key to McIntire's Studebaker on the table.

"How's the knee doing? Must have been one hell of an experience. You coulda died."

"I could have, along with a young woman from halfway round the world with two babies whose husband has lost his job and is being hounded out of the country that has been his home all his life." It was all the misery McIntire could fit into a single breath.

"Having a wife and kids don't make Pelto any less communist. Whether he goes or not is up to Immigration. But one less commie in this country is okay by me."

"We know that, Melvin."

"Particularly those with a subscription to…." He pulled a thin magazine from his pocket and slapped it on the table. *"Science and Society."*

"He's a science teacher."

"This rag has nothing to do with science, unless you call Karl Marx a scientist."

So why was Fratelli bringing the evidence of Pelto's treachery to McIntire?

"John." The agent pulled out a chair and sat. He placed his hands on the table. "I know you aren't taking this very seriously, and I'm concerned about that. It's a serious business and we could use your help. That's why I brought this." He picked up the magazine. "And now I'm going to tell you something else. Something in strictest confidence."

So McIntire had made the transition from suspect back to prospective colleague. He wasn't sure he cared.

"Does this mean I should leave?" Leonie's eyes grew round.

Fratelli studied her face for a minute. "You appear to be a sensible woman. Just remember this is top secret." At Leonie's solemn nod, he continued, "Certain documents have been found. Maps. Maps of this area, showing mines, railroads that carry the ore, docks they carry it to. This is information the Russians would love to get their hands on."

"So why don't they get their own map?" Leonie asked.

"These are their maps, or would have been if we hadn't intercepted them. What we want to know is where the information came from."

"Perhaps from the Michigan State Highway Department?" Leonie was indeed a sensible woman.

"State highway maps don't show mines."

"But that information isn't private," Leonie pointed out. "They could look in the phone book. Or just drive around and—"

"Have you noticed anyone doing that?"

"Driving around?"

"Maybe slow, keeping their eyes open. Like they were looking for something."

"Only you, Mr. Fratelli."

McIntire sighed. "Melvin, if you have some specific evidence that one of us is a Soviet spy, get back to me. Otherwise, this is still a free county."

"And people who don't like it are damned well free to leave. Not like some of those places your precious Erik Pelto and his bunch would like to turn us into." He stood up brusquely. McIntire pulled back his bare feet.

"Mr. Fratelli," Leonie inquired, "wouldn't you like to purchase one of the church's cookery books? Only one dollar. The money is going to help a family in need."

Fratelli opened his wallet. "I don't really have anything smaller than a five—"

"How very generous of you!" Leonie gently removed the bill from his fingers and replaced it with five shiny new copies of *The St. Adele Zion Lutheran Church Ladies Auxiliary Recipes and Household Hints.* Fratelli opened his mouth, then closed both it and his coat.

"Happy hunting," McIntire told him. He closed the door on Agent Fratelli's back. For a long time, he hoped. "Better hide that before it dawns on him who the needy family is."

Leonie folded the bill and stuffed it into her neckline. "I believe you were going to tell me about a trip to New Jersey."

TOKYO—American and British troops
rolled northward as far as seven
miles in west central Korea yesterday.

Chapter Fifty-Five

"Can I borrow your wife?" Pete Koski, in three layers of wool, filled McIntire's porch.

"What did you have in mind?"

"We got to search Touminens. It's just a formality since the woman confessed, but it's gotta be done. Sulo's home now and he ain't gonna be pleased."

"So you want Leonie to wrestle him down? Sure thing, we'll drive over." If Koski wanted Leonie to exert her placating influence on Sulo, her husband would be part of the deal. The sheriff didn't argue, only asked, "Can you get around?"

"Well enough." McIntire would have crawled if that's what it took to participate in the search of Irene Touminen's house. Her confession to McIntire—killing the doctor and the ensuing collusion with Eban Vogel to cover it up and protect Rose's good name—had satisfied the sheriff and the state police, but they hadn't been there to hear it. McIntire was still unsettled by Irene's demeanor during their encounter, and by the lack of hard evidence. She had only to plead not guilty, deny it all, and it would be McIntire's word against hers. He swallowed four aspirin and got into his coat.

There was nothing tougher than an old Finn, except maybe a relatively young one. Sulo's twenty-four hours in the ice house seemed to have left no lasting physical effects. He peered around McIntire's shoulder to the car. "Shit, I thought you were maybe bringing Irene home."

Leonie moved forward. "It could be a while, Mr. Touminen. You'd be wise to be prepared to be on your own for a time."

"Who's going to do the milking?"

"We'll all help out where we can. You'll do fine."

When he heard that the sheriff intended to search the house, Sulo swore and added, "Irene ain't gonna like somebody snooping through her stuff." McIntire was relieved to watch him stalk off to the barn. He would as soon have Sulo well away while he snooped through his sister's stuff.

Koski was accompanied only by Cecil Newman. This mission was no doubt another considered too sensitive for Adam Wall.

Cecil, by virtue of his stature, or lack of it, was assigned to explore the attic.

"We'll leave the kitchen for last," Koski decided. "Anything she wanted to keep to herself would probably be in her bedroom. I'll take a look." He followed Newman up the stairs. That left the living room for McIntire.

There was little to search. The room held a sofa, two chairs, a floor model radio, a good-sized bookcase and, snugged up to the coal-burning heater, the sewing machine. He pulled open one of its two drawers. Thread, scissors, pincushion. Nothing criminal. The other held more of the same. He turned to the glass-fronted bookcase. Its top shelf held a thick stack of letters from the Finland Touminens. Letters that McIntire had translated. Proof, at least, that Irene might have expressed some surprise at Rose Falk's postcard. Not much help but every little bit—

"Mac, come on up here a minute, will ya?" Pete Koski sounded about as excited as McIntire ever heard him.

Irene Touminen's bedroom was like herself, all contrast. Stark white walls, a chest lacquered in gleaming ebony and deep blood-red, smooth globular lamps. The bed was covered with a patchwork quilt, jewel-colored scraps of velvet joined with gold and silver braid. It was on this that the sheriff's attention was fixed.

He pointed to a russet-toned triangle. "That look familiar to you?"

McIntire's heart gave a leap. "It's what the watch was wrapped in."

"That's what I thought." Koski scooped the quilt into his arms.

It wasn't a lot, but it was something. Maybe they would be able to match the shape of the fragment with the watch to one on the quilt. Maybe the remains of the garment it was cut from was still in that attic. Maybe some shreds of it were with the sewing materials.

Koski opened the closet door, and McIntire returned to the living room and the bookcase. The volumes were unremarkable. A smattering of novels, classic and contemporary; a bible; textbooks that must have been from Irene's nurses' training.

The middle shelves were filled with more of the sewing implements. Knitting needles, balls of yarn, folded bits of fabric, none of them velvet. He opened a polished wood box. It held—he recognized them this time—crochet hooks. He closed the box, then opened it again. There were five of the hooks in graduated sizes, each in its own spot. Five hooks and an extra indentation; a space for a sixth. A larger one. Except for the loop on its end, it would not be much different from the knitting needle Mia had mentioned as an alternative to Hudson's services.

He ran his hand along the spines of the books. *She begged me to do it.* Twice she'd said it. She wasn't talking about the note, or the roses on her grave. She wasn't talking about keeping Rose's secret.

"Sulo seems to be behaving himself. I may as well go home." Leonie stood at his elbow.

"These are crochet hooks," McIntire told her.

"I can see that."

"The biggest one is missing."

"Too bad. Irene will probably have plenty of time for handiwork for the next few years."

"Mark Guibard had it. It was with Rose's body." Not just in the well, *with her body,* with those things that were bundled into the blankets and quilts.

"She was pregnant. Maybe she was making…."

"Rose wasn't crocheting booties. She didn't want to have a baby. She was terrified. The needle belonged to Irene. Irene was her only friend. Irene was a nurse."

Leonie put her hand to her mouth and turned the sickly pale shade that McIntire felt. "Are you saying it was Irene? That she did the abortion?"

"And fetched in the doctor when things went bad. It was too late."

"It must have driven her over the edge."

"It might have. On the other hand killing the doctor might only have been a way out of an awkward situation. Even if she realized that it was too late, that Rose was going to die, it wouldn't have been too late to go for the notorious abortionist. The perfect scapegoat. All she had to do was get him there. She had a car. Sulo had gone to Escanaba. It would have been easy. She might have told Hudson Rose was having a miscarriage. He'd have known better. When Rose died, Irene had to make damn sure he didn't tell how it really happened. That turned out to be pretty easy, too. Jarvi's old shotgun was behind the door, loaded and ready."

Irene had set out to conceal Rose's death before it even happened, composing that ambiguous note to Teddy. Sitting at her friend's bedside, waiting for her to die, she'd have had plenty of time to plan how she could dispose of evidence, how she'd handle Cedric Hudson, sending him into the well, hanging on to his clothing.

"The only thing she had to worry about was if people started wondering why they didn't hear from Rose. There might be awkward questions. But she duped Eban Vogel into helping her out, keeping quiet, and Teddy played right into her hands." McIntire closed the lid on the box. "Irene must have been ecstatic when she got that postcard from New York City."

NEW DELHI—a suggestion that
President Truman and Prime
Minister Stalin meet in the nude
for peace talks was made by the
50,000 naga (nude) sect monks and
nuns.

Chapter Fifty-Six

McIntire stood back from the circle of people gathered around the grave in the newly thawed ground. The trees were still lifeless and, among the pines, patches of white gleamed in the weak sunshine. But it was over. Whatever snow fell now would be drunk up by the earth.

Accompanying herself on the kantela, Gilette Karvonen's *Finlandia* was counterpoint to the exultant chorus of frogs. Neither her plaintive song nor the naked branches could quash McIntire's spirits. The dead were at last in their proper place, the living were muddling along, and spring would not be denied.

The Reverend Peters smiled beneficently upon his congregation and turned to the bereaved husband, a signal that the formal element of the ceremony had ended.

Ended. Over. Was it over? McIntire felt that the events of the winter had only been the awakening of the seeds sown so many years before. They had yet to come into full bloom. But this respite, however brief it might be, was all the more welcome for that, and he wouldn't question it. The faces around him wore the same self-satisfied expression he felt on his own. Was it the triumph of having survived another winter? Smugness that it was not they being laid in the ground? Delight over the restoration of items lost under last autumn's first snowfall?

Teddy Falk left the minister's side and strolled to McIntire. His thin hair was trimmed short, and he wore a black suit.

"I'll be on my way now." He spoke softly. "Thank you."

"I'm sorry for the loss of your wife." McIntire shook the extended hand. "And of your children."

"They've forgot me by now." He walked to his car, passing by the grave without a glance in its direction.

Mrs. Falk's burial would do nothing to put an end to the parade of sufferings the discovery of her body had set in motion. Erik Pelto and his family were still in exile. Teddy Falk was caught in a web from which he'd never extricate himself. Nelda Stewart was still dead.

McIntire walked the few steps to her grave.

Irene Touminen might have taken advantage of the terror that Nelda felt, but McIntire had prompted that fear. Irene, at least, had the excuse of self-preservation. McIntire had acted out of cowardice. Maybe they were the same thing.

He raised his eyes from the mound of soggy soil and its handful of decomposing lilies, and met Mia Thorsen's. Another casualty. Mia had to live with the knowledge that her father had died protecting a murderer. She held his gaze for a moment, then bent to brush the winter's debris from the flat white stone that bore her daughter's name. She stayed only a moment, then straightened up and strode, on two good legs, to where her husband leaned against a wrought iron rail.

"Thank you."

It was Sulo Touminen. McIntire was on the verge of becoming a hero. If he wasn't careful he'd be re-elected. *"Pozhaluysta,"* he responded loudly, "don't mention it."

Sulo ignored the suspicious word. "I could of froze to death if you hadn't come along. When Irene gets home...." He shook his head and walked away.

"Is he really naive enough to think she'll be back?" Leonie stood at his side.

"Spring hopes eternal," McIntire told her.

"But she tried to kill him."

"Love conquers all."

"I don't think that refers to siblings."

"Blood is thicker than water."

"I'm not sure about that." She took his arm. "I suppose we'll find out in time."

Author's Note

During the early part of the twentieth century, an estimated six to ten thousand Finnish-Americans left the United States and Canada to take part in building a socialist workers' Utopia in the Soviet republic of Karelia. The largest numbers came from the Finnish communities of northern Michigan and Minnesota. "Karelia Fever" peaked in 1931 and 1932, when groups of hundreds made the crossing. It was almost immediately apparent that the idealistic society they planned to join did not exist, and many of those who had retained their non-Soviet citizenship left within a short time to go back to North America or to settle in Finland. They typically did not return to their original home communities, nor did they speak of their experiences. The exodus, and the people who made it, was largely forgotten.

In 1986, a contingent from Duluth, Minnesota, traveled to Karelia to organize a sister-city relationship with Petrozavodsk. They were astonished to be met at the train station by an excited group of people whose families had left the Great Lakes region more than 50 years earlier. Old ties were renewed and details of their experiences began to emerge.

Life had been harsh. Hundreds of the emigrants were executed in Stalinist purges. Many more starved or died in labor camps.

One of the survivors was Kaarlo Tuomi, who'd emigrated from Rock, Michigan, at age 16 with his mother and stepfather. Tuomi's mother died of starvation and his father was taken away and executed, but Kaarlo lived and settled into the Soviet society, becoming an English teacher. In the early 1950s, Tuomi was coerced into leaving his family behind and returning to the U.S. as a spy. From the day of his arrival, he was under surveillance by the FBI and was eventually arrested and given the choice of going back and facing the KGB or turning counter-agent. Tuomi spent many years as a spy, eventually retiring, marrying a Minnesota woman, and lecturing on his experiences. In the late 1980s he was reunited with his three Russian children.

The Internal Security Act of 1950 (McCarran Act), passed over the veto of President Truman, gave the government the tools for an anti-communist crusade that affected citizen and non-citizen alike. Hundreds were called to appear before the House Un-American Activities Committee, the Senate Internal Security Subcommittee (the Senate's equivalent of the HUAC), and the Senate Permanent Subcommittee on Investigations (Senator Joseph McCarthy). While the investigations resulted in few prosecutions and even fewer convictions, thousands of people throughout the country lost their jobs and their reputations.

Likewise, the government's attempts to deport aliens on charges of violating the McCarran Act mostly resulted in failure, especially when those accused had the stamina and resources to fight the order. Knut Heikkinen, mentioned in this text, editor of a prominent Finnish-American newspaper, was first arrested in 1948 and again in late 1950. The case dragged on until he was exonerated by a Supreme Court decision in 1958.

To receive a free catalog of Poisoned Pen Press titles, please contact us in one of the following ways:

Phone: 1-800-421-3976
Facsimile: 1-480-949-1707
E-mail: info@poisonedpenpress.com
Website: www.poisonedpenpress.com

Poisoned Pen Press
6962 E. First Ave., Suite 103
Scottsdale, AZ 85251